MAGGIE MAY AND MISS FANCYPANTS MYSTERIES

BOOKS 4 – 6

BOOKS BY ALEKSA BAXTER

MAGGIE MAY AND MISS FANCYPANTS MYSTERIES

A DEAD MAN AND DOGGIE DELIGHTS

A CRAZY CAT LADY AND CANINE CRUNCHIES

A BURIED BODY AND BARKERY BITES

A MISSING MOM AND MUTT MUNCHIES

A SABOTAGED CELEBRATION AND SALMON SNAPS

A POISONED PAST AND PUPPERMINTS

🐾🐾🐾

A FOULED-UP FOURTH

A SALACIOUS SCANDAL AND STEAK SIZZLERS

A PUZZLING POOCH AND PUMPKIN PUFFS

NOSY NEWFIE HOLIDAY SHORTS

HALLOWEEN AT THE BAKER VALLEY BARKERY & CAFE

A HOUSEBOUND HOLIDAY

TABLE OF CONTENTS

A MISSING MOM

AND MUTT MUNCHIES

A MAGGIE MAY AND MISS FANCYPANTS MYSTERY

ALEKSA BAXTER

CHAPTER 1

"Where's Fancy?" I asked my grandpa as I toweled my long blonde hair dry with one hand and rooted in the fridge for a Coke with the other. Normally when I took a shower she went to sleep at his feet, but he was seated at the kitchen table and there was no sign of Fancy anywhere.

He set aside his pen and half-completed crossword puzzle and reached for his non-existent cigarettes. (He'd stopped smoking when my grandma got sick, but lifelong habits don't die easy. He'd started smoking when he was twelve so that made close to seventy years of reaching for that pack of cigarettes tucked away in the breast pocket of his tried and true flannel shirt.)

"Where do you think, Maggie May?" He nodded towards the hallway that led to the backyard.

I sighed. "Bunnies."

"Rabbits. And wouldn't be a problem if you'd let me take care of 'em."

"You are not going to shoot a bunch of bunnies, Grandpa. One, because the neighbors would probably call the cops on you for using a gun in your backyard.

Two, because even if they didn't, the police station is only a few blocks away and there's at least one cop there who would love to throw you in jail. And, three, because they're bunnies. Who shoots bunnies?"

"A homeowner who wants to protect the foundation of his house from varmint, that's who." He leaned back in his chair and glared me down.

I crossed my arms and glared right back at him. "They are not varmint. They're bunnies."

"They're rabbits. And where there are two rabbits there are ten and then a hundred."

"We are not going to have a hundred rabbits. There are what, two, living back there?"

"More than that." He took a long sip of coffee, still glaring at me.

I just shook my head. "They're bunnies, Grandpa. No shooting, poisoning, or otherwise harming them."

As I made my way towards the backyard I wondered what I'd done in my thirty-six years of life to warrant my current situation—living with my eighty-two-year-old grandpa who most definitely did not feel a need for me to take care of him (although his predilection for using guns when he shouldn't indicated maybe he was wrong about that), running a not-yet-successful café and barkery in a small Colorado tourist town with my best friend (who had decided it was the perfect time to fall in love and get married), and trying to keep my precocious three-year-old Newfoundland, Miss Fancypants, from inadvertently killing a bunny in her desire to "play" with it.

This was nothing like the life I'd had just a few months before in Washington, DC. And even though it was one I'd chosen for myself, it wasn't exactly peaches and cream.

Was it too much to ask that my grandpa actually need my help, that my business actually thrive, that my best friend not go and get all moony over some guy, and that my sweet-natured dog not turn into a stone-cold bunny killer?

I mean, honestly.

I stepped out on the back porch and spared a moment to admire the clear blue sky and the mountain covered in evergreens and aspen trees that rose behind my grandpa's house—a view worth all the frustrations in the world. But I didn't take too deep a breath. That time of year there was a yellow-flowered weed of some sort that grew all around and smelled decidedly musky.

Fancy was stationed on the bottom section of the ramp that led off the porch, her one hundred and forty pounds of furry bulk squeezed across the space over the last two slats. She was crammed in there so tight I wasn't sure how she was going to manage to stand back up.

She looked up with a "please help me" look and a small whine before returning to licking the slats and snuffling at the space between them.

I sighed. "Fancy…"

I could never decide whether she was licking the slats because she wanted to make friends with the little furry creatures hiding underneath, or because she wanted to eat them. I'm honestly not sure she knew.

Whichever it was, I was just glad they were separated from her by two slats of very sturdy Trex decking. And glad, too, that my grandpa hadn't used wood to build the ramp or we'd be making frequent emergency trips to the vet to have splinters removed from Fancy's tongue.

I'd tried putting a welcome mat over the end of the ramp but she just pawed it away so she could get closer to the bunnies.

I was about to shove Fancy off the bottom of the ramp and tell her to go play in the yard and "leave it"—a command she usually obeyed—when I looked past her.

There in the grass, hunkered down not a foot away from Fancy, was a tiny little bunny about the size of my closed fist. It met my eyes and hunched its shoulders, pressing itself closer to the ground, not even smart enough to run away when it should.

I laughed. Once.

I know. I'm horrible, but I couldn't help it. There Fancy was, frantically licking at the slats on the ramp, crying her head off as she tried to get to the bunnies underneath it, and right behind her was one of the very bunnies she was looking for.

Fancy looked at me again and cried, pawing at the slats with both feet like she could somehow dig through the decking.

"Treat?" I said, hoping to lure her inside.

Her head tilted a bit at the magic word but then she went back to snuffling at the spot between the slats. Seemed there was something Fancy liked more than food. Who knew?

"I bet there isn't even a bunny under there, you big goof." I sat down next to her and peered between the slats, expecting to see nothing, but right there on the far right side was just a hint of brindled fur. So two bunnies. At least. Seemed my grandpa was right.

(And I should mention here that I call all rabbits bunnies. It's a quirk I have. To me rabbits belong on a fancy dinner menu at some four-star restaurant. Bunnies are the cute little things that infest your yard with their furry white tails and complete lack of survival skills.)

I stood up. "Come on, Fancy. Let's go inside."

She didn't budge.

Since she doesn't wear a collar at home I grabbed her by the ruff of her neck and tried to pull her towards the door. She cried out like I was torturing her and rolled onto her back.

Which was not an act of surrender, I might add, although it might look like it to the uninitiated. Oh no, Fancy and her rolling on her back because she doesn't want to go somewhere is straight out of the pacifist playbook.

It's like she's saying, "Look, I'm showing you my belly and making it so you can't actually get ahold of me to move me anywhere. Why don't you just give up on what you had planned and pet me instead?"

Normally at that point I would've started a countdown because I was not about to fall for that one, but unfortunately the foolish little bunny that had decided to hang out a foot from a very large predator chose that moment to make a run for it.

Away from the ramp.

Fancy scrambled to her feet and chased after it while I chased after her shouting "Leave it" as loud as I could— a command that had absolutely no effect on Fancy because there was a small scurrying thing running along the ground and she was no longer an overweight domesticated house pet but instead a descendent of wolves who needed to catch her prey or else risk starving to death.

Fortunately, the bunny somehow managed to dart past Fancy—baby bunnies are really fast—and through the slats in the deck. At which point Fancy started very loudly voicing her opinion about being defeated in her efforts to eat a bunny by crying at the top of her lungs.

My grandpa poked his head out the door. "What happened?"

"She chased a bunny under the porch." I tried to push her towards the house, but she dug in and wouldn't budge.

He opened the door wider. "Fancy. Here. Now."

Fancy hesitated for half a second, but no one refuses my grandpa when he uses that particular tone of voice. She slunk up the ramp, glancing back at me once before going inside.

"That was far too close," I told my grandpa.

"You need to let me take care of 'em. One of these days she'll get ahold of one and then what will you do?"

I didn't even want to think about that. I knew she wouldn't kill one on purpose, but you take a tiny bunny and a big dog and put the one in the other's mouth and it's not going to come out well.

My life. I swear. Why couldn't it be simple and perfect? Was that really too much to ask?

CHAPTER 2

I followed my grandpa into the kitchen for breakfast. For some reason I'd decided I was getting old and losing my mind so I'd started trying to eat healthier, which meant breakfast consisted of oats soaked in yogurt with blueberries, bananas, shredded coconut, and some cinnamon sprinkled on top.

It wasn't bad, but it wasn't the bacon and eggs I wanted.

(And, yes, there was still a Coke involved. I am quite well aware of my hypocrisy, thank you very much. I figure baby steps are better than no steps at all.)

"So what are you up to today?" I asked him. "Lesley coming over?"

He shook his head. "Her husband's in hospice. I don't expect I'll see her until he passes."

"Oh, Grandpa, I'm sorry."

He and Lesley had an awkward situation. They'd once dated and been in love, but then he'd been sent away to prison for killing her sister's abusive husband. While he was gone she'd met her current husband and married him. (With my grandpa's blessing. He'd thought he'd be in a lot longer than he was.)

It had all worked out in the end. Lesley's husband was a good man. He'd even given my grandpa a job when he got out of prison for the second time, and my grandpa had ended up with my grandma and been happily married for forty years until she died of cancer.

But since then he and Lesley had spent a lot of time together because her husband was in the end stages of Parkinson's and she needed to get away sometimes. Being a caretaker is not easy.

Nothing had happened between them as far as I knew, but there was definitely a more than friends vibe to what they had. Which meant staying away from Lesley had to be killing my grandpa.

But even worse was probably trying to figure out what happened next. Small towns are not always forgiving when you cross the invisible lines of propriety. And since their special friendship was well-known after the Jack Dunner incident, all eyes would be on them, watching and judging.

My grandpa shrugged it away. "Lesley's the one you should be sorry for, not me. But because she's taking care of Bill I'm stuck making twelve dozen cookies for the end of season baseball party."

"End of season? So soon?"

He nodded. "House will be full of pretty much everyone in town Saturday when we have the big end of season awards and pot luck."

(Not that that was a lot of people. Creek only has about forty homes total.)

I wanted to ask him if Matt had said anything more about whether he was going to stick around or not, but I didn't dare. My grandpa would read way too much into my question. Honestly. Just because I asked a question about a guy did not mean that I was in love with him and desperate to know if he was going to re-enlist or not.

(Even though I was. Not that I was going to let Matt or anyone else know. And if they did figure it out that didn't mean I was going to act on it. There were reasons I was single. Reasons with a capital R. And being in love with a gorgeous, decent, intelligent man didn't change any of them.)

My grandpa glared at his crossword puzzle and set it aside half-finished. "I also have to mow the yard and weed out that plot on the north side of the house. What are you up to on your day off?"

I grimaced. "I was planning on reading a book. My favorite author just released the final book in her latest series, so I figured I'd spend the day devouring it."

I'd really wanted to read that book, too. There's nothing I love more than getting lost in a good story. But...

"I don't need to, though," I added. "I'll mow the yard for you instead."

"Mow the yard? Why would I let you do that?"

"Because it's hot out and you're..."

"Old?" He shook his head. "I may be eighty-two-years-old but I am perfectly capable of mowing my own yard." (There was an extra word in there before yard that I'm not including here. My grandpa doesn't mince words and doesn't appreciate having anyone question his health or stamina.)

"I'm just saying, Grandpa. I'm here. Use me. I moved in with you to help out around here. And mowing the yard is part of that."

Ever since I'd moved in I'd been feeling like a burden more than a help. Half of the reason I'd moved to Creek was so he'd have someone to take care of him, but he wouldn't let me.

He snorted. "You want to help out?"

"Yes. Please."

"Fine. You can bake the cookies. Here's the recipe. Ingredients are in the fridge." He slid a piece of paper across the table.

Walked right into that one, hadn't I?

I sighed. The last thing I wanted to do on my day off from working at a bakery was to bake. But I wasn't about to say no and my grandpa knew it. "Great. Love to. I'll get right on that after I finish breakfast."

My grandpa winked at me before picking his crossword puzzle back up with a smug little smile.

CHAPTER 3

Twenty minutes later, with Fancy out back on alert for bunnies and my grandpa out front mowing the yard, I stared at my grandpa's kitchen, hands on hips, prepared to do battle with an ancient oven and warped cookie trays. All for a bunch of kids that weren't even mine or related to me in any way.

What had my life become?

But when my grandpa actually voiced a need for my help, I wasn't going to turn him down, so there was no turning back.

I grabbed my phone, started Rebecca Ferguson playing, cranked up the volume, and went to work.

I do actually like to bake. I find it relaxing, especially when I have good music playing in the background. It's just when I'm forced to do so that I get a little cranky.

But within minutes I'd settled into my rhythm and was happily singing about how nothing's real but love (ironic, I know, given my own aversion to the feeling) while I mixed my ingredients and pre-heated the oven.

I'd just finished stirring in the chocolate chips when I turned to find Matt standing in the doorway, grinning at me. He wasn't in uniform but was instead wearing a pair of well-fitting and well-worn jeans with a blue t-shirt that matched his eyes.

Honestly, it's not fair for a man to look as good as he does without even trying. Check the dictionary under tall, dark, and handsome and you'd probably find a picture of him.

Not that I cared. I was too busy coughing my head off because I'd stopped singing so abruptly I almost choked myself to death.

"Need some water?" he asked, still smiling at me.

"I don't drink water." I grabbed a Coke from the fridge and took a deep gulp. "How long were you standing there?"

"Long enough to hear you make it through a song or two."

"Seriously?" I could've melted into the floor right then. I love to sing but I try not to torture others with it. I've been told nails on a chalkboard sound better. "I'm sorry. Why didn't you say anything? I would've stopped."

"Why would I want to stop you?"

"Because I'm horrible."

He shrugged. "A little off-key, but I didn't mind. It's not often I see you so relaxed and happy." He grabbed himself a Coke and sat down at the kitchen table as he cracked it open. "Where's Fancy?"

"Out back. She's developed an obsession with bunnies."

"That's not going to end well."

"Tell me about it." I started scooping cookie dough onto the cookie sheet, needing something to do so I wouldn't start thinking about those poor bunnies.

Matt came over and snagged a bit of cookie dough. "Mm. That's good. What are you baking for?"

"Your team as it turns out. My grandpa guilted me into doing it since Lesley can't."

"Ah, yeah. Sad news about Bill. He's had a rough time of it the last month or so."

"Do you know everyone in this town?" I'd visited in the summers, but hadn't grown up in the Baker Valley. Matt had, though. And now he was a police officer which probably put him in contact with even more people.

"Not everyone. Just the troublemakers, like you, and family friends, like Bill and Lesley. Bill was best friends with my grandpa. Spent a decent amount of time around him when I was growing up. Good man."

"Small towns, I swear. There's, what, three degrees of separation between any two people here?"

"More like one."

He reached for another taste of cookie dough and I slapped at his hand. "Take a beater if you're going to keep eating my cookie dough."

"Yes, ma'am."

As he helped himself to one of the beaters and started to lick it clean—something I tried very hard not to pay attention to—I put the first cookie tray in the oven. "Why are you out of uniform anyway? Thought you worked today."

He grimaced and sat back down at the kitchen table, stretching his legs out. "I decided to take a little time off. Lots of decisions to make now that the baseball season is wrapping up."

Suddenly my throat felt too dry. I grabbed my Coke and took a nice long swallow. "What kind of decisions?"

He leaned against the wall. "Jack's decided to stick around for a bit. Said he wants to get on the straight and narrow. Asked if he could crash with me while he does. Figured I can't say no since it's our dad's place."

That sounded like a non-answer, but it wasn't. One of the things Matt struggled with most as a small-town cop was the fact that he had to arrest or investigate his friends and family. And since his brother Jack was a criminal to the core—a good-looking, fun-loving, not going to hurt someone if he could steal their television while they were out sort of criminal, but a criminal nonetheless—his deciding to stick around town meant Matt was probably going to have to arrest him at some point.

Not to mention Jack's bizarre statement that when he was healed up he was going to make a pass at me, something that Matt most definitely hadn't been happy about. (Even though he'd yet to make a real pass at me himself.)

"Okay. So you're just taking a couple weeks off so you won't have to be the one to arrest Jack when he changes his mind?"

"That's part of it."

I grabbed the other beater so I'd have an excuse not to look at him as I asked, "And the other part of it?"

"I got a re-enlistment offer. It's a pretty good one."

I turned to stare at him, wanting so much to tell him to tear it up and throw it in the trash. But I couldn't. That wasn't fair to him. I couldn't ask him to make that decision for me when I knew I wasn't going to be there for him if he did.

I forced myself to sound casual as I asked, "You think you'll take it?"

He held my gaze for a few seconds more than was comfortable until I turned away to wipe down the counter. I'm the type of cook that can get flour on the ceiling, so there was a lot to wipe down.

"I'm considering it," he said.

I gotta tell you, I hate conversations with subtext to them. There he was, sitting in my kitchen, basically telling me he was going to leave and re-enlist in the military and what he was really doing was asking me if I wanted him to stay, poking around at the edges trying to figure out if there was some sort of a possibility of there being an "us" at some point.

We both knew that's what he was doing, but neither one of us was going to come at the issue head on. Heaven forbid.

Of course, that's what *I* figured was going on. There was always the chance that his interest in me was all in my head and I was just making up feelings that weren't there. I swear, I have spent far too many moments of my life trying to figure out if there's anything happening below the surface of a conversation when nine times out of ten there probably isn't.

Most people are not as complex as I give them credit for. But with Matt…

It didn't matter. I couldn't tell him what he wanted to hear from me. Matt was pretty much the perfect guy. Good-looking, good-hearted, smart, and with that undefinable something that drew me in. But relationships…

They're just not my thing.

Especially since I'd been forced to watch my best friend and business partner Jamie act like a lovesick fool the last couple of weeks. Honestly, I swear, if it was possible to float from happiness she would've been. And that kind of giddy, out-of-control foolishness was not what I wanted. Not at all.

But I didn't want him to go either.

"You're a good cop, you know. This town needs you."

"You really think so?"

Before I could answer, my grandpa stomped into the kitchen. "Maggie, you burn those cookies you're not going to do any of us any good."

I whirled around to check on the cookies and by the time I was done getting them out of the oven and onto a cooling rack Matt and my grandpa had disappeared out back to have a talk. I desperately wanted to know what my grandpa's advice was going to be, but instead I busied myself with getting the next cookie tray ready and in the oven.

I swear, life was a lot simpler when I was just a self-absorbed workaholic who lived alone and had no romantic prospects.

CHAPTER 4

That Saturday I actually managed to attend the final baseball game of the Creek Coyotes, the town baseball team that my grandpa coached and that Matt had been helping out with most of the season. Normally I would've been working, but Jamie told me to take the afternoon off—we weren't exactly slammed with business even on a Saturday afternoon.

Putting aside thoughts of destitution and bad life choices, I settled Fancy and myself in a spot of shade along the first baseline.

I loved the baseball field in Creek. The whole town was surrounded by mountain ranges that thrust into a clear blue sky and the grass was brilliantly green, which for the mountains wasn't always the case. There's far more scrub brush than grass the higher up you go. But the town prided itself on its ball field.

There were even cute little white-washed dugouts for each of the teams, something that hadn't existed when I was a kid. And two sets of wooden bleachers painted a bright blue.

It was like an image straight out of a post card of

small town America.

Fancy and I hadn't been there two minutes before Jack Barnes, Matt's older brother, came to join us.

Jack's trouble through and through. Setting aside his criminal proclivities, he's also the type of guy to make a woman lose all sense of reason and rationality. He's got the same tall, dark-haired, blue-eyed good looks as Matt, but he also has a mischievous streak a mile wide. One grin and suddenly running away to Cabo for the weekend to pick up a package for a friend starts to sound like a fun adventure instead of the life-threatening criminal enterprise it is.

"Maggie May Carver. To what do we owe the pleasure?" he asked as he settled in next to me.

Fancy rolled on her back as soon as he came close and Jack obliged by giving her a thorough tummy rub. (She's such a sellout it's ridiculous.)

"Figured I baked all the cookies for the end of year party, least I could do is make it to a game." Before he could make some smart comment about my cookies, I added, "And what brings you out?"

"Didn't you hear? I've decided to become a fine upstanding member of society. Means I have to interact with people and let them see how I've changed. Can't do that at the Creek Inn. Plus, I figured I could show my brother a little support."

"He said you're going to be living with him."

"I am. Which is going to make things really awkward when you and I get all hot and heavy." He leaned close enough he was almost touching me, but I wasn't looking at him. I was watching Matt watching us from the dugout, his hands fisted at his sides—until my grandpa whapped him in the back of the head, that is.

I glared at Jack. "You're not a very nice person, you know that?"

He leaned back on his elbows with a chuckle. "How so?"

"Matt's right over there. He can't do anything about it. And yet here you are hitting on me when you know…"

"What do I know, Maggie? That you pretended you guys were dating when I first met you. That doesn't make you off limits."

"You know that he…" I pressed my lips together.

"That he actually likes you? Hm. Seems you do, too." He leveled a look at me that reminded me of Matt's pin-you-to-the-wall interrogation stare. "So why are you playing my brother?"

"I'm not playing him. I just…" I shook my head. "Tell me you've never liked someone you *knew* you'd be no good for. It has to have happened to you."

"Never stopped me, though." He winked.

"Yeah, well, that's where we differ."

"So that's why you're keeping him at arms' length? Because you think you'd be bad for him? Why do you think that?"

Who knows where that conversation would've gone from there—nowhere good, that's for sure—but right then the kid playing first base—a small boy with red hair peeking out under his baseball cap and more freckles than any single person should ever have—missed a simple grounder when it ricocheted off his glove.

The other team erupted into cheering as the kid chased after the ball, and the batter, who'd thought he was out, continued on towards second.

The poor kid had to scramble under a car to get the ball. By the time he threw it back to the catcher what should have been a simple out had turned into a triple and the kid was crying his eyes out.

That would've been bad enough. But then a large hulking man in a stained white t-shirt, ratty jeans, and steel-toed boots stumbled over to the kid and started to scream at him. We were close enough to catch the reek of alcohol and body odor. A lovely combination, let me tell you.

"What was that?" the man shouted, looming over the poor kid. "And why are you crying? Man up. You've got a game to win."

The poor kid crouched into himself as if expecting a blow.

The dude was a good six inches taller than me, probably twice my weight, and muscled in a way I most definitely am not. Plus, something told me he didn't have qualms against hitting women, but I was about to get up and give him a piece of my mind.

Fortunately, Fancy beat me to it. She started barking her head off at him and even lunged in his direction.

By the time I got her under control, Jack was on his feet ready to throw a punch. That wouldn't have helped his new plans to become a good law-abiding citizen but before anything else could happen Matt, my grandpa, and the other team's head coach all converged on us.

So did a skinny woman with bright red hair and freckles to match the kid's. She grabbed at the man's arm "Come on, babe. Let's go home. Sam can get a ride after the party. Come on, baby. Let it go."

He shook her off. The way she flinched I was pretty

sure that in another time and place he wouldn't have just shook her off, but hit her.

She didn't give up, though. She grabbed at him a second time and leaned into him, urging him to come away with her, murmuring something in his ear that finally had him calming down and stepping back.

We all watched them go, Matt with his hand on his cellphone. "I swear, he gets in that truck of his, I'm calling it in," he muttered.

But they didn't get in a vehicle. Just stumbled down the road towards a small set of rundown trailer homes a few blocks away.

Too bad. That was one man who deserved to be locked away from others from the little I'd seen.

Surprisingly, it was Jack who led the boy away towards right field, leaning close to whisper to him as my grandpa, Matt, and the other coach got back to the business of playing small town baseball.

Jack knelt down to talk to the kid, gently wiping away his tears. Who knew he had that side to him? Within moments he had the kid calmed down and smiling. Not bad for a grifter and drifter.

As they made their way back towards us, I showered Fancy with a bunch of kisses and ear scratches because she was still a little wound up. "Good girl, Fancy. Way to bark at the bad man."

Jack nudged the kid back towards his dugout and dropped down next to me. "You going to give me a bunch of smooches and caresses, too, because I stood up to the bad man?"

I smacked him on the arm.

Hard.

He just grinned back at me and winked.

Men. I swear.

CHAPTER 5

The end of year party was a madhouse. Take a bunch of sugar-hyped kids that had just won their final game of the season and add all of their parents and their parents' friends and you have loud, crowded, and insane. Exactly the type of situation I wanted to avoid at all costs.

Normally, I would've used Fancy as an excuse and locked both of us away in my room until everyone was gone, but she was still on bunny watch. So while the kids ran through the house and filled up the front lawn she was out back stationed in the middle of the yard staring at the spot where that baby bunny had fled under the porch.

I leaned against the railing. "Fancy, would you give it a rest?"

She didn't even look at me. All else had failed to exist for her except for those stupid bunnies.

Matt came out to join me. "Your grandpa said I might find you out here. She still looking for bunnies?"

"Unfortunately. I don't know what she's going to do if she actually manages to catch one. Why is it that we make dog toys look so much like animals?"

He grinned at me. "Because that's what they like to chew on. Buck, the dog we had when I was growing up, was a great birding dog. He'd retrieve those things like no one's business."

I stared at him. "Why are you telling me this? Why are you okay with that? I want a dog that lays on her bed, snores funny, and eats bon bons. Not a…bunny killer."

He just laughed. "Be glad you don't have a cat. They can climb trees. And get under decks like this one."

I shuddered at the thought. "So why are you out here with me instead of in there celebrating with the kids?"

"We just finished giving out all the awards so my part's done. And it just didn't seem right to leave you alone out here. Who knows who might corner you."

Ah, so that was it. He was keeping me company so Jack wouldn't. I did not need to be stuck between those two. But saying anything about it meant walking on very thin ice. So I chugged down the rest of my beer and shook the empty can. "I need another beer. Want one?"

"Sure."

Matt and I made our way out front to grab a couple cans of Coors from a big metal vat filled with ice. I let him play the gentleman because no way was I putting my hand in water that cold if I didn't have to. As he dug around for two cans of beer under all that ice I glanced over to the side of the house where Jack and the little boy from the game, Sam, were sitting off to the side talking.

"That's odd, isn't it?" I asked as Matt handed me my beer. "I never thought of Jack as being good with kids."

He followed the direction of my gaze. "Not really. Jack dated Trish last time he was around this way. Sam would've been maybe four or five at the time? Not sure how things were between Jack and Trish—she's a volatile one—but I know Jack really got a kick out of spending time with Sam. Bought him his first baseball glove."

"Really? I would've never guessed."

Matt took a long swig of his beer. "That's my brother. A man of hidden depths."

Of course, Jack chose that moment to wink at a woman I happened to know was very much married. I turned away, shaking my head. He was going to get himself shot (again) if he wasn't careful.

Three boys ran by us screaming at the top of their lungs and I winced. "I'm going inside and hiding from all this mess."

I wanted to just flee, alone, but I remembered how Matt had saved me at the charity thing so instead I added, "I guess you could come along if you want. I'm just going to be in my room listening to music."

He glanced around. "Alright. Sure. Sounds fun."

🐾 🐾 🐾

Matt and I spent the next two hours in my room listening to various songs and discussing our favorite music, me sprawled on the bed, him sprawled on the floor.

I felt like I was in high school again. Not that I'd ever actually had guys over to the house in high school. I'm not sure if it was a rule that they couldn't come over or if it just never happened. (Knowing me, it probably just never happened. Are you really surprised?)

All the same. It felt very high school. All that was missing was me wearing my hair in a high ponytail and chewing some form of fruity bubble gum while my parental unit checked that everything was "okay" every fifteen minutes.

We even left the bedroom door open so no one would think anything hinky was going on. Last thing I needed was to be the subject of small town gossip.

It was fun, though. Matt was definitely one of those rare guys I could spend hours with without getting bored or annoyed.

But eventually everyone headed out and so did he.

CHAPTER 6

The next morning I found myself in a battle of wills with Fancy. Normally I take her into work with me, but that morning she was having none of it. I went out back when it was time to go and she actually ran away from me.

"Fancy, what are you doing?"

She glanced towards the ramp where the bunnies were hiding and cried her little head off at me. She may not speak English but it was perfectly clear she did not want to have to abandon her bunny watch post.

"No. Leave it. Come on." If I let her stay home she'd sit there all day even when it was far too hot for her to be outside. Not to mention the chances of her actually snagging one, something I did not want to have happen.

I cornered her on the far side of the yard, but then she pulled her rolling on her back act. Even a nudge with my foot wasn't enough to get her to flip back over.

"Fancy, you have ten seconds." I stood over her and glared as I started my countdown. "Ten. Nine."

She wiggled and cried and rolled around on the ground like I was performing some sort of exorcism on her as I continued to count down towards one.

When I reached three I paused to glare at her. Was she really going to push it this time? If so, I wasn't quite sure what I'd do. Wrestling a collar onto her would probably be a lot like trying to wrestle a bear. Not a good idea.

"Two," I continued, as I leaned down. "One."

She cried one last time and then jumped to her feet. "Thank you." I put her collar on her before she ran away again. "Come on. We're going to be late."

She strained towards the ramp as we walked by, but at least she followed me back inside and out to the van.

As you can imagine, not being a morning person and then having to fight my dog to take her into work with me—something that she should have seen as a privilege and not a punishment—I was not in the best of moods when I finally pulled up outside the Baker Valley Barkery and Café, the business I ran with my best friend Jamie.

Which meant as I stared at the cute little sign with the barely-legible script and Newfie heads on either end that I wasn't feeling all that positive about things.

It had seemed like such a good idea when we came up with it. Part café for people—that was Jamie's side—and part bakery for dogs—that was my side. (Barkery. Get it? Haha.) What could be better than running a business with my best friend, living in a small town, and finally getting away from corporate life?

(Money, as it turns out. A steady paycheck is actually a nice thing to have. When you work for some large soulless corporation those paychecks come nice and steady, but when you're running your own place sometimes those paychecks don't come at all.)

It wasn't all bad. Jamie's cinnamon rolls had been a definite hit. And I did well with online sales at least. And I did have some regular customers—Greta and her Irish Wolfhound, Hans—but I was scared. Scared that I wasn't pulling my weight—Jamie could've probably run the café without the barkery and made twice as much. And also scared that now that she'd met Mason she wouldn't want to be there anymore. What would I do then?

I'd started a "Name the Treat" fundraiser for the local boys and girls club, figuring it would be a good way to get word out about the barkery and garner us some goodwill at the same time, but unfortunately I'd only had a grand total of five dollars donated in the first week and the names they'd suggested were just plain awful.

(One person had literally suggested "dog treats" as the name for my newest dog treat. Yeah, no.)

Take it from me. Never, ever, ever let strangers name your product.

Anyway. As I walked in the door I was already having a bad morning. Even the delicious smells of coffee and cinnamon rolls didn't help.

Nor did seeing Jamie singing to herself like some scene out of Snow White, her long brown braid swinging happily back and forth with each step she took as she cleaned the tables.

It got worse when I saw the paper.

It was just the *Baker Valley Gazette*, the local paper, so not like the statewide paper or anything, but still. The headline on the front page was *Local Police Too Incompetent To Solve Murders On Their Own*. And right below that, as part of the article, was a picture of yours truly.

I snatched the paper off the table and started reading as Jamie waved to me. "Hey, Maggie. Want a chocolate croissant? I think I've perfected the recipe."

"Better make it two. And can you bring me a Coke?"

I didn't even bother to put Fancy in her cubby in the back of the barkery, just sat down at the nearest table and devoured the article.

It seemed that Peter Nielsen had gotten wind of the fact that I was involved with solving the last few murders in town. Rather than applaud me as a Good Samaritan helping out a hard-working police force (which was the truth) he'd used it as an opportunity to question their competence while painting me as an interfering busybody.

Jamie set a Coke and a plate with a delectable-looking chocolate croissant on the table in front of me. "Hi, Fancy girl. How are you this fine morning?" She gave Fancy a kiss on the nose and a good ear scratch while I finished the article.

I threw it aside and glared at the plate. "I thought I said two croissants?"

"You did. But part of being your best friend is knowing when you mean something and when you don't. You'll be fine with one."

No I wouldn't.

But she was so darned happy I didn't have the heart to argue with her. Instead I took a bite of croissant. For a moment all my worries and anger disappeared, replaced by the sheer heaven of flaky, buttery pastry dough and real chocolate.

"Mmm. Delicious. You nailed it. This could've come straight from a street vendor in Paris."

"Thanks. Mason's mom helped me with the last little

bit. She attended the Sorbonne when she was younger and still keeps a pied-à-terre in central Paris that she said Mason and I can borrow anytime we want. Wouldn't that be amazing? To live in Paris for like six months?"

I was surprised she didn't float out of her chair out of sheer happiness, which is why I didn't point out to her that living in Paris for six months would make it a little challenging to run the café on a daily basis.

Instead I said, "So you're getting on with the family, too, huh?"

"Oh, absolutely. They're all wonderful."

Call me jaded (I am), but I figured they probably weren't all wonderful all the time. But love will do that to you. It's why it's best avoided like the plague. Clouds the senses.

"So you saw the article?" Jamie asked, sitting down across from me.

"Yeah. Doesn't paint a very flattering picture does it? Of any of us."

"I don't know. Depends on how you choose to see it. I think it's pretty impressive really that someone with no investigative training at all has been such a help to the police force."

I laughed. "You would see it that way, wouldn't you? I bet Matt won't. And I bet his boss won't either." I took a long sip of Coke and another bite of croissant to steady myself. "Well, it doesn't matter. Because I am not going to get involved in any other police matter ever. I swear, if I see another dead body I'm stepping over it and going on my merry little way. Let someone else deal with that mess. And if I get accused of murder again, I'll just confess and do the time."

"Mmhm. Sure you will." She gave me that knowing look she has.

"What does that mean?"

"It means I know you, Maggie. And if something else comes up and you think there's a way you can help, you're going to do it. You're not the type to turn away. And, heaven help the police if you think they're not doing a good job."

I lifted my chin in disagreement. "You're wrong. From this day forward I am keeping my nose in my own business."

Not even Fancy was buying it. She gave me a skeptical look from where she'd sprawled at my feet.

Jamie just laughed. "If you say so. Hey, when you're done here I need some help in the kitchen. I'm trying out a new recipe and I could use your input."

"For what?"

"*Lavender* creme brulee."

"Lavender?"

"Mmhm. It's going to be delicious." She bounced out of her chair as a customer walked in.

I winced but fortunately she didn't see it since she was already headed back to the kitchen.

Lavender creme brulee? Why lavender? I know a lot of people like the scent and maybe the taste is nice, too, but ugh. There were so many other choices if you were going to make creme brulee. I'd had an amazing mango one once. But lavender? What ever happened to vanilla? Or chocolate? Or even coconut?

Ah well. It was Jamie. I knew no matter how odd it sounded to me she'd make it taste delicious. And at least she still needed my help with something…

CHAPTER 7

It turns out that a well-made lavender creme brulee is incredibly delicious. It has this delicacy to it that's absolutely heavenly. The iterations before that final sample were less so, but it was all worth it for the final product which Jamie, Greta, and I enjoyed while catching up that afternoon.

Hans, Greta's Irish Wolfhound, rested at her feet, as stalwart as ever, but I noticed that she slipped him a few treats here or there, something she'd never done before. And that she reached down to pet him frequently. He was also lying close enough to her to keep in touch with her foot at all times.

They'd been through a rough situation. I couldn't blame them for wanting the comfort of their closest companion. I'd had a hard enough time dealing with it and it wasn't even my dog that was hurt.

Greta was doing well, too. She looked as polished as ever in a bright purple silk top and trim black slacks, her white blonde hair pulled back in a simple chignon at the base of her neck. She was insanely wealthy, but she kept the jewelry to amazing but subtle pieces. I figured she was only a couple years older than me, but it was hard to tell. She could have just had very good work done.

We talked about Jamie and Mason's wedding options for a bit—a topic that fascinated Jamie and Greta far more than it did me. Who cared what flowers were in season? Or what the latest trend in bridal colors was? Or if there had to be a vegan food option just in case?

And did it really matter if there was a chocolate fountain and a photo booth? Would people care any less if they weren't adequately entertained?

It wasn't that I begrudged my friend a public celebration of finding the love of her life, or even the fact that she'd found someone. It was just that, well…

I hate weddings.

For some reason I'm always getting invited to weddings by close friends who seem to have all these other friends that I've never met. And I never have a plus one to bring, which means I generally get put at the "extras" table with a bunch of folks I've never met before who also don't have a significant other to bring and were probably only invited for arcane social reasons.

Basically, I fall into the same category as the second cousin twice removed who Aunt Betty insisted had to come but no one in the family even knows, and who was only invited because they figured she wouldn't come but then she did.

It's not that my friends don't want me there. They do. And it's not that I don't want to be part of the wonderful joining of their lives. I do. It's just that they're stressed and busy and not available the whole time and I get stuck making conversation with the weirdo next to me who's into something like bug collecting.

And there is never, ever a good-looking, intelligent, funny, interesting single man at one of those things. You'd think there would be, but no. At least not all four qualities in one. (Usually I can't even find a guy who has two of those qualities at a wedding, and if he does have two of them, single isn't one of the two.)

I was prepared to suffer through for Jamie, but that didn't mean I wanted to spend the next few months of my life hearing all the little details that led up to it.

So I was zoned out and brooding about the stupid article and how Matt was going to react when he read it when Greta turned to me. "How is your cop?"

"He's not my cop. He's just…a friend. And he seems to be fine. I mean, I don't know. I don't keep track of him. I'm not his keeper. But last time I saw him he seemed fine." I knew I sounded a little defensive, but he wasn't my cop. Not really.

Greta raised one slender eyebrow as she took a delicate bite of her creme brulee. "So you are still single then? I could bring my friend, Eduard, by to meet you?"

"No."

"You are not single?"

"I am not interested."

Greta had an unfortunate belief that a woman's first husband should be very old and very rich. Since she was probably in the double digits husband-wise and already obscenely rich herself that meant pushing men who met her criteria in my direction instead.

"I have better things to do with my time, Greta. Like figure out how to make the barkery actually thrive."

"Money would help with this, no? Eduard would help with this. He is a very generous man. And very smart.

Very good at business."

"Greta…"

I was on the verge of saying something extremely impolite when I saw Sam, the red-headed freckled kid from the baseball game, ride his bicycle into the parking lot. His cheeks were decidedly pink under his baseball cap and there were spots of sweat on his t-shirt.

I pushed outside. "Sam, right? What are you doing here? Did you ride all the way from Creek? How long did that take you?" It took me twenty minutes by van, it had to have taken him a couple of hours on his battered red bike.

He tried to gather his breath to answer me, but I could see that he'd been crying so I immediately shuffled him inside. "Let me get you something to eat and a drink. You like Coke?"

He nodded. "Yes, ma'am, Mrs. Carver. Thank you."

I pointed him to a table near Greta and Jamie as I ran to the kitchen for a Coke and a chocolate croissant. I figured he probably wouldn't appreciate the buttery delicacy of what Jamie had accomplished, but chocolate and fat are always good choices for anyone remotely human, especially kids.

When I came back he was seated with Greta and Jamie. I was about to shoo him back to the table I'd pointed out to him, but Greta put her hand on his back and shook her head.

Instead I dragged a chair over to join them and set the Coke and croissant in front of him. "Sam, what are you doing here?"

He didn't answer right away. He was too busy drinking down half the Coke and tearing into the croissant. When he finally looked at me he had a smear of chocolate on the corner of his mouth. He'd somehow managed to get chocolate on his fingers, too.

"I need your help, Mrs. Carver."

"It's Miss Carver, not Mrs., but you can just call me Maggie. What's wrong?" I tensed as I remembered that ugly scene from the game the day before.

"My mom's missing. I saw that article in the paper about how you solve crimes." He reached for his backpack and pulled out a baseball-shaped piggy bank that jangled with change as he hefted it onto the table. "I want to hire you to find her."

I opened my mouth to tell him no, but how could I? He was staring at me with those big brown eyes of his like a lost puppy.

"Sam…Ummm. I think you got the wrong idea from that article. But Matt, Mr. Barnes, your coach, I'm sure he can help you. He's a cop. It's his job to find people who go missing."

He hunched his shoulders and looked at the floor. "I called the cops. They won't listen to me. Said to leave it to the adults. But Vick won't do anything. He doesn't care. Said it's just like her to run off. Not the first time she's done it either. She'll come back eventually."

"Is Vick the guy from the game yesterday? The one who yelled at you?"

He nodded, but still wouldn't look at me. I was pretty sure he'd started crying again.

"And the woman? Was that your mom? The one who pulled him away when he got mad?"

He nodded again.

I flicked a glance at Jamie and Greta. "And she's gone?"

"Yeah. She wasn't there when I got home last night. And she wasn't there this morning either. Sometimes she's gone at night, but not in the mornings usually."

"Well, maybe she just needed to get away for a few hours. Vick seemed pretty mad yesterday. I know I wouldn't want to be around a man who was angry like that."

He hunched further into himself. "He's always angry. She doesn't seem to mind."

"But she has gone away before?"

He kicked the table. "You're just like them. You're just like the cops. It's my birthday tomorrow. We were supposed to go shopping today. She's never been gone for my birthday. Never. Something happened to her."

I pressed my lips together. I was way out of my depth on this one. The kid didn't need me. He needed the cops.

I mean, it was pretty obvious to me what must've happened. Only question was whether Sam's mom had run off to get away from her abusive boyfriend for a while or whether the ugly fight I'd seen coming when they walked away from the game had turned into something permanent.

Either way, I was not the person to handle it.

"Tell you what. I'll call Matt for you. And he'll look into it. I promise."

When Sam looked up at me I swear his eyes had doubled in size until he was like one of those cartoon characters that are all just sad eyes and floppy ears. "I want *you* to help, Miss Carver. Not him. I'll pay you." He pushed the piggy bank at me. "There's twenty-two dollars and thirty-one cents in there. It's all I have. Please. You have to help me."

My heart almost broke for the poor kid. "Sam…"

"Please." His eyes filled with tears. "I know she wouldn't leave me. I know it. She's hurt. You have to find her."

I sighed. "Okay. Fine. I'll help."

What else could I say? I would've happily and callously stepped over the body of a dead person to avoid getting sucked into another police investigation, but how do you turn your back on a sad little boy who just wants to find his mother?

"Thank you, Miss Carver." He flung himself out of the chair and hugged me.

I winced, wondering what kind of mess I'd gotten myself into now.

CHAPTER 8

The first thing I did, of course, was call Matt. Sam might not want the cops involved, but I did. And I was still hopeful that there was a chance I could pawn the whole thing off on someone more qualified.

"Maggie May. To what do I owe the pleasure?" Matt practically purred when he answered the phone.

I stepped out back with Fancy so Sam wouldn't hear me. As Fancy ran around sniffing everything and doing her business, I filled Matt in on what had happened.

I loved that space back there with its view of the mountains in the distance and the stream running by at the edge of the grassy area. Only Jamie and I ever used it, since it was fenced off on both sides, so it was like a little private oasis. A perfect spot to sit with a beer at the end of the day.

When Fancy was done with the basics, she gave me a quick look and then ran for the stream, settling herself into the middle of it with a happy little look as I glared at her. I swear, that girl knows how to take advantage of a situation, and she knew I wasn't going to yell at her or try to wade in and bring her back out when I was on the phone.

She is one smart little Newfie. (Smarter than me, I'm pretty sure.)

When I finished telling Matt about Sam's mom I asked, "Do you think Sam's right? That the cops aren't going to look into it?"

"I do. She's an adult. And she hasn't even been gone a day. Plus, from what I hear this isn't the first time Trish has pulled a runner. She's taken off at least once that I know of."

I paced back and forth. That was not what I'd wanted to hear. "Did Sam call about that one, too?"

"No. I don't think anyone did. I heard about it when I was hanging out at the Creek Inn. It seems a couple months ago Trish walked in, a fresh shiner on her eye, looked around the place, zeroed in on some out-of-towner having a beer with his buddies, and within half an hour had the man convinced to take her to Wyoming with him when he left town the next day. Didn't come back for a week."

That wasn't a good sign. How do you tell a kid his mom won't be there for his birthday because she's a bit of a tramp that runs off with strange men?

I pinched the bridge of my nose, thinking.

Maybe this time was different. "Sam said his birthday's tomorrow. And that his mother has never been gone on his birthday before. Maybe this time it's worth investigating."

There was a long silence.

I waited Matt out as I watched Fancy come out of the stream and shake herself off and then go lie down in the shade along the fence. She was going to be a muddy mess. Good thing she seemed to miraculously clean up from even the worst messes after a few hours. If not, my grandpa was going to have something to say about it.

I could almost picture Matt trying to figure out how to get me to drop the whole thing. But that wasn't going to happen, so I finally said, "I've gotta at least try to find her, Matt."

"No, you need to stay out of it. She probably got in a fight with Vick, took off, met someone else, went home with him and spent the day sleeping it off. She'll be back for the kid's birthday tomorrow. Just let it go."

"Sam rode his bike here all the way from Creek. That had to take hours. And you should've seen him, Matt. He probably cried most of the way here. I can't just let it go. He's a little boy who wants his mom there on his birthday. Doesn't he deserve that?"

"Maggie."

"Please help me. At least go by Vick's with me."

Matt sighed.

"Please?" I don't like to beg, but in this case I was willing to make an exception.

There was a long silence on the other end of the line, so I continued, "You're taking some time off, right? Isn't this a better way to spend your time than fishing or watching Jack to see what trouble he'll get into? It's Sam's birthday tomorrow, Matt. He said she's never been gone on his birthday before. And you saw the way that man was with her at the game. I think he did something to her. What if she's injured and we could save her?"

"You need to stay out of their business, Maggie. It could be dangerous."

I didn't say anything. Of course it was going to be dangerous. The man had probably killed his girlfriend.

But didn't Sam deserve to know what had happened to his mom?

"Maggie…"

I shook my head even though I knew Matt couldn't see it. Why did he have to be so darned stubborn?

"Don't you know me by now? I'm not going to stay out of it, Matt. You can come along and help me ask the questions that need to be asked, so we can find this little kid his mother. Or you can sit at home with Jack and worry about what's going to happen to me when I show up at Vick's door accusing him of murder. Your call."

"That's not fair."

"It may not be fair, but those are your choices."

Fancy watched me from where she'd laid down in the shade, one eyebrow raised. Even she knew I was playing dirty, but I didn't really care. This was about a little kid and his mom. I'd play as dirty as it took.

And I really needed Matt to say yes. If he didn't I was going to have to ask my grandpa for help, which I did not want to do.

As impetuous as I might be, even I knew that it wouldn't be smart to confront Vick alone.

"Damn it, Maggie. Why can't you just leave things be?" Matt growled.

I knew when he cussed that I had him. "So you'll meet me at my place in an hour?"

"Yeah. See you there."

"Thank you," I practically sang into the phone. I should've probably toned it down a bit given Matt's reluctance to get involved, but I was so happy I wouldn't have to rope my grandpa into helping out that I couldn't help it.

CHAPTER 9

I sincerely apologized to Jamie for leaving her—yet again—to take care of things at the barkery. It's a good thing she's such a go-with-the-flow even-keeled sort of person or I was pretty sure I'd have lost her as a friend by that point.

She just smiled and said, "We should've put some money on your statement that you wouldn't get involved in another police matter."

"Well, *technically*, it's not a police matter since they wouldn't look into it. But I am sorry to do this again."

She laughed. "Don't worry about it, Maggie. I completely understand. He rode all the way here. His mom is missing. You have to help. If you didn't, I would. Now go. I've got this."

"You're sure?"

"Positive."

"Thank you." I gave her a quick hug before shuffling Fancy and Sam out to my van.

Jamie is one of the best people I know. And competent as all get out. She could run the café, the barkery, and the world without breaking a sweat if she wanted to, so at least I knew the place was in good hands and I could focus on Sam and his mom.

During the twenty-minute drive home Sam talked non-stop. I heard about what he and his mother had done on every single birthday since he'd turned five, the names of all of his friends at school, the names of the three older boys who bullied him at lunch each day, what those boys had done to him over the last school year, his plans for when he was grown up and could fight back, as well as the fact that he planned on being a superhero, a cop, an astronaut, and a fighter pilot. Oh, and a billionaire. And…

It was a lot.

By the time I walked in the front door at home I was ready for a nap or a Tylenol or maybe both, but that wasn't going to happen. Because sitting together at the kitchen table, their faces grim, were my grandpa and Matt.

I should've known Matt wouldn't keep my grandpa out of it, but I gave him a really nasty glare anyway.

I grabbed ice cream from the freezer for Sam, Fancy, and myself (puppy ice cream for Fancy) and in an artificially cheery voice said, "Hey, Sam, why don't you go out back with Fancy. I need to talk to these guys for a minute."

Once they were outside I turned to deal with the dual threat of my grandpa and Matt. I figured I needed every advantage I could get, so rather than sit at the table I leaned against the fridge as I carefully unwrapped my ice cream bar. (Technically a salted caramel gelato bar—yum—but whatever.)

"Maggie May." My grandpa folded his hands on the

table, giving me flash backs to being grounded when I was a kid.

"Don't even try to talk me out of this, Grandpa. I am not letting that little boy spend his birthday wondering where his mom is if I can do something about it."

My grandpa tapped his fingers together as he glared me down. "Vick Kline is the worst sort of scum. You think he won't hurt you if he did this? He will. You even suggest he did it, he'll hurt you. Just for fun."

I barely stopped myself from rolling my eyes. "It's not like I'm going alone. Matt's coming with me. And this Vick guy can't be stupid enough to go after a cop."

My grandpa raised one eyebrow as if questioning that assessment. "Matt isn't going with you."

I stared at Matt, hurt. "You're not? But you said you would."

"I'm a police officer, Maggie." He rubbed the back of his neck with a wince. "And after that little newspaper article today my boss told me very specifically to keep you out of any and all police investigations."

"But it's not a police investigation. If it was, I wouldn't need to do this. Why don't you tell him that?"

He laughed. "Because I don't really want to push back on him right now. That would not be good."

"Look, all I'm asking is that you come along while I ask a guy a few questions. That's all."

He shook his head. "I can't do it, Maggie. Especially if you're planning on accusing him of murder. How am I going to explain that if he goes and complains?"

"I don't know. You're smart. You can think up something."

"I can't do it, Maggie."

I looked back and forth between them. "So you guys just want me to drop it? Well, that's not going to happen."

My grandpa reached for his non-existent cigarettes and then glared at his coffee like he wished it were whiskey instead. "We know. That's why I'm coming with you."

"Grandpa…I don't think that's a good idea."

(I know. If Matt had turned me down originally I'd planned on turning to my grandpa, but the more I thought about getting him involved with confronting a potentially dangerous man, the more that seemed like a really volatile combination that could end up with my grandpa in jail. Or worse.)

"Maggie May, don't you even start with me. I may be old, but I survived years in prison surrounded by men like Vick Kline. I know how to handle a man like that."

"That's what I'm worried about."

He snorted.

"Promise me before we go that you aren't going to do anything that would require someone to call the cops."

He very deliberately took a sip of his coffee instead of answering.

Great. So now my choices were go on my own—which was not a good idea and we all knew it—or take my grandpa who was likely to do something I'd regret witnessing and that might make me an accessory to something I didn't want to be an accessory to.

Or I could just let it go. Walk away because it wasn't my business if some woman who ran off on a regular basis happened to do so the day before her kid's birthday.

Even if her kid had ridden his bike all that way to find me and ask for my help.

But that wasn't me. Jamie was right. If I could help Sam, I was going to do it.

Just then Fancy ran inside followed by Sam who was screaming and trying to slap at her. I was about to tell him that no one, and I mean no one, yells at my dog. And certainly no one hits my dog unless they want me to hit them. But then I saw the two little paws sticking out of the side of Fancy's mouth.

She'd caught a bunny.

As if things weren't bad enough.

"Fancy, drop it. Right now," I said, my voice whipping out at her.

She did.

But then it moved. So she picked it back up.

The look she gave me said, "I dropped it like you asked me to, so don't glare at me like that." (I swear, sometimes she is too clever by half. It's like having a mischievous twelve-year-old boy around all the time.)

"Drop it," I snapped again.

She did.

"Leave it," I said before she could pick it back up. I stepped forward. "Go. Outside. Now."

Fancy cried at me, but she went outside, tail tucked down and head bowed. She knew she was in trouble, she just didn't know why.

"You too, Sam. Go back outside."

He looked at the slobber-covered bunny at my feet, but then followed her outside without argument.

I glanced down at the bunny, part of me hoping that it was already gone so I wouldn't have to figure out what you do with a baby bunny that your dog has scared half to death but hasn't killed.

Unfortunately, it was still breathing.

Or fortunately. I mean, I was glad it was alive and that Fancy hadn't killed it. But now I had one more thing to deal with. And I couldn't just put the thing back out in the yard. It was making no effort to go anywhere, just lying there on its side breathing fast. If I put it in the yard and it didn't recover it would certainly be dead.

But what else was I supposed to do with it? I was pretty sure there weren't a bunch of bunny rehabs out there. And I certainly didn't know the first thing about raising a bunny.

Plus, I didn't want a pet bunny. I just wanted my dog to have not killed the wild bunnies living in our yard.

I shook my head. "Someone get me a box."

I grabbed a dish towel from the drawer and turned back but neither Matt nor my grandpa had moved.

"Did you hear me? Someone get me a box."

Matt looked at the bunny and back at me. "Maggie, what are you going to do with a box?"

"Put the bunny in it. Give it a safe place to recover. When it's better I'll put it back outside."

He and my grandpa exchanged a look.

"What?"

Matt looked like he wanted to say something, but instead he stood up. "You have a good box for rehabbing a bunny?" he asked my grandpa.

My grandpa nodded towards the hallway. "Should be something on the top shelf in the front closet."

When Matt came back he took the dish towel from me. "I'll take care of this. Why don't you and your grandpa go deal with Vick Kline before it gets dark. He should be home from work by now. He works the early shift at the mine."

"Are you sure?"

He nodded. "Yeah. Go."

I left, glad I wasn't actually going to have to deal with the bunny.

(I kinda knew there was probably nothing to be done for the poor bunny and that Matt was sparing me having to see that, but I pretended that he really was going to create a little home for it in that box and that in a few hours it would be back under my grandpa's porch hopping around with all its little bunny friends. The alternative was just too sad to contemplate.)

CHAPTER 10

Vick Kline lived in one of a cluster of rundown trailer homes a few blocks from the ball park. There were no yards to speak of—the trailers were clustered too close together on a single lot. And no road either, just a dirt track that ran between them.

We parked on the street and walked towards the cluster of trailers, my grandpa leading the way. Clearly, he knew where he was going. I certainly didn't.

A woman in a big muumuu with bright flowers on it watched us with narrowed eyes. She was smoking a cigarette, her other hand wrapped around some sort of alcoholic beverage that probably consisted of cheap whiskey and generic soda on the rocks. A couple of kids a little older than Sam played in the dirt in front of her trailer and I wondered if one or both of them were the bullies Sam had told me about.

She nodded to my grandpa. "Lou. What brings you around?"

"Nat. Here to see Vick. Sam said Trish is missing. You seen her today?"

"No, but good to know where that kid got to. I was

supposed to be watching him but he lit out of here on his bike a few hours ago." She took a long drag on her cigarette as she eyed me up and down.

I opened my mouth to ask if she'd bothered to be worried about him at all, but my grandpa grabbed me by the wrist and squeezed. He knew me too well.

"By the way, Nat, this is my granddaughter, Maggie May. Maggie May, this is Nat."

She nodded. "Seen you around. You have that dog thing in Bakerstown with the Green girl, right?"

"The Baker Valley Barkery and Café. Yes."

"Right. The dog thing." She narrowed her eyes as she blew out a stream of smoke. "People actually pay for that stuff?" (The word she used was not in fact "stuff" but it started with the same letter.)

"Some people do." I tried not to sound offended, even though I was. I failed.

"Huh. Who would've thought it."

My grandpa dragged me away before I could say anything else, calling out, "Thanks, Nat. Give my best to Don."

Nat nodded and went back to watching the kids who were jumping around and kicking at each other, shouting back and forth as they tried to re-enact some movie they'd seen somewhere. I heard a smack as one of the kids connected a little too hard and turned back to see Nat take another drag on her cigarette, completely unconcerned as the two kids rolled on the ground pummeling at one another.

My grandpa led the way to a faded green trailer at the end of the line. There were some rusted spots, but overall it looked well-tended for what it was. The curtains in the window were crisp and white with little edges of dark green lace.

He stepped up the wooden stairs and thumped on the door with his fist three times.

Vick answered the door in a white tank top and what looked like the same jeans from the day before. He scratched at his belly and I was treated to the sight of way too much hair in places I didn't want to know it existed. "What?"

"We're looking for Trish. She here?"

"No." Vick looked like he'd just woken up from a nap, the creases from the couch still visible on his face and what remained of his hair sticking up in at least three places.

"Where is she then?"

"How'm I supposed to know? I'm not her keeper."

I wanted to make some smart aleck comment about Sam and whether he'd even noticed the kid was gone, but my grandpa glared at me before he stepped into the trailer, forcing Vick to step back to avoid touching him.

My grandpa filled the doorframe as he looked around the living area. "It's Sam's birthday tomorrow. He says they were supposed to go shopping today. Make sense to you that she's not here for that?"

Vick ran a hand through his greasy, receding hairline, smoothing it down. "No. She loves that kid more than anything."

"Then where is she?"

"I don't know. Look. Trish took off yesterday. We had a thing. Said some words. And then she tore out of here. I figured she'd be back last night. When she wasn't, I figured she'd be back today. She does that sort of thing."

"But she's not."

Vick met my grandpa's gaze for a brief moment and hunched his shoulders. "She does that sort of thing, too. Always looking to trade up. But she comes back eventually. I'm good to her. Better than most of the losers she finds for herself."

I stepped up to the base of the stairs. "Mind if we look around?"

Both he and my grandpa glared at me, but I glared right back. "What? You're going to take his word for it that she just took off like that? Do you know what she's done for each of Sam's birthdays? Treasure hunts and special picnics at the park. That sort of thing. And now we're just supposed to believe him that she didn't care this year because they got in a fight?"

Vick's eyes were black with hatred as he glared down at me.

My grandpa very deliberately braced his arm across the doorway between us. "She could be a little more polite about it, but she has a point, Vick. Show me around."

I stepped forward to join them, but my grandpa shook his head. "You stay out here. I'll be back in a minute."

I wanted to argue, but I knew I'd lose. Instead I walked around the perimeter of the trailer looking for any signs of foul play.

(And, no, I really had no idea what that would be. Pretty sure most killers don't intentionally leave a big pool of blood visible for anyone to see.)

There was nothing that looked the least bit suspicious.

No broken furniture. No rolled up rugs. No bloody baseball bats. Just a bunch of weeds and some rusted out car parts around back. The little bit I could see of each of the windows looked well-tended and clean, though. Seems wherever she'd disappeared to Trish had taken some pride in her home.

My grandpa didn't find anything either. He just shook his head as he stepped back outside.

He turned and shook Vick's hand. "Thanks, Vick. You'll let me know if she comes back?"

Vick nodded. "And if you find her you'll let me know?" He actually sounded concerned.

My grandpa nodded. "I will."

As we walked back to my grandpa's truck, I muttered, "You didn't have to be so friendly to him, you know. Even if he isn't the reason she's missing, he probably still beats her. And he's most definitely a drunk. I mean, look at that woman who was supposed to be watching Sam today. A cigarette in one hand, a drink in the other…"

My grandpa grabbed my arm and pulled me to a stop. "Maggie May. Not everyone has a charmed life like you did."

I opened my mouth to protest that my life had been far from charmed, thank you very much, but the look he gave me made me snap it shut again.

"I know. You're life wasn't perfect." He leaned closer. "But you ever been hit?"

I shook my head. "No. Of course not."

"You ever had a parent gone for months or years because they were in jail?"

"No."

"You ever had to add water to your ketchup to make it last longer?"

"No." My dad had before my grandpa came into his life, I knew that, but I never had.

"Or sleep on a friend of a friend of a friend's couch because that was the only way to have a roof over your head that night?"

"No." I muttered the answer, wanting him to stop already. I got it. Other people were worse off.

"Then don't judge, Maggie." He gestured at the trailers. "You look at these people and you see what they aren't. So what if they don't have pretty yards in front of their homes. Or they drink and smoke a little more than you think is right. Or maybe they get so worn out and run down by life they lose it every once in a while. That doesn't make them bad people, Maggie May. It just means they're living in bad circumstances."

"Fine. Okay. But…If he was hitting her, that isn't right. And if he ever hit Sam…"

"Agreed. But I walked through that place and it was clean as a button. And that kid had three times as many clothes as either of them. I'm not saying Vick isn't a violent man or that he couldn't stand to lay off on the drink. But I don't think he did this. Wherever Trish is, it isn't because Vick put her there."

I pressed my lips together. I wasn't so sure. I mean, come on. Drunk man threatens woman and kid in public and then woman goes missing, how can you not think the drunk man is responsible?

But there was no point in arguing with my grandpa about it. Not after I'd just insulted his friend. "Okay. So if she did leave on her own, then where'd she go?"

"That's the question isn't it? Let's go home. Vick gave me a list of numbers you can call."

CHAPTER 11

We headed back home to regroup. I was surprised to find Jack there when we arrived. Especially since he was seated at the dining room table working a puzzle of a mountain meadow with Sam.

He glanced up when we walked through the door. "Hope you don't mind. We dug this out of the closet. Thought it would be more interesting than watching that big mutt wait to catch another bunny."

"Where's Matt?" I asked.

Jack glanced at Sam but the kid was focused on putting together a section of the puzzle border, his tongue sticking out of the corner of his mouth.

"He went to take that bunny to a friend of his who specializes in that sort of thing. Asked me to keep an eye on Sam while he was gone."

For a moment I got my hopes up about the fate of the poor little bunny Fancy had gotten ahold of. But when I caught my grandpa's smug look I realized Matt had taken it elsewhere to spare Sam knowing what had happened to it.

My grandpa leaned close and whispered, "*Now* are

you going to let me take care of the rabbits?"

"No," I whispered back. "Because you'd take care of all of them. Fancy isn't fast enough to get more than one or two."

He shook his head and walked towards the kitchen. "You hungry, Jack? Want to stick around for dinner?"

"Sure. Why not?"

I was fine with having Matt over for dinner on a regular basis, but Jack was another story. Then again, he did seem to be doing well with Sam. At least the kid wasn't crying anymore. And since we'd found absolutely no sign of his mother, he needed someone to look after him.

I followed my grandpa into the kitchen. "What are we going to do with Sam?"

"He can stay here or go with Jack until his mom's back."

"Vick didn't care about that?"

He shook his head. "Naw, he just wants Trish. If Sam comes along for the ride, fine. But when she's not there…He could care less what happens to that boy."

"Doesn't she have a mom or other relatives that can look after him?"

"Her mom is out of state. No other family. A few friends here or there. But usually when Trish disappears for a while Vick dumps Sam on Nat. The woman you met today."

"Oh."

He gave me a look that had me ducking my head in apology. "You have that list of numbers for me to call?"

He reached into the breast pocket of his flannel shirt and handed it over. I turned it around, trying to figure out which direction was up.

"What?"

"I'm just wondering if I'll be able to decipher your handwriting. Is that a two or a seven?"

"A two. Now get out of the kitchen and make those calls while I put something together for dinner."

As I grabbed my phone, my grandpa pulled a box of macaroni and cheese from the cupboard and rooted out some hot dogs from the fridge. I paused and stared at him. "You are not seriously going to fix mac n cheese with hotdogs for dinner are you?"

He nodded. "Yes, I am. It's the perfect dinner choice for kids."

Maybe in the seventies it was.

"There's not even a vegetable in that."

"Vegetables are over-rated. But you want a vegetable there's some canned peas in the cupboard."

He knew how much I hated canned peas. I'd once spent three hours sitting at the dinner table because I refused to eat those mushy, gushy nasty things and my grandma wouldn't let me leave until I'd cleaned my plate. I'm not really sure who won that battle of wills since I swallowed each one whole rather than eat it and she had to sit there the whole three hours to make sure I didn't ditch them down the drain when she wasn't looking.

I glared at him for a long moment, but my grandpa was in a mood, and when my grandpa was in a mood there was no point arguing with him because he could dig in harder than a diamond.

We'd all survive one night of bad food.

But hotdogs? This was one of those times when I wished I lived somewhere that had a Pizza Hut right around the corner. Unfortunately, delivery of any kind of food was non-existent in our little town or the neighboring towns for that matter. It was eat what you have on hand or drive to the next town over for a meal.

And since I didn't want to do that...

I took my phone out to the back porch so I could make my calls and check on Fancy at the same time. She'd stationed herself on the porch, her nose poked through the slats, chin resting on the bottom rail as she watched the yard, completely motionless.

There was nothing to see, but that didn't seem to bother her. Clearly she'd found a spot she thought gave her a good vantage point for if or when another bunny showed up.

I walked to the other end of the porch and leaned on the side rail to dial the first number, the one for Trish's mom.

As the phone rang I glanced down to see two baby bunnies and two adult bunnies gathered together in the shade happily munching on the grass, having what looked to be a nice little family picnic.

I snorted. Of course that's how it would be. Fancy was so intent on looking for bunnies in one direction she'd completely missed the family gathering happening in the other direction.

No one answered at Trish's mom's house. The answering machine kicked in—and it was definitely a machine that I'd bet probably ran on tapes and everything—and informed me that she was sailing the seas in Mexico and wouldn't be back for a week.

I winced, but hung up without leaving a message. No point in worrying her when Trish would probably be back before she was. But hadn't anyone ever told her not to announce to the world that she'd be out of town and to please stop by and steal her things while she was away? It was like the people who posted on Facebook about all of their travel plans.

"Hey, world, look, I'm in Europe right now having an amazing time. Yes, of course that means that my house is unprotected because I even complained on here about having to board my dogs. Oh, and yes, that fancy schmancy TV I posted a picture of at Christmas is absolutely sitting in my front room right now."

Especially since most of the people who did that sort of thing also had seven hundred and fifty "friends" on Facebook. I'm sorry, but no. Those people are not all your friends. And if they are your friends, well, you probably aren't a very good friend to them.

(Sorry for my rant. I'm the small, close circle of friends type of person and take it personally when I run up against the "everyone is my friend" type who is more performing for an audience than forming friendships. But I digress. To each their own.)

After missing Trish's mother, I quickly worked my way down the rest of the list. There were two friends from high school who hadn't heard from her in days but agreed she'd never miss Sam's birthday, as well as an ex who hadn't heard from her either but did try to hit on me by inviting me to come over and check out his place if I wanted, because according to him I sounded like sunshine on the phone.

Seriously? Did that line ever work for him? It's about as bad as "Is your father a thief? Did he steal the stars and put them in your eyes?" Although not near as unique as the guy who once stopped me on the street to tell me he liked the shape of my upper arms. (That one was probably a cannibal or something weird. Not my legs? My arms? Okay. Whatever.)

I even tried Trish's work, but that just earned me a long rant from the boss who said the only reason he'd given her two days off when he was short staffed was because of Sam's birthday. He threatened to fire Trish if she'd pulled a runner rather than do what she'd said she was going to do which, according to him, was take Sam down to Denver for a day at the zoo.

After I hung up from that call I needed a long moment to recover my sunny disposition (ha), so I stared at the bunnies as they happily munched on the grass without caring at all that I was right there watching them. Fearless little things.

I didn't know what else to do about Trish. We'd tried her home and struck out there, I'd tried her friends, I'd tried her work, I'd even tried her worthless ex.

But then I remembered that Trish had pulled her last runner by picking up a random guy at a bar. I figured the dive bar in Bakerstown where Marla worked was more her speed, but that the Creek Inn was closer and more likely to have the type of easy mark Trish could charm. She might have bad taste in men, but she was still an attractive woman so could pull a higher class of guy if needed.

I dialed Abe, the not openly gay but so gay owner of the Creek Inn, and also one of my favorite people in the entire county.

"Hello?"

"Hey, Abe, it's Maggie Carver. How are you?"

"Good, Maggie. When are you going to come in and

visit us at the Inn? I'm starting to feel hurt that you haven't dropped by. Maybe I'll just have to make my next barkery order a delivery."

Abe was also one of my best customers. He and his partner Evan came by on a regular basis to pick up dog treats for their St. Bernard, Lucy Carrots.

I'd yet to make it to the Creek Inn to return the favor, though. Probably because I was in my pajamas curled up on the couch by six most nights. And bars are just…not my scene. Too much noise. Too many drunks. And men who try to grope you before they even talk to you…

Yeah, not a place I'd willingly go.

Not that Abe would run a place like that. But in a small town where the pickings were slim I figured a reasonably attractive woman walking into a bar was going to attract some attention no matter how nice the place. And after being as charming as I could manage at work all day I didn't have much left for random creeps. Even well-meaning ones.

"I will someday, I promise. Might even do so tonight, depending on what you have to say."

"Really? Do tell."

"Um, do you know Trish Mullens? Redhead with questionable taste in men?"

He laughed. "Yeah, she's in here fairly regular."

"Was she in there last night by any chance?"

He took a moment to think about it. "Yeah, I think she was. We have a group in right now and I remember her talking to one of them. Last night was the only night they've made it to the bar since they've been here."

"Any chance she left with one of them?"

"Can't say I noticed. Why?"

"She's missing. Didn't come home last night. And it's her son's birthday tomorrow so he's convinced something bad must've happened to her."

"I didn't know you and Trish Mullens were friends."

"We're not. But the cops won't look into it yet, so I said I would."

He harrumphed. "That article go to your head? You taking on clients now?"

"No. But that stupid article is why Sam Mullens rode his bike from Creek to the barkery and offered me all the money in his piggy bank to look for her. What was I supposed to do? The cops won't look for her yet because she's not considered missing for at least a day. And even if it had been a day they wouldn't be all that concerned because it seems she likes to take off on a regular basis."

"That she does. She'll probably be back tomorrow."

"Yeah, probably. But I have to give it a try for the kid, you know. You think those guys will be back tonight?"

"Maybe. They're staying here and not much else to do unless they want to drive all the way to Masonville."

"You mind texting me as soon as they show up?"

"Sure. Happy to."

"Thanks."

I hung up and turned to look at Fancy, because she was still staring intently out at the yard while the bunny family picnic continued at my feet. "You are not a very good bunny dog, do you know that?"

She ignored me.

"Do you understand that there is a whole family of bunnies that has been having dinner over here while you're staring off into space over there?"

She still ignored me.

I pointed over the railing. "Bunny, Fancy. Bunny."

She turned to look at me.

"Bunny." I pointed again.

She slowly stood and looked in the direction I was pointing.

(Don't worry. I had no expectation that she'd catch any of them. She's slow. And most bunnies are fast. Turns out the only reason she'd caught that bunny earlier in the day was because it had frozen out in the middle of the yard and all she'd had to do was duck her head and pick it up from the grass.)

(Plus she was up on the porch and I figured they'd run as soon as she made a move towards them.)

I didn't want her to catch them, but I did figure they needed to be just a little bit more scared than they were. Maybe scared enough to stop hanging out in my grandpa's yard before he took matters into his own hands.

"Bunny, Fancy" I said, again, nodding my head towards the bunnies who'd finally deigned to notice my existence but still hadn't bothered to run away.

Fancy finally came over to see what I was pointing at and saw the bunnies. She turned and ran for the ramp and then galumphed after them but they scattered and hid without even breaking a sweat.

At which point she started to cry very loudly and look at me like it was all my fault somehow. Shaking my head, I went back inside to have the kind of dinner I hadn't had since I was a kid. (And hadn't wanted to have since I was a kid either.)

"Enough, Fancy. Dinner."

CHAPTER 12

My grandpa was gone when I walked back inside, but the food was ready.

Turns out Lesley had called and asked him to come over. Bill had passed earlier that day and she wasn't doing so well being alone in their house all by herself. (She had kids and grandkids but they'd left her alone because she'd asked for the space. Plus, I think sometimes it takes talking to someone who's been through what you've been through at a time like that and my grandpa had, unfortunately, been there himself just a couple years before.)

It was good for Lesley that she had my grandpa to turn to, but I worried about him. As much as I liked Lesley—and I did, she was a good, kind woman—I wasn't entirely happy with the thought of my grandpa moving on.

I mean, he'd been married to my grandma for forty years. Is it even possible to move on from something like that? And what does it say if you can?

Those were my thoughts at the time. What can I say, I can be petty sometimes.

But I knew deep down that if someone moves on after losing a love like that it isn't because they didn't love deeply. It's because they were once loved so much that they crave that connection with another person and can't live without it.

Once I'd acknowledged that I also acknowledged that I should be grateful that my grandpa actually had the potential to find that type of connection again with Lesley. It's not often that people have a chance at that kind of love twice in their life.

Still, though.

My grandpa was all I had left. I didn't want to lose him and I didn't want to see him hurt.

🐾 🐾 🐾

We squeezed four chairs around the kitchen table because the dining room table was still covered by the half-finished puzzle. It was a little tight moving around in the kitchen with the table pulled away from the wall and Fancy sprawled next to my chair, but we made it work.

We couldn't talk about Sam's missing mom over dinner. At least not in the sort of "where do you think she ran off to" way I wanted.

At least Fancy did actually join us for dinner. She laid down next to me and daintily ate mac n cheese and hot dogs off her sharing plate I put on the floor. I had to tell Sam not to feed her, though, because he would've probably given her half his meal just for the fun of watching her eat each bite and then gaze up at him with her sad amber eyes begging for the next one.

She didn't make it through the whole meal, though. About halfway through I hiccuped. (It happens sometimes if you drink as much Coke as I do.) When I did that Fancy jerked her head up and stared at me with horror in her eyes, her entire body tensed to flee.

Hiccups being hiccups, I did it again, and she scrambled to her feet and ran outside, looking back at me like I was suddenly possessed.

Who knew a hundred and forty pound dog could be scared of someone with hiccups? But she was.

At least it made Sam laugh. He giggled his head off and wouldn't stop talking about it for the next five minutes.

After that Sam and Jack pretty much dominated the dinner conversation with a debate about the various superheroes and which was the best one.

I would've never expected it, but Jack got right down in there with the details, debating whether super strength was better than the ability to fly, and what x-ray vision could really be used for.

I caught Matt's eye at one point and raised my eyebrows as if to say, "Look at that? Who knew Jack would be so good with kids?"

He nodded and watched Jack with a thoughtful, but slightly sad look on his face.

After dinner I asked Jack to check Trish's Facebook account to see if she'd made any posts, but she hadn't. He also sent her a private message to let her know he had Sam with him, just in case.

I found it interesting that Jack had stayed Facebook friends with her even after they'd broken up and he'd left town. I tried to talk to him about it, but he shrugged me off. Whatever his reasons, there was more to it than "Never occurred to me to unfriend her."

I would've pushed more—just to annoy Jack more than for any other reason and because I'm always curious about those sorts of things—but Abe texted me to let me know the guys who'd been talking to Trish the night before were there.

I showed my phone to Matt. "I should go talk to these guys and I don't know if or when my grandpa's going to be back. You think you can go to a bar with me without getting in trouble? Otherwise I'll have to take Jack with me."

"No way are you and Jack going to a bar together."

"Is that so? And why not?"

Jack winked at me. "It's alright. Maggie and I'll get our alone time some other day. Sam and I can hold down the fort here until you get back."

Matt glared at him, but didn't say anything.

"Come on, Matt. Let's get going. No idea how long those guys are going to stay there."

As I grabbed my purse, Jack added, "You two don't do anything I wouldn't do."

I turned to look at him. "*Is* there anything you wouldn't do, Jack?"

"Good question." He swaggered towards me. "I figure you should never rule out any possibilities. Who knows what fun you'll miss?"

"Come on, Maggie, let's go." Matt frowned as he led me out the door, but I just laughed. Jack was trouble, no doubt about it, but he was amusing, too.

CHAPTER 13

As we were walking towards Matt's truck—a blue Ford F-250 extended cab that I always had to hop to get into—my phone rang.

It was my old boss, Karen. When I'd quit I'd told her to call me if a question came up that she thought only I could answer. I didn't want to leave her in the lurch, and even though I'd tried to pass on as much as I could before I left, I knew there'd always be a few things that I could answer in a minute that would take hours or days for someone else to track down.

Even though I had no intention of ever going back to that job or that city I also didn't believe in burning bridges. So I answered as Matt held the door for me.

"Hey, Karen. What's up?"

"Hey, Maggie. How are you? How's the dog bakery going?"

(She wasn't the type to ever use the word barkery. It was too cutesy for her.)

"It's going well," I lied. No point in telling her I was feeling like a failure. "And how are you?"

We made some polite chit-chat for a few minutes as

Matt drove through the winding canyon between Creek and the Creek Inn.

The whole time we were talking I was wondering what on earth was going on because Karen was not the type for small talk. I remember the first time I met her I asked if she knew someone who had worked at her old employer. As you do. Trying to form connection. She'd said "Yes," and then immediately changed the topic to something business-related.

I'd worked for her for five years and she'd been like that the whole time. Not an easy fit for someone as unfiltered as myself who actually likes to be friends with the people I work with.

Which meant that her taking the time to chit chat the way she was before she got to the point did not bode well.

Finally, I couldn't stand the suspense anymore. "Look, Karen, I'm headed somewhere and going to have to get off the phone in a minute. Was there something specific you were calling about?"

She almost sounded relieved when she said, "Actually, yes. Remember the Devinson project?"

"Yeah."

It was one of the most challenging and annoying projects I'd ever worked on. I'd liked the challenge part of it, but the rest…Ugh. Probably part of the reason I'd finally hit my breaking point and decided to leave.

"They want to do a Phase II to build out what we proposed in Phase I."

"Congratulations. That's great. How many years of work is that going to be for you?" I put a subtle emphasis on the *you* part of that sentence.

"Three. But they had one condition."

My gut clenched. I did not like where this conversation was heading. "Oh?"

Matt pulled the truck into the gravel parking lot in front of the Creek Inn and killed the engine as Karen said, "They won't hire us to do the project unless you're involved."

"What? That's ridiculous. You don't need me." I gave Matt a quick sorry glance as he settled in to wait for my call to end.

"We tried to tell them that. But Craig is convinced that it just won't be the quality he wants it to be if you aren't involved."

(He was probably right. That didn't mean the project wouldn't be a success, though.)

I drummed my fingers on the dash. "Did you tell him I quit and moved to Colorado to start a barkery?"

"I did."

"And?"

"He told me to make you an offer you can't refuse. So here it is…"

Before I could stop her she'd laid out the details.

It was good money. *Really* good money.

I'd earned enough before to comfortably live on my own in DC, which is not a cheap city to live in. This offer was three times that. *And* they'd include housing right by the client site. *And* they'd pay for day care for Fancy.

It was a dream offer.

If going back to what I'd been doing before was in any way what I wanted to do with my life.

I opened my mouth to tell her no, but she beat me to the punch on that one, too. "I don't want an answer right now, Maggie. Think about it. I'll call you back in a few days. Just remember, we don't get this project without you. So we're all counting on you. I'll email a copy of the contract for your review."

"Karen…"

"Just in case. Give it some serious thought, Maggie. Please. We need you on this." She hung up.

I stared at the phone for a long moment. It would've been easier if I could just tell her no instead of having to think about all that money. And how they needed me.

She knew just how to push my buttons.

I could probably turn down the money even if that made me a fool and I regretted it in five years when I was begging space on my friends' couches.

But to let down a team? To cost them a three-year project? That was going to be a lot harder to do.

It would've been one thing if I thought Jamie needed me, too, but with her comments about Paris it was pretty clear she was looking for a way out. Or at least, dreaming of something other than running a small town café with her best friend.

So I had Jamie who probably wanted out and didn't know how to say it, a barkery that wasn't living up to my expectations, and now a job offer that was almost too good to refuse where other people would suffer if I said no.

I shook my head when Matt opened his mouth to say something. "Later. Right now let's see if we can't find Trish and get this over with." I forced myself to sound cheerful even though a sick ball of stress had settled right in my gut.

CHAPTER 14

The Creek Inn was a valley staple. It had existed in one form or another since the first families showed up and built their first cabins. Abe and Evan hadn't owned it all that time, obviously. They'd only been around for the last five years or so. What on earth had possessed them to abandon their life in suburban Atlanta to run a small town bar and hotel in the mountains of Colorado, I do not know. But they seemed to like it. And being the owners of the Inn gave them an instant acceptance they probably wouldn't have found otherwise.

The Inn in its current incarnation was a tall white-washed building with green trim along the sloped roof and downspouts. Inside the bar portion it was one giant room with a long bar that stretched the length of the back wall, polished wooden tables scattered around the place, and a single dilapidated pool table (bar size, not regulation) and dart board tucked in the corner near the restrooms.

Everything was worn but clean. The walls were covered with Colorado paraphernalia of one sort or another, including a large selection of the old Colorado license plates (white lettering on green) that I would always think of as the real version. That new white with green lettering deal? Yeah, no. Those were not Colorado plates even if it had been twenty or so years since the changeover.

Abe waved at us as soon as we walked in. "What can I get you?"

In the interest of looking like Matt wasn't there helping me with what should be a police investigation, we each ordered a beer. They had Laughing Lab on tap so I went with that. It's a nice brown beer made by a brewery in Colorado Springs that I've always enjoyed.

Matt ordered a Coors Light. I was going to tease him about it, but before I could he pointed out that he was driving us back so he needed to keep the alcohol content as low as possible. That made enough sense that I didn't give him a hard time about the fact that his beer could likely be confused with yellow-tinged sparkling water.

We chatted with Abe and Evan for a few minutes as Abe poured our beers. They were headed to Canada for a week of heli-hiking on Monday which sounded like a ton of fun to me. Imagine being helicoptered to the top of some mountain peak it might take days to reach and then getting to hike around from there. I'd wanted to do something similar in New Zealand with a helicopter that dropped you at the top of a glacier, but the weather hadn't cooperated. Someday I'd get back there and make it happen.

Or I'd go to Canada where the weather was more predictable and heli-hike there instead. Right after I won the lottery. (Or completed a three-year project I didn't really want to do that would take me away from my family, friends, and Colorado…)

I reached for my purse to pay for my beer but Matt handed his card over before I could even get ahold of my wallet.

"Thanks. Next one's on me," I said, but he shook his head.

"You're not buying your drinks as long as I'm around. My mom would never forgive me for it."

I was tempted to launch into a lengthy discussion of how frickin' complicated it was to figure out when to pay for your beer or not when you're a woman. When I was younger men just bought my drinks, so I got used to that. But then I went to work out of college and most of the guys I worked with treated me like one of the guys and expected me to chip in, which I did. But it was my MBA program which really messed me up, because the guys would each buy a round and it was hard to get in there to pay for a round myself. But if I didn't manage to do so then the guys in my study group would give me a hard time for mooching off of everyone. Which I wasn't trying to do. But if someone puts a beer in your hand, what do you say?

You want me to pay, I'll pay. You don't, I won't. But what am I supposed to do? Hit people to be allowed to buy the next round?

I finally got to the point where all I wanted to do was run my own tab, buy my own drinks, and everyone who wanted to give me a hard time for making it all so confusing could just go jump in a lake somewhere.

Of course getting to that point then messed things up when it came to dating…

So…

Ugh.

Best to drink at home alone and not even deal with it.

To avoid going off on that rant on poor Matt who didn't deserve it, I took a long, long sip of my beer instead. Matt wanted to buy me beers? Good for him. One more mark in his favor.

As we leaned against the bar, Abe pointed to a group of four men sitting in the corner by themselves and told us those were the ones Trish had been talking to the night before.

They looked like yuppies with their nice shoes, khaki pants, collared shirts that had little brand emblems on the chest, and close-cut hair-dos that were trim but not military trim. (If such a thing as yuppies still exists. It does in my world. Basically they looked like a bunch of guys who probably wouldn't try to change a tire if they got a flat but would instead call an Uber to pick them up and AAA to fix it for them.)

"How should we do this?" Matt asked. "You want to take the lead, or you want me to?"

"How about you hang back and let me go chat with them."

Matt frowned at me. "A woman's missing. One of those guys could be responsible."

"Really? Look at them. You think one of those guys could take Trish? Please."

"If I'm going to hang out here at the bar while you do all the work why'd you have me come along at all?"

I gave him my best smile. "Because you're good company. Plus if they're not the citified types they look to be you can rescue me when I get in over my head." I batted my eyes at him.

He just took another sip of his beer but I could see the annoyance in his eyes. Probably figured that was exactly what was going to happen. But, seriously, this group was not going to be a problem. Not unless someone scratched their Mercedes.

I strolled over to them and they perked up when they caught sight of me. Couldn't blame them. It was a small town and they weren't anywhere near where single women were likely to hang out, so I was pretty much their only viable option if that's what they were looking for.

"Mind if I join y'all?" I asked.

(I don't know why, but it seems I turn Southern when I'm flirting with strangers. It's some weird thing I've never understood, but there you have it. It works in some odd way, though, so I've never bothered to fix it.)

One of the guys looked me over while another pulled over a chair and the other two shuffled to the side to make room for me.

"So," I asked, "what brings y'all to town?"

Within a few minutes I had the whole story. It seemed they were a group of high school friends who liked to take a trip together each year even though they'd now scattered to various big cities along the east coast. One of the guys had just relocated to San Francisco for work so they'd moved that year's choice of location to Colorado to cut him a break. They'd been hiking that morning, rafting the day before, and fishing the day before that and were headed back home in the morning.

I teased them a bit about a boy's trip in a town that didn't offer a lot more than fishing and rafting. No night life. No ladies to flirt with.

Turned out three of the four were happily married so that was a big part of it. Best to avoid temptation as one of them put it.

"Lance has done alright for himself, though," one of the guys added, elbowing the guy who'd grabbed me a chair.

He blushed as he ran his hands through his dark hair. "Not really."

"What about that chick last night? The redhead. You were getting pretty friendly when I left."

I perked up. "Trish? She's a good friend of mine. Not a lot of redheads around these parts. You guys hook up?"

He scratched his chin. "Nah. It was definitely headed that way but then this guy walks in, throws an arm around her shoulder, and pulls her away. Said it had been a long time and they should catch up but she didn't look too happy about it and he didn't look too friendly."

I described Vick to him, but he shook his head. "No, that wasn't him. This guy was really tall and skinny with stringy blonde hair."

One of the other guys elbowed him in the ribs. "And you just let her go that easy, huh? No wonder you're still single."

The first guy shuddered. "If you'd seen this guy, you would've let her go, too. One look and I knew I wanted nothing to do with him. Reminded me of *Deliverance*."

I stared him down for that one. I swear, one movie with crazy people living in the mountains and suddenly anyone who isn't the type to blend in a city reminds a guy of *Deliverance*.

"That's a bit extreme, don't you think?"

"Sorry, but he was scary." The guy crossed his arms and looked away. Clearly not the type to hurt a fly let alone a woman.

I looked around, but no one matched that description. "Hm. I wonder who it was. You catch a name?"

He shook his head.

"Did she seem scared at all?"

"No. Didn't seem happy about it, but didn't seem scared either. I waited around for another ten minutes or so, but she never came back in, so I called it a night. Like you said, not a lot of choice around here."

"Never came back in? So they went outside to talk?"

He nodded. "Yeah, they did."

One of the other guys interrupted, "Enough about your friend. She lost her chance. But here you are, and here Lance is, and one last night to…"

I laughed and shook my head. "Can't, sorry. I'm not the one night kind of girl. Plus, my ride wouldn't appreciate it much if I ditched out on him." I nodded towards Matt who was watching us very intently. "Speaking of. Better get back to him. Nice meeting you."

I made my way back to the bar certain that Lance was not the one responsible for Trish's disappearance. Which meant we needed to figure out who Mr. Stringy Hair was and what he'd done to Trish.

CHAPTER 15

I told Matt and Abe what I'd found out.

"You see anyone like that here last night?" I asked.

Abe shook his head. "No. But we were busy. I could've just missed it."

Matt looked at the table of guys one more time. "You're sure it couldn't be one of them? Maybe they just lied to you."

"I'm not usually that off about people."

He raised an eyebrow at me.

So I'd accused a few people I shouldn't have of murder and completely missed a few others that really were murderers. That didn't make me a bad judge of character.

Resisting the urge to stick my tongue out at him, I said, "You want to go talk to them yourself, feel free Mr. Super Cop."

He thought about it. He really did. But then he shrugged it off. "You're probably right." But that didn't keep him from watching them until they finally left.

I looked at Matt. "Well, what now? You have a database of skinny men with stringy blonde hair who might know Trish?"

"Not one I can access." He glanced at the pool table. "But since we're here, how about we play a game of pool or two?"

I bit my lip. Me and pool….

It was tempting. Very tempting. But Sam's mom was missing and I was no closer to finding her. What would I tell him if he found out I'd stopped to play pool instead of trying to find the guy who'd taken his mom?

Matt leaned closer. "Maybe that guy will come back in tonight. Don't want to leave too soon, do we?" He flashed me a wicked smile. "Plus, you know you want to beat me at something. Since you've failed with Scrabble, maybe you can make it up with pool."

Maybe…

I studied the table, moving into hustler mode. "What makes you think I can even play?"

"Way I heard it your dad was a pool shark back in the day."

I shook my head. "My grandpa talks too much. But, yeah, my dad could hold his own with a pool cue."

"I can't believe he wouldn't have taught his daughter to play, too."

I eyed the table. It had been years since I'd played, but some things you never lose, and I was pretty sure pool was one of them.

There'd been a time in my life when playing pool was my personal form of meditation. I'd go to the local pool hall, pay for an hourly table, and sink into the zone for a couple of hours as I tried to clear the table in as few shots as I could.

I loved pool. And it had been far too long. I rolled my shoulders. "Alright. Let's do this. But don't be surprised when you lose."

He'd probably beat me, but pool's a mental game as much as anything. And if I could put him off his game with trash talking, I was going to do it.

"Oh, I'm not going to lose. Trust me on that." He led the way to the table.

The cues were warped, of course. I don't think I've ever been to a bar that didn't have warped cues. I rolled the two choices we had across the table and instead of smoothly rolling along the felt one of them thumped its way across and the other veered sharply to the side.

I chose the one that veered over the one that thumped. Figured it was the less warped of the two.

"You can break," I told Matt as I chalked my cue getting pale blue chalk dust on my hand.

"You sure?" he asked.

"Unless you're good enough to clear a rack off the break?"

If he was that good, I was going to lose. And badly. Unless he was too pampered to manage on a bar table with a warped cue. I'd once played with a guy who could only make shots if he was using his own custom graphite cue that required him to wear a special glove. Nice enough guy, but really? That's not playing pool. That's…something else entirely.

As I watched Matt chalk his cue and line up the cue ball I could see he was more than just a casual player, but I still didn't want to break. I've never been particularly good at it and I figure it's always better to have the balls spread out than clustered together. Let's you focus more on the shot you want to take than on what to do about the mess that's still left.

It was a good break. He made two balls right away and at least three others reached the far end of the table. He sunk another two before it was my turn.

I'll give it to him. He had solid skills. And he knew how to set up his shots.

A lot of guys have no finesse when they play. It's all about hitting the ball as hard as they can and then hoping the ball lands somewhere good for the next shot. But Matt didn't play that way. He never used more force than was needed to get the ball in the pocket and the cue ball where he needed it for the next one.

Actually, other than his preference for bank shots he and I played a lot alike.

Me, I'm all about the cut shot. Geometry was not my favorite class, by far, but I can always see those angles no matter how unlikely they might be.

A few times early on I saw Matt raise an eyebrow in question when I went for a side pocket cut shot instead of the end of the table straight-in shot. But after I made the third or fourth one, he expected it.

The first game was a close one. It got down to just the eight ball.

But I won. Of course.

"Best of three?" Matt asked.

I nodded. "But I need another beer. Be right back."

"I got it." Matt got Abe's attention and signaled for two more beers.

We were close on the second game, too, but Matt won that one. He'd adjusted his leaves to account for my preference for cut shots which made him a really smart player, but didn't make me particularly happy.

That meant we had to play a third game, but I didn't

mind. I was enjoying myself in a way I hadn't in a long time.

The third game went down to the eight ball, too.

As Matt leaned in to take his final shot, I leaned close (on the side where he wasn't holding the pool cue, thank you very much) and let my hair fall along his arm as I whispered in his ear. "Hm. You think you can make that? I mean it's not the easiest of shots, is it?"

What can I say? All's fair in love and pool.

He paused and looked at me, our faces inches apart. "Maggie. Stop trying to cheat."

"What are you talking about? I'm just saying it's not an easy shot."

"And you have to do that from right there?"

"How else could I see it? Why? Am I distracting you?"

He held my gaze as he took his shot. "No. Not at all." And…

He made the shot.

Jerk. Some guys just can't be ruffled that easy.

I would've probably challenged him to best of five and upped the flirting another notch but just as I was turning to order another round from Abe a tall guy with stringy blonde hair walked in.

"Looks like our guy just got here. You want to take this one?" I asked. Even from across the room I could see what Lance had been talking about. The man who'd just walked in did not belong in the Creek Inn. He probably didn't belong anywhere that didn't involve illegal everything or four walls of concrete and some steel bars.

Matt glanced around. There was only one other woman in the whole bar and she was very clearly with a large man with a big beard and big arms. While we'd been playing pool a few guys had been watching us. I wasn't sure if they wanted the table or me, but clearly Matt had his opinions on the matter.

"How about we both go chat with him?"

"Okay. But you take the lead."

CHAPTER 16

The man leaned against the end of the bar as he waited for Abe to pour him a shot of Jack Daniels. He sized up the room with a narrow-eyed look that put my teeth on edge. This was not a nice man, that was clear. Physically he didn't look like he could do harm to anyone, but there was something about the way he stood and the way he looked at people that made me think he'd play dirty and vicious if it came to a fight.

Reminded me of that Jim Croce song about how you don't mess around with Slim.

I didn't see any obvious weapons, but his belt buckle was big enough to do in a pinch.

(A little trick my grandpa had told me about once.)

"You sure you want me to come with you?" I whispered to Matt as we approached.

"Absolutely. Easier to keep you safe that way. But stay behind me."

The man focused in on Matt as we came closer, but didn't move from his not-so-casual slouch.

Matt held out a hand. "Matt Barnes. I'm local police around here. And you are?"

The man looked down at Matt's hand and back up at his face, but didn't take the hand. "Ted Little."

Matt crossed his arms but braced his feet shoulder-width apart. I stayed behind Matt's shoulder, ready to move out of his way if things became physical, which I honestly believed was possible.

"So, Ted. What brings you to Creek?"

"Grew up around here."

"Really. I don't recall seeing you before."

Ted smiled. It was not a nice smile. "Been away a while. You know how it goes."

Matt nodded. "And what brings you here tonight? If you don't mind my saying, the Creek Inn doesn't exactly seem like your type of place."

"It's not. But I ran into a friend here last night. Thought I'd come back and see if she was here again. You have a problem with that?" His voice dropped at the end, threatening.

"Nope. Free country. Who's the friend?"

Ted tensed up even though he was still slouched against the wall. "I don't have to tell you."

"True. You don't. But you'd be helping me out a lot if you would. Turns out a friend of ours was in here last night, too. Trish Mullens?"

He grunted. "Huh. Same friend." He flicked a glance back and forth between us. "But you don't look like the type to be friends with a girl like Trish, if you don't mind my saying."

"I coached her son in baseball. Trish made every game. She may have her faults, but she's a good mom. I respect that."

Ted's eyes went flat and hard. "Not so sure I agree

about her being a good mom. She's shacked up with Vick Kline, isn't she?"

Matt shrugged his shoulders. "Bad taste in men, but she loves her kid. As far as I can see, she's doing the best she can."

"Except she took off again, didn't she? Kid's birthday's tomorrow and where is she?"

I leaned around Matt. "How did you know that? How did you know that Sam's birthday is tomorrow?"

He transferred those black eyes to me and I was suddenly reminded of a cobra about to strike. "Kid's mine."

"Sam's your son?"

"Surprised? Yeah, well, so was I when she told me. *After* I was sent up for arson and couldn't do a thing about it."

Seems Trish was smarter than she looked if she'd kept this man out of her son's life.

Matt nudged me back. "If he's your kid, how come I've never heard anything about you before this?"

"I just got out. Was trying to figure out how I was going to handle things. Went to Vick's looking for Trish last night and he said she'd split but might be here, so I came by. Walked in the door and saw her draping herself all over some loser in a polo shirt. Day before her kid's birthday and she's in here trying to pick up some new guy?" He spat on the ground.

The Creek Inn was not the kind of place where you spit on the ground. But Abe just gave me a subtle head shake. No one was looking for trouble with this guy.

"So you pulled her away for a talk." Matt leaned forward slightly, challenging him just a bit.

He sat up a little straighter, returning the challenge. "I did. Someone needed to remind her what her priorities should be."

"And then you roughed her up. Wanted to make the lesson stick."

"Nope."

When Matt just stared at him, Ted leaned forward until his face was inches from Matt's. "That woman is the mother of my child. It's his birthday tomorrow. I wasn't going to hurt her because that would hurt him. And I don't need fists to get my point across. Trish heard what I had to say and then she got out of here just like I told her to."

I leaned around Matt again. "So you guys just talked then?"

"Yeah, we just talked."

"In here?" I was hoping to trip him up. Catch him in a lie.

"No. Out in the parking lot. Where it was quiet enough for her to hear what I had to say."

I swallowed, not liking to have his attention on me, but wanting to get all the information I could out of him. "And what exactly did you have to say?"

"That she needed to get home to her kid. And that I was back and I was going to be a part of his life from here on out so she'd need to be sure she kept his best interests in mind. Or else."

"What did she say to that?"

He laughed softly. "She didn't appreciate my interfering in her life. It seems I'm a no-good loser who doesn't know the first thing about being a father. That I couldn't help out before so what made me think I had the right to be part of his life now."

"And you didn't do anything when she said that?"

"Like I said. My kid's birthday's tomorrow. He doesn't need to have his mom all black and blue in all the photos. Been there, done that myself."

"And she wasn't beat up already?"

"No."

"What happened then?"

"She left. Called me a bunch of names as she was storming towards her car and then tore out of here and headed back towards town. You're awfully full of questions. What's *your* name?"

I opened my mouth to answer, but Matt interrupted, "Thanks for your time. Appreciate it."

He led me straight outside. I didn't even have time to wave goodbye to Abe before we were out the door and headed for his truck.

"What did you do that for?" I asked.

"Get in, Maggie."

"But…"

"Get in." He held the door for me and waited until I was seated and buckled in before going around to the driver's side. I could see Ted Little standing in the doorway of the Creek Inn, watching us.

"What's wrong?" I asked as Matt got into the driver's side and started up the truck.

He held up a hand as he dialed his phone. When the person on the other end of the line answered he said, "Hey, it's Matt. Ted Little? That the guy I think it is? The one who went away for burning down the house of a guy he'd had a fight with? Mmhm. Yeah, well, he's out and back in town. Figure it won't be long until you're dealing with him again. At the Creek Inn right now. Yep. Gotta go."

He hung up and pulled out onto the highway. "That man in there is a vicious criminal. The last thing you need to do is get on his radar, Maggie."

"Granted, he's not someone I'd invite over for Sunday dinner, but…"

"Maggie. Ted Little went away for arson, but he was suspected of a lot more. There were three women who went missing while he was around. The disappearances stopped when he was sent away. Cops always figured he'd done it, but no one could find them and no one was talking back then. Until he's back in jail I want you to be very careful. No walking Fancy unless I'm with you or your grandpa is."

"Don't be ridiculous. What does that man care about me?"

"I'm not." He was so serious, the smile dropped from my face.

"Look, I'm sure I'll never cross paths with him again. I mean, it's not like he and I are going to be running in the same circles. And do you really think he'd risk getting bit by a big dog like Fancy when there are easier targets out there?"

"Fancy? Fancy who loves all men and wags her tail and snuggles up against anyone who rubs her ears? She's not a good guard dog, Maggie. Maybe if it was Hans I'd feel differently, but Fancy is not going to protect you from the likes of Ted Little."

There was no point in arguing with him about it. A few weeks would pass, he'd forget about it, and I could go back to living my life like I wasn't surrounded by dangerous killers. He was a cop. He should know that most people do violence to people they already know.

"He's probably the one who took Trish, you know," I said to change the subject.

Matt shook his head. "No. I don't think so. If he'd hurt Trish last night he wouldn't be at the Creek Inn today. It's not his kind of place. Only reason he'd be back there again tonight was to make sure she wasn't."

"I guess that makes sense. So now what?"

"Now I take you home. You tried, Maggie. You talked to Vick, you called her mom and friends, you talked to the city boy, you talked to Ted. There's nothing left to do."

I stared out the window as we wound our way through the canyon, even though it was pitch black and I couldn't see a thing. Why they'd never bothered to put lights in the canyon I'd never understand. And why the most popular bar in the valley was on the other side of that canyon…Yeah, that didn't make a lot of sense to me either.

"I can't just let it go, Matt."

"Well, you come up with some other idea of where Trish is, you let me know. But for now I think you're done."

He was right. I'd exhausted all my leads. But I wasn't ready to quit.

I had to find Trish. For Sam.

CHAPTER 17

I didn't sleep well that night. Not at all. The house was completely silent. Matt and Jack had taken Sam home with them and my grandpa was still over at Lesley's when I went to bed. Being alone in that big house gave me the jitters.

And since I'd built those stairs for Fancy I rarely had a perfect night's sleep. She'd sprawl so far across the bed that I was left with a narrow strip across the very top. The only thing that saved me from falling off onto the floor was the headboard. I could've probably pushed her to the bottom half of the bed but she was just too darned cute when she started doing that snuffling cry thing in her sleep.

But the real issue was the job offer from Karen.

I knew Jamie. She'd never just walk away from the café and leave me in the lurch. She wasn't that type of person. So as much as she might talk about living in Paris with Mason, she wouldn't do it. Not as long as we were running a business together.

But was it honestly fair of me to ask that of her? I knew we both loved parts of running the place. Being in charge for once and being able to choose who we worked with was a big part of what I loved about it. And living where we both wanted to live.

I also knew, though, that Jamie was sick and tired of making the same thing every day and there was no chance she'd be able to get away from making cinnamon rolls anytime soon.

Sure, we could hire staff, but that's the worst thing to do when you're a brand new business and can do the work yourself. Better to do things ourselves and fund it with our sweat equity. Plus, no employee will care as much as the owner.

Oh, some people come close because that's just who they are, but when it's your business…It's a whole different level of care and concern.

They always say to figure things will cost twice as much, take twice as long, and earn half as much as you plan. And so that's what we'd planned for. But it was still going to take twice as long and cost twice as much as *that*.

Wasn't it better to just take Karen's offer and let Jamie off the hook so she could move on with Mason and whatever exciting plans they'd made? At least one of us would be happy.

And then there was my grandpa. He said he didn't need me. And he certainly acted like he didn't need me. But if I went back to DC how many dinners and casual conversations would I miss? There was no amount of money on this planet to make up for that. Was there?

Because what if I said no to Karen now and three years from now she said it was too late to come back there. I'd be without the barkery and without a career.

Of course, I might lose all those dinners anyway now that things had changed with Lesley. I wouldn't be surprised if my grandpa pulled out his old battered RV and took to the road with her for a while. Out of sight out of mind, you know.

And what about Fancy. I knew she'd go along with anything. I'd already dragged her halfway across the country once and she'd settled into her new normal just fine. She'd do it again if she had to. But what was best for her? Being with me or my grandpa all day or going to some day care with a bunch of other dogs? I think she liked having a yard, but maybe she'd prefer taking walks with me three or four times a day if that also meant getting to play with other dogs more.

Of course, when she'd been in day care they told me most afternoons after her lunch break she'd refused to go back to the playroom, preferring to stay by herself instead.

And then there was Matt.

The best thing for him was for me to leave so he didn't miss some great opportunity at love and happiness that was right there in front of him because he was too busy thinking he could make something happen with me. (I just knew if I wasn't there he'd quickly find a wonderful woman who'd love him for the amazing man he was. She'd probably even like cleaning the house and doing laundry.)

But it was hard to walk away from that potential. There was something there whether I wanted there to be or not. And no amount of fighting it would change that fact.

Not that I'd ever go there…

Disgusted with myself and my inability to know what I wanted out of life after thirty-six frickin' years on this planet, I stared at the ceiling and tried to distract myself with thoughts of Ted Little, Vick Kline, and Trish Mullens.

Had Trish gone back home? Had Vick done something to her when she did? If so, why hadn't there been any sign of it? Vick didn't strike me as the sharpest blade in the drawer. Or had Ted Little done something to her? He did strike me as smart enough to go back to the Creek Inn the next night to give himself an alibi. And nasty enough to have harmed her. Both of those men did.

Honestly, you'd think you cross paths with one man like that you figure out how not to do it again, but like my grandpa had said, I'd never been there so I shouldn't judge. Maybe you chose one to get away from the last one and just kept on making bad decisions on down the line until you forgot there was anything better out there than what you had. Or until you got so scared of what might come next you figured the devil you knew.

Finally, I gave up on falling asleep and pulled out the book I'd been dying to read. Fancy took herself to the living room when I turned on the light, clearly indicating with her disgusted departure exactly what she thought of humans who turn on bedroom lights in the middle of the night.

🐾 🐾 🐾

I'd only been reading for a few minutes when my grandpa came home.

"Maggie? What are you still doing up?"

"Just have a lot on my mind."

I told him what we'd found at the Creek Inn.

He shook his head. "Ted Little's back, huh? That's a man you wish would've been shivved in the shower. If I'd known you'd be here at the same time as him I might've tried to arrange it myself."

"Grandpa!"

"He's a bad man, Maggie. You…" He settled himself on the edge of the bed and looked at me. "You've never truly seen evil. I have. In prison, some guys are just in there trying to do their time and get out and get back to their lives. Some make mistakes that they regret almost immediately. But others…They're proud of what they've done. They relish hurting other people. They don't see someone like you as human or worth protecting. You're prey."

I wanted to roll my eyes at what he was saying, but I knew every single word was deadly serious. My grandpa didn't talk about his time in prison often, but when he did it always was.

"I already promised Matt I'd keep away from him. We have no reason to cross paths."

"Doesn't mean he won't find you. Listen to Matt on this one. Don't go out alone until Little is back in prison."

This time I did roll my eyes. "I have to drive to work, you know. And run the barkery."

"I know. Just…Be as safe as you can, Maggie May. Please."

"Fine. I will."

"So that's what had you up in the middle of the night? Not being able to find Sam's mom?"

I shook my head and told him about the call from Karen. I'd tried very hard not to talk to my grandpa about the kind of money I was earning in DC because it was so foreign to how we'd grown up and what most of the people I knew were used to, but I couldn't get his advice if I didn't tell him what I was dealing with. So I told him what she'd offered.

"For all three years?"

"Nope. That's per year. And they're going to pay housing and doggie day care for Fancy on top of it."

"So after three years you'll have earned…"

"Yep." My stomach clenched because I knew what he was going to say.

"You have to take it, Maggie May. You can't walk away from that kind of opportunity."

"But…you. And the barkery. And…"

"Maggie May, how many times in your life is someone going to offer you money like that?"

I clenched my pillow to my chest. "Probably never again."

"Exactly. Take it." He patted my leg and stood up. "And now I better get to bed because I am not used to being up this late anymore and I need my beauty sleep."

He turned off my bedroom light as he left, but I didn't fall asleep immediately. I'd been leaning towards taking the job because it made the most sense, but when he told me to take it all I could do is feel this dropping sensation in my stomach. Like I was walking away from my only chance at having the life I wanted.

Sure, I'd have money. Enough money to go heli-hiking, that's for sure. But what would I lose that had nothing whatsoever to do with money?

With that happy thought, I finally drifted off to sleep.

CHAPTER 18

As much as I wanted to find Sam's mom, I unfortunately had a business to run, too. So even though the disappointment I knew I'd see in Sam's big brown eyes haunted me, Trish couldn't be my priority. Especially if I was going to leave soon. I owed Jamie more than that.

I gave up on taking Fancy in with me when she pulled out of her collar for the third time as I tried to drag her out of the backyard. I gave her a stern lecture to leave the bunnies alone before I left, though. Not that she was going to listen, but fortunately they were all faster than her. At least the ones that ran were. I hoped they'd all learned the "don't freeze near the big black dog" lesson when bunny number one went down.

I didn't tell Jamie about the offer. I wasn't going to tell her about it until I'd figured out which way I was going to go. No need upsetting her one way or the other until I knew if it was an actual option for me.

I was in back dealing with some online orders when someone rang the bell for the barkery counter. Usually if we're slow Jamie will hop over and catch any customer while I'm in back, but it was still a pretty busy time for us on the café side, so I rushed out to see who it was before she had to try to juggle both at once.

Ted Little leaned against the counter with that same predator's slouch he'd had the night before at the Creek Inn. Only a fool would miss just how dangerous he was.

I stopped about a foot away from the counter. "Mr. Little. This is a surprise."

"Isn't it, though?" He glanced down at the bakery display case where I had barkery bites and doggie delights showing. "People pay for this sort of thing, huh? Dog treats priced like chocolate truffles."

"Yes. Some people do. You have a dog, Mr. Little?"

"Oh, call me Ted." He smiled at me and I wished my grandpa and Matt were right behind me, one on each side.

"Ted then. You have a dog, Ted?"

"No."

"Then how can I help you." If it had been anyone else there would've been a lot more bite in my words. But the last thing I wanted was to trigger him to take more of an interest in me than he already had.

He stood up straighter. "I think we should become friends. You and I could get along real nice."

Every instinct in my body was screaming at me to run away. Now.

But I'd long ago decided that I wasn't going to let anyone use fear to intimidate me or force me to do something I wouldn't do otherwise, so instead I looked him in the eye. "Hate to disagree, but I don't think you and I have all that much in common."

He pressed his hands into the glass on the counter as he leaned forward. "We could."

Jamie was just feet away helping café customers. I could shout for her and she'd come running. But I didn't need to give Ted Little another target. Having me was bad enough. Plus, he wasn't actually doing anything other than being incredibly intense and scary.

I crossed my arms and leaned against the wall. "You know, Matt believes what you told him last night. That you didn't take Trish. That you didn't hurt her."

"But you don't?"

"I think you're a smart enough man you could have taken Trish and come back the next night to give yourself an alibi."

He chuckled. "That would be mighty convoluted of me, don't you think?"

"Maybe. Maybe not."

His grin vanished as he stared at me with those black, black eyes of his. "I didn't hurt Trish. Like I said before. She's my son's mother and I'm not going to do something like that on the day before my boy's birthday."

He looked me up and down, a slow smile spreading across his face. "But you on the other hand…"

I did my best to hide how much he scared the living daylights out of me. If I shuddered in front of him, I knew I was gone. Whether it was in that moment or some other moment, he'd eventually come after me.

Fortunately, Matt walked in the door just then. I saw his hand go to where his gun would normally be if he was in uniform.

"Matt. Be right with you," I called, forcing a smile on my face. "Can I get you anything else, Mr. Little?"

Ted Little turned and leaned his elbows on the display case as Matt approached. "What do we have

here? Well if it isn't the friendly officer from last night."
He stood up, glancing back at me. "Thank you for your
time, Miss Carver. Sometime soon we'll have to get to
know each other well enough you can just call me Ted."

As he strolled out, brushing shoulders with Matt, I
saw Matt's hands clench into fists. I fully expected Matt
to clock him one, but he didn't. What he did do is turn
and watch until Ted got in his old gray sedan and drove
away.

Only then did he turn towards me.

I stood with my hands braced on the edge of the
counter, trying to catch my breath.

Only one other time had I felt that sort of primal fear
that makes you shudder against your will. It was
watching one of those shows on serial killers. I can't
remember which one, there are so many. But this one
had footage of an interview with the actual killer. It
wasn't a re-enactment. It was real live footage. And when
that man spoke…I'd had this visceral, gut-deep reaction
to him. Thousands of years of evolution screaming in my
mind to run and hide even though the footage was
twenty years old and the man was on my television.

"You okay?" Matt asked.

"I will be once that man is back in prison. Or dead."
I shook myself until the feeling went away. "I need a
Coke. Only because it's too early for a straight shot of
whiskey. You want one."

"Sure. That'd be great."

As I grabbed us both a Coke, Matt studied me. "I
didn't know you drank whiskey."

"I don't. Other than an unfortunate period of time
when I thought it was cool to drink Malibu rum straight

up, I've never been much of one for hard alcohol. I figure that's taking your drinking way too seriously. But this would've been symbolic."

He chuckled, but we were both still on edge and we knew it.

CHAPTER 19

Matt stuck around for a bit, but he eventually had to leave. He made me promise before he left that I'd call him if I saw Ted Little again.

"It's a small town, Matt. How many times a day do you want me to be calling you?"

"As many as you need to. I don't care if you see him when you're at the grocery store, Maggie. You call me."

"So you can what? Run over there and glare at him?"

"Just call me, Maggie. Please."

"Fine. But better be prepared to hear from me a dozen times a day."

I knew it was a good idea. I knew that for whatever reason Ted Little had fixated on me. But what can I say? When I'm scared I become obnoxiously sarcastic.

After Matt left I kept wondering if Ted Little was the reason Trish was missing. I had no doubt he was capable of murder. None whatsoever. But he seemed sincere when he talked about not ruining Sam's birthday. And it was pretty convoluted for him to go back to the Creek Inn the next night just to establish an alibi when probably no one knew he was out of prison.

He was an option, about the only option we had, but not a clear-cut one.

🐾 🐾 🐾

Business on the café side was steady throughout the rest of the morning. The barkery side, not so much.

A woman did come by and ask if we had boarding available, but I had to tell her no. She wasn't the first who'd done so. Early on I'd had to actually put up signs over the cubbies along the wall informing people that no, they could not just walk in and leave their dogs for a couple hours while they went for a hike. The cubbies were for when someone wanted to bring their dog but not have them at the table. Or for when they ran to the bathroom real quick. Not as some unsupervised drop-off doggie day care.

Since I had nothing better to do, I spent most of my time contemplating Karen's offer.

Finally, I couldn't wait anymore. Our lunch rush was almost over and we still had someone in to watch the counter so I dragged Jamie out back with me. She hadn't brought Lulu to work—she said Lulu preferred to stay at her mom's house where she had full access to the backyard all day but I wondered if it wasn't just part of pulling away from the business—so it was just the two of us.

Jamie sprawled on the bench against the wall and wiped a hand across her flour-dusted forehead as I stared out at the distant mountains.

"Phew. It's nice to get out and see the sun for a bit. I swear, I'm cooped up in that kitchen so much I almost forget how enjoyable summers can be here." She took a long drink of water. (Unlike me, Jamie actually worries about her health and her figure.)

I paced towards the stream and back. "That's kind of what I wanted to talk to you about."

I couldn't bring myself to sit, so I loomed over her, my arms crossed.

"What? What's wrong? Sit down, you're scaring me."

I shook my head. I couldn't sit down.

I turned away. It was so beautiful with the mountains rising in the distance and the stream and the trees. (If you forgot that there had very recently been a dead man found in those trees...) There were birds singing somewhere and it was quiet enough you could actually hear the water burbling along. And it smelled so crisp and clean. So pure.

I loved it. I loved it so much.

And it was nothing at all like DC.

But…

I bit my lip and turned back around. I didn't want to cry. This wasn't bad. Not for Jamie, at least. Not even for me, really. (So why did it feel so bad?)

"Jamie, look. I, um…"

"What is it?" She leaned forward, studying my face, ready to leap to her feet and solve whatever the issue was like the ultra-competent friend she was.

"Um. Karen called me last night."

"Karen? As in your old boss, Karen?"

I nodded.

"What did she want?" Jamie hadn't been a fan of Karen's since I told her about the time Karen called and woke me up at three in the morning to participate in a two-hour conference call where I hadn't even been needed. When I'd told her about that she'd informed me that anyone who couldn't value their staff more than that didn't deserve staff as dedicated as I was.

I kind of agreed. Especially since Karen had never even acknowledged that participating in that call was anything less than what should've been expected from me.

Man, I did not want to go work for that woman again. (And to be fair, it wasn't just her. It was the whole company. Probably the whole industry. Working long hours was some sort of badge of pride. It all came down to how much you earned, who your clients were, how nice your clothes were, and how many hours you worked.)

But my friend deserved to be let out of the situation she was trapped in. She deserved to enjoy a sunny day if she wanted to.

Plus, Karen and her team needed me. They weren't going to get the project without me. And I couldn't let them down like that.

And there was the money. And the fear of failure if I stayed and the barkery went under. That inevitable slide into insignificance.

So, pacing back and forth, I told Jamie about the offer. And about why I was going to take it. About how it would free her up to go to Paris with Mason or to go wherever else she wanted with him, even if that was just home for lunch on a nice summer's day.

"You're the best baker in the world, Jamie, but I also know you hate having to make cinnamon rolls every single day of your life. This…It isn't what we thought it would be."

I almost did cry then. I'd wanted it so bad. To live in a small town in Colorado with my dog and my grandpa and my best friend. To run a silly little business that was anything I wanted it to be. To have something that was completely mine.

But life changes on you. And it wasn't working. Not anymore. Maybe it never had been.

Jamie sat forward, studying me with an intensity that made my skin itch. "You're right, Maggie. It isn't what we thought it would be. And while I do love that people love my cinnamon rolls, I don't want to have to spend the next twenty years of my life getting up before the sun baking them."

I'd been right. I turned away.

"But…" She stood and grabbed my arm, turning me back around to face her. "I am not okay with my best friend moving states away and going back to a career that made her miserable. Maggie, how many weekends did you spend Saturday in the office and Sunday shopping for crap you didn't even need just to make yourself feel better?"

I shrugged one shoulder. "Too many. But less after I got Fancy. I'll be better this time."

"No you won't. You don't have it in you to give less than a hundred percent. And since Karen will ask for a hundred and ten percent you'll end up giving everything. You can't go back there."

"But you agreed. This isn't what we thought it would be. It isn't what either of us want. You can stay because you have Mason now. I have…nothing."

Jamie snorted, a not very lady-like sound for someone I was used to seeing as classy. "Nothing? Your grandpa. Matt. That's nothing?"

"My grandpa has Lesley now. And Matt's probably going to re-enlist."

"He wouldn't re-enlist if you asked him to stay."

I glared at her. "I can't ask him to stay when I know I can't be with him."

Jamie opened her mouth to argue with me but I held my hand up to stop her. "I'm not discussing that with you, Jamie. I love you to death. You're my best friend. But we have very different takes on love and all of that and I'm just not going there. You won't convince me to feel differently than I feel about it so just leave it alone."

She tapped her foot on the ground as she studied me. "Okay. But promise me this. You'll give me two hours before you call Karen and accept this ridiculous offer that she should've never made to you."

"It's not ridiculous. They need me."

"It is, too, ridiculous. You'd gotten out, Maggie. Don't let them pull you back in."

"But the money…"

"Oh, screw the money. Like you care about that. Two hours." She held my gaze. "Promise?"

I nodded.

After she'd run back inside I collapsed onto the bench and stared at the mountains. I loved this place. It was my home. But logic told me taking Karen's offer was the best choice.

CHAPTER 20

I spent the next hour calling all of Trish's friends and family one more time. I even called Abe to see if she'd shown up at the Creek Inn after we'd left or if he'd remembered anything new. But nada. No one had heard from her, no one had seen her. It was Sam's birthday and he was going to spend it without his mom because I couldn't figure out what had happened to her.

I hung up the phone—I'd been using our office phone—and stared at all the little to-do lists and checklists on the poster board on the wall. Jamie was nothing if not organized. She had an opening checklist, a closing checklist, and even a checklist for preparing cinnamon rolls. I wondered if after all these weeks of making the rolls every morning she still followed it.

Knowing Jamie, yes. She liked completing tasks. Putting that little x next to each one as it was finished.

She knocked on the doorframe. "You done with your calls?"

I nodded.

"Good. I need to speak with you. Betty went home and I closed up early. But you have to promise me something first."

I frowned at her. "What?"

"You won't be mad at me."

"If you want me to promise you I won't be mad, I can't."

"Why not?"

"Because the fact that you're asking means I'm going to be. And you know me, I'm not exactly good at hiding my emotions."

She nodded. "Good point. Well, just promise me you'll try. Come on. We're set up out front."

I followed her to the front of the store where Greta and Mason were seated side-by-side at one of our larger tables.

They both looked perfect, as always, Greta in black slacks and a bright blue top, Mason in gray slacks and a black t-shirt I figured cost more than my whole wardrobe. (Which isn't saying much. I'm cheap and I like to buy things that are on sale. It's just clothes. As long as I'm not in danger of being arrested for lewdness I figure I'm covered. Literally and figuratively.)

But they also both looked nervous.

Jamie kissed Mason's cheek and squeezed his shoulder. I had to admit, he was a good-looking man even with his salt and pepper hair. He was one of those men who have presence when they walk into a room. Women always turned to take an extra look and really, who could blame them?

Still. He'd always struck me as a little bit too uptight for my tastes.

That day he was in full-on stick mode, his spine as straight as humanly possible.

I didn't know why they were there, but it felt very much like an ambush. I glanced towards the front door and saw that Jamie really had locked up.

"I thought we weren't going to close early anymore," I said as Jamie ran back to the kitchen for a tray with a Coke for me, coffees for each of them, and a gorgeous cake with delicate white piping.

If you have posted hours you should keep them even if you know no one will come in for the last two hours you're open. Otherwise, why bother staying open that long. All it takes is that one time that person who would've come in on a regular basis at three each day drops by to find you closed to lose them.

"Don't worry. It'll be okay. You're talking about leaving anyway, remember? And if you do that, the fact that we closed two hours early one Monday afternoon isn't really going to make a difference."

"I guess not." I grudgingly sat down at the table as Jamie passed around drinks and sliced up the cake. It was lemon. One of my favorites. "Hi Mason. Hi Greta."

They both said their hellos, but there was still that nervousness to them. Like they thought I was going to suddenly attack them or something. I turned to Jamie. "What's this about?" I snapped.

Greta let out a sound that was part exasperation, part disgust as she passed Hans a small treat that he took with all the dignity of a true gentleman. "Honestly, Maggie. You will find out soon enough, yes?"

Couldn't fault her logic even if it did feel like an ambush. I took a quick bite of the cake. It was delicious. Moist and tangy and just sweet enough. Jamie truly is a genius in the kitchen.

But then I put my fork aside and waited to see who was going to do the talking.

They all looked at each other, none wanting to be the one that started. Finally, Jamie turned to face me. "We were waiting to talk to you about this because we wanted to iron out some final details. To make sure it was going to happen before we sprung it on you. But since you're talking about taking that offer from Karen I figured we better tell you about it now."

"Tell me about what?" I glared at all three of them, my appetite gone.

The thought that the two women I considered my best friends in town and my friend's fiancé had been talking about something important behind my back made me feel ill.

"Remember the two plots of land that Janice Fletcher left? And how Mason had wanted to buy them so he could turn this area into a resort?"

I glared at Mason. "Mmhm. But he didn't buy them. I checked. It was some corporation no one had ever heard of. So we're safe from him tearing down our business and ruining our lives."

"Maggie."

I shrugged one shoulder. "I know you love him, Jamie. But that would've ruined everything."

"Not necessarily."

I narrowed my eyes at her and then looked at Mason and Greta before finally turning my glare on Greta. "It was you? You own the corporation that bought the plots of land?"

She nodded.

"And now you're working together. You and Mason.

You're going to build that resort. You're going to tear down the barkery. Well, guess it's good I decided to take that offer of Karen's then, isn't it. Gets me out of the way all nice and neat." I took a sip of Coke but my hand was shaking.

Jamie grabbed my wrist when I set the can back down. "No, Maggie. You've got it all wrong. *We're* going to build the resort. All four of us."

"All four of us? Then why am I the only one that didn't know about this little plan until now?"

She bit her lip. "Because I wanted to give it a little time between the engagement and telling you about this. I didn't want you to think we were doing this because of that."

"But aren't you?"

"No. It's…" Jamie seldom looks flustered, but she was definitely struggling to keep calm and explain things to me in a way that would get through effectively.

She sighed and tried again. "Look, Maggie, we can both agree that this place is far more of the type of work that neither one of us enjoys than we'd anticipated, right?"

I shrugged my shoulders, not wanting to agree with her on anything at that point. What can I say, I'm stubborn when I'm angry.

"But there are parts of it I think we both like. You love coming up with new ideas for dog treats. And I love experimenting with different recipes. And the idea is sound. I really do think there's a need for a place where tourists can go with their pets."

I nodded.

"It could be more, though. So much more. And we can find a way to do the fun parts without having to do the parts we don't like."

"Who says there are parts I don't like?" I crossed my arms and refused to look at anyone at the table. If there was a job to do, I did it. Sure there were some parts I wasn't a great fan of, but…

Jamie laughed. "Come on, Maggie. You know that you and customer service are not a good fit. The customer is not always right in your world."

"Well, yeah, some customers are idiots. Or jerks. And I refuse to let someone use anger to get what they want."

I shook my head. "I don't even know why we're discussing this. You've obviously come up with a plan that doesn't need me. And now I have that offer from Karen. So, great. Tear this place down and build your fancy resort with your fancy husband. I'll go back to my old life and we'll all be just as happy as can be."

"Maggie May Carver. Enough. The reason we are here telling you about this now instead of letting you take some ridiculous job offer that takes you back to DC where you are going to be miserable is because we want you to be a part of it. Now sit back, quit being a spoiled brat, and listen."

I was so surprised to see my normally mellow-mannered friend snap at me that I did exactly that as Mason laid out an architect's rendering of a beautiful resort property.

He put on his serious lawyer face as he turned to me. "Here is the plan. We are going to build a pet-friendly resort. Top to bottom. We will have big dog and small dog areas as well as cat areas. Each room will have top of the line sound-proofing. There will be a cat café on one end and a dog barkery on the other. We will offer pet spa services, even acupuncture and chiropractor services, as well as boarding. And there will be a novelty shop that's three times the size of what you have here. Think Dylan's Candy Bar but for pets. High-end everything. Top quality. It will be a pet-lover's dream. Anyone who views their pet as part of the family can take them on vacation just like any other member of the family. Full service, luxury, all-inclusive."

It sounded amazing. Like our little barkery idea on steroids. I leaned back and crossed my arms. "Sounds great, but I still don't understand why you need me."

Greta leaned forward. "We don't need you, Maggie, we want you. You are our friend and you are smart and you will help us run this place."

Mason nodded. "This is the plan. We will buy out your interest in the barkery with an interest in the resort. You will run the barkery, retail store, and online sales for the new resort. As a salaried manager. Starting the day this place closes. Your main role will be strategy and management. We will hire staff for the store and order fulfillment. Jamie will do the same for the cat café and restaurant as well as overseeing the hotel staff. Neither one of you will ever have to man a retail counter again unless you want to. And Jamie won't be stuck in the kitchen all day every day."

"We'll get to work together more, Maggie. And on the parts of things that we actually enjoy doing."

It sounded good, but…

I shook my head. "Look, this is a great idea. You've come up with something brilliant here. I think people will love it. And you'll have made a place that people who love their pets will love to go to. But I'm not like you guys. I'm not…flashy. I'm silly Newfie heads on a sign

with a bad script font that no one can read. I'm…this."
I gestured at the rest of the barkery with its cheesy but
adorable displays that didn't scream luxury no matter
how you looked at them. "It's a brilliant idea, but it's not
for me. It's you guys."

"Maggie…"

"No. It's fine." I stood up and focused on Jamie. "I was
worried about taking that offer from Karen because I
didn't want to let you down, even though I knew it was
the best thing to let you out of this. But now I know you'll
be fine. Now I can take it without feeling guilty."

I glanced at Mason and Greta. "Thank you. Truly.
For considering how to include me. I'm sure this will be
incredibly successful. But…" I shook my head and
turned back to Jamie. "I have to go, okay?"

I raced to grab my purse and get out the door before
I lost it.

CHAPTER 21

I didn't know where I was headed, I just knew I needed to get out of there.

You might be wondering why I was so upset. I mean, they'd made space for me, hadn't they? It was probably thanks to Jamie and Greta that the resort was going to be a pet-friendly one that could incorporate the barkery. And they hadn't had to include me even then. Not like I had rights to the idea after all.

It was likely inevitable that the minute Janice Fletcher died the barkery would be torn down to create a resort. I mean, not like Mason was earning high rent on the existing building. Not the kind of money he could earn on a luxury resort.

But it just felt like a betrayal.

Like my best friend and my only other real friend in town had been conspiring behind my back. It was *their* idea. Not *ours*. I hadn't been part of coming up with what should be included or not. I hadn't helped with the artist's rendering.

Which is why it felt so horrible. Like I was an afterthought.

It didn't help that Mason was involved. Jamie loved him and I was happy for her, but it was hard enough to lose her to love and marriage. Having him take my business, too, was just that last little bit that pushed me over the edge.

As I drove towards home, trying not to lose it, I reminded myself that it was fine. At least I had the offer from Karen. I'd take that, go back to what I was good at, and leave the people who didn't really need me to their lives.

I barely noticed the beauty of the valley as I sped by. The grass was kind of dried out by that part of the season, but the aspen trees scattered among the evergreens on each mountainside colored the world with yellows and oranges and even some reds.

It was a perfect day, too. No clouds in a blue, blue sky. I'd miss it.

Of all the east coast cities I'd spent time in DC was probably the best of the lot when it came to nature and greenery, but it wasn't the Colorado mountains. It wasn't wild. It was cultured and controlled. Everything trimmed and tidied. Nature as backdrop instead of centerpiece.

But it was what it was.

And what other choice did I have?

🐾 🐾 🐾

I stormed in the door at home, wanting desperately to talk to my grandpa about everything. He'd understand. Or if he didn't understand he'd at least listen and give me some practical advice and a knock upside the head.

But as soon as I walked in I saw that he had company. He and Lesley were seated on the worn old goldenrod couch. He had his arm wrapped around her shoulders;

she'd clearly been crying.

I hate to say it, but Lesley looked terrible. She's usually a very polished woman. She has this beautiful white hair that she pulls back into a flawless bun, but that day the bun was falling apart. And her normal red lipstick looked like she'd smeared it on without checking the mirror. She'd lost a good ten pounds since I'd seen her last and there were dark shadows under her eyes.

She had a pallor to her skin that made me want to tell her to get some rest and good food.

Despite it all, at least she'd still made the effort. Good for her.

Fancy was there, too, and came over to say hi. I rubbed her ear and she leaned into my hip with a contented groan. "Lesley. I'm so sorry about your husband."

"Thank you, Maggie. I appreciate that."

"What are you doing home so early?" my grandpa asked.

"We decided to close up. No customers. Thought I'd get in a hike."

I hadn't actually wanted a hike, but Lesley clearly needed time alone with my grandpa. Plus, it would be good to get out and move. Sometimes I think better when I can be active. It was too hot, though, for Fancy. "You okay with Fancy staying here while I'm out?"

He nodded.

"She give you any trouble with the bunnies today?"

"No. I had a man come out this morning and round them up. He set some traps for the ones he couldn't get, but I expect we'll be varmint free in a day or two."

"Aw, Grandpa. Look at you, choosing the humane option."

He harrumphed. "Figured it was easier to do that than listen to you complain about the poor bunnies for the rest of my life. You sure you're okay?"

"Yeah, I'll be fine. Rough couple of days, that's all. I better get changed."

I threw on some hiking pants, a t-shirt, and my hiking boots, and then slathered on sun screen on any exposed skin. No point in getting burnt if I could avoid it. I topped it all off with a Rockies baseball cap. Not the most hiking-worthy of hats, but at least it shielded my face some.

I threw my new book and a can of Coke in my backpack along with the small first aid kit I always carry and figured I was ready to go. I opened the front door to find Matt standing there, just about to knock. "What are you doing here?"

"Jamie called. Told me you might need someone to talk to."

I was torn between anger at Jamie for interfering in my life and gratitude that Matt was there.

"Well, I don't. I was just about to head out for a hike, actually."

"Then I'll come with you. She said you hadn't eaten lunch yet, so I brought some sandwiches for us. I was going to suggest we take them up to that big rock you like so much."

"How'd you know about that?"

"You'd be surprised what I know. Come on." He stepped back to let me out the door. "Mr. Carver. Lesley." He nodded at them before closing the door firmly behind me.

CHAPTER 22

We walked up the mountainside in silence, picking our way towards the large rock on the side of the mountain that I'd always considered my true home. It was harder to get to now that Mr. Jackson was gone. While he was alive he'd kept the trail that led up the mountainside nice and trimmed (so he could reach his pot stash), but now it was largely overgrown.

Forcing my way through helped me work off some of my anger so that I was mostly calm by the time we finally reached the rock and sat down cross-legged to look down on the town of Creek.

It might not be much to look at, but I loved the view anyway.

"What did you bring?" I asked Matt as he opened up his backpack. As far as I knew the only things he ate at home were fast food, burgers cooked on the grill, and cans of tuna fish.

"A couple of sandwiches. Turkey and cheddar with tomatoes, lettuce, and mayo. I remembered you don't like mustard. And a bag of chips and a couple of apples, too."

"Not bad."

"I try." He grinned at me and my heart gave a little tug, taking the last of the anger with it.

I didn't want to be mad at Matt. He didn't deserve it. He hadn't betrayed me. And he hadn't made me an offer I couldn't refuse but desperately wanted to. His only fault was that he was such a good person I couldn't just write him off.

I pulled out my Coke and cracked it open.

"Water's better for a hike, you know."

"Yeah, well, I often do what isn't the best for me."

He let that go and we sat in silence as we ate our sandwiches. Finally, Matt said, "Nice view."

"It is, isn't it? One of my favorite places in the world. I used to come up here in the summers and count the number of cars in each of the freight trains that passed by."

"Me, too."

"From here?"

"No. From my dad's place. There's this little spot right at the edge of our property that's good for fishing. I used to sneak down there as often as I could. This was before we moved, of course. I could see the train tracks from there and I'd count the cars as they went by."

We sat there for a moment in silence, both of us looking down on the town of Creek. It's not a big town. There are maybe forty houses in the whole town and half of those started off as mobile homes. There's the creek running along the edge of town, the ballpark, the county seat, and the shiny new library building at the edge of town and that's about it. But it's beautiful. And it's peaceful.

And it's home.

I sighed. "I love this town."

"Me, too."

"But you're thinking of leaving." I glanced at him sideways.

He finished his bite of sandwich before answering. "So are you. Aren't you? That offer you got last night?"

"Yeah. They need me."

"Doesn't Jamie need you, too?"

"No."

I told him about the resort offer and how it was clear Jamie, Mason, and Greta had been working on it for a while without me.

"Sounds like they'd planned for you to be involved."

"But they don't *need* me to be involved. Karen on the other hand said they won't get that project without me. So if I don't go back to DC I cost all those people I used to work with a lot of money. I'd rather be needed than some charity case."

"Hm."

"What's that mean?"

"Nothing. It's your choice. But maybe give it another day. Let your temper cool before you make your final decision."

"My temper?" I asked as I felt the anger flare back to life.

He nodded, not looking away or down which is what most people do when I'm in that kind of a mood. It made it a little hard to sustain when he refused to let it affect him.

I crumpled up the paper towel I'd used as a napkin. "I need to walk this off. You up for more of a hike?"

"Sure. But, Maggie?"

I glanced at him. "Yeah?"

"People here, they need you, too. More than you think they do. Just remember that when you're making your decision. Now, come on. There's a gorgeous spot right at the edge of the canyon where you can see for miles on a day like this." He held out his hand and I took it, letting him pull me to my feet.

CHAPTER 23

It only took us about ten minutes to reach the spot Matt had wanted to show me. I liked hiking with him, he kept his pace steady but didn't leave me behind when the altitude (and probably my choice of beverage) made me slow down a bit.

And he was right. It was a gorgeous spot. Breathtaking as a matter of fact.

Off to the right I could see the entire valley stretching off into the distance, the mountains rolling along like they'd never end. It was just…stunning.

To the left was the canyon. I couldn't see as much of it as I could of the valley because of how it twisted and turned. But there was still the sky and that feeling of being part of something larger than myself. Something so powerful I could barely wrap my mind around it.

I closed my eyes, took a deep breath, and let it wash over me.

"Can you really walk away from this?" Matt asked, standing close enough that I could feel the heat of him.

"Can you?" I answered. I sat down cross-legged and stared out into space.

I didn't want to leave. I didn't want to do that work anymore. I didn't want to put Fancy in day care every day. And I didn't honestly care about the money no matter how much it was.

But they needed me. And one of my biggest weaknesses is my inability to say no when someone really needs my help. Like Karen did.

Matt sat down next to me, our knees almost touching. The silence stretched between us for a long moment and then he said, "You know, there's another way to think about what you told me earlier about Jamie, Mason, and Greta."

"Is there?"

"There is. Instead of thinking about what you're going to lose with the barkery being torn down, you should think about the fact that Greta and Mason, two people who didn't have to make room for you in their lives if they didn't want to, have decided to do so. Think about how you came here to open a business with one person, Jamie, and how you made enough of an impact in that short period of time that both Greta and Mason want you to be part of this amazing resort they're building."

I pressed my lips together.

"And your grandpa? He doesn't show it, but he loves having you here. Sure, Lesley will probably be a much bigger part of his life going forward, but nothing can replace you. You're his only granddaughter. Having you around makes him proud."

"He thinks I should take the project in DC."

"He thinks you should have a life. And he doesn't want to be the one who holds you back from that. Did you tell him about the resort offer?"

"No. I didn't get a chance to. Lesley was there when I came home."

"So he doesn't know that you have a perfectly good choice here, too. Maybe if he did he'd change his mind." He nudged me with his shoulder. "Do you really want to give this up? For any amount of money?"

I made a small pile of pebbles and knocked it back down. "It's not about the money. If I don't go, they won't get the project."

"Too bad. If they can't convince that company to hire them anyway, then that's on them." He leaned close and I could smell the faint hint of aftershave. "Maggie, it might not be as obvious, but the people here need you just as much as those people back in DC. Maybe more."

Our eyes met.

It was one of those moments. One of those moments where that potential between two people can tip over into something more. The possibility hung there between us as I met his eyes. Eyes so blue I could drown in them.

All it would take was opening up to him. Leaning forward. Letting our lips touch.

That's all it would take…

But I turned away. "We better get back. I still haven't found Sam's mom." I didn't look at him as I stood up and dusted off my pants.

It would've been better if he'd gotten mad at me. If he'd called me on it. But he didn't. He wasn't that type of person. He just quietly started back down the trail.

I paused and took one last look at the view. It really was stunning.

I was going to miss it.

🐾 🐾 🐾

I hated the distance that had suddenly grown between me and Matt. A distance I'd created by turning away.

I knew why I'd done it, but he didn't. He just knew he was this good guy who couldn't get the girl he liked and he probably thought it was about him when it absolutely wasn't.

I hurried to catch up to him.

"You know, when I was little Tina's mom would walk us to the center of the canyon for fresh spring water. It bubbled out of this little spot in the canyon wall and we'd take one of those plastic jugs with us and fill it up. Tasted so sweet. So pure. Better than anything you can get with even the best filter."

He nodded, but didn't look back at me. "I remember that. She'd take me along sometimes, too."

"Probably be suicide to do that now, there's enough traffic through the canyon these days I'd never let a kid walk through there. You just never know when someone will veer off the road that little bit."

I carefully stepped over a large rock before adding, "You know I always admired her for having such confidence even though her leg was all mangled up from that car accident. Never let it stop her, though."

"That accident…" Matt stopped so suddenly I almost ran into him. He turned to look at me. "It was in the canyon, wasn't it? Their car rolled down the canyon."

"Yeah. Probably only reason they survived is how drunk they were. At least that's how I heard it."

"That's it."

"What's it?"

He grabbed my shoulders, grinning like a fool. "Trish was driving back from the Creek Inn. *Through* the canyon. Late at night. In the dark. Probably upset because her kid's worthless father just got out of prison and wants back in his life. All it would take is missing one curve."

"You think she drove off the edge?"

"Could've. It's worth looking at."

"Wouldn't someone have noticed?"

"There's no guardrail. So what is there to notice? People zip through there so fast no one's going to see a tire track on the side of the road and think someone went off the side. And there's nothing at the base of the canyon except for the river and the train tracks."

"A train could see her."

"There's some switch issue. Hasn't been a train through in days."

I nodded. "It makes sense. And she isn't anywhere else." I gave him a hug. "Quick thinking. Come on. Let's go see if you're right."

I raced down the mountainside, Matt on my heels.

CHAPTER 24

I wanted to go straight to Matt's truck, but I was in desperate need of another Coke by the time we got to my grandpa's, so I veered towards the house instead. As I walked through the front door I saw that Jack and Sam were there working the puzzle they'd started the day before. They almost had it done.

A cute, bright package with little dumpster trucks sat at the end of the table.

"Where'd that come from?" I asked.

"I brought it. It's Sam's birthday after all, isn't it, buddy?" He ruffled Sam's hair. "I thought we could throw him a little party here. Your grandpa said it would be okay."

My grandpa joined us from the direction of his workroom. It seemed Lesley was gone. "He even brought a cake."

I eyed Jack like I'd never seen him before. "Well look at you, Mr. Fine and Upstanding Citizen. Who knew that all it took was one little kid to turn you around?"

"I'm not little." Sam frowned at me. "You found my mom yet?"

"I'm working on it. Matt and I were just about to go check something out actually."

"What?" For a little kid Sam had quite the in-your-face attitude.

"Well, your mom was at a place called the Creek Inn the night she went missing. It's on the other end of the canyon. We thought maybe she'd had an accident coming back home. Missed a turn in the road."

Jack stood up. "You think she rolled her car down the canyon."

"Maybe."

He glanced down at Sam. "You think you'll be okay here with Lou, buddy? I'd like to go help them look."

"Can I come?"

"No."

It was a good thing Jack had to be the one to tell that kid no, because I would've probably caved and let him come along. But Jack was right. If she'd rolled her car down the canyon, chances were she was going to be in rough shape. (If she was still alive.) No need for Sam to be there when we found her.

Sam pouted, but Jack waited him out. "So you okay staying here?"

"Fine."

"And you okay looking after him for an hour or so?" he asked my grandpa.

"You can help me finish the puzzle," Sam added.

My grandpa snorted, but he nodded his head and sat down in the chair Jack had vacated.

"Then let's go."

"Just give me a second to get a Coke would ya?" I said, heading for the kitchen.

Jack didn't look too pleased to have to wait that whole thirty seconds, but he didn't say anything.

Matt did, though. He called after me. "A bottle of water would be better. Grab me one, too?"

Rather than argue especially when I knew he was right, I grabbed three bottles of water. But I did mutter a few choice words about interfering men as I handed Jack and Matt their bottles on the way out the door.

🐾 🐾 🐾

As we piled into the truck, me in the front passenger seat, Jack in the seat directly behind me, I looked at Matt. "What are you thinking? What's the best way to do this?"

"I say we drive through the canyon and you two keep an eye out for any signs that a vehicle went off the edge. If we don't spot anything on the first pass then we'll park and walk back through on foot just in case."

I had no desire to walk through that canyon on foot. Walking along the side with the canyon wall would be scary enough. Walking on the side with the sharp drop off? Ugh. Not worth considering.

I was so nervous about finding Trish I kept twisting and untwisting the cap on my water bottle until Matt finally reached over and put his hand on mine long enough to get me to stop.

He took his hand back when we reached the canyon and I turned to focus all my attention on any sign of a car going over the edge.

It wasn't much of an edge. In some spots there was no more than a foot or two of loose dirt between the asphalt of the road and open air. There were two, maybe three pull outs in the canyon, but they were all on the other side up against the canyon wall.

Trish would've been coming from the other direction, but at night it would be easy enough to miss a turn and go across a single lane and off the edge. No lights. No guardrail. To think we all drove through that canyon like it was nothing…

I wasn't exactly sure what to look for but I figured it was one of those situations where I'd know it when I saw it.

The speed limit through the canyon was only forty miles per hour, but that didn't keep the locals and visitors from winding their way through the canyon at a much less reasonable sixty on most days. Since Matt was probably doing thirty-five he had a long line of angry people piled up behind him and nowhere for them to go.

Someone in the string of cars behind us honked loudly and Matt's grip on the steering wheel tightened. "Anything yet?"

"Nope. Sorry. You just keep your eyes on the road, though. Jack and I will spot anything there is."

We were almost at the edge of the canyon when both Jack and I cried out at the same time.

"That looks promising," I said.

"Definitely. Find a place to park Matt and we'll go back and check it out."

Matt sped up to reach the end of the canyon since that would be the closest place to pull over. You could almost hear the cheers from the cars behind him.

The road curved over a small bridge at the end of the canyon and just past that there was enough space for a single vehicle to pull over—a scenic viewpoint that fortunately didn't have anyone in it at that particular moment. We piled out of the truck and lined up along the bridge rail to see if we could spot Trish's car, but the canyon curved before the spot where we'd both seen sign someone might have gone off the edge.

Watching the traffic whiz by I did not want to walk back into that canyon, not even a hundred feet. Especially since we'd have to do it on the open air side if we had any hope of spotting Trish's car.

Fortunately, Jack had a better idea. He scrambled up the side of the embankment above where we'd parked the truck, the ground giving way beneath his feet. I held my breath until he'd reached the top edge. That put him on the opposite side of the canyon from the road and let him walk along the ridgeline until he could get a view of where the car might be.

"Careful, Jack. We don't want to lose you, too."

I'm not even sure he heard me. He was a man on a mission.

Finally, he stopped and crouched down. "I see a car," he shouted down to us. "I think it's Trish's. Call it in, Matt."

Matt didn't have signal on his phone. Before I could offer him mine, he said, "I'll just drive for help. You stay here."

He hopped in his truck, flipped a U-turn, and drove back towards Creek, leaving me to watch with fear as Jack made his way back down the embankment.

I don't think I managed to breathe until he put his foot down on the side of the road once more.

"You know that's all we needed, you falling into the canyon yourself."

He winked. "Don't worry about me little lady. I have nine lives."

I snorted. "Please. And if you do have nine lives, I'd

lay money on the fact that you've used at least seven of them by now."

"Probably six. But who's counting?"

CHAPTER 25

As we stood there waiting for Matt to come back with the cavalry, Jack said, "Jamie told me why you don't do relationships."

I crossed my arms, suddenly wishing I'd gone with Matt. We didn't need two people standing on the side of the road and I'd rather be with him than having this conversation. Not to mention how angry I was with Jamie for talking about me behind my back. The resort thing was bad enough. This…

This was unforgivable. I knew she meant well, but my issues were no one's business but mine. Of course, Jamie didn't know my reasons, so…

I shook my head. "Nice try. But she can't tell you what she doesn't know."

"She's your best friend. Of course she knows."

"Just because she's my best friend doesn't mean I've had that conversation with her. My general reaction to 'Gee, Maggie, why don't you date someone?' is to say, 'Because I don't want to.' That usually ends the conversation right there. We never get into the hows or whys of it because most people aren't stupid enough to press the point."

I gave him my best death stare, but he just shrugged it off. "You may not have spelled it out for her, but she knows."

"She's wrong."

"I don't know. Makes sense to me. You lose your parents in a car accident and the love of your life in a skydiving accident within a year, it's bound to make you a little gun shy about love."

A wave of fury ran through me. It was not Jamie's business to tell Jack about any of that. It didn't matter if that wasn't my reason for avoiding relationships, it was still personal and none of his concern. But I pushed the anger away because he'd just keep coming at me if he saw it.

I laughed instead. "You think that would shut me down for fifteen years? Lose enough people and that's it? Done forever."

People who know me would've let it drop right then and there. I don't do violence but I certainly know how to lash at someone with my words. Enough for them to back off.

Not Jack though.

"Yeah. I do. Can't be easy to lose so many people you love so close together. And when you're not even out of college."

I took a deep breath and shoved the emotions that were threatening to swamp me back where they belonged.

Death is funny that way. Someone can be gone for ages and then one little comment or one little thing will bring it all right back like it was yesterday. I could go weeks without consciously thinking about my parents or

Alex but Jack brings it up and suddenly all I wanted to do was go have a good cry.

I turned to face him, because that was the only way to make him hear what I said. "It wasn't easy. But that's not my issue with relationships." I stepped right up in his face. "And I swear to you, if you tell Matt about this, that that's my reason, I will gut you."

I've never gutted anyone in my life, of course.

I've never punched anyone. I'm pretty sure I've never even slapped anyone. I might've deliberately jostled someone in a crowd once. And I certainly didn't hesitate to use my body to shove a few players around when I played basketball, but overall I don't actually have a violent bone in my body.

In that moment, though, I was absolutely, 100% sincere that I would inflict bodily harm on Jack Barnes if he took those painful moments from my past and used them like that.

And I know it showed.

Jack held his ground, though. The problem with dealing with criminals. They've actually been there and are prepared to take the hit if they have to. "Are you sure? You going to tell me that didn't impact you? That that didn't make you hesitate the next time you met someone?"

I sighed and let go of the anger boiling in my gut.

I wanted to stay angry. Especially with everything that had happened over the last day or so. But I refuse to live life feeling that way. It would eat me up just like battery acid if I let it. So I don't. I feel that rancid feeling building in my gut and I wash it away before it can consume me.

Jack cared about his brother. It wasn't his business, but that's all it was about.

"Yeah, sure. That was a serious double-blow. You know, honestly, I had the exact opposite reaction of what you're thinking when I lost my parents. Losing them is why I fell so hard for Alex. I had this great big gaping hole where they'd been and then I met Alex and BOOM. I was all in. One hundred percent. Right away. Would've been forever, too. But then I lost him. And you know, for a while there it just didn't seem worth the risk to go through that again."

"Exactly. See? I get that. I was head over heels for Trish. Loved that kid, Sam. And then she just left me one day. Tore my heart out. It's not easy to trust like that again."

"But you do eventually. It's what makes us human. It's how we survive. We forget how much it hurt and we try again."

"You haven't."

"No. I haven't. But it wasn't because I lost them."

"Then what was it? Why won't you let Matt in?"

I sighed. "It's not your business, Jack."

"It is, too. Because if he re-ups…"

I closed my eyes. "If he re-ups, that's *his* choice. Not mine."

"He'd stay for you."

I shook my head. "I can't ask him to make a decision like that because of me. He needs to choose to stay here because it's what *he* wants."

"If he does choose to stay, will you let him in?"

"I won't be here. I'm leaving. I got a job offer I can't refuse and they're tearing down the barkery to build a resort." I turned to look down the canyon. "Oh, look who's back."

Matt drove through the canyon with a police car, an ambulance, and a fire truck hot on his heels.

I stepped away from Jack, pretending that I was doing it to make room for everyone to park where they could but really because I wanted to get away from him. It was no one's business but mine why I was the way I was. They just needed to accept that I wasn't going to be like them and leave me to it. How hard was that?

CHAPTER 26

Turns out trying to send someone down into a canyon with sheer walls to figure out if the occupant of a car that went over the side is still alive isn't all that easy.

The emergency vehicles set up a command center across the highway along a rutted service road no one ever used. And then everyone proceeded to gather around and debate the best option for getting down to Trish's car. For thirty minutes.

They discussed having someone rappel down the canyon wall where we'd found the tire tracks, but the rock that made up the canyon wasn't the type to rely on for that sort of thing. If they parked a vehicle for someone to anchor to that meant blocking all traffic through the area for as long as that took.

We all knew the horror stories out of Glenwood Canyon every time there was a rock slide there. It was hours and hours to detour around and no one wanted to mess with traffic that way.

Abe and Evan might've appreciated the extra business but we would've been hearing about it for weeks from every single business owner in the valley. Not to mention the horror stories the tourists would spread of how they'd been trapped for hours in the Colorado mountains with nowhere to go.

Live by tourism, die by tourism.

The longer they took to debate things the more agitated Jack became until he stormed off to demand rappelling equipment and a wet suit from one of the mountain rescue guys. The guy would've probably said no and Jack would've probably decked him if Matt hadn't stepped in and vouched for him.

There was some tense back and forth and then the guy handed over his gear and helped Jack set up to lower himself from the edge of the bridge at the end of the canyon.

By the time anyone else noticed what was happening Jack was already over the side and halfway down. He'd taken a headset with him so we all gathered around the speakers in the command tent to listen as he relayed his progress back to us.

Things were no easier at the bottom of the canyon. The river flowed pretty fast through there and half the time there wasn't a bank, at least not on the side where the car had gone over, just the steep-sided canyon and the river. Jack could've crossed to the railroad tracks but then he would've had to risk getting back across to the car once he reached it, which depending on how wide the river was at that point might've been impossible.

Instead he scrambled over sharp rocks and waded through the river, trying to get to Trish without being swept away.

It was slow going and there was lots of creative cussing that I wouldn't want my grandma to hear. It was so colorful at times it might've even made my grandpa blush. (Who am I kidding? Nothing can make my grandpa blush.)

But finally he radioed back that he'd reached the car. He was clearly tense as he said, "Car is on its side. Passenger side is in the water. Driver's side is clear. There's a chance."

We all went silent. No one spoke waiting for the next transmission.

"I'm approaching the vehicle. It's a bit of a scramble here, there's lots of big rocks. I can't see into the car. The windshield is busted up, but still in one piece."

Whatever else he was, Jack obviously still cared for Trish. I could hear it in every strained word.

I didn't even realize I'd done it, but I grabbed Matt's hand and squeezed it tight, praying that Trish had somehow miraculously made it through but knowing she probably hadn't. He squeezed back with just the right amount of reassurance.

"I'm almost there. I..." We could hear it as Jack slipped on a rock and cussed up a blue streak. He was clearly in pain, but he got it together. "I'm lifting myself up now. Looking in the window…"

I didn't even want to breathe.

"I can see her. It's Trish. But she isn't moving."

It had been two days. And she had rolled her car into a canyon. What were we expecting?

I buried my face against Matt's shoulder. I'd wanted to find her. But not like this. What was I going to tell Sam? And what kind of life was he going to have now without his mom? Who would take care of him?

But then…

"She's alive! I tapped on the window and she turned her head to look at me. Get some EMTs down here. Now."

We cheered. Matt hugged me tight and we both laughed with joy. Only for a minute though, because then we had to figure out how to get Trish—who had to be seriously injured—out of that car and to the hospital. She was alive, but if they didn't do things right, she still might not make it.

As the mountain rescue team consulted with the paramedics, Matt and I stood off to the side.

"Should we go home and tell Sam?" I asked. "Or should we stay here and wait?"

He glanced towards the canyon. "I say we wait. Better to do that than go home, tell Sam his mom is alive, and then find out she didn't make it. And…Jack's there."

"Of course. I'd forgotten. Sorry."

He ruffled my hair. "No need to apologize. It's a lot to take in."

We moved ourselves out of the way and settled in to wait, sitting hip to hip in companionable silence.

CHAPTER 27

When it became obvious that it was going to take hours not minutes to get Trish out of the canyon, Matt drove me down the road so I could call my grandpa and fill him in on what we knew so far.

I asked him not to tell Sam.

"The kid's smart, Maggie May. You're not back yet, he knows something's up."

"I know, but…I don't want him to get his hopes up."

"Understood. Hey, you doing okay?"

I shrugged even though he couldn't see it. "Sure. Why do you ask?"

"You seemed awfully upset when you came home earlier. Anything I should know about?"

I debated telling him about the resort idea, but I just didn't have it in me to talk about it right then. Instead I asked, "Do you like having me here, Grandpa?"

I'd already decided I was going to take Karen's offer, but I still wanted to know the answer to the question. A "yes, but you're a pain in the patootie" answer would've helped cement things for me.

"What kind of question is that?"

"An honest one."

I could almost see him frowning at me through the phone. "This about that job offer you got last night?"

"That and a few other things. I mean, I moved here to help you out but you don't seem to need it. And now with Lesley, I figure I might just be in the way more than I'm a help. You won't even let me mow the yard."

"Maggie May."

"Well. So, do you like having me here? Or…not."

There was a long silence. My grandpa isn't the most eloquent of men at the best of times and I knew with a question as loaded as the one I'd just asked he'd want to be very careful about what he said.

Finally, he answered. "Maggie May. I don't have any family left other than you. I never had kids of my own. Your dad was as close as I came. And now that he's gone…Well, there's just you. So of course I want you around. You're my only family. And with Bill passing away that just reminds me how precious the ones we love are and how little time we have with them no matter how long that time is."

"Oh." I don't know why, but I hadn't expected him to say that. He's not one for emotion or regret most times.

"But," he added.

"But?"

"But I don't want to be the reason you don't take a once-in-a-lifetime opportunity. That offer you got? The amount of money you're talking. That's not something to pass up. You won't be young and healthy forever. And people won't be making offers like that to you when you're sixty. So as much as I love you and want you to stay around here, I think the best choice you can make is to take that offer. Think about what that money could mean for your future."

"It's just money, Grandpa. Isn't family more important?"

"Depends on how much money you have. When you're broke and can't feed yourself and robbing a bank seems the only option? No. Family is not more important. Not unless they have money to help you out."

I forgot sometimes how rough he'd had it as a kid. Never having been that bad off myself, I couldn't grasp just how bad things can get.

"Maggie May, I know you love that place you started, but, honestly, do you really think it's going to make it?"

"Oh, didn't I tell you? They're tearing it down to build a resort."

"What?"

I told him about the plan Greta, Jamie, and Mason had put together and how they'd made room for me in it but how I also felt like some afterthought add-on they could do without. And, of course, even though they were going to pay me a salary as part of the deal that salary was nothing compared to what I could earn if I went back to DC.

I bit my lip. "So, knowing that, what do you think?"

"I think *you* have to make this choice, Maggie May. No one else can make it for you. I love you. I love having you here. But it seems to me you have a sure thing with that offer in DC. The resort option is better than the barkery. But is it something you can bank your future on?"

A very good question.

I would've talked to him about it further, but my phone beeped to signal an incoming call. It was Karen.

"I've got a call on the other line, Grandpa. Better take this."

"Love you, Maggie May."

"Love you, too, Grandpa."

I thumbed the screen to answer Karen's call. "Hey, Karen. What's up? Thought you were going to give me a couple of days."

"I was, but I'm getting a lot of pressure here to let them know if you're in or not. I might lose some team members to other projects if we don't nail this down now."

That's how it always worked there. They made it seem like there was room and flexibility, but there never was.

"Maggie? We need you on this project. You say no, it's going to cost us millions."

I watched Matt sitting next to me, pretending not to listen, but clearly hearing every word.

"It's a big decision, Karen."

"Why? You're wasted there, Maggie. I mean, honestly, a dog bakery? And do you really want to spend the rest of your days in some small town with people who wear overalls and drive pick-up trucks? I mean, come on."

"Actually…yes."

I realized in that moment that what I wanted was to spend my days around people who wouldn't look down on something like that. Small towns and pick-up trucks wasn't all of who I was, but it was a part of me. And I wanted to be around people who could accept that. Not mock it or dismiss it.

I thought I'd already decided. I thought I was taking the job. But when Karen pushed me I realized that wasn't at all what I wanted my life to be. I'd rather be poor in small-town Colorado, surrounded by my quirky friends and family who weren't perfect but were mine, than in some flash job in DC where I felt like I could only be half of who I was.

Or worse, where I was changing into someone I didn't want to be.

"What did you just say?" Karen asked.

"I can't do it. I can't take the offer. I'm sorry."

"Take a few more days to think about it…"

"No. A few days won't matter. I'm staying here."

"You'd turn this down? Do you know what kind of an opportunity this is?"

"Yeah. One I don't want."

"What if we up the hourly rate? I can go up another fifty an hour."

"It's not about money, Karen. It never was. You're just going to have to convince them you can do this without me. I gotta go."

I hung up on her.

I didn't even care if she was upset with me or if I'd burned that bridge and could never go back, because I finally realized I didn't want to go back. Ever.

This was where I wanted to be.

Matt grinned at me. "I knew you weren't going to take it."

"Did you?" I asked. "Because until right then I thought I was."

"Yep. I knew it when you stood there on the edge of the canyon and looked around and your entire face lit up. No way you could walk away from that."

"Well, glad one of us knows me so well."

He just laughed.

CHAPTER 28

They still hadn't brought Trish out by the time I finished my calls, but at least the medics had reached her and gotten an IV into her so she was being hydrated.

After about an hour of debate and back and forth and throwing out more and more absurd ideas they figured out some ingenious plan to get a platform under the car and get it across the river to the railroad side where they could then transport it out of the canyon. It wouldn't have been possible if Trish drove some rugged truck, but she drove a lightweight little compact that four of the guys swore they'd picked up and moved once just as a joke.

(I'd had a car like that once. A Geo Metro. Cheap and reliable, but not all that sturdy. Certainly not a mountain car.)

It took another hour to get everything ready. By then it was starting to get dark in the canyon, but it's not like they could wait until the next day, not with Trish trapped inside.

The whole time Jack stayed by Trish's side. He'd moved the microphone away from his mouth, but I could hear the murmur of his voice as he talked to her, keeping her at ease, letting her know she wasn't alone.

Despite his criminal ways, I had to admit Jack Barnes was a pretty decent guy when he wanted to be.

Finally, they were ready to act. Those of us not down in the canyon huddled around the command center as they coordinated the rescue. It didn't go perfectly. One guy fell in the river and was swept downstream about twenty feet until he managed to rescue himself. He was bruised up but otherwise uninjured.

It also took more than four guys to maneuver the car onto the platform since Trish was inside and they couldn't just tip it over and there was the tiny little matter of a river to deal with. But after a tense forty-five minutes, they had Trish and her car on their way out of the canyon.

From there it was a pretty straight-forward rescue. They cut Trish out of the car and loaded her into a helicopter bound for Denver, Jack at her side. She was in rough shape, but still alive. So there was hope.

🐾 🐾 🐾

As Matt and I drove back through the canyon I shuddered to think how Trish had driven off the edge like that and no one had known.

And then to be stuck there, probably trapped, no cellphone signal, knowing her son would think she'd abandoned him on his birthday…

Ugh.

Matt squeezed my hand. "We found her, Maggie. That's what counts."

"You reading my mind again, Mr. Barnes?"

"Maybe." He kept ahold of my hand.

I didn't pull it away until we reached my grandpa's. I

knew I should, but I just needed that little bit of connection. That knowledge that I wasn't actually alone. That someone might notice I was missing and care enough to find me if something similar happened.

Sam ran out of the house as soon as we stopped moving. "Did you find her?"

I nodded. "We did. But she's not in the clear yet. She was hurt pretty bad."

"Where is she? I want to see her."

"They had to take her to the hospital in Denver. Did you see that helicopter earlier?"

He nodded.

"That was for your mom. Jack's with her. And we'll get you down to see her, but probably not until tomorrow."

He stomped his foot. "Why not? I want to see her now. It's my birthday."

Matt knelt down in front of him. "Your mom was badly hurt. She's going to be in surgery most of the night. There's nothing you can do for her right now and you wouldn't be able to see her even if you were down there. But I'll take you down tomorrow, okay?"

Sam nodded. He wasn't happy about it, but it was what it was.

Fancy started crying her head off, so I went into the house to calm her down. When Matt and Sam eventually joined us I said, "How about some cake? If finding your mom isn't a reason to celebrate, I don't know what is."

"But mom should be here. And Jack, too."

"Tell you what. We'll wait until your mom's better and Jack's here and we'll have a big party for both of you. But this cake isn't going to last that long, so we might as well eat it now."

"Fine." He wasn't that enthused, but I'd seen him eat sweets before. I knew once that slice of cake was in front of him, he'd scarf it right up.

We lit the birthday candles and sang happy birthday to Sam. Even my grandpa joined in and he usually won't, but he at least has a better voice than I do.

"You make a wish?" I asked Sam after he blew out the candles.

He nodded, staring at the cake with an expression much older than his years. If I had to guess, I'd bet he'd wished that his mother would be alright now. That's what I would've wished for. Or maybe that Jack would stick around. That would've been a good choice, too.

Sam may not have wanted to eat cake originally, but once he got started he was all about it. He had three slices and I let him. I figured why not. He'd had a rough enough day and it was his birthday after all. (I had two slices myself.)

I wondered, watching him, if I had blue frosting around my lips the way he did. It was one of those sheet cakes you get from the store that always have that colored frosting that stains everything. With Sam that meant a blue spot on his cheek, one on his nose, stains all over his lips, and on at least four of his fingers. And we all had blue tongues, too. It happens.

Sam might've been a mess, but at least he'd enjoyed it.

We'd been silent as we ate, each of us lost in our own thoughts, but finally Sam set his fork down and turned to me. "You didn't tell me what happened to my mom. Did she run away like Vick said?"

In other words, had she abandoned him on his

birthday?

"No. As a matter of fact, she was coming home to you. But she had an accident. Her car went off the road. No one saw it happen so they didn't know she was down there." I squeezed his hand. "If it wasn't for you, we may have never found her in time. It was your faith in your mom that kept us looking. You saved her, Sam."

He started crying and all I could do was let him crawl into my lap and cry himself out. He fell asleep with his head pillowed against my shoulder.

I glanced across the table where Matt was watching us, his expression unreadable.

"Since Jack's in Denver, you guys can just stay here tonight if you want," I said.

"That's okay, thanks. We're all set up at my place. Here, I'll take him. We better get going. It's been a long day."

It felt like there was so much more we needed to say to one another, but I didn't know where to start, so instead I just handed off Sam to Matt and walked him out to his truck.

"Thanks for everything today," I said as I held the door open and he belted Sam into the back seat, still half asleep.

"What are friends for?" He didn't quite look at me. "I'll catch you later?"

"Sure. Sounds good. Safe drive tomorrow."

🐾 🐾 🐾

My grandpa looked at me when I walked back in the door. "You okay?"

"As good as I can be." I joined him at the table. He and Sam had finally finished the puzzle. "I told Karen

I'm not taking that job. I don't want to leave here. I know it might not work out, but I can't imagine going back there."

"You sure that's what you want?"

I nodded. "Absolutely."

"And what about Matt?"

"What about him?"

"Now that you're staying…."

"Grandpa." I shook my head. "Between you, Jamie, and Greta, I swear. I better make some calls. Let Trish's friends know we found her."

"I'll call Vick."

I winced. I knew the man needed to know that Trish was okay, but I really hoped for Sam's sake, and Trish's too for that matter, that when she woke up it was Jack by her side not Vick.

Jack had his issues. He certainly wasn't perfect. But I couldn't imagine Vick climbing into that canyon or staying by her side all those hours. Jack really cared for her. And for Sam. I just hoped Trish was smart enough to see it and to see that the life she could have with Jack was a lot better than the one she had with Vick.

CHAPTER 29

When I walked into the barkery the next morning Jamie wasn't singing. She wasn't even smiling. I should've called her the night before but I'd been so tired after everything that had happened. Plus, apologies like the one I needed to make are best made in person.

"Hey, Maggie. Wasn't sure you'd be in today."

I grimaced. "Sorry. About yesterday. About what a brat I was. You guys had really put a lot of thought into everything and it's such a great idea and…"

"We really do want you to be a part of it, you know. It won't be the same without you. And I'm sorry that…"

I help up my hand. "Wait. Just let me get this out, would you?"

She clearly wanted to keep talking, but she pressed her lips together and instead grabbed me a chocolate croissant and a Coke. (There's a reason she's my best friend. More than the fact that she's one of the few people in this world willing to put up with me.)

I laughed. "A bribe?"

"Maybe." She almost smiled.

Leave it to Jamie to feel bad about things when I was

the one who'd been horrible.

"Look. You caught me by surprise yesterday. And I know you didn't mean it to be but it felt like you were all in on this secret and I wasn't. Which was hard. You're my best friend. And I'm losing you to Mason already and then…"

"But you aren't!"

"I know. That's just how it feels sometimes. You know how people get married and then disappear into their new married, coupled lives. So I took it poorly when you showed me those plans that were so well-developed and that I knew nothing about."

"We didn't want to tell you if it fell through…"

"I know. I know you'd never hurt a fly. Which, thank God, because it's probably the only reason you're still my friend after all these years. Any sane person would've written me off long ago." She looked like she was going to object, so I just plowed ahead. "Anyway. Long and short of it is this. I was horrible yesterday. I'm sorry. And I told Karen I don't want to take that job. So, if you guys still want me, I'm in."

"You are?" She almost squealed she was so happy about it.

"I am."

"Yes." She hugged me and did a little jig around the café before launching into a non-stop discussion of all the ideas she had for the new resort.

I was able to finish both my Coke and the croissant before she finally stopped for a breath. "This is going to be so great, Maggie. Think of everything we can do with an entire pet resort!"

I was. And there were certainly some interesting

possibilities. I still wasn't as sure as she was that everything would work out perfectly, but I was cautiously optimistic.

"As long as I don't have to wear heels," I told her.

She laughed. "Deal."

CHAPTER 30

Matt sent a few texts over the next couple of days keeping me updated on Trish's condition. She was in rough shape. Broken bones and lacerated organs. But having Jack and Sam there helped a lot. Matt decided to stay down there with them rather than come back home. I wondered why but I was too scared to actually ask.

Nothing had changed. He was still a great guy and I was still unable or unwilling to let him get any closer than he already had, no matter how I felt about him.

I was working at the barkery when Jack and Sam walked in.

"Hey, Maggie," Sam called, running over to say hi to Fancy.

"Hey, Sam. Hey, Jack. What brings you here?"

Sam answered for both of them. "We just came home to grab a bunch of stuff and then Jack and I are going to go back down to Denver to be with my mom. She's hooked up to all these machines all the time and her leg and her arm are in a cast and she's all bruised all over her face. But she was so happy to see us. And one of the nurses gave me this really cool truck. See? It lights up and everything."

"Nice."

I looked to Jack. "Where's Matt?"

"Home. We went there first to pack up some things and grab my truck. Sam and I are headed back to Denver now."

"Oh. Makes sense." I tried to hide my disappointment, but I'm not sure I did a good job of it. "You guys want some cake? Maybe a Coke to go along with it?"

"I'll take a coffee. Squirt here can have a milk, not a Coke. And just half a slice of cake. For both of us to split."

Sam ran over and grabbed his hand. "Ah. Come on, Jack. Can't I have a whole slice?"

"No. You're hyper enough as is. Half a slice. And we're splitting it."

I joined them at the table by the window, taking the other half slice of cake for myself. "So what brought you in here today?"

"Business." Jack said. He looked at Sam. "Go ahead, buddy. It's yours to settle, not mine."

Sam dug into his backpack and brought out his piggy bank. "I wanted to pay you for finding my mom."

"You don't need to pay me, Sam. It's okay."

"Yes I do." He got that mulish look kids get right before they throw a loud temper tantrum.

"Really, Sam…"

He crossed his arms and glared at me. "I asked you to find my mom. I told you I'd pay you. You found her. So I'm going to pay you. Here."

He pushed the piggybank across the table at me, hard enough I had to stop it before it fell off the table.

I looked to Jack for help but he shook his head. "I'm with the kid. He hired you to find his mom and you deserve to be paid for services rendered."

The last thing I wanted to do was take the last twenty bucks from some poor kid for something I would've probably done for free. Although, offering to pay me had been a nice touch. That last little nudge I'd needed to listen to him. And it was good to teach him that services have value…

But, really. Twenty bucks.

I glanced at the piggybank and then at the very empty name-a-treat fundraiser jar. "Tell ya what. We'll compromise on this one. I'll take the money, but I'm putting it towards the fundraiser. Which means you've contributed the most to the fundraiser and you get to name my new dog treat. Deal?"

"Can I name it anything I want?"

"Within reason. No cuss words. It can't be 'dog treat'. It has to have something to do with dogs. And I'd prefer if it be two words that use the same letters. Like Barkery Bites and Doggie Delights and Canine Crunchies. Other than that, it's up to you."

Sam narrowed his eyes at me as he thought about it, but then he nodded. "Deal."

"Okay, then. You let me know what name you come up with."

I left Jack and Sam to discuss their choices as I cleaned up a little on the café side. Jack came over to me as I was dipping a rag in a bleach bucket.

"There's another reason we came by," he said, keeping his voice quiet.

"What's that?"

He held out an envelope to me.

"What's this?" I dropped the rag back into the bucket and dried my hands off before taking hold of it.

"Matt asked me to mail this for him. It's been sitting on the kitchen counter unsigned for a week, but when we got home he signed it and put it in the envelope."

I glanced at the address. "He's going to re-enlist."

Jack nodded, watching me intently.

It was like a gut punch, but I didn't let it show. "Well, good for him. If that's what he wants to do, he'll be excellent at it. We need men like him, you know. This country."

"This town needs men like him."

"Jack…" I tried to hand him the envelope back, but he held his hands out to the side, refusing it.

"Since you're the reason he's leaving, you should mail it."

I opened my mouth to protest, but Sam came running over just then. "I have it. I have the name for the treat."

"Yeah?" I forced myself to smile. "And what is it?"

"Mutt Munchies."

"Mutt Munchies?" I could feel my eyes go wide with shock.

"Yep. Mutt Munchies." Sam didn't notice, he just grinned like it was the best name in the world.

Jack laughed as I stood there, not sure what to say. I mean, Mutt Munchies? Really?

Of course, what did I expect leaving the name up to a young boy?

It was okay. Maybe not everyone would see it the way I had. Maybe it would seem perfectly normal to them. I sure hoped so, because there was no way around using it. Not with Sam looking at me that way. I wondered what Mason Maxwell was going to think of having a treat named Mutt Munchies in his new fancy pet resort.

Thinking of it that way…
"That's great, Sam. Mutt Munchies it is."

CHAPTER 31

As soon as Jack and Sam left, I did too. I needed to think. I wanted to be in Colorado. I wanted to be running a business with my best friend and spending time with my grandpa and with Fancy.

But without Matt…

I hadn't meant to let him become a part of my life. I hadn't wanted to fall for him. And yet, I had. Which meant I didn't want to lose him. I believe in serving your country and I'm proud of every man and woman who chooses to do so. But I'd be a fool to think that it doesn't come with risks. Or consequences.

I still firmly believed that Matt needed to make his own choices. That he couldn't choose to stay for me. It's not fair to ask that of someone.

But…

I didn't want to lose him. I'd walked away before. Turned my back on other men at other times. Chosen to stay on my path, alone. And yet with Matt, the loss was too big to bear.

I couldn't let him go that easy.

So I went to find him. I dropped Fancy off at the

house and went to Matt's.

His truck was parked in front of his place, but he didn't answer when I knocked on the door. I peered through the windows I could reach, but no one was there.

I was about to leave when I heard the sound of a train and remembered the fishing spot he'd told me about. I looked around and found a faint path through the grass behind his place that led in the direction of the river.

I followed it as the train came closer, the breeze blowing my hair back and carrying with it that scent of water and freshness I always associate with Colorado.

He was seated on a folding chair—one of those ones with striped colored strips of plastic woven to form the back and seat, this one in red and white—his fishing rod propped in the mud at his side. An opened beer sat on top of an old cooler that could've probably fit a couple cases.

He couldn't hear me over the sound of the train.

I stood there, frozen, about ten feet away, watching as it passed. I didn't want him to leave but I didn't want to ask him to stay either. It was such a moment of vulnerability, such a moment of potential loss. Easier to turn and walk away before he saw me.

But then the train was past and I stepped forward. Matt glanced over his shoulder and gave me a nod, "Maggie. To what do I owe the pleasure? Have a beer. Have a seat." He reached into the cooler and held out a beer to me, keeping his own in his hand and gesturing towards the cooler which was the only other seating option available.

I nodded towards where the train had disappeared. "I counted thirty-five cars," I said, taking the beer and sitting down facing him.

"You must've missed the first few. There were forty-two."

"Ah. Still not a record-breaker." I opened my beer and took a long sip. "Jack and Sam came by the store today on their way back to Denver."

"Really?"

"Sam wanted to pay me." I told him about Sam naming the new treat and we had a good laugh about it, but then lapsed into silence.

I stared at the river, not sure how to turn the conversation where it needed to go. Finally I decided the best way to deal with it was head on. I looked him in the eyes. "Don't go."

"What?"

I pulled the envelope Jack had given me out of my back pocket and ripped it in half. I figured worst case scenario he could always fill out new papers. "Jack gave these to me. Said you asked him to mail them for you. But I don't want you to go."

Matt frowned at me. "What…?"

"Look. Just listen would you? You have to stay. Jack is ten times more likely to stay on the straight and narrow with you around. And Trish and Sam need him. So you're helping there, too. And my grandpa's going to need your help next summer. And you're the best cop I know. And…"

I rushed on before he could stop me.

"And *I* need you to stay. This place won't be the same for me if you go."

Just saying it made me want to cry. I don't like to be vulnerable. I don't like to need people. Needing people means losing people and then hurting.

But if I couldn't be vulnerable in that moment to keep Matt then there was no hope for me. No one is actually perfect, but he was probably as close as you can get.

He just continued to stare at me so I rushed on. "I…Oh damn it. I think I love you, Matt. You can't go. Not when there's something here. You just can't."

I stood and started pacing, lost in my own thoughts. "I'm not a relationship person. I'm just…Not everyone can do that juggling thing where you let someone else in without smothering them or being lost in them. It's too easy for me to change when someone wants me to change. And there's so much I want to do that I'm not ready to be changed by someone else."

I stopped and frowned at him. He'd stood up and was staring at me. "Jack probably told you about Alex? About how he died?"

Matt nodded.

"But see, that's what no one gets. It wasn't him dying that broke me. It was realizing that his dying was probably the best thing that ever happened to me. That's what scared me away from relationships. I mean, I was going to give everything up for him. He wanted to move to Sweden to be a skydiving instructor and I was just going to go with him. I was almost done with college. I had plans of my own, but I was just going to walk away from everything I'd ever dreamed of being so he could pursue *his* dream. The only reason I didn't is because he died."

I crossed my arms tightly across my chest. "See, *that's* what love does to me. It sucks out who I am and replaces it with whoever the guy I'm with wants me to be. And I don't want that. But I can't lose you either."

Matt put his hands on either side of my face. "Maggie, I don't want you to be anyone other than you are, sharing plate for your dog, off-key singing, and prickly personality included. I'm pretty sure I love you, too. And I'm not going anywhere. I never was. I knew I was going to stay here the minute you decided to stay."

"What? But, Jack…"

Matt took one half of the torn up envelope and pulled out the blank piece of paper inside. "Jack knows how to get what he wants out of people. He played you."

"That…" (I called him a few words I won't repeat here.)

"I think we can forgive him just this once, don't you?" Matt smiled down at me as he brushed a piece of hair back from my face. I looked up, drowning in those blue eyes of his. Yeah, I could forgive him. Just this once.

Maybe.

And then…

Matt kissed me.

It was a good kiss. A *really* good kiss.

The type of kiss you want to be your last first kiss.

Oh yeah, I could definitely forgive Jack for this one.

EPILOGUE

It was my day off and I was finally going to have a chance to read that book I'd been dying to read for weeks. I grabbed myself a Coke from the fridge and went out back to join Fancy while it was still cool enough to read outside.

She was passed out on the grass at the base of the ramp, snoring quietly. I glanced over the rail to check on her, careful to keep from disturbing her, and had to keep myself from laughing when I noticed the tiny little bunny curled up against her tail, also sound asleep.

I desperately wanted to take a picture, but I knew that the minute I clicked on the camera option on my phone Fancy would wake up and the moment would be lost.

Well, at least I knew she wasn't a stone-cold bunny killer after all...

Now to just hope that one little bunny wasn't the first of a hundred or else I'd be back to restraining my grandpa from "dealing with the situation".

I tell ya, the fun never ends.

HALLOWEEN
AT THE
BAKER VALLEY
BARKERY & CAFE

A NOSY NEWFIE HOLIDAY SHORT

ALEKSA BAXTER

CHAPTER 1

It was early afternoon on a gorgeous late fall day in the Colorado mountains. Fancy—my three-year-old Newfoundland—was sound asleep in her cubby behind the barkery counter (you read that right, barkery, as in bakery for dogs), her legs thrust towards the ceiling as she happily snored away.

I was all alone. It was Jamie's day off and our shop assistant had already left for the day. I wasn't expecting any more customers, so I cranked the music up as I wiped down the tables and belted out how there's no one like me right along with Taylor Swift.

I can't sing to save my life, but I honestly, truly did not care. Just like I didn't care that I was cleaning—something I normally hate to do. Because, well, I was hopelessly, pathetically in love. It was a horrible feeling, all giddy and gooey and happy. But in that moment, filled to the brim with thoughts of Matt, a/k/a Officer Handsome Distraction a/k/a *Mine*, I didn't care that I was infected with some sort of brain-eating insanity that stole all my self-respect.

All I cared about was the fact that I, bitter, jaded, crazy person that I was had found a boyfriend that I really, really liked. That thought alone made me crinkle my nose, smile, and add an extra little bootie shake as I wiped down the last table in the corner, my blonde braid whipping back and forth as I really got into it.

Life was good. Life was *very* good.

Sure, there were some changes coming, including the fact that we were going to have to close down the barkery soon so that it could be replaced with a top-notch luxury pet resort catering to not only dogs but cats and probably geckos, too. But that was okay.

I was almost excited about it. Me and luxury don't exactly go hand in hand, so that scared me some. But I'd still get to run a business with my best friend, Jamie. And with her fiancé Mason and with Greta, my newest friend and a woman who had one of the most colorful pasts I've ever encountered.

Also…And this was maybe the best of all. I'd get to keep designing fun new dog treats but I wouldn't have to work the counter and be "on" all the time.

Not that I'd been having a problem with that lately, because I had a boyfriend (!) and it made me all giddy, happy, friendly. It was a very odd feeling. Like an out of body experience, really. But that had to end at some point. You can't stay on a love high forever.

Which meant eventually I'd be very happy for that pet resort and my new role as Chief Treat Developer even if it would probably be best for the business to keep me locked away in a dark backroom somewhere.

But that was in the future.

In the present it was time to work on my plans for the first (and only) Halloween Pet Parade at the Baker Valley Barkery and Café. I figured if we were tearing the place down we should go out with a bang. So our last day of business was going to be the Saturday before Halloween and we were going to have a big, huge costume party for pets and people.

Which meant figuring out what to make Fancy.

Not the easiest of tasks. You see all these dogs in these cute little costumes and you think, "Oh, I love that. I could totally do that with my dog." And then you try it on your hundred-and-forty-pound dog and it doesn't really turn out so well.

I once bought Fancy those little snow booties to protect her feet when she was a puppy because we lived in an apartment and they put that awful deicer stuff all over the sidewalks and I didn't want her to get it on her paws. Yeah, that lasted about five minutes.

She tore one off with her mouth, kept shaking her feet to get the front ones off, and wouldn't even let me near her to get the fourth one on, all the time giving me one of those looks that asked "Why would you do this to me? What have I done to deserve this sort of torture?"

So nothing on the feet. Which ruled out the cute little bowtie and cuff set I'd found.

The Halloween before I'd tried one of those bee costumes on her, the type that come with a little hat and wings that attach around the back. She was okay with it for a minute or two—long enough to get a cute picture. But then…

No.

She kept spinning in circles trying to get the wings off her back. And clawing at her head to remove the hat. It took all I had to get her calmed down enough to get the outfit off of her.

And don't even get me started on the Santa hat…

Of course, it did make noises and turn psychedelic colors if you pushed the little white ball at the tip so I really can't blame her on that one. She did actually tolerate it. She just looked so miserable the whole time I felt like the worst dog parent on the planet.

It seemed I'd have to get my fill of clever dog costumes from my clientele.

But I so wanted to make Fancy into a loofa. Or an Energizer Bunny. Or a teddy bear. Or a panda.

(I really wanted to make her a panda…)

Seriously, I needed to stay off Pinterest.

But they had such cute pictures. It made me want to have like ten Newfoundlands instead of one. And then I could dress them all up for a Mad Hatter-style tea party with funky little hats and giant-sized tea cups with dog biscuits on little colorful plates and…

Yeah, I know. I was losing it. Love, I tell ya. Fries the circuits.

But, hey, at least I wasn't as bad as the woman I knew who dressed her dogs up as a bride and groom and had them get married. Not that there's anything wrong with that if you yourself have done so. Not even if you sent out embossed invitations, hired the best caterer in the county, and had a swing band perform at the reception.

You are perfectly normal. No one is judging you. Really. Truly. I swear.

(Okay, so I'm not a good liar. Whatever.)

Anyway. I needed to figure out a costume for Fancy. But first I wanted to figure out a new treat to give out at the party, because of course a pet Halloween party has to have trick or treating.

We already had our staples: Doggie Delights, Canine Crunchies, Barkery Bites, and Mutt Munchies. (I still winced every time I said that last one, but it was what it was and they did actually sell well—to my surprise and amazement.)

But I wanted something new for the party. We were going to keep the online store open during construction and the party would be a perfect opportunity to get some fun photos for the website and introduce a new product.

I figured it should be Halloween-themed, though. Which meant finding an appropriate name. Maybe Ghostly…something.

Or Devilish…Delights. No, I'd already used delights. Devilish Delishes? No. That didn't work. Too much sh-ing.

But maybe Boolicious…?

Bites?

Or Booberry Bites?

Or Boolicious Booberry Bites? That was a mouthful.

And it used bites again which I'd already used for Barkery Bites.

I frowned out the window, trying to work it out. Boolicious, Booberry, ba, ba, ba, ba, ba. I found myself tapping my foot along with the sound and made myself stop.

And then I had it.

Booberry Biscuits. *That* would work. A little bit of blueberries, maybe some banana…Yeah, that would definitely work.

I did another little bootie shake and headed for the kitchen. Time to create a treat that would live up to its boolicious name.

CHAPTER 2

Fancy was definitely a fan of the end product. Then again, Fancy would probably eat saw dust on the off chance it was tasty so perhaps she's not the best judge of quality. Although she has declined to eat cauliflower, so she does have some standards. Albeit low ones.

Because I'd wanted to finish baking the last batch of biscuits, I was running late when I finally left the barkery. Not that traffic was bad.

That was one of the best perks of living in the Colorado mountains. No real traffic to speak off. I mean if we'd lived along I-70 we'd have been faced with some crazy tourist traffic where people drive like they're in some sort of speed-based death race weaving in and out of large semis hauling produce cross-country, but we didn't.

We were on one of those highways that shoot off of I-70 and are considered a scenic byway, so things were a lot more relaxed and calm. Even though it was technically a highway it was only one lane going in each direction so the real insane drivers who had to get somewhere fast stayed away—get stuck behind a cattle truck and a double-yellow line once and you learn your lesson.

So the twenty-minute drive from the barkery to my grandpa's place in Creek was beautiful and relaxing. The whole valley was surrounded by mountains and capped with a blue sky covered with filmy clouds that were colored pink and purple as the sun set.

Heaven.

Absolute heaven. And so far removed from my old life in DC it was hard to think about. But I'd made my choice. And I was...happy with it. Nervous. More nervous than I'd been about anything in my life, ever. Probably because this was the first time I'd decided to stay somewhere instead of moving on to the next, best choice. It's surprisingly hard to say, "Yeah, this is what I want" when your nature is to explore and try new things.

But it *was* what I wanted. I had Fancy. I had my grandpa. I had time with my best friend. I had Matt, which made me smile to myself and then blush even though no one was around to see it.

I had it all. For now. Which is all anyone can ever hope for.

Of course, when I finally walked in the front door and my grandpa gave me "that look" I was reminded that no matter how perfect life is it's never actually perfect.

"Maggie May..."

"Sorry I'm late. I really am. I got caught up making a new treat for the party." I kissed him on the cheek as he grumbled at me. He was my rock. In his faded jeans and flannel shirt—long-sleeved now in honor of the changing seasons—his hair still a light brown despite his eighty-plus years.

He patted my arm. "Don't tell me. Tell Lesley."

I made my way towards the kitchen and the smells of some delicious concoction I couldn't identify. "Hey, Lesley. How are you? Sorry I'm late."

Lesley, my grandpa's friend who was probably now his girlfriend but that was too weird a term to use for two people in their eighties, was at the stove, stirring some sort of sauce that bubbled with the scents of red wine and mushrooms.

She looked as polished as ever with her white hair pulled back from her face and her impeccable makeup. The only concession she'd made to cooking was to remove her jewelry and leave the rings and bracelets in a small pile on the kitchen table. She had an apron tied around her narrow waist, and if I wasn't mistaken the cute little coffee cups dancing along the edge were cross-stitched by hand.

"It's okay, Maggie. Matt called to say he was running late, too, so we're probably ten minutes from dinner being ready."

"It smells delicious." I leaned in for a deeper whiff, but Lesley's flinty look told me not to try for a taste.

I'm not a bad cook. I can make a Crockpot recipe or a simple casserole with the best of them, but what Lesley had done in that kitchen was a whole level of sophistication above anything I can pull off. There were crisped potatoes with real fresh herbs of some sort and that wine sauce along with some form of beef that looked tender enough to melt at the first bite.

I sniffed the air.

"Is that an apple pie?"

She nodded.

"I tell ya, Lesley, if we weren't demolishing the café and barkery I'd argue for hiring you to come run the place."

She laughed. "Oh, I'd never want that. Retirement is good for me." She smiled at my grandpa who was standing in the doorway.

When he smiled back at her I suddenly felt like the odd one out. "Well, then. I think I'll sneak off to change real quick if that's okay with both of you."

They didn't even notice as I raced out of the kitchen before they did something crazy like kiss. I no longer begrudged my grandpa his relationship with Lesley—I'd come to see that he deserved to move on now that my grandma was gone and that Lesley was a great fit for him—but I still had that childhood cooties reaction to the thought of anyone older than me kissing or…well, let's leave it at kissing.

And I did need to change. When I get to baking it's a mess. I don't know why I find it so hard to run a blender and not kick up flour in every direction, but I do. I'd also somehow managed to sit in the batter. How had I done that? When had I done that?

I'd just finished throwing on a new pair of jeans and a different t-shirt when someone knocked on my bedroom door. I opened it to see Matt standing there and sighed in pleasure.

He's a great man. Solid as a rock. Kind. Funny. Intelligent. But he's also darned fine looking. All tall and lean with these great blue eyes and dark hair and that smile and…

Alright, enough. I know how annoying people in love can be, because I'm not usually one of them so I have to suffer through it a lot myself. But he is very attractive. And he was mine. And he was standing there in the doorway and my grandpa and Lesley were off in the kitchen somewhere.

So I kissed him.

Which made me smile all that much more. Seriously, they really need a cure for that stuff. It's just not healthy to live like that.

CHAPTER 3

At dinner I told everyone about my dilemma trying to figure out what to make Fancy that she'd actually wear at the party.

"Honestly," I said as I took another bite of the most delicious meal I'd ever eaten in my life, "the only thing Fancy has ever worn without complaint was a doggie GoPro I got her when she was about a year old."

"What's that?" my grandpa asked.

"A GoPro is a camera that a lot of athletes use. I used to know a bunch of skydivers who used them to film their jumps. They're small and pretty tough so good in situations like that. Mountain bikers like to use them, too. Anyway. Turns out they sell a harness that dogs can wear so you can strap a camera to your dog's chest or their back and see the world from their viewpoint."

My grandpa took his time finishing his last bite of food. "Let me get this straight. You spent good money to buy a camera that you strapped to your dog so you could see how things looked from her perspective?"

"Mmhm. I actually had this whole idea where I'd take Fancy to different dog parks in the area and have her wear the GoPro and capture footage of the place and then I'd start a website where I rated each dog park and had a video for each one that was partially footage from me and partially footage from Fancy. I actually wanted a friend of mine with a little dog to come along so we'd have the big dog perspective and the little dog perspective and they could see each other in the footage and…"

I stopped talking because my grandpa was looking at me like I'd lost my mind.

"What? It could've totally worked. Fancy is adorable. People would absolutely watch a show that involved her."

"You think so. You think people have nothing better to do with their time than watch your dog go to dog parks?"

"You'd be surprised, Grandpa. But I didn't know enough about filmmaking to pull it off. The footage was so bumpy it made me nauseous just to watch it. I'm sure there's some way to fix it, but I never bothered to find out what."

Matt dropped a piece of potato on Fancy's plate where she sprawled on the floor between the two of us. "You know…You could have her wear the GoPro that day."

"And?"

"Maybe that's all you need. Put a pad of paper and a pencil on her harness or something and call her an intrepid reporter."

"Well, Peter Nielsen is a dog, that's for sure." (He was the local reporter for *The Baker Valley Gazette* and had tried to ruin my business with a few unwarranted smear articles that I hadn't appreciated one little bit.)

I pouted. "But I wanted to make her a panda. Wouldn't she make an adorable panda? I could put white pajamas on her and leave her feet bare and then a little white hoodie with her ears poking out of the corners and her nose in the middle?"

Matt just looked at me. "You could certainly try that."

"But it won't work, will it?"

Fancy watched us both with attentive interest but I knew that was more out of a desire for another bite of food than any actual understanding of what we were discussing. I looked down at her and frowned. "You'd never let me do it, would you? As much of a slug bug as you are, why won't you let me dress you in silly costumes?"

She raised one eyebrow at me in that way she has.

"I know. Dignity. It's the same reason I never trained you to do tricks. If only I'd started on you when you were young…"

Fancy harrumphed and put her head on her paws, still watching me out of the corner of her eye for another bite of food. I snuck her a green bean as I turned back to the conversation.

"Intrepid reporter, huh?"

Matt nodded. "And it will give you video footage of the event. You might even be able to use it for the website if we can find someone to solve that shaking issue for you."

"Okay. Fine. It's a good idea. And possible, which is most important of all."

My grandpa smiled at both of us. "Now, the real question. What are you two going to wear?"

I stared at him in horror. "Nothing. It's a pet party, not a human party."

Matt cleared his throat. "I happen to know that Jamie and Mason are going to wear costumes."

"Oh no. Don't tell me that. Jamie loves wearing costumes. What is she coming as?"

"I can't say. I'm sworn to secrecy."

I glared at him, but when he makes a promise he keeps it. "Just because they are, doesn't mean we have to."

"It'll be fun." He leaned back in his chair. "I was thinking you and I could go as Elvis and Marilynn Monroe?"

I laughed. "No."

"You'd make a great Marilynn."

"No, I would not, but that's very sweet of you to say. I usually just put my hair in two braids, wear some peace symbol jewelry and a long dress, and call myself a hippie."

"That's no fun. Come on, we have to be creative about this."

"We?"

"Well, now that we're a couple we should match."

"We should?" I squeaked.

I tried to hide it but the thought of being one of those people who dresses up in matching costumes with my boyfriend made me want to break out in hives. It was like being made into one of the pod people. Who does that?

"It'll be fun."

"It will?"

How had I ended up with someone who thought that would be fun?

See, this is the problem with real, live relationships. The other person has all these weird ticks and traits you never imagined and suddenly you have to make the choice to go along with them (the easy route) or to resist (the awkward one) or to just flat-out run for the hills because if this is what they're letting you see now then who knows what they're hiding under the surface.

I really wanted to run. But he had such gorgeous blue eyes. And he'd pulled a Bridget Jones on me and told me he liked me just the way I was, flaws and all. How could I run from that?

Instead I bowed my head in defeat. "We can go in costumes, but please, keep it within reason? And no Marilynn."

"Hans and Leia?"

"No."

"Ah, darn. I thought you'd look good in a chainmail bikini."

"Matthew Allen Barnes, my grandpa is sitting right here."

My grandpa chuckled and patted my hand. "It's alright. It's good to see you two together."

He'd campaigned for it pretty much from the day I opened the front door to find Officer Barnes in uniform ready to take my statement on the dead body I'd found up the hill. Of course, he'd known Matt for a lot longer than that. It seems I had, too, since I'd written his name on the wall in permanent marker when I was a little girl.

I stared at the spot where those letters were still scrawled. Destiny? Maybe. If you believe in that sort of thing.

In a sense the party would be our first outing as a couple, so we really should play it up some. But I was not going to do something like hamburger and fries or two halves of a heart or ketchup and mustard. No, no, no.

CHAPTER 4

Since it was our big send-off party I figured there'd be a pretty good turnout, but I didn't want to leave things to chance, so I paid a visit to Matt's. I wasn't there to see Matt, though. I was there to see one of his current roommates—Sam.

I figured any kid willing to ride his bike across the entire valley and offer up every penny in his piggy bank to get help for his mom was a kid with a good dose of chutzpah. And that's exactly what I needed to drum up contestants for the pet parade.

I knocked on the metal screen door of their converted mobile home, listening to the sounds of some shoot 'em up game coming from the living room and took a moment to enjoy the gorgeous view. Matt's place, which he inherited when his dad passed away, wasn't much to look at. Just a brown on brown former mobile home that had been turned into what could pass for a house. But the view behind it was a million-dollar view.

"Come in," Jack shouted.

I stepped inside to find Jack and Sam sprawled on an old brown couch in identical positions of laziness, both slouched down halfway with game controllers in hand. Sam was wearing a baseball cap over his bright red hair, but it did nothing to hide all the freckles on his cheeks. That kid had more freckles than there are stars in the sky.

Jack had the same dark good looks as his brother, but a rogue's casual charm. You just knew looking at him that more than one woman had lost all sense and reason at one flash of that smile. To make it worse, he didn't have his shirt on.

I promptly tried to ignore that fact, but Jack being Jack, consummate conman and eagle-eyed expert on women, smiled a slow, lazy smile.

"Hey, Maggie. You here to see Matt? Or maybe you waited until he was gone so you and I could have some quality time together…" He wiggled his eyebrows.

"Oh, shut up, Jack." I knew better than to fall for that kind of charm. Ever.

"I know. Matt's the only man for you. You know…I do believe you owe me for that one."

I *was* grateful to him for manipulating me into finally confessing my feelings to Matt, but the thought of owing him a favor made me very nervous. He'd supposedly decided to clean up his act and was doing well so far—especially now that he was responsible for Sam—but I wouldn't put it past him to show up on my front door one night with something body-shaped wrapped in a tarp and ask if I had an extra shovel he could borrow.

"Yeah, well, just keep it reasonable would you? I'm very happy to be with Matt, but I am not going to jail for you Mr. Jackson Barnes."

He guffawed. "Yes, ma'am. Now what brings you by?"

"Actually, I have a business proposal for Sam. You

want a chance to replenish that piggy bank of yours?"

Sam perked up. "Yes."

Jack pushed him gently back. "Now, now. Let's not be too eager. What do you need? What are you willing to pay?"

"Oh it's going to be like that, is it?" I narrowed my eyes at them but couldn't hide my slight smile. (I do not have a poker face. Only reason I win at that game is because I'm so unpredictable seasoned players can't figure out my range.) "Alright. Here's the deal. We're going to have a store closing Halloween party at the barkery. And part of the party is going to be a pet parade. I'm thinking cute dogs in cute costumes. And I thought that if you were to recruit for me I could pay you…fifty cents per entrant."

"Okay." Sam bounced in place.

"Hold up, sport. Not so fast. Fifty cents? That's not enough. Five dollars."

"Per pet? Are you kidding me? We're not even charging anyone to enter. I'll give you a dollar for each one."

"Let me consult with my client." Jack leaned over and whispered to Sam who whispered back with a sly little smile on his face. Great. Instead of Sam helping Jack clean up his act Jack was going to corrupt him.

Jack nodded to Sam. "It's your deal."

Sam sat up looking very serious. "Here are our terms. We'll accept one dollar per pet. But we also want a slice of cake each."

"Hm. I can do that. But every entrant has to be in costume. It's not enough that they show up, they have to be dressed to impress."

Jack smiled. "Oh, don't you worry about that part. It'll be a pet parade you'll never forget."

He was up to something. I just didn't know what. "And keep it legal, please."

"Of course. I am a new and reformed man after all."

He winked as I turned to leave and I shuddered to think what I'd gotten myself into. But at least that was one less task I had to worry about.

I hoped.

CHAPTER 5

At last the big day arrived. I tried not to cry as I pulled the van up at the far edge of the parking lot and looked across at my well-loved but short-lived adventure in running a business. I didn't care what anyone said, I still loved that sign with its hard-to-read cursive script and its cheesy little Newfie heads on either end.

And I'd miss retreating out back at the end of a long day to have a beer with Jamie while the dogs ran around in the fenced area and Fancy made a mad dash for the creek, wallowing in the water like it was a second home.

We hadn't done bad for a first business. Jamie had done particularly well with her cinnamon rolls. And I'd managed a decent online following. But Mason and Greta had seen the real potential. High-end. Flashy. Slick. The type of experience that attracts people who don't bat an eye at a two-hundred-dollar chiropractor appointment for Fifi, their teacup poodle.

It was time to level up.

But first, a party.

When I walked inside, Jamie was in full drill instructor mode, directing a slew of volunteers in setting things up just right. She's the one with style so she was in charge of the decorations and activities. We were using not only the area out back of the barkery but the interior and half of the parking lot, too. It was going to be a madhouse.

Assuming anyone showed. Which I really hoped they did. Sam and Jack had been walking around like cats with a canary so I assumed we'd be okay although some part of me was very, very nervous about why they seemed so smug.

Out back there were all sorts of games for the dogs. Instead of bobbing for apples we had bobbing for balls. And there was a little obstacle course for them to run with a ramp and one of those hollow tubes that Fancy would never ever get near. There was also a game where they had to retrieve the stuffed pumpkin while navigating a minefield of tasty treats.

(Did you ever see that video of the golden retriever that failed the obedience test miserably but had so much fun with all the toys that it was supposed to ignore? I was kind of hoping for that to be honest. Better to have fun than to "win".)

And, of course, there was the costume contest with a grand prize of a Booberry Biscuit crown held together with peanut butter.

Out front was for the human contingent. We had hot cider and hot chocolate for drinks and then fresh cotton candy, caramel corn, and funnel cakes. We'd rented the little carts you see at amusement parks. That was definitely not going to be my role, though. I've made cotton candy before and had the sugared-over hair to prove it. And I wasn't allowed near a funnel cake machine ever since an incident that involved a pair of tongs and hot oil running down the back of my hand.

Inside would be seating for everyone who decided it was a little too chilly outside. It was late October in Colorado after all. Honestly, we were incredibly lucky there was no snow on the ground or in the forecast. But that didn't make it warm.

Before I could get too teary about it being our last day of operations, Jamie put me to work. For the next two hours we arranged and cleaned and debated logistics and rearranged until everything looked perfect.

And then it was time to change and get the party started.

CHAPTER 6

I got Fancy into her costume first. It wasn't hard. Just get her into the harness and start up the GoPro. We'd already strapped the fake notepad and pen to the back of it. She wasn't going to win any prizes and she wasn't a panda like I'd wanted, but she actually looked pretty good.

Of course, I'm biased.

Before I could sneak off to Jamie's to put on my costume Matt showed up. After all that debate we'd settled on the couple from *Grease*, so he had his hair slicked back 50's style, with tight jeans, a white t-shirt, and a black leather jacket. It was a good look for him. A very good look.

He was holding something behind his back, but I didn't really care what because I was too busy gawking. I felt another little thrill at the thought that this amazing man was mine, but shook it off.

"It suits you," I said.

"Thanks. Can't wait to see your outfit."

I winced. I'd wanted to do Sandy as she was at the start of the movie—all poodle skirt and ponytail—but Matt had argued for Sexy Sandy in puffed out hair and slim-fitting black outfit. I hadn't let him see it yet, though. I don't know why. Nerves I guess. I have a few more curves than Olivia Newton John ever did. (Not that the outfit looked that bad on me. More just self-conscious silliness that I normally don't feel but did when it came to Matt.)

Anyway.

"Speaking of. I better get over to Jamie's to change." I leaned in to give him a quick kiss on the cheek.

"Wait. I, um, I have something for you."

I tilted my head at the nervousness in his voice. "What?"

He blushed and waved whatever it was in his hand. "I, um. I knew this was kind of a hard day for you with the barkery closing and all and that you'd really wanted Fancy to dress up as a panda and…well…Here."

He shoved one of those brown plastic grocery bags into my hand, the type that are all thin plastic that tears apart at the slightest effort.

"Sorry for the wrapping. I forgot and then I was running late and…"

"That's okay."

I opened it up and had to almost bite my lip to keep from crying. I would've bit my lip if Matt hadn't been watching me.

This is going to sound stupid. I know you won't get it. Who would? I mean, I was thirty-six-years-old for crying out loud.

But what he'd given me was…

Perfect. And sweet. And absolutely adorable.

Somehow, I don't know how, he'd managed to find a stuffed Newfie and then he'd put that Newfie into a panda costume. It was a mini Fancy. In costume.

I wanted to melt. I wanted to go all soft and fuzzy and cry-ey right then and there. But I couldn't. Because to him I was this strong, capable, sarcastic woman and seeing me go all gooey would probably scare him right back into enlisting.

So I flashed him a smile instead. "Thank you. It's…I love it. But I better get changed. Don't want to be late."

I fled to the office and took a quick moment to collect myself, staring at that stupid stuffed dog that was so ridiculously perfect for me that it made my heart ache trying very hard not to cry. When I'd finally wrangled my feelings into submission I tucked it away on the top shelf and ran off to Jamie's to get changed, pushing Fancy aside as I snuck away before I could see Matt again.

CHAPTER 7

Of course, I couldn't hide how emotional I was from Jamie. And I didn't need to either. She was my best friend. She knew when something absolutely wrecked me. So we bounced around her living room like teenagers as I told her what Matt had done.

I don't know how to describe to you why that hit me so deep. Maybe because it showed that he really got me? I mean it was a stuffed animal. Who gives a grown woman a stuffed animal? But it was perfect *for me*. Because it was about Fancy and about her dressing up as a panda and it was because the barkery was closing and he'd remembered and he got that this was a big day for me even though I was supposedly moving on to something bigger and better with the pet resort.

And…

I know. All this silly relationship stuff, right?

I'll stop now, I promise. It's perfectly normal to have a boyfriend. And for that boyfriend to give you caring gifts. And from here on out I will pretend that was perfectly normal for me, too—that I wasn't some spinster-bound misanthrope who was insanely lucky to have found a man who was actually worth my time.

So anyway. Great, caring gift. Whatever.

Time to get dressed.

I slipped into a ridiculously fitted pair of black slacks and off-the-shoulder black top and then added red heels that were going to break my ankle before the end of the day. Then to top it all off I let Jamie destroy my hair in a way I hope to never repeat again. I'm pretty sure she used an entire can of hairspray. I have no doubt that had anyone come within five feet of me with a match I would've gone up like a torch.

That's what dressing up for Halloween will get you.

I still didn't know what she was going as until she ducked into her room and came back out with her hair in pigtails tied with ribbon, a cutesy blue dress, a basket with a fake little dog in it, and ruby red slippers.

"Dorothy from the Wizard of Oz?"

She nodded. "Lulu is going to be the lion and Mason is going to be the scarecrow."

"Tell me that involves wearing bib overalls."

"And a plaid shirt."

I clapped my hands together. "And is Lulu going to have one of those lion ruffs like on that commercial with the baby?"

"Yes. She looks so cute. I can't wait until you see it. Mason's bringing her. I figured otherwise she'd run herself ragged before things even got started."

"Makes sense. Fancy was definitely ready for a nap when I headed over here. Then again, Fancy is always ready for a nap."

We stood side-by-side in front of her mirror. It was an interesting contrast. Me in my skin-tight outfit and ratted out hair and her in her pigtails and bobby socks.

She pulled out her camera. "Here. Selfie time. And then we have to get back before things fall apart."

"Tell me about it. I can't believe I left Jack in charge of registration for the pet parade."

"Neither can I." We leaned our heads together and she took the photo. She showed it to me. "What do you think?"

I laughed. "I think that's us to a T. Opposites that are somehow complements."

I took a deep breath. "I'm scared, Jamie. Things are changing so fast and…"

She squeezed my arm. "It's going to be okay, Maggie. You'll see. Now come on. We have a costume contest to judge."

CHAPTER 8

I had to deal with the usual complement of hubba-hubbas and wolf whistles from Jack when Jamie and I made it back to the barkery. It's quite possible I said a few things to him my grandma wouldn't want to hear, but he deserved every single one.

He wouldn't let us see the contestants before the parade. Claimed that it would bias our judging. Instead he led us to a raised platform off to the side of the little parade path that wound its way through the parking lot.

There were maybe a hundred people gathered to see the "parade", but a lot of familiar faces were missing, so I assumed they were signed up to participate.

I looked towards the end of the lot where the parade was going to start, but I couldn't see anything past the very large vehicles that were parked there. I counted at least three horse trailers. And one cattle trailer?

I looked back at Jack. "What did you do?"

He grinned. "You said it was a pet parade. And that they had to be in costume. Those were the only rules you gave us."

"Pets, Jack. Pets. Like dogs and cats."

Jamie caught my look of concern. "What? What is it?"

I glanced towards the end of the parking lot one last time before sitting down with a huff. I knew I should go investigate but already I hated my red high heels enough that I wanted to torch them when I was done. "I think we're about to watch a very interesting pet parade…" I glared at Jack. "This goes wrong, it's on you Jackson Barnes."

"Don't worry. Matt wouldn't let me do anything too drastic. It's why you don't have an elephant in a tutu in the mix although I'm sure Tootsie would've won the grand prize."

He winked at me and left to get things started.

I wanted to believe he was joking, but I was pretty sure he wasn't.

🐾 🐾 🐾

The parade started out relatively normal. First in line was Greta with her Irish Wolfhound, Hans. He's such a dignified old soul I was surprised to see him in any costume at all. Then again, he's infernally well-behaved, so he was also capable of pulling off any costume. (Unlike Fancy. Who I love. Dearly. I swear.)

Greta had dressed him like a king with a deep purple cape and a crown and a little scepter sewn to the front of the cape.

He carried it off like a champ. She'd set aside her customary black slacks and bright tops for a matching ball gown that looked like it was actually real, right down to the delicate tiara resting on her pale blond hair.

Right behind them was Mason with Lulu. Not only was he wearing ratty old bib overalls and a flannel shirt with straw poking out of it but he also had on scuffed up boots that looked like they were a hundred years old. It was great.

And Lulu made for an adorable lion. She was a little excited by the crowd and didn't want to walk along the actual parade path, especially when she saw Jamie up on the podium, but she did really well for a puppy.

Behind them came Evan and Abe and their Saint Bernard, Lucy Carrots. All three were dressed as pirates. Abe even had a fake parrot on his shoulder. How he'd managed to get Lucy to wear her pirate's hat I do not know, but she did.

By that point I was already overwhelmed with adorableness.

But the next contestant in line had me almost choking on my Coke. It was Sam and Jack walking along with a miniature horse. Not a dog dressed like a horse. Oh no. It was an actual horse.

And she was dressed like a hippie with a little peace symbol headband running across her forehead and flowers braided into her mane. Her little feet even had beaded fringe that jingled when she walked.

Sam ran over to me, grinning ear to ear. "That's Lady. Isn't she great? We didn't have a dog to bring. Although I want one and Jack said maybe we can get one but not now. Maybe later. Maybe a big one like you have. But in the meantime he said we could bring Lady. She's Jack's new boss's best friend's horse. He normally uses her for kids' parties, but we were able to borrow her for today. And isn't she just the greatest? Now I think I want a horse instead. Can we get a horse, Jack?" he called.

Jack just smiled. "Maybe, champ. We'll talk about it more later."

"She's going to win. I just know she is." Sam ran back to Lady who continued to plod along, her warm brown eyes full of endless patience and a surprising amount of intelligence.

The next few were more normal.

James, the fishing guide, had dressed his dog up as a trout. (It didn't work very well.)

Dean, manager of the conference center and resort, brought a Chihuahua dressed as a monkey. (That one was pretty clever.)

Russell surprised all of us by dressing his old hunting dog up as a peacock. (Very bright if nothing else.)

And Darryl the hunting guide dressed his dog up as a pumpkin. (He got points for effort if nothing else.)

Fancy made her appearance, too, with Matt leading her along the parade route through the surreptitious use of a never-stopping supply of treats in his left hand. I was pretty sure most of the video footage we were going to get of the event would just be of Fancy eating something, but that was okay.

Next came a handful of cats in various costumes. A lion, as you might expect. (Although not near as cute as Lulu.) An Ewok. (*That* was beyond cute.) And a sunflower and a dinosaur and a few others I'm sure I've forgotten.

And then things got interesting again.

There was a llama dressed as a loofa. And a cow dressed as a hippo that didn't really want to move and never actually made it off the starting line. And three goats in bow ties, one of whom tried to eat a funnel cake, plate and all, that some little kid held too close to him.

And last, but not least, an emu dressed as a football player which was not the least bit happy about it.

"Jack! Your problem, fix it," I shouted when the emu started to fight its trainer and the crowd realized that maybe they wanted to be somewhere not so close to a big angry bird.

Fortunately, Matt jumped in, too, and between the three of them they got the emu back in its cage.

It was quite the assortment. And a miracle that they all seemed to behave themselves more or less. I had planned to get a big group picture of all of the contestants, but realized that was just not going to happen if I wanted to avoid an actual incident.

At least everyone had seemed to enjoy it.

CHAPTER 9

Jamie and I decided we needed one more pass through the contestants before we chose our winners. There was a lot of cuteness involved and it deserved some serious consideration. Plus, I just wanted to pet the dogs. And Lady.

I ran into Greta first. She was studying the chaos as one of the goats—probably the same one who'd gone after the funnel cake—chomped away on the llama's loofa costume and the cow adamantly refused to return to its trailer.

"This was fun, yes? I think we will do this again next year at the resort. Jack has promised me an elephant in a tutu."

I laughed. "It was fun. But maybe we skip the elephant."

Greta shrugged one shoulder and I knew that I better start planning for an elephant in a tutu at next year's parade.

I made my way to where Fancy had plopped down on her side in the shade. She looked thoroughly done with the whole thing. Lady stood next to her chewing on some grass she'd snuck from the side of the parking lot.

Matt stood between them, arms crossed.

I stepped closer. "Well done with leading Fancy. I told you she'll do pretty much anything for a treat."

"Yep. Here." Matt shoved Fancy's leash and Lady's reins into my hands and strode away.

I watched him go, baffled. What had I said?

He joined in with the group wrangling the cow into its trailer and I relaxed some. So it wasn't about me. It was just he wanted to help out. But then he kept going, helping get all of the animals back in their pens or cages. Finally, he returned.

I tried again. "Quite the parade. I knew your brother was up to something, I just didn't know what."

I smiled at him but he didn't smile back. "You okay?" I asked.

"Yeah. Fine. Here. I've got Fancy if you want to go back and announce the winners."

"Matt?" He hadn't even said something about my costume and he wouldn't meet my eyes. "What's wrong?"

"Nothing."

Before I could push him further Jamie came over. "We better announce the winners so everyone can get out of here."

"Right." I glanced back at Matt as we returned to the judging platform. He was watching me, but the look in his eyes was most definitely not happy.

Relationships suck. Seriously. How does anyone navigate their way through one?

But I put that all aside as I stood on the platform. "Sam, come here." I motioned for him to join us.

He ran up the steps, cheeks pink with excitement.

"Ladies and Gentlemen, you have Sam here to thank

for the wide variety of participants in today's pet parade, so I'm going to let him announce your winners."

I handed him the microphone and whispered in his ear what to say.

He stumbled a few times in that breathless way kids have, but he managed. "The judges have chosen three winners. One dog, one cat, and one other. The dog winner is…"

Jack made a fake drumroll noise for him.

"Lucy Carrots as a Pirate of the Carrot-be-an." (That would be pronounced like Caribbean but with carrot in there instead. Yeah, it threw me, too.)

Abe and Evan led Lucy on to the stage where Jamie handed them the Booberry Biscuit crown. They swapped it out for her pirate hat but she promptly shook it off her head and devoured it, leaving a big puddle of crumbs and drool in her wake.

"The second winner is The Amazing Miss Maisy as an Ewok."

That was the cat. She was given a small bowl of cream which she delicately lapped up as her owner watched in pride.

"And the last winner," Sam jumped in place when I told him, "is Lady as a Groovy Granny." He ran over to Lady, still holding the microphone, and gave her a great big hug around the neck. Lady for her part just stood there until Sam showed her the apple she'd won. That she took and delicately chomped to pieces.

"And that concludes our pet parade," I shouted. "Thank you everyone and please enjoy the food and drinks."

I turned away, wanting desperately to cry now that it

was really over, but forcing myself to walk down the steps of the platform and mingle with the remaining guests.

I tried to remind myself that this wasn't the end of everything. It was just the end of a chapter, that's all. But it was hard to make myself actually believe it.

CHAPTER 10

After the party we gathered all of our volunteers and friends inside for red chili, cornbread, and a viewing of the Fancy parade footage.

I quickly changed out of that ridiculous outfit and put on shoes worth walking in, but the hair was going to take at least a shower or two to get back to normal.

I stood by the counter with Jamie as everyone talked and laughed and ate. It was a good feeling to see all those people who were a part of our lives gathered together.

"We didn't do that bad with this place, did we?" I asked.

"No. We didn't." She hip-checked me. "We would've made it work, Maggie. You know we would've."

"Only because of your cinnamon rolls."

She laughed. "No. Because you'd never let us fail."

"Neither would you."

"Exactly."

I crossed my arms and studied Matt who'd managed to wedge himself in a corner with Jack on one side and Sam on the other.

"Matt's mad at me."

"What for?"

"I honestly don't know."

"Well, make him tell you. You guys are good together, Maggie. But no relationship is perfect. You're going to have bumps along the way."

I raised an eyebrow. "Oh really. I haven't seen you and Mason have any bumps."

"Oh we have them, believe me. You know he wants to invite five hundred people to our wedding? And have it at the country club?"

I shuddered. "That sounds like my idea of a horror movie."

Jamie laughed. "Well, when you find someone you love, you make those kinds of sacrifices for them. Go on. Don't let this fester. Find out what's wrong."

I made my way over to their table with four slices of cake on a tray.

"Well, Sam, it wasn't what I expected, but you certainly delivered on the deal we made. Here you go. Twenty-five dollars and two slices of cake."

"Twenty-five? But we only…"

Jack shushed him. "Thank you very much. Pleasure doing business with you."

I shook my head. "Jack, I swear if you corrupt this boy…there will be hell to pay."

"Yes, ma'am. Come on, Sam. You can eat your cake while I get the Fancy footage going."

He led Sam to the barkery counter where we'd placed a television, and started working on hooking up the GoPro from Fancy. I didn't expect it would show anything useful, but hopefully it would be entertaining.

I sat down next to Matt. "Are you going to tell me what's wrong?"

"Nothing's wrong."

I might have said a word I won't repeat here that said he was lying. "I can't fix something if you won't tell me about it, Matt."

"Nothing's wrong. I think I'll go help Jack."

"Fine. I think I will too."

He glared at me, but what could he do? It was my store and my television and my video footage.

Just as we reached Jack, the video started to play. And it was completely focused on me. I'd never realized until that moment how much Fancy followed me around or watched me.

A room full of people and I was her world.

"Awww, look at that." I glanced towards where Fancy was sleeping in her cubby. "You silly goof."

On screen Matt walked up to me, the brown plastic bag tucked behind his back.

Next to me Matt tensed. "You can fast forward through this. No one wants to see it."

"I do," I snapped, giving Jack a glare as he reached towards the fast forward button.

Somehow Fancy had been positioned perfectly to capture the entire moment. So I saw the shy pride on Matt's face when I pulled the stuffed animal out of the bag and smiled.

And then the way his face crumpled when I turned away from him so abruptly afterward and hurried away.

I was going to say something to him. Apologize. Try to explain.

But the footage on the screen continued as Fancy followed me into the office and I stood there, wiping away a tear and pulling myself together before kissing the stuffed animal on the nose and tucking it away on the top shelf.

"No one will mess with it there, will they, Fancy?" I said on screen with one last sniff, clearly overcome with emotion.

"So you didn't hate it," Matt whispered.

"Of course I didn't. It was perfect." I turned away, trying not to cry again, but Matt spun me around and pulled me close.

I buried my face against his chest and then looked into those oh-so-blue eyes of his. "I'm sorry. I didn't want you to see me blubber. I thought you might run for the hills if you did."

He kissed the tip of my nose. "You can blubber all you want. I'll still love you."

I stopped breathing. It was the first time he'd used the L word for real. I didn't know how I was supposed to respond.

On screen a dog barked and right behind us Fancy jumped to her feet, barking, which set off Lulu and Lucy Carrots.

By the time we got them all calmed back down the moment had passed.

I turned back to Matt. "So we're okay?"

He nodded. "We are."

I rubbed the back of my neck. "You should know I suck at this. At relationships. But, I do love you, alright?"

He laughed and pulled me in for a kiss. "Alright."

We spent the rest of the night surrounded by family and friends watching Fancy's view of the most bizarre pet parade I'd ever seen.

It was a good night. A really good one. A bootastic one, if I do say so myself.

A SABOTAGED CELEBRATION

AND SALMON SNAPS

A MAGGIE MAY AND MISS FANCYPANTS MYSTERY

ALEKSA BAXTER

CHAPTER 1

It was a Thursday morning at eleven and I was still in the same pajamas and sweatshirt I'd worn the day before and I honestly did not care. They were comfortable and when you have absolutely no reason to change into "real" clothes, pajamas are the best clothing option out there in my humble opinion.

They don't pinch. They're soft. And they don't point out to you that you've probably gained five pounds since you stopped working in a real job by digging into your belly. In other words, I think we should all wear pajamas all the time and we'd be much happier.

But, alas, that is not the world most of us live in.

Fortunately for me, at that point my world consisted of my dog, Fancy, who was a three-year-old Newfoundland and perfectly fine with me no matter what I wore, my grandpa, who had run away to Las Vegas to spend a drama-free few days with his new love before Christmas, and my boyfriend, Matt, who had run down to Denver with some friends to see the Avs game, do some shopping, and pick up my grandpa and Lesley from the airport.

Which meant I, at least, could get away with pajamas as non-stop daywear. It's also why I wasn't too concerned with the stain or two on my sweatshirt from trying to eat fruit cups without a spoon. (They work a lot like bottles of ketchup. Nothing's coming out and then suddenly all of it wants to come out at once.)

Anyway.

Since the closing of the barkery I had discovered that at heart I was really a slob, something I'd never known before since I'd been working or in school since I was fourteen-years-old. It turns out those twenty-two years of hard work and accomplishment weren't because I was inherently motivated, they were instead just a product of others' expectations and a failure to question my own direction.

But with the barkery closed and nothing better to do but read books, invent dog treats, and develop an addiction to computer games, I'd found my true happy state.

One little problem. Fancy was not on board with my newfound slothfulness. As she made very clear, standing in the doorway, yipping at me to get off my butt and go outside with her.

"Fancy. It's snowy outside. And it's cold. I don't like snow. Or cold."

She barked—one loud, short demand for attention.

"Fancy…Ten minutes. Okay? I promise."

She plopped down in the doorway and gave me that look she has that says she'll lay there and be quiet because she knows she has no other choice, but that she's very broken-hearted and disappointed by her horrible, awful mother who won't even come out and play in the snow with her.

A Sabotaged Celebration and Salmon Snaps

If I'd had something meaningful I was doing—like campaigning for world peace—I would've felt better about ignoring her. But since all I was doing was trying very hard to place in the top five of that day's solitaire tournament, I felt horribly guilty.

Not guilty enough to stop, though. The way those stupid tournaments were set up if I stopped it might just keep on counting time against me. And it certainly wouldn't let me continue that particular game where I'd left off. I'd have to start all over again and I was not going to do that on an expert-level Spider that I'd already spent five minutes on.

Fancy whined so softly it was practically subsonic. I spared her a quick glare because I knew she would do that for a half hour straight if she was so inclined, which she clearly was.

"Give me a break, Fancy. It's cold out."

That was the one part of living in a small town in the Colorado mountains that I hadn't given quite enough thought to. The winters. That came with snow. And freezing temperatures.

Oh sure, I was aware that's what happened in Colorado in the wintertime and especially in the mountains. But I'd had some naïve notion that a town situated at seven thousand feet was somehow going to have a winter like Denver where it snowed on Monday but everything had melted and it was back to fifty degrees Fahrenheit by Wednesday most of the time.

That was not the case.

Fancy whined again, staring me down with those sad amber eyes of hers.

"Fine." She jumped to her feet. "But. I have to finish

this game first." She dropped back down to the ground with a loud huff.

I was sorry to disappoint her, but I did have to finish. Didn't I? I mean, this was about proving the kind of person I am. And I am the type of person who finishes what I start, even when it is a meaningless computer game.

Fancy obviously didn't think so. She flopped onto her side with a gusty sigh.

"Almost there. I promise. Just one more stack…"

I growled at the screen. All I needed was a seven of spades. How hard was that?

Fancy huffed at me again and then stood up and left.

"Fancy…I'm sorry, but…"

I turned my attention back to the screen. Almost there…

It took another two minutes which pretty much destroyed my chances of placing in the top ten for the day. (Top ten of my measly little group of a hundred out of three hundred thousand, but let's not go there.)

At that point I figured I might as well stop and go walk Fancy because even if they did add on time to my game it wasn't going to change things enough to matter.

Fancy was ecstatic when I came out into the living room. She ran around with her favorite zippo hippo dangling from her mouth as I layered on enough clothes to survive the arctic chill outside.

(Not that I know that it was technically an arctic chill in Colorado. But it's one of those things you say and then some goodie goodie comes along and tells you you're wrong and spends five minutes of your life you'll never get back explaining to you the real word you should've used when it honestly doesn't even matter. Can you tell I've been spending a little too much time around Lesley's library friends who know *everything* and insist on correcting anyone who gets any little thing wrong? Actually, I think I was that way when I was a kid. Might be why people didn't always like to be around me.)

Anyway.

By the time I'd added a sweatshirt to my long-sleeved shirt and then a winter jacket and scarf on top of that, Fancy was raring to go. She'd already run five laps of the living room and finally settled for standing in front of the door like a statue, just waiting, waiting, waiting like that old Mervyn's commercial with the lady saying open, open, open.

I leashed her up which was the point where she'd normally drop her toy, but not this time. She was taking it with us. A sign that she was truly desperately in need of some attention.

I opened the door onto the part of Colorado I don't like. The cold part. The icy part. The part that unfortunately exists in the mountains for a good chunk of the year.

I'd seriously underestimated the amount of days that could involve snow falling out of the sky or crowding up the streets when I'd made my decision to move to Creek to take care of my grandpa.

(A man who it turned out did not need my care.)

Left to my own devices, I would've hibernated for the entire winter, not leaving the house except for when I had to buy groceries. But weather like this was Fancy's happy place. The more it snowed, the more she wanted to be outside. Preferably with me in tow.

So as I miserably trudged through the snow, Fancy frisked along like a puppy, head held high, her little tail swishing back and forth, her bright blue toy dangling from her mouth as she looked for fun and adventure.

Newfies, I tell ya. I think they live in an alternate world where snow is actually a white sand beach and blizzard-level winds are just a pleasant breeze.

At least it wasn't nostril-freezing cold out…

But it was close.

Which is why I shuffled her around the block and back home within about ten minutes of our leaving. I loved her. And I knew she loved to be outside in that kind of weather. But she had a backyard now. She didn't need me out there freezing to death keeping her company.

Love. It has to have some limits, doesn't it?

CHAPTER 2

I'd just removed all of the layers of clothing and snuggled myself up for the last game of the solitaire tournament when my phone started ringing.

I not-so-silently cussed at it. Probably some solicitor trying to scam me out of my hard-earned money.

I'd been receiving calls lately from some woman who left these complicated voicemails about this horrible thing that was happening to her that sounded like a wrong number. I'd almost called her back the first time because she was so good at it, but then she called again with some completely different sob story and I realized what was happening.

She wasn't being sexually harassed at work or about to get evicted from her apartment or desperately trying to reach her cousin because his aunt was in the hospital and on the verge of death. She just wanted me to call her back so she could somehow scam me.

Just in case it was someone I'd actually want to talk to (unlikely but possible), I glanced at the phone, losing two precious seconds from my game time, and cussed again.

It was Mason Maxwell, fiancé of my best friend Jamie

whose wedding was only nine days away. I sighed.

Mason was not exactly someone I wanted to talk to—he's a bit uptight for my tastes—but I had to. Jamie had been too fragile since the whole Ted Little affair and I couldn't afford to ignore it if Mason was calling for my help.

I know. You're thinking to yourself, what Ted Little affair? I don't remember her telling me about that.

And you're right. I didn't. For two reasons. First, there was nothing funny or entertaining about what happened with Ted Little. That man was truly evil and he almost took away my best friend. Second, because I was just a helpless observer who didn't do anything useful to bring him down, so my part of the story would have been really boring.

But since you should probably know what happened, let me give you a quick recap.

I ran into Ted Little when I was looking for Trish, Sam's mom, after she went missing. (I did tell you about that.) He really scared me the first time I met him even though I was with Matt. But he scared me even more when he came walking into the barkery one day when I was all alone even though he didn't own a dog.

Matt and my grandpa insisted that I not give him any chance to get at me since he'd been suspected in the disappearance of three women before he went to prison for burning some guy's house down. So when he showed up, I called Matt and let him know. And I kept doing so until Ted Little finally backed off.

I thought that was the end of it. But it turns out that when he couldn't get me alone, he focused in on Jamie instead. And before any of us realized what had happened, she was missing.

A Sabotaged Celebration and Salmon Snaps

If it hadn't been for a very strange woman who was passing through town—she talked to herself a lot but it was like she was having actual conversations with other people, multiple other people—we might not have found Jamie at all.

Fortunately, Mason and Matt were desperate enough they followed the crazy woman when she led them down some remote mountain road to a cabin tucked away where no one even knew it existed.

And they found Jamie. *Before* Ted Little had a chance to do anything serious. (They also found the bodies of five other women, so we know what *would* have happened. That strange woman saved Jamie from…a lot.)

Like I said, nothing funny or entertaining about it. And I wasn't even there. So not my story to tell. Maybe Ruby will write about it someday. (That's the crazy woman. According to Matt she found Jamie because she followed the ghost of one of Ted Little's other victims. Yeah, right. Like ghosts really exist.)

Anyway. Scary situation. But all over. Everyone safe. Ted Little back in prison.

Unfortunately, Jamie's way of coping was to move the wedding date up to New Year's Eve and insist on doing everything herself. Two hundred guests and she wanted to not only plan and coordinate the whole thing but make all of the food, too.

Fortunately, I'd talked her out of making the five-course sit-down meal, but she'd still insisted on making the wedding cupcakes. And some sort of hand-made party favors that I didn't even want to know about.

If it was anyone but Jamie I would've sat her down and said, "Don't you even think about it." But this was

Jamie and Jamie is Wonder Woman. She can do anything she sets her mind to. So I just stepped aside and let her go.

(I did offer to help, before you think too poorly of me, but Jamie knows how much I hate weddings so she told me it was fine. Everything was fine. I knew she was probably lying, but you only push people so far, you know?)

But if Mason was calling…

Well, that was a bad sign. So yet again I closed out of my tournament.

"Hey, Mason. What's up?" I said.

"Maggie. We have a problem."

"With the wedding?" I grimaced. I really do hate weddings. I'd go, because Jamie was my best friend, but until the day of I was trying to ignore the fact that this big awful social event was hurtling my way. So many awkward conversations…Ugh.

"With the wedding dress, actually. It just arrived."

"And?" I asked, showing great restraint in not demanding to know why was he calling me and ruining my chance to win my solitaire tournament over a wedding dress.

He sighed. A very un-Mason-like sound. "From what I can gather between sobs, it is the wrong size."

"So you get a seamstress to fix it, right?"

"I suggested that…"

"Didn't go over well?"

"No. Something about custom beading and seams that I did not understand. Maggie, I have never seen Jamie cry. And I do not know how to get her to stop."

"Well, for what it's worth, I've only seen her cry once.

And I'm not sure I was much help getting her to stop then. But I'll come over and see what I can do."

"Thank you."

As I bundled up yet again, I shook my head. The things we do for friends…

CHAPTER 3

Fancy was not happy when I left her at home. But I figured she'd never been to Mason's house before and a crisis was not the time to introduce a hundred-and-forty-pound dog who liked to be muddy into the house of a man who was best described as fastidious.

And, wow, what a house it was. *All* wood and stone.

It wasn't as fancy as Greta's house—that was a flat-out mansion meant to impress—but it was definitely memorable. Three stories of what could best be described as "rugged mountain chic". There was a lot of wood that you knew was absolutely not hand-carved like it appeared to be.

And lots of artful use of river stone. There were beds of stone along the driveway and stone incorporated into the façade as well. It was like someone wanted to say, "I may be rich but I am also a part of these here mountains."

It was…interesting. Tasteful even. For what it was.

But once again I found myself contemplating the odd fact that so many people I knew had found happiness with someone I would not have lasted through a first date with. Mason had turned out to be a decent guy and I liked how he was with Jamie, but…yeah, not my type.

I didn't even reach the front door before he yanked it open. "Maggie. So glad you're here."

He was in what I figured most rich men wear when lounging around their mountain homes. Black slacks, a soft black sweater that was probably cashmere, and black shoes that weren't slippers but clearly weren't outdoor shoes either. It all fit very well with his salt and pepper hair and rugged good looks.

"Is she still crying?" I stepped inside, wondering if this was the type of home where outdoor shoes weren't allowed and, if so, what Mason would think of my socks that had little Newfie heads on them and were bright pink.

"Worse. She's in my office looking up flights."

He nodded to a shoe rack off to the side of the entryway and I reluctantly removed my shoes and then had to bite my lip when he handed me my very own pair of house shoes. Well, at least I wouldn't slip and fall on the spiral staircase made of more wood and stone.

There was that, at least.

"Flights to where? Does she want to elope?" I asked as I put on the surprisingly comfortable shoes.

"No. The wedding is still on. But she wants to go to New York."

"New York? Why?"

"She wants to find the wedding designer and have them fix the dress."

"I take it they're in New York?"

"That is the return address on the box the dress came in. But I don't know if that is really where the designer is located."

I nodded. "Got it." Clearly Jamie had entered full-on crazy mode where rational thought no longer existed.

I took a deep breath, preparing myself to handle something I'd never had to deal with before—my best friend in panic mode—and turned to Mason. "Where's your office?"

Mason visibly relaxed as he pointed me up the stairs and down a hallway paved with larger stones I was just sure would be Colorado-sourced.

Give me carpet any day. It's a lot more comfortable on bare feet. (Not that I could picture Mason walking around barefoot, ever. He probably wore shoes in the shower. But still.)

I found the office easily enough. It continued the theme of high-end mountain man with its deep rich browns and greens and leather, not to mention a desk that looked to have been custom-made from a large slab of wood. (Bet that didn't come from Colorado, though. We have tall trees, but I don't think we have trees that big around. Probably a California redwood or something like that.)

I paused in the doorway to study Jamie.

She's normally so put together with her brown hair styled perfectly and a touch of makeup and color-coordinated outfits. But that day…

Her hair was a greasy, ratted mess and if the circles under her eyes were any indication she wasn't sleeping and hadn't bothered with makeup. And the clothes she'd chosen were…clothes. I'll give her that.

They weren't pajamas, so she hadn't sunk to my level. Yet. But they definitely weren't Jamie clothes.

I wondered where she'd even found them since I

didn't expect her closet or Mason's had such a shabby selection. No wonder Mason was concerned.

"Hey Jamie," I called, putting as much forced cheer into my voice as I could manage.

"Oh, hey Maggie. What are you doing here?" She barely looked away from the laptop to greet me.

"Just wanted to stop by and see how things are going." I dropped into the brown leather chair across from the desk. "So…How are things going? Everything on track? You finalize the menu with the caterer?"

I figured I'd ease into the whole wedding dress issue, but that backfired, big time.

She stared at me, eyes wide with panic. "The caterer. I'm supposed to meet with him at one to go over the final details. What time is it?" She glanced at the computer. "It's already noon. He's in Bakerstown. I can…" She stood and then froze like her mind had overloaded. "I need…But I have to…"

"Sit."

She obeyed me, eyes still too wide for normal.

"Do you have the caterer's number?"

She nodded.

"Okay. Good. Give it to me. I'll call him. We'll reschedule for tomorrow."

She shook her head. "But I'll be in New York by tomorrow. My dress…I have to…"

"No. You will not be in New York tomorrow."

"But I have to go. The dress was the wrong size. I have to fix it."

"Yeah, well, you're not going to fix it by going to New York. Did you book a ticket yet?"

"No. I was just about to…" She turned back towards

the laptop.

"Don't. Close that computer down. Now."

"But…"

"Close it."

She closed the laptop.

"Good. Now where is your room?"

"Down the hall."

"Okay. Let's go." I stood and waited for her.

She stood up, looking very confused. "Where?"

"To get you cleaned up."

She looked around again, lost. "But…There's so much to do. I can't…"

"It will wait until after you brush your hair and take a shower. Trust me."

I wasn't one to talk since I'd been lounging around at home for the last couple days without bothering to shower myself, but she needed it. Badly. This was not the Jamie I knew. She needed to get back to her old self and then we could tackle this whole issue of the messed-up wedding dress.

CHAPTER 4

While Jamie took a shower, I dug up the caterer's number from her collection of five three-ring wedding binders that were neatly arranged on a small desk in the sitting area of the ginormous bedroom she shared with Mason. (Honestly, I think that bedroom was bigger than some people's houses.)

The binders took planning and organization to an entirely new level. There were tabs and spreadsheets and sample products and who knew what else in there. She could've probably sold the system for thousands of dollars it was so amazingly cross-referenced and detailed.

And right there under the caterer tab was the number of The Baker Valley Catering Company. (The only independent catering company in the valley. Fortunately, they made truly excellent food.)

That section included a detailed menu with Jamie's notes about what she'd chosen as well as a listing of all known food allergies and food preferences from the RSVPs, cross-indexed to where each individual was going to be seated. She'd gone so far as to put all of the nut allergies at their own table as well as all of the vegans together at another table.

It was…something, alright.

(Me, I would've honored the allergies because you don't want anyone dying at your wedding, but I would not have paid for ten different menu selections just to honor people's food preferences. Vegetarian or vegan is fine enough, but some of the preferences she'd received back? Oh hell no. You want to be that particular, honey, you find your own meal.)

Anyway.

I dialed the number and when a woman answered on the second ring I asked for James, the head caterer.

He picked up a moment later. "James Kingston."

"James. It's Maggie from the Baker Valley Barkery and Café. How are you?"

"Good, Maggie. To what do I owe the pleasure?"

"Well, I know Jamie had a meeting scheduled with you at one to finalize the menu, but is there any way to move that to tomorrow? She's a bit frazzled at the moment. A wedding dress snafu has thrown her for a loop."

There was a long pause on the other end of the line.

"James?"

"Um, Maggie, we're not catering Jamie's wedding."

"But you're right here in her wedding binder. Who else would be doing it if it isn't you guys?"

"I don't know. That's why I was so surprised when she cancelled on us a week ago."

"She cancelled on you?"

"Yep. Sent an email. Said she'd decided to do it herself and sorry for the late notice. Offered to pay the full cost of any supplies we'd already bought."

I glanced towards the bathroom door where I could hear Jamie singing in the shower. "Jamie would never do something like that via email. Are you sure?"

"Positive. I've got the email right here."

"Can you send that email to me?" I rattled off my email address for him.

"Sure. Give me a minute."

I made my way back to the office and opened up Jamie's laptop so I could access my email. A few seconds later the email arrived. At first glance it did look like Jamie's email—it had the right name on it—but when I looked closer I realized that the email address had a period between the first and last names and Jamie's real email address doesn't.

"Huh. That's interesting," I said.

"What? What is it?"

"This email didn't come from Jamie. The address is wrong."

Another long silence on the other end of the line.

"James…Any chance you can still do the wedding?"

I knew the answer before he gave it.

"I'm sorry, Maggie. We booked up immediately afterwards with another event. I can't do both."

"But she didn't *really* cancel on you, you know."

"I know. But…"

"Is there anyone else that you can think of that could handle it?"

"Not anyone local, that's for sure. I was gonna be stretched to the limit trying to do it myself."

I stared at the bookcase in Mason's office that had a whole set of books on procedural law that looked like they'd make good paperweights but poor reading. "And you probably cancelled all of the ingredient orders already?"

"Yeah, I did. And some of that stuff…No way to get it all in now."

"Okay. Thanks."

"Sorry, Maggie, I…I wish I could help."

"So do I." I hung up and stared out the window for a long, long moment. What were the odds that both the wedding dress and the caterer were messed up and nothing else was?

I did not have a good feeling about this.

CHAPTER 5

When I walked back to the bedroom I could hear Jamie singing *Joy to the World* through the bathroom door. (Not the Christmas song. The 70's classic by Three Dog Night.) Fortunately, she has a much better voice than I do.

As I listened to how happy she was I realized there was no way I could tell her about the caterer. Not after the dress fiasco.

She came out of the bathroom with more Jamie-like clothes on and a big smile on her face. "Oh, that felt so good. I needed that. Thank you."

She gave me a quick hug and I hugged her back, wincing inwardly at what I was going to have to do.

She glanced at the wedding binders. "Were you able to reschedule with James? When do I have to meet with him?"

I took a deep, painful breath. Friendship. Sometimes it requires sacrifice. "Actually, you don't."

"What? Why not?"

"Because I'm going to take care of it. All of it."

"But, no. It's my wedding. I wanted to plan it."

"And you have. Look at these binders. They are a miracle of hard-work and planning. But you're the bride,

Jamie. You can't work yourself into the ground before your big day. Take the time between now and the wedding, book a spa appointment, run away for a few days with Mason, catch up on some reading...Just relax."

She shook her head. "No. Maggie, I can't just sit around. I can't. I'll...No."

But she couldn't keep planning this wedding. Not if what I suspected had happened, had happened.

"I'll tell ya what. You keep the cupcakes. And whatever fancy party favor you're doing. I'll take the rest." I forced my best smile. "I have the binders. I know what you want, I know what you've set up, and I will make sure this goes off without a hitch. I'll even figure out the wedding dress situation."

"You're sure?"

"Absolutely. You only get married once, right?" (One would hope and one will certainly pretend while preparing for a friend's first wedding.) "Let me help you make this the best day ever."

I continued to smile even as my gut clenched in dread.

"Oh, Maggie. Thank you!" Jamie threw her arms around me, clutching at me more than hugging me. "It's...Everything has been so awful lately, and...I thought working on the wedding would help, but...Oh, thank you. You don't know what this means to me."

I patted her awkwardly on the back. "You're welcome. That's what friends are for, right?"

She nodded as I pulled away from her. "I owe you. When you and Matt get married..."

"Whoa, there. Don't go talking crazy. Matt's great and I really love him...But...No. No, no, no. Just, no."

I did love Matt. And I couldn't imagine being with someone else or not being with him. But, marriage? I was just getting used to the idea of having an actual plus one for a wedding for the first time in my life. That would be plenty for me for the next, say, five years?

I patted the stack of binders. "Now. I do need one thing from you. I need you to look through these binders and make sure they're completely up to date so that I have all of the information I need to make this come off perfectly."

"Okay. Sure. I can do that." She smiled and was the old happy Jamie. That alone made the hell the next week of my life was about to become all worthwhile.

"Great. While you're doing that, I'm just going to run downstairs real quick and tell Mason about the change in plans and find myself a Coke. Okay?"

"Okay! There should be a few Cokes in the main fridge. I bought them just for you."

Somehow I managed to keep the fake smile on my face all the way out of the room. And then I ran.

CHAPTER 6

I found Mason in the "kitchen"—an expanse of space with even more wood and more stone, two ovens, two fridges, and a mini fridge. (What single man has two ovens in his house? Seriously.)

"Mason."

He spun around at my tone of voice. "What? What is it? Is Jamie okay?"

I glanced around, making sure Jamie hadn't followed me into the kitchen. "Jamie's fine, but we have a problem. A big one. I think someone is trying to sabotage your wedding."

He laughed. "Because of a wedding dress? Don't be ridiculous."

"It's not just the wedding dress. Someone emailed the caterer pretending to be Jamie and cancelled. He already took on a new client for that night."

"But we have two hundred guests coming."

"I know. And let's hope that you still have a venue and flowers and a pastor and whatever else goes into a wedding. Not to mention the guests."

I'd never seen Mason lost for words before, but he just

stared at me and then finally said, "Why wouldn't we?"

"Because if someone cancelled the caterer and sent the wrong measurements to the dress manufacturer, what else might they have done?"

He paled. "Who would do something like that?"

"I don't know. That's what we need to find out. Do you have any exes or enemies that might do something like this?"

He rubbed his hands through his hair, the most nervous I'd ever seen him look. "I might have one."

"Really? An ex or an enemy?"

"An ex. We, um, we were engaged." He rubbed the back of his neck. "And I broke it off."

I hadn't heard about this. "When?"

He licked his lips and wouldn't meet my eyes.

"When did you break off this engagement, Mason?"

"The first time I saw Jamie."

"You broke off an engagement to ask my friend out?" I had to struggle to keep my voice down.

"No. It wasn't like that. I…" He paced away from me and then back. "I saw Jamie when she came in to sign the lease for the barkery. It was about a year ago. We didn't even speak. I just…" He shook his head. "I saw her and I realized that if I could feel that kind of spark for a woman I didn't know that I should not be marrying Elaine. That it was not fair to her for me to do that. So I broke it off. It was months before Jamie and I actually went on our first date."

"Does Jamie know about this?"

He shook his head. "No. It never came up."

"It never came up that you were engaged less than a year ago? How does that not come up?"

"Jamie did not want to know about my exes. She said all that mattered was the future we were going to make together, not the past. So I didn't ask about hers either."

(That was probably a good thing. Jamie had a lot of exes. A lot.)

I shook my head, marveling at the fact that Jamie and I were such good friends when we were also such polar opposites in so many ways. I couldn't imagine marrying someone not knowing that they'd been engaged before.

If I was getting married I'd want the name of every single girl my future husband had ever kissed as well as a rundown of everything about her and why they hadn't worked out. And then I'd want to talk through each one in detail to make sure that none of those issues were going to be our issues.

(There are reasons I've stayed single so long. Many, many reasons.)

I put on my best interrogator's face. "Have you been *married* before?"

"No."

"Do you have some random kid hidden away?"

"No. Why would you ask a thing like that?"

"Well, if you were previously engaged who knows what else you're hiding."

Mason pinched the bridge of his nose. "Being engaged is not the same as being married or having a kid."

"I don't know about that. They're all serious life commitments. I mean, whoever this woman was you got down on one knee and asked her to marry you, didn't you? Only difference between that and being married to her is saying some vows in front of an audience."

He huffed out a breath, but before he could say something caustic about my weird perspective on the world, Jamie came into the kitchen to join us, setting down a box overflowing with the wedding binders. "All done. Everything is exactly as it should be."

She gave me a big hug. "Thank you so much for doing this, Maggie. I can't tell you how happy I am that you're helping out with the wedding."

"Of course. What are friends for?" I met Mason's eyes. I hoped Jamie still thought I was amazing when this was all over. Because I had a feeling I was going to be planning a wedding for two hundred people from scratch with only nine days to make it happen. And that was not going to be easy in small-town Colorado in the middle of winter on New Year's Eve.

CHAPTER 7

Mason carried the box of binders out to my van for me. It was getting colder, the wind whipping around and blowing hints of smoke towards us. (From fireplaces, not forest fires, thankfully.)

He put the box in the back. "I will keep Jamie distracted until the wedding while you figure out how bad it is."

"Sounds good. She's still making all the cupcakes and wedding favors, so that should help. But keep an eye on things there, too. I don't know how close this person is to you guys."

"I want to find them."

"We will. But in the meantime, I suspect we're going to be planning this entire wedding from scratch. So…um…How much do I have to work with money-wise? I assume most of the deposits you guys already made are going to be lost."

"Whatever you need."

"Mason…This could be very expensive. I'm trying to put together a wedding for two hundred people with nine days' notice."

"Like I said. Whatever you need. I love her and there is no amount of money I would not spend to make her happy."

"While that's a nice sentiment, most people's bank accounts and mortgage payments put a practical limit on these things. So at least give me a number that when we hit it I should let you know."

"A hundred thousand."

I coughed. "A hundred thousand. On top of whatever you may have already lost?"

"I told you. She is my world. And that is not the upper limit, Maggie. That is just the number where you should call me and tell me how bad it is going to be."

I shuddered. "I can't imagine spending that much on a single day's event. For that much money you should get gold-plated silverware to take home with you and be carried around on the shoulders of five Sherpas the whole day."

He laughed. "Hardly. You are about to learn just how expensive these kinds of things can get. The meal alone will probably be half of that."

"Not if I can help it."

"Maggie…" He caught my gaze and held it. "This is Jamie's wedding. Give her what she wants. Please."

"Fine. I will do everything in my power and your bank account to give her the wedding she thought she'd already planned."

"Thank you."

I shuddered once more as I got into the car. Why on earth would anyone spend that kind of money on a single day?

Yet more proof that I am simply not wired like a large

part of the population. There is nothing about weddings that appeals to me. Not the big party, not the fancy dress, not the ring that catches on your hair for the rest of your life, not wearing white, none of it.

And yet there I was. Planning the social event of the year.

What can I tell you? Life is ironic.

CHAPTER 8

The first thing I did when I got home was give Fancy some ear scratches and a handful of Salmon Snaps, my newest and greatest dog treat invention.

What? You thought the first thing I did when I got home was call to see how royally messed up the wedding plans were? Then you've obviously never had an incredibly spoiled dog that's about as big as you are and very demanding of attention when she's been left alone for any period of time.

Only after I'd given Fancy a sufficient amount of hugs and kisses to make up for my absence did I sit down at the kitchen table and start making calls.

First call was to the dress manufacturer. Sure enough. They'd received an email with updated measurements. I asked why they hadn't bothered to call when the measurements were so completely different from the original measurements they'd been given, and was lectured on how "it wasn't their problem, lady, sometimes people gain weight before a wedding", by someone with a very strong Bronx accent.

Who knows? Maybe Jamie could've flown to New

York and resolved the issue, but I suspect an in-person conversation would not have gone any better than my phone call did. The dress was a loss. They couldn't and wouldn't make any changes at that point. Didn't I know how long it takes to make a wedding dress? I mean, really, lady, not their problem.

Next was the florist. They too had received an email cancelling the order and couldn't possibly get the baby pink roses that Jamie had wanted in on such short notice.

Good news on the hotel. They still had a reserved room block for the wedding and it was full up with confirmed wedding guests. I made them promise not to cancel any of the reservations without talking to me first.

Bad news on the reception venue. It too had been cancelled via email with no way to rebook. I asked why someone hadn't asked Jamie about it, or Mason about it. I mean, this was a small enough community they had to have crossed paths with one or the other of the two since the email was sent.

I was told that no one wanted to risk offending Mason's family by appearing to be ungrateful so they'd just sucked it up and kept silent.

(Although it was very clear there had been some private conversations about the type of bride who books a wedding with only a month's notice and then turns around two weeks later and cancels all of her arrangements. It seems Jamie, Mason, and I were probably the only ones involved with the wedding who hadn't known about all of the cancellations.)

At least we still had a pastor and a church. I warned him not to pay attention to any emails he might receive from Jamie, Mason, or anyone else, including me, because the only way his participation in the event was going to be cancelled was if I showed up in person to do so.

After that call I put my head down on the table and let myself have a minor breakdown.

It could've been worse. We had a pastor and guests at least. And those guests had somewhere to stay while they were in town. I wasn't going to have to ask them to couch surf or stay in a heated barn or anything. So there was that.

But I still needed somewhere to have the reception. And food to feed everyone. All *two hundred* of them.

And a wedding dress, of course.

Not to mention I needed to figure out who had done this to Jamie. Because if I didn't figure that out there was a good chance they'd keep trying to sabotage the wedding and then I or Mason might end up doing something regrettable that would *really* ruin the wedding.

But before I could do any of that…

I glanced at the clock.

Matt, his brother Jack, my grandpa, and Lesley were due back from Denver in half an hour and I hadn't even bothered to set the table yet. At least I'd put a chicken bacon potato spinach soup in the slow cooker that morning so there'd be food to eat.

(One of the problems of living in a really small town is you can't just run out and grab something for dinner at the local fast food restaurant or pizza joint. You have to actually prepare for meals. It was an adjustment, especially compared to living in a big city like DC.)

I gathered up the five lovely three-ring binders and put them aside. Nothing more I could do on the wedding front until the morning, but that wasn't going to stop me from worrying about how to pull this all off with less than ten days to go and Christmas smack dab in the middle of that.

CHAPTER 9

It was a good thing I'd already decided to put the wedding disaster aside until the next day, because my grandpa and Lesley threw me for such a loop that night that I was pretty much useless for anything but staring at them with my mouth wide open.

I knew something was up when Matt came in the door first—as tall, dark, and handsome as ever—and immediately pulled me into a big embrace. Not that we don't hug when we see each other—we are a couple after all—but this was one of those "pull you close so I can whisper something important" hugs.

He buried his mouth against my ear and said, "Play it cool, Maggie," before pulling away.

"Play what cool?" I muttered as my grandpa escorted Lesley through the door. They were both glowing and giggling like kids. Which is saying something for a man who's normally taciturn and a woman who is never anything but perfectly put together.

"Guess what?" My grandpa took off his coat and I saw that he was wearing nice slacks and a sweater rather than his standard jeans and flannel shirt.

"What?" I asked, knowing already I didn't actually want to know.

Lesley held up her left hand and flashed a wedding ring. "We got married!"

I couldn't breathe for a second, but I forced a smile.

"Congratulations!" I hugged them both, looking at Matt with horror eyes over their shoulders.

Wasn't this sudden? It was sudden, wasn't it? It was really sudden. I mean, her husband had just passed away a couple months before. And, sure they'd known each other forever and even dated before Lesley met her husband, but…This was sudden, yeah?

I mean, my grandpa was eighty-two-years-old and Lesley was probably right up around there, but still…

Was I the only one in the world who thought it was a good idea to at least date someone for a year before you married them? I mean, how could you know what you needed to know about them if you didn't at least spend a year with them? What if they disappeared fishing every summer? Or turned into a shouting beast every football season? Or spent the month of January in a depressed stupor?

How could you know you wanted to spend forever with someone you hadn't even spent a year with?

And putting that aside, what did my grandpa getting married mean for me?

I know it was selfish to think, but…

Was Lesley going to move in now? Should I move out? Where would I go? It was way too early to move in with Matt, not to mention he had a more than full house with Jack and Sam and Trish.

It was awkward enough living with my grandpa, but

with some strange woman who was always perfectly coiffed and put together? What was that going to be like?

The only good thing about their news—other than their obvious happiness, of course—was the fact that it cleared all thoughts of Jamie's wedding completely out of my mind.

Lesley beamed at me. "I know it's sudden, Maggie. But we're not young either one of us. And we knew we wanted this. So why wait? Who cares what other people think?" She looked at my grandpa with such adoration I didn't even know what to say.

So I made it up. "Hey, I understand. When you find that person you want to be with for the rest of your life…Why wait, right?"

My laugh probably sounded a bit panicked, because Jack, Matt's brother, who'd snuck his way inside and was leaning against the wall watching the whole scene with far too much amusement, said, "Really? Is that how you feel, Maggie? Once you know you've found the one, just get married? Right away?"

I glared daggers at him. He knew me better than that. And Matt did not need to go getting any ideas, thank you very much.

I swallowed my panic. "Well, when you're the age my grandpa and Lesley are, and you've known each other as long as they have…Sure. Why not?"

Matt kissed my cheek and rubbed the back of my neck. "Don't worry, Maggie. No one's trying to force you into anything crazy like marriage."

I smiled up at him with probably too much relief, but I knew Matt. He was decided already. And all this talk of love and marriage was just going to make him wonder why I wasn't. And, true, I wasn't going to find a better man, ever. But…

Give me a year, would ya?

Ugh.

Lifelong commitments are…well, *lifelong*. I mean, at our age, that was fifty-plus years of your life.

Living with one person. Day in. And day out. Hours a day together…

I'm sorry, but no one is so perfect that you're going to like them while living in close proximity with them for *fifty years*. At least, not if you're me. Heck, there are people I can't stand for five minutes let alone fifty years…

To stop my spiraling desire to sprint for the door and never return, I turned it back on Jack instead. "Speaking of lifelong commitments, Jack. How you and Trish getting on? You headed for the altar anytime soon?"

He winked at me. "As a matter of fact, I'm planning on proposing New Year's Eve. Matt helped me pick out the ring while we were in Denver."

I froze, not daring to look at Matt. Please, please, someone tell me that he hadn't picked up on all of this wedding insanity. I loved him, but if he proposed to me on New Year's Eve…I'd…No. Just, no.

"Aren't you going to be at Jamie's wedding?" I asked.

"I thought that was moved to some other date."

"What? Where did you hear that?"

He shook his head. "I don't know. Someone mentioned it somewhere."

"Oh no." I buried my head against Matt's chest.

"What's wrong, Maggie? What is it?" he asked.

I pulled away. "Let's get the food served up and I'll tell you all what's going on with Jamie's wedding. Because I am going to need some serious help if I'm going to pull this one off."

🐾🐾🐾 257 🐾🐾🐾

CHAPTER 10

Rather than dealing with the lack of a caterer, lack of a venue, lack of flowers, and lack of wedding dress the next morning, I found myself at the kitchen table with my portion of the guest list making calls to confirm who was coming and who wasn't.

My grandpa, Lesley, and Jack worked their own portions of the list at the same time. (Matt was at work or he'd have helped out, too.)

It turned out whoever our saboteur was, they didn't have the guest list. That was the good news. All of the out of town guests were still planning on being there.

But…

Someone had started the local rumor mill going. And it turned out that almost every local guest who wasn't family or a very close family friend had thought the wedding was cancelled. Some were still willing to come—it was the wedding of Mason Maxwell after all and his family was very important in the valley—but others had made other plans and weren't willing to cancel them.

When I tried to point out that this was a wedding and their other plans were likely far less of a life milestone than that, more than one told me they were going to a different wedding that night. The wedding of someone named Margaret Kepper who was going to have a six-foot ice sculpture and ride into the ceremony on live horses. A wedding it turned out these people had originally planned on attending until Jamie's wedding was announced when they'd changed their minds because Jamie's sounded fancier.

(It seems that was before the addition of the ice sculpture and live horses.)

Sigh.

By noon the two-hundred-person guest list was down to one-twenty-five. Looking on the bright side, it made finding a caterer and venue easier at least…

Or so my optimistic, turn-lemons-into-lemonade side had decided. But my pessimistic, this-is-only-going-to-get-worse side was wondering what next. Locusts? Balls of fire falling from the sky?

If Jamie hadn't been through that disaster with Ted Little and if she wasn't already planning to spend the entire month of January in Paris for her honeymoon (not the best of months to be in Paris, by the way, but, it was still Paris) I would've probably just called her up and urged her to move the wedding. To spring, maybe? (Give it a full year before she committed her life to Mr. Stone and Wood Everywhere.)

But she needed this win.

So I spent the next three hours calling every caterer I could find in a four-hundred-mile radius.

Unfortunately, all of the good ones were already booked up because: New Year's Eve. Which left me with one of two choices: hire someone who'd probably give all the guests food poisoning or really awful-tasting food, which for someone like Jamie who knew how to cook would be devastating and ruin the day, or…

Swallow my pride and reach out to the one person I knew could probably step up and make this happen, Jean-Philippe Gaston, invited wedding guest, acclaimed French chef, and my freshman year mistake.

(Technically, he was also Jamie's freshman year mistake. Although she didn't consider him a mistake. More a fun diversion. When he moved on to *her* roommate she just laughed it off and moved on to his roommate to make things convenient. Me, I spent the rest of the semester brooding about how he'd suckered me into thinking I actually meant something to him and second-guessing the motives of every single guy who tried to hit on me.)

Not someone I wanted to talk to or ever see again. But he was already coming to the wedding. And he did know how to cook if that Michelin star meant anything. So he really was the ideal solution.

But…Ugh.

Rather than do what I knew I needed to do, I took Fancy for a walk instead, relishing the feel of ice-cold wind blowing against my cheeks as we shoved our way through the six inches of snow that had fallen overnight.

Sometimes if I give my mind time, I come up with better ideas. But at the end of a blisteringly cold thirty-minute walk that had Fancy practically bouncing with joy and me so frozen I made a cup of peppermint tea instead of reaching for my usual Coke, the conclusion was the same: I needed to call Jean-Philippe and ask for his help.

A Sabotaged Celebration and Salmon Snaps

I sighed and sank into the kitchen chair, staring at my phone. Best to just get it over with. Like pulling off a Band-Aid, right?

He owed me. And her.

CHAPTER 11

With each ring of the phone I desperately wanted to hang up, but I didn't.

"Oui?" He answered with that sexy accent and deep voice that had so mesmerized me when I was eighteen.

"Jean-Philippe. It's Maggie Carver. Remember me?"

"But of course, Maggie. How are you? I am looking forward to seeing you at the wedding. You are still single, yes?"

(I might have also repeated the mistake of falling for his charms at my friend Julie's wedding as well as my friend Kate's wedding, but let's not go there.)

"No, actually. I will be there with my boyfriend." And, man, did that feel good to say.

"Ah, this is so sad. Have you just called me to break my heart?"

"No. Actually, I need a favor. A very big favor."

"Ah, yes? And what favor can I do for you, Maggie, who is no longer single?" he purred.

I rolled my eyes. Some people never change. "I need you to do the catering for Jamie's wedding."

He laughed but when I didn't say anything else, he

stopped. "Mon Dieu. You are serious? You want me to cater a dinner in some itty bitty town in Colorado with no notice? Maggie…"

Time to turn on the charm. "It's only a hundred and twenty five guests, Jean-Philippe. And I know if anyone can do it, you can. Actually, you may be the only one who can save this wedding. Jean-Philippe, please…"

He chuckled. "Ah, you always knew how to get to my heart, Maggie."

I snorted.

"It is true. You are special to me."

"Just not special enough for you to keep your attention focused on just me, yeah?"

(I know, I was trying to convince him to do me a favor, so I shouldn't have pointed out his flaws, but I am what I am and that includes someone who is not always guarded with their opinions.)

"The world is full of beauty, Maggie. Am I to deny that beauty for the love of one woman?"

"That's pretty much how it's supposed to work, yeah."

"Pah. That is so provincial. My love for you is pure, Maggie. The rest…It is something else, yes? It is a celebration of life. Of the beauty of a woman. Of the way two people…"

"Oh, seriously. Stop. Just stop." I took a deep breath. "Will you do this? Please. Jamie needs you."

His accent mellowed as he turned serious. "This is not a simple thing. And I will not use some other man's menu. It must be my own creation. I am an artiste not a copycat."

"Of course. Understood. At this point I'm just trying to avoid feeding Jamie's guests mac 'n' cheese for dinner.

Let me know what you need and we'll get it for you, okay? But there are some guests with food allergies and diet preferences, so if you can account for those as well…"

"Diet preferences? What is this?"

"Some people don't like red meat. Or dairy. Or carbs. Or sugar. Or any of those things."

"You want me to feed these people cardboard? I cannot use cream? Or potatoes? Or beef? Or bread?"

"It's just a few people. Please. No one is asking you to make them cardboard. But if you could have a couple options that take into account those dietary preferences, it would be very much appreciated."

He huffed. "I will try. But you tie my hands. I cannot be the genius I am when my hands are tied."

"Understood." I rubbed my forehead to keep from saying anything damaging. "Just, please do the best you can. And, Jean-Philippe?"

"Yes?"

"Do not let anyone else tell you this is cancelled or that there are any changes. I am the only one you should listen to. And only if I call you. Do not take orders from me via email."

"What is going on here, Maggie? What are you not telling me?"

I briefly told him about the person who was trying very hard to cancel Jamie's wedding.

"Why did you not tell me about this at first? I would have immediately said yes. And who would do this to Jamie? She is the sweetest."

"I don't know. But I'm going to find out. Until then…Talk to me and only me. Got it?"

"Yes, of course. We will make this work. You and me, Maggie," he made a kissing noise, "we are good together..."

"Haha. No. No, we are not. See you soon, Jean-Philippe."

I hung up the phone wondering what I had ever seen in that man. All I can say is I guess we all have that phase where a sexy foreign accent and intense interest can override common sense. But at least he'd help. That meant a lot.

Next step, figuring out *where* to host the wedding. Like that was going to be easy.

CHAPTER 12

Before I could start making calls to find somewhere to host the wedding, my grandpa came home. He's normally a reserved sort of man, calm like a good country lake. You know there's depth there and things you're not seeing, but it seldom ruffles the surface. So to see him agitated like he was made me immediately set aside everything and focus on him.

"Hey, Grandpa. What's wrong?"

"Lesley's grandkids are going to be staying with her for the rest of the week. Last-minute request by her daughter." He sat down across from me at the dining room table which was now my war room, all five of Jamie's binders spread across its surface along with all of my notes and ideas.

He didn't even look close to his eighty-two years of age. More like sixty, probably because his hair was still a light brown and he was trim and active in a way most men his age weren't anymore. I was glad to see he'd switched back to his standard flannel shirt, this one long-sleeved in honor of the season, and jeans.

It was good to have him around. To have something

in life that felt like it would always be there even though that's absolutely not the way life actually works.

I tilted my head to the side and studied him. "Do you think this was some move by Lesley's daughter to keep the two of you apart? I mean, kinda pointless now, isn't it?"

He shrugged one shoulder. "Could be. She doesn't know we're married yet."

"Why not?"

"Lesley wanted to wait a bit. At least until the new year. You know how some of her family doesn't exactly approve of me."

Sort of understandable given the fact that he'd shot her sister's husband when the man tried to kill her, a set of facts that not everyone in the family agreed upon. At least some didn't agree about how that man, who'd shown up with a gun and threatened everyone in the room, deserved to die. (That was the first time my grandpa went to prison.)

"Well, not like it's going to get any better unless you find a way to bring them around to your side. You could stay with Lesley and help take care of the kids…"

He snorted. "No. Those kids are spoiled brats. Last thing I need is to alienate Lesley's daughter by putting one of them in their place." He glanced around the house. "Maybe I'll clean up here a bit instead."

I hunched my shoulders as I followed his gaze. It wasn't *dirty*. There weren't weird smells or anything. But it was certainly much more cluttered than my grandpa normally allowed. What can I say? If a surface is free it seems like the perfect place to set a coat, the mail, or whatever else happens to be in my hand when I feel like setting it down.

"No, don't do that. I should do it. It's my mess. Why don't you work on one of your miniatures?"

My grandpa loved to assemble miniature planes. He was very good at it even though it took him a lot longer than it had in the past. But he still had the patience for it. He'd sit there for minutes working to place just one little piece when his hand started shaking.

"Nah. I'm too wound up for that. It's okay. I need something to do. I'll just dump whatever's yours on your floor and then you can deal with it from there."

I grimaced, wondering if I'd have any space left on the floor when he was done. At least the steps I'd built for Fancy were free to use. After the first couple weeks she'd decided she didn't like them and never set foot on them again.

"Just don't move anything from this table, okay?"

"Where are we supposed to have dinner?"

"In the kitchen. Or on the couch. I mean, Lesley's family now, right? And Matt is…Matt. We don't really need to eat at the dining room table anymore, do we?"

"Maggie May. Unless you are married to that man we are not going to have him over for dinner and make him eat it on the couch or in the kitchen. That is not acceptable. Your grandma's probably rolling over in her grave right now at the mere suggestion of having a guest sit on the couch for dinner."

I wanted to object, but his house, his rules. So I just nodded instead. "Yes, sir. If Matt comes over for dinner, I promise I'll clear the dining room table."

"How's it coming along? You find replacements for everyone yet?"

"No. Not yet. I've only taken care of the caterer so far."

"You found someone?"

I nodded. "Jean-Philippe Gaston. Thanks to our saboteur Jamie's wedding is now being catered by a Michelin-starred chef."

"Isn't he that French fool who messed up your head when you were in college?"

I shrugged. "He may be a lot of things, but he's also a good cook who was already coming to the wedding. And most important, he was willing to help."

"Hm." My grandpa was not a fan of Jean-Philippe. He'd heard just enough over the years to probably want to have a private chat with him about how you treat a man's granddaughter. A chat I would love to witness but also hoped never happened. "I look forward to meeting him."

"Just promise me you'll wait until after the food is served to put him in his place?"

He chuckled, finally relaxing. "Promise. Anything I can do to help?"

"Do you know someone who can get their hands on enough baby pink roses for a wedding in less than ten days?"

"Hm. No, not the roses. But I might be able to put something else together. Especially if you're okay with a Christmas theme."

"At this point? I'll take anything. Now to find a venue…"

I reached for my phone, hoping I'd have better luck with finding a venue than I'd had with finding a caterer.

CHAPTER 13

I didn't. Every meeting hall, conference space, ballroom, and barn in the entire valley was booked up for the holiday. Why Jamie had decided to get married on New Year's Eve, I did not know. I was pretty much ready to pull my hair out by the time Matt came by for dinner.

Like the dutiful granddaughter I am (or at least pretend to be) I cleared off the dining room table and set it with the nice china. Why I had to do so when it was just Matt coming over, I did not know. But my grandpa's house, my grandpa's rules.

I realized as I did so that I still hadn't even started on figuring out who was responsible for the mess I found myself in.

After I'd served up fifteen-minute chicken chili and my grandpa had cut up chunks of corn bread I asked, "Either of you know Mason Maxwell's former fiancée, Elaine something or other?"

"Oh, so you've heard about Elaine?" my grandpa asked.

"You knew about her then? And you didn't tell me?"

"Maggie May. What was the point? Mason had

moved on and was clearly madly in love with Jamie. And I know you. You'd want to tell Jamie, and I saw no point in that."

"Well, then. Tell me about her. Do you think she's the type to sabotage his wedding in revenge?"

"Elaine?" My grandpa shook his head.

"Definitely not." Matt slipped Fancy a bit of cornbread before taking a bite of the chili and making a pleased little hum in the back of his throat.

"Why not? What's she like?"

Matt and my grandpa exchanged a look before Matt answered. "Forgettable? Quiet? Mousy?"

"Hey sometimes the quiet ones are the crazy ones."

"Not really. That's usually only on television shows or in books to keep it interesting. In my experience, and I am a cop, most people who do something like that, there were signs beforehand. A little flash of temper, a fight here or there, or they just made people feel uncomfortable for no good reason. But Elaine? Nah."

"What does she do?"

"She's a bookkeeper. Works for the Mason family trust."

"So he still sees her on a regular basis?" I asked, outraged.

"Oh calm down, Maggie May." My grandpa shook his head. "Some people can date and move on like it was nothing."

"They were engaged!"

"Eh. Small town. Not a lot of choices, especially if you wait too long. She was nice enough, pretty enough, and his family liked her. So he asked her to marry him. But there was no spark."

What a horrible description of a future marriage. Nice enough? Pretty enough? Ouch. Let me never have an "enough" marriage.

"Well, the same about not having a lot of choices must go for her, too, right?" I asked. "Mason Maxwell, and I hate that I'm saying this, is quite a catch. She must've felt resentful when she lost him."

Matt shook his head. "Pretty sure she's just not capable of that kind of emotion, Maggie."

"Yeah, well, I'll see for myself. Where can I find her tomorrow?" Both Matt and my grandpa gave me disapproving looks, but I ignored them. "Well?"

My grandpa answered, "She should be at the Y. She's in charge of the charity clothes drive."

"Thank you. I'll swing by with Jamie on our way to Greta's."

"Greta's? Why are you going there?" Matt asked, slipping Fancy a bit of shredded cheese.

(I have to admit my heart swelled every time he gave her a bit of food from the table because it meant he loved my dog as much as I did. Even if it probably wasn't the healthiest choice for her. I was pretty sure I wasn't the only one who'd put on a few pounds since the barkery closed.)

I gave Fancy a rub on the top of her head as she looked to me for even more food, a thin line of drool coating her chest. "To fix the dress issue, hopefully. We'll see if Jamie is as willing to think outside the box as I am when it comes to weddings."

Matt raised an eyebrow. "How so?"

"Well, Greta has an insane number of gorgeous gowns in her closet. She had them shipped here after she decided to stay. But I doubt most of them are white.

Which means if Jamie is willing, we can find her an absolutely beautiful gown to wear on her wedding day, but it may not be a traditional color."

"That's probably not going to work. Doesn't every bride want to wear white?"

"Not me. White gets dirty. I would not want to spend what's supposed to be one of the biggest days of my life worrying about whether or not I sat in something. And I certainly don't want to eat food in a white dress." (Not to mention sweat stains.) "Honestly. Why would I wear a color I haven't worn since I was a teenager just because it's tradition?"

"So you're thinking about marriage, are you? About being a bride?" Matt grinned.

I choked down my last bite of chili. "Only because I'm planning this for Jamie. And let me assure you that the more planning I do, the more I realize that a wedding is absolutely not what I want."

He leaned back, arms crossed as my grandpa glared daggers at me. "How so?"

"Well, take the expense, right? For *one* day. I'd rather use that money to go visit my friends and let them meet my husband that way than have them all fly in for a day where I'm so stressed and busy I barely have a chance to speak to them. Plus…I mean, I lost both my parents. There is no way I could have a wedding and not be reminded of that fact. Sure, my grandpa could probably walk me down the aisle, but I'd be thinking about how my dad wasn't there to do it the whole time and I'd be aware every single step down that aisle that my mom wasn't in the front row crying happy tears. Who wants to be that sad on one of the happiest days of their life?"

"Okay, making sense so far. What else?"

I didn't trust the mischievous gleam in his eye, but I figured I better get it all out while he was willing to listen.

"Well, we already talked about the white dress thing. So not me. Give me a brilliant blue any day of the week. And wedding rings? Again, why? Do I really want to spend the rest of my life with this gigantic rock on my hand that will snag on everything? I have no objection to making a commitment to someone and wearing a symbol of that commitment for the world to see, but I'd far rather it was a simple band than what every other girl seems to want."

"A commitment to *someone*, huh?" Matt asked. "No one in particular?"

I rolled my eyes. "Matthew Allen Barnes, do not even get me started. I love you. I have told you that. Right now, in this moment, if there were anyone who was that someone it would be you. But I am a woman of many, many layers and you have barely scratched the surface so don't go getting all forever on me when you don't know what you're getting yourself into."

He grinned. "You're not supposed to know everything about someone when you marry them, Maggie. That's what the rest of your lives are for."

"Ha. You are so like a girl." I stood up from the table even though I probably would've had another serving if Matt hadn't thrown me so bad. "If you'll excuse me, I have to go make a list of people who might want to sabotage my friend's wedding. You two…I don't know. Bond or whatever."

My grandpa shrugged and looked at Matt. "What do you say to a game of Scrabble?"

"Sounds good. I'll get the board." Matt squeezed my shoulder as he walked past me. Part of me wanted to shrug him off but an equally big part of me wanted to bury my head against his chest and just let him hold me for a while.

This relationship business was not easy.

CHAPTER 14

While Matt and my grandpa engaged in a fierce game of Scrabble that I was surprised didn't draw blood, I tried to brainstorm who might want to ruin Jamie's wedding.

I had Elaine from Mason's side of things, but I figured it was much more likely that one of Jamie's exes had decided to get a little payback.

Jamie's a great person. And she loves everyone. It's one of her more endearing traits. But, well, let's just say that when it comes to affairs of the heart she's not always the most thoughtful. (Refer back to the fact that she loves everyone.)

Unfortunately for her there are men out there who just like me nurse their wounds after a relationship ends, no matter how casual. And Jamie, well, she's never really realized that.

So I wasn't surprised that she'd invited Ed to the wedding. A love interest from high school who chose to go to CU because Jamie was going there even though he had a full-ride scholarship to MIT. Also the guy she broke up with on Valentine's Day their freshman year so she could spend the rest of the day with a guy she'd met two weeks before and fallen head over heels for.

He went on my list for sure.

Then there was Brad. The first guy who'd ever asked her to marry him. She broke his heart when she said no even though how he could've thought she'd say yes I don't know. He followed her around like a lost puppy dog for the next three months until she finally set him up with one of her co-workers. They'd dated for two years until that woman also turned down his proposal.

So he went on the list.

So did Caroline, one of Jamie's friends from high school and sorority sisters in college who was the very definition of frenemies. At first glance you'd think they'd make perfect friends. They looked a lot alike, had the same interests, had the same taste in men. But that was exactly the problem. Every time Caroline took an interest in some guy, Jamie would accidentally steal him away.

(And I promise you, it was never intentional. Jamie would just shrug and move on if anyone ever told her they were interested in some guy, because plenty of fish in the sea and all. But just because Jamie moved on, didn't mean the guys turned their attention back to Caroline. It was ugly.)

And, of course, if they both joined a club Jamie ended up President and Caroline ended up Secretary. That was just the way it was. And since Caroline had announced her engagement a month before Jamie's and Jamie's wedding was now going to occur six months before Caroline's, she definitely had to go on the list.

As did Bethany who was trashy enough to ruin someone's wedding just because, why not, sounds like fun, especially if it involved poking at someone as put together as Jamie.

(Why Jamie stays friends with certain people, I will never know. Me, I'd kick them to the curb. But Jamie just shrugs it off. I guess I should be grateful for it, since she's also stayed friends with me all these years despite my sharp edges.)

I also had to consider the local angle. Who else was local that would want to see Jamie and Mason's wedding ruined? Because someone had started those rumors. And only a local could've pulled that one off.

I put Katie Cross's mom, Georgia, on the list for good measure. There'd never been love lost there and after everything that happened with Katie…Well.

I debated putting Lucas Dean on the list, but what was the point. He wasn't the type to do something like that and I didn't have time to bother with him. Knowing my luck, he'd demand an apology and he wasn't going to get it.

(One of his oh-so-accommodating defenders—i.e., a middle-aged woman he flirts with like the rabid dog he is—had the audacity to pull me aside the last time I was at the library and hand me a copy of Colorado's age of consent statute, because she didn't think it was fair that I kept calling what he'd done with Katie illegal when it was perfectly acceptable under Colorado law. I informed her that, thankfully I had never personally had to look up that law seeing as I wasn't trying to sleep with high schoolers, but thanks for the info. I also added that just because the law said a man of any age could legally sleep with a seventeen-year-old *girl* didn't make the whole thing any less skeevy and disgusting in my opinion. She walked away in a huff and hasn't spoken to me since. I consider that a good thing.)

Anyway.

I couldn't believe Jamie invited Lucas Dean to the wedding. But I didn't think he was behind this. So I put it aside.

That gave me six people to start with, which was plenty. I figured I'd run the list by Jamie the next day and see what she had to say about them.

(I wasn't planning on telling her about the sabotage, but I could ask, "Why did you invite that person?" without rousing any suspicions. Or so I hoped.)

CHAPTER 15

The next day dawned cold and crisp. Being in the Colorado mountains in wintertime is wonderful if you're there to ski, which I don't. Or if you can stay inside the whole day, because then you get all that snowy beauty without having to deal with the cold. But between Fancy wanting to go for yet another freezing-cold walk and then having to pick up Jamie and drive to Greta's, that wasn't an option.

It was still beautiful. That snow-capped mountains' majesty is not just some lyric in a song. And the roads were actually clear enough to drive on without danger. But cold and I do not go well together. At least I was lucky enough to have some extra padding here or there from my lifestyle choices so I wasn't completely freezing.

(How do skinny women do it? I used to work with a woman who was always cold even in the middle of summer. Body fat has its uses, you know.)

Jamie, at least, was looking much better. She was back to her put-together self, her hair pulled back into a jaunty ponytail and wearing subtle makeup that gave her a bit of a cat eye. Her bright pink snow coat topped it all off with cheer.

For that alone, I was glad I'd taken on the role of wedding planner.

As we drove the twenty minutes towards Greta's, Jamie babbled on and on about the party favors and the cupcakes she was going to make. She'd decided to forego the traditional wedding cake in favor of five flavors of cupcakes formed to look like a wedding cake and had been experimenting with flavors the last few days.

Her final list included carrot cake, vanilla cream, and chocolate peppermint for the traditionalists. And then lavender pumpkin and basil strawberry balsamic for the more adventurous.

She'd tried a bunch of much crazier flavors than that—including a habanero chocolate caramel pecan— but decided that maybe her wedding wasn't the time to roll them out to a mass audience, so she was saving those for the café at the new pet resort instead.

"Thank you so much for this, Maggie," she said as we drove into Bakerstown. "I would've never thought of asking Greta if she had something that would work for the wedding. I mean, the dress I ordered was so perfect, but…"

"Right. No way you can gain fifty pounds in a week. Although, worst case scenario, we could stuff the dress until it fits you…"

She laughed. I was glad to see she was feeling better about the whole situation. I was pretty sure a few days ago she would've burst into tears at my joke instead.

"Hey, do you mind if we swing by the Y?" I asked. "I have some old clothes I want to drop off for the clothing drive."

(I'd already told Greta we were going to be delayed while I checked out Elaine.)

"Sure. No problem. I wish you'd told me. I could've brought some of my own."

"Like that hideous outfit you had on the other day? I mean, not that I can judge since I pretty much wear jeans and plain t-shirts anymore, but it was definitely not you. Where did you even get it?"

"My mom sent over all my old clothes from high school. And I was so bummed that morning I just wanted something familiar and comfortable to wear."

"That's what you used to wear in high school? Weren't you a cheerleader?" (Jamie and I hadn't become good friends until college.)

"I was. But I did wear clothes like that sometimes. Mostly on the weekends when I was helping my dad out around the cabin."

"Ah, that makes sense." I pulled into the parking lot for the YMCA. It was more crowded than I'd expected and I wondered how I was going to manage to find this Elaine woman and confront her long enough to determine if she was the saboteur.

(I think I'd been watching too many episodes of *The Mentalist* lately. That's the problem with binge watching shows, they stick in your head until you start to think like the main characters. So I was all Patrick Jane as I walked through the door, ready with a witty, "Are you the killer?" type question and a keen eye for deception.)

Fortunately for my diabolical plan, Elaine was the one in charge of the clothing drive, so the lady at the front desk sent us right to her.

"Are you Elaine?" I asked as Jamie and I walked up to

a long folding table at the back of the gym with two large bags of clothes in our arms.

"I am."

I tried not to stare. *This* was the woman Mason Maxwell had been engaged to before Jamie? She really was mousy. I mean, nothing wrong with being that way, but it was hard to believe that a man who'd been drawn to my friend's bubbly effervescence had at one point proposed to this quiet and reserved woman.

She had dishwater brown hair, pulled into a bun at the nape of her neck, and small mud-colored eyes. She was wearing makeup, but not well. At least her clothes were nice enough.

"I'm Maggie Carver. I don't think we've met." I held out my hand.

"No, we haven't."

Her hand hung limp in mine when I shook it. (I hate weak handshakes. I don't know why. They make me want to wipe my hand off on my pants afterward like maybe that lack of strength will somehow transfer to me like a bad virus.)

"And this is my friend, Jamie Green. Have you two met?"

They both shook their heads. "But I've heard good things about you," Jamie beamed at Elaine. "Elaine works for Mason's aunt at the family trust office. She says you're highly competent."

Elaine nodded, but didn't make eye contact. I couldn't rule her out as our mystery saboteur. I needed to get to know her better.

I glanced at the waist-high bins behind the table. "So do you take the donations and then sort them into those bins?"

Elaine nodded and waved towards a huge pile of unsorted clothes and bags off to the left. "I have to get through all of that today. It's the last day for the drive and they're going to pick everything up at five."

"Well, let us help you then. If that's okay?" I looked back and forth between Elaine and Jamie who both nodded.

"Great." I took off my jacket and gloves and hid them away where they wouldn't get accidentally added into the donation bins. "Let's do this."

CHAPTER 16

An hour later I was convinced that Elaine was exactly what she appeared to be—a kind but unassuming woman who really did not have it in her to hurt anyone for any reason. Either that or she was the most cunning psychopath to walk the earth. Because her persona did not change for that entire time.

Jamie being Jamie she managed to draw Elaine out probably as much as it was possible to do. They talked about high school and growing up in the area and going tubing and being a member of the local girl's adventure group as kids and how absurd that had been. (Elaine was a bit younger, so they hadn't been in the group at the same time, but the pack leader or whatever she was had been the same and it sounded like she was quite the character.)

By the end of the hour Jamie had invited Elaine to the wedding. I opened my mouth to suggest that wasn't the best idea, but Elaine beat me to it with a demure comment about how she really didn't like big social events.

"Oh, I'm right there with you," I said. "If it wasn't my best friend getting married I'd be at home on New Year's Eve snuggled up with a book and my dog."

That was the one time I saw Elaine smile. It was a bright flash that transformed her face for just a moment and I realized that maybe under that quiet surface was a woman Mason Maxwell could've fallen for.

"That's where I'd like to be," she offered.

We then, of course, had to show each other photos of our respective dogs. She had a cute mutt that was part Australian Shepherd named Zela.

"I'll envy you on New Year's," I said, putting away my phone.

"Oh, I'm actually going to be at Margaret Kepper's wedding. We grew up together. I'm one of her best friends." She blushed as I tried to reconcile this quiet woman being friends with a woman who it seemed was anything but quiet.

"I heard it was going to be quite the event," I said.

Jamie paused in winding a bright turquoise and yellow scarf around her neck. "I didn't know Margaret Kepper was getting married that night, too."

"Oh, yes. It's been all anyone could talk about for months. It's going to be at her father's estate, which is absolutely amazing. They're even bringing in some fancy chef from New York to cater the whole deal."

I pursed my lips. "So she's not using anyone local? Like the Baker Valley Catering Company?"

"Oh no. She wanted better than that."

Well then she hadn't been the one to take Jamie's caterer away.

I nodded. "Someone told me her wedding dress is from some exclusive couture house in Paris. Supposedly it took seven months to do all the hand beading on it."

"That's what they say." Elaine was back to not making

eye contact.

I turned to Jamie. "Do you know her?"

"Not really. She was a few years behind me in high school. She, um…They used to call her Mousy Margaret."

Elaine nodded. "Yeah. They actually called us the Mouseketeers when we were in middle school. But that all stopped after Margaret got her braces off and spent the summer with her aunt in New York. She came back looking amazing." Elaine ran a hand over her frizzy hair. "From that point forward, she ruled the school. All the boys wanted her and all the girls wanted to be her."

Jamie laughed. "Well, good for her for turning things around."

"Yeah. It was…awesome."

"So you guys have kept in touch then?" I asked.

"Sort of. Um. Yeah. We'd lost touch but then, um…" She glanced at Jamie. "We started hanging out again the last couple years you know after, um…Anyway. I better let you guys get going if you're going to make your lunch."

On the spur of the moment I grabbed a business card from my wallet and scrawled my phone number on the back. "Hey, you ever want to take your dog for a walk or something, call me. I'd be happy to join you."

Elaine nodded and tucked the card away. "Okay. Thanks."

I knew she probably wouldn't call, but she struck me as the type of person who could use another friend or two. And I have a weak spot for social orphans. I'm always reaching out to that person hiding in the corner or against the wall. Probably because I am that person more times than not and I know a kindred soul when I meet one.

As we got back in the van I mentally crossed Elaine off my list of suspects. One down, five to go. But first, time to find a wedding dress for Jamie.

CHAPTER 17

As we drove up the winding road that led to Greta's mansion, I wondered who on earth thought it was a good idea to live on the top of a mountain in a snow-packed area like this one. Sure the views were great, but the drive had to be hellish a lot of the time when it wasn't downright impossible.

But then I realized that most of the houses we were passing were probably used as tourist rentals and what would be unpleasant and annoying after three months of fighting through it was probably considered part of the adventure for someone in from Florida for the week.

At least the roads were well-plowed so my van didn't slip or slide at all.

I drove slowly as Greta's place came into view. It was definitely stunning with the two wings of rooms branching off of a central entryway and the Italian-style fountain (that was of course not running at the moment) in the center of an arched driveway with pristine snow in every direction until it hit the tree line. (In the summer that snow was a beautifully manicured lawn.)

After I parked I took a moment to stare out over the

valley and admire the literally breathtaking view. Mountains on either side, covered in snow and evergreens, and Bakerstown and the valley spreading out below us like a picturesque little village scene you'd see on a postcard. Truly a million-dollar view.

Greta had the door open by the time I turned around, Hans, her Irish Wolfhound, at her side as always. "Greta!" I called. "How are you?"

I missed seeing her since the barkery closed. She'd come in with Hans almost every single day. And even though we still met at least once a week to discuss the plans for the pet resort, it just wasn't the same.

She made for an interesting friend. She was an ex-thief who'd been married so many times she'd lost count and was now worth hundreds of millions of dollars as a result. You wouldn't know it from her demeanor, but if you looked closely at the black slacks, jewel-toned tops, pale blonde hair, smooth skin, and tasteful diamonds they all pretty much screamed money.

We said our hellos as she led us into the sprawling entryway. I shuddered, remembering the last time I'd been there—a memory I'd rather forget.

"Where's your help?" I asked as she led us into the massive living room with a twenty-foot tall live tree in the center, festooned with white and silver ornaments punctuated with flat little red wooden horses and snowflakes.

"I did not need them today. I have made us lunch. It will be good, just us girls, no?" she said with her German accent.

"Oh, absolutely." I slowly turned, taking in the amount of space. "Hey, Greta, just out of curiosity, how many people could you host for a party in this place?"

A Sabotaged Celebration and Salmon Snaps

I already knew she had an amazing kitchen, which Jean-Philippe might need to borrow to prep. But if we could also use her place for the reception, that would be perfect, seeing as I still hadn't found a new venue.

"Two hundred? Two hundred and fifty, perhaps?"

"Really? In here?" Jamie asked.

"Oh, no. There is a ballroom. You have not seen it. Come. I will show you."

She led us to a corner of the house I'd never seen and opened a pair of double doors. Sure enough. There was a full-sized ballroom attached to the house. And it was as stunning as the rest of the place, all warm wood tones, pale marble, gold, and crystal. Something like that could easily be tacky if overdone, but she'd struck just the right note with it. (As she did with everything.)

Jamie stared. "Wow. You know, Greta, if I'd known you had this I might've asked to have my wedding here instead of at the convention complex. That space is functional, but this is…Amazing."

Greta and I exchanged a look. She knew about the wedding fiasco. The whole thing, not just the dress.

"Then we will do so."

"What? But…I've already booked the convention complex, I can't cancel now."

"She does not know?" Greta asked me.

Jamie turned to stare at me. "Know what?"

"Um, no, not yet."

Jamie looked back and forth between us. "What's going on? What aren't you telling me?"

I put an arm around her shoulders. "Well, I have some good news for you and some bad news for you. But first, let's get some drinks and food in hand, shall we?"

Anything to delay the inevitable moment when I ruined my friend's day.

Jamie gave me a sidelong look, but she didn't ask anything else as Greta led us to her amazing kitchen that looked like it had come straight out of a design magazine. Nor did she ask any questions while Greta dished us up an incredible breakfast-style casserole with eggs and bread and cheese and sausage that looked positively sinful but at least was balanced out by a bowl of fresh-cut fruit.

For drinks we had Bellinis. Who can go wrong with a drink made of peach and sparkling white wine? (Although I was sorely tempted to ask for just the wine. Or even better, the hard stuff. Not that I drink the hard stuff hardly ever, but shooting back a shot of whiskey seemed like a good plan in that moment.)

Jamie, not knowing what we were up against yet, watched Greta fill each champagne flute with a bit of skepticism. "It's not even noon yet. We should probably skip the alcohol, Greta."

"Nonsense. This is a ladies' brunch and a ladies' brunch always must have a bit of alcohol. It is not enough to get you drunk. It is just a polite amount to go with the meal."

We tapped glasses and dug into the food which was decadently delicious. "Greta, we're going to need to get this recipe from you for the resort," I said, trying not to shovel it all in at once.

"Thank you. It is my mother's recipe. Now. We must tell Jamie, no?"

"Tell me what?"

I set down my fork and downed the rest of my Bellini.

"Turns out, the dress wasn't the only problem with your wedding."

She set her fork down, too, a panicked look in her eyes. "What do you mean?"

I opened and closed my mouth a few times, trying to find the best way to explain things. Greta beat me to it. "Someone is trying to ruin your wedding, my dear. They cancelled your caterer and your reservation at the conference center. They ruined your dress. And they spread a rumor that the wedding had been cancelled as well."

So matter of fact. I flinched.

"But good news," I added, "is that we have a venue now, thanks to Greta. And will hopefully have a dress by the time we leave here. Also, thanks to Greta. And I've arranged for a new chef to cook for the wedding, so that's covered. And my grandpa is going to do something for the flowers. And we still have the pastor and the church and all of the out of town guests. So we're fine. It's all handled."

She bit her lower lip and I could see her struggling to be calm. "*Something* for the flowers? You mean I'm not going to have the baby pink roses I wanted?"

I clenched my fists under the table. Best to be as honest as possible. "No. You're not. But you are going to have a wedding. And it is going to be beautiful. And that's what counts."

"I've been dreaming about my wedding since I was six-years-old…"

When Greta refilled my champagne glass with straight Prosecco I cast her a grateful look before downing it in one gulp. She moved over to the second fridge and came back with an ice-cold can of Coke in hand. For that I wanted to kiss her. Instead I just said, "Bless you," before cracking it open and taking a long sip.

I grabbed Jamie's wrist and gave it a small squeeze. "Your wedding is going to be amazing, Jamie. I promise you."

"Is it? I mean, your wedding day is supposed to be so special and…Now I'm not going to have the dress or the flowers or the reception area or the food I wanted…"

"It *is* going to be special, Jamie. As a matter of fact, it's going to be even more special than you'd planned."

"How?"

"Well, you already said Greta's ballroom is even better than the reception space at the convention center, right?"

"Yeah. I guess."

"And do you know who's going to cook the food for your wedding now?"

She shook her head, tears in the corners of her eyes.

"Jean-Philippe."

"Jean-Philippe? How did you manage that? I mean he's invited, but I would've never asked…"

"Exactly. But I did. So instead of a local caterer who is a nice man and makes good food you will now have a world-renowned chef feeding your guests. Although, I can't promise he's going to honor all of those dietary preferences all your friends had. But there will be food. And it will be good." I took another sip of my Coke. "Jean-Philippe may be a lot of things, but he's a damned fine chef. And with Greta's kitchen here, he should be able to put together a masterpiece."

She nodded, coming around a bit but not there yet. "But the dress…And the flowers…"

"Trust us, Jamie. And remember what matters most about your wedding day. You and Mason. Promising to spend the rest of your lives together. As long as that happens and you are strong in your love for each other, everything else is just window dressing. We'll make it beautiful window dressing, but the only thing that actually matters is you and Mason exchanging vows. And, fortunately, no one cancelled the pastor, so that's still good."

She nodded one more time, the panicked look finally leaving her eyes.

"Any chance you know who might have wanted to do this to you?" I asked.

"No. No one. I don't have enemies. And neither does Mason."

I pulled out my list of suspects. "This is who I came up with. Based on that, anyone else who should be on here?"

She glanced through the list and laughed. "You think Ed would try to sabotage my wedding? Why? He loved me. And what is Elaine doing on here? I don't even know her."

"Uh, well. Mason does."

"Through the family trust, but why would she want to sabotage my wedding for that?"

I winced. I hadn't planned on telling her about Elaine. "Because Mason broke off his engagement with her the first time he saw you."

Now, me, in that moment I would've turned white hot furious at the fact that the man I loved had been engaged and not told me, and the wedding would've probably been called off. (Many, many reasons I am single. Many.)

But not Jamie. She smiled. "Really? He never told me that. Oh, how romantic. It really was love at first sight for both of us, wasn't it?"

She put the list on the table, all sappy and happy. "I don't care who's trying to ruin the wedding. Let them. Nothing can come between us. What we have is true love."

I nodded. Sure it was. And, of course, love conquers all, right? Even horrible people trying to ruin your wedding. You just smile and voila it all works itself out.

Yeah, no.

But let Jamie think that. She was the bride-to-be. Let her have her illusions. I would be the dark enforcer who tracked down this horrible, awful person and got them to back off of my friend's special day.

"Well then," I said, forcing a smile. "That's settled. Let's find you a dress, shall we?"

CHAPTER 18

You know how on some of those home shows a person has a well-organized walk-in closet where all their clothes are on display on hangers and their shoes are lined up like artwork? Yeah, well compared to Greta's walk-in *room* of clothes that was a paltry, pathetic attempt at glamour.

The room we found ourselves in had to be ten foot by twenty foot. And it was all gowns, evening shoes, and little bejeweled bags on display stands. I don't even know where she kept her normal clothes. Probably in another equally-sized room.

There was one of those round seat things in the center of the room that comfortably sat all three of us and could've probably sat five more. And a large three-way mirror in one corner and a dressing screen in another.

I immediately sat down while Jamie slowly moved around the circumference of the entire room, almost but not quite touching all of the shiny and beaded dresses that hung from satin-padded clothes hangers. For Jamie, this had to be heaven. I knew she desperately wanted to try everything on and immediately wondered if I'd starve before I was allowed to finally crawl my way to freedom.

Not that I don't like fashion or looking nice. And some really high-end clothes do feel absolutely exquisite on, like they're made from some perfect body-hugging material that will hide every flaw with finesse. (All for the measly cost of a house in some portions of the country.)

It's just that I have a very low girly tolerance. And then I'm done. And ready for my pajamas and a good book and a Coke.

I hunkered down for a long afternoon while Jamie sighed in pleasure. "Greta…I just want to spend a day in this room watching you try on all of these clothes. They are amazing."

"You are going to spend a day in this room, but *you* will be trying on the clothes, no?" She poured each of us a glass of champagne and plunged the bottle back into the waiting ice bucket. "Now. Are we set on the color white? Is that the only choice?"

Jamie looked around the room at the rainbow of colors and then turned back to us, her eyes pleading. "I really would like to wear white for my wedding. Or maybe ivory. If I have to. But I've always pictured a dress that was snow white and like a cloud…" She glanced towards the one visible ivory dress in the corner.

Greta nodded. "Of course. Do not despair. We have many choices. I hide the white dresses. They are not as pretty to look at, no?"

I shook my head as Greta went to the far wall and pressed a button which rotated one of the rows of dresses until the entire visible wall of dresses was just gowns in shades from the purest white to the most delicate ivory.

"Greta, do you just come sit in here some days and stare at all of your beautiful clothes?" I asked.

She laughed. "Some days. But I like to look at my art more."

I still hadn't seen the painting that had led her to marry her last husband. I suspected not many people had since the painting was quite probably the original that she wasn't supposed to have based on his will. (She'd claimed when he died that his copy had been a forgery, but I knew better. She'd just pawned off a forgery on the museum he'd left it to so she could keep the original and actually see it. I guess once a thief, always inclined to blur the line as needed.)

She pulled three dresses and hung them facing outward so that we could see their silhouettes. The first was a long graceful sheath of pure white. The second was a princess-style dress in a softer shade of white with gold laced throughout the bodice and poofy skirt. And the third one was a short lacy affair of lightest ivory. "We will start with these."

Jamie stared, her mouth hanging open in awe.

"Careful there, Jamie. You might drool on the carpet." I took another sip of champagne, glad to see things were coming together so well.

That broke Jamie out of her trance. She grabbed the first of the three dresses like a kid in a candy store and went to the dressing screen to try it on.

🐾 🐾 🐾

It took two hours for Jamie to try on each and every dress that had any chance of working for the wedding. I honestly think she knew which one she wanted from the beginning, but decided to have fun with it. And why not?

How often do you get the chance to try on that many beautiful dresses?

I wanted to be annoyed, but it felt so good to see my friend happy and carefree for once that I just smiled and drank.

I would've probably been drunk by the end of it if I hadn't switched back to Coke halfway through.

Jamie finally settled on the princess-style dress with the gold laced through the bodice and skirt. It suited her. And, better yet, only required minimal alterations, which Greta herself had volunteered to do.

(I silently wondered whether she was qualified to do so, but when she pulled out her sewing kit and got to work pinning the hem it was clear she was an experienced seamstress on top of everything else.)

"Greta," I said as she made her final checks and adjustments, "I have to say I'm surprised you owned a dress like this. I can't see you in something so…poofy."

She laughed. "Ah, yes. I do not believe I ever wore this one. My sixth husband? Perhaps my seventh? I can never remember. Dominic. He bought it for me." She took a sip of her champagne as she walked around Jamie looking for any last-minute adjustments to make. "That is when I realized that we were not as well matched as I had first thought."

She shrugged slightly. "He was a magnificent man, but not for me. And I, clearly, was not for him. But now we have Jamie's dress for her wedding, so it all works out eventually, no?"

"So it does."

"Would you like to try anything on, Maggie?"

I laughed. "Jamie tried that with me at one point. It

turns out that you women are a lot more slender than I am. But thank you for the offer."

"Wait. I have not always been slender. And I have a dress that I think is perfect for you. One moment." She pushed a button to rotate the dresses on one of the other walls where all the blue and green shaded dresses were and then pulled out a dress and turned to show it to me.

It was stunning. A gorgeous sapphire blue that had a fitted V-neck bodice with no sleeves and then a multi-layered skirt that flared out from the hips but not so much that it felt princessy.

"It's…Wow, Greta. *That* is definitely my kind of dress. But…"

"Try it on. You may be surprised."

"I don't know…" It was gorgeous, but if it fit Greta it would probably not even fit over my head. Maybe I could wear it on one thigh.

"Just try it. You will not show us if it does not fit."

"Okay." I gingerly took the dress and disappeared behind the dressing screen. I really wanted it to fit, but I wasn't holding my breath. I figured I'd step into it, just in case. As I pulled it up to my hips I clenched my teeth, waiting for that moment when it would stick and go no farther, but it slid right on up.

Turns out it fit. Perfectly. Like it was made for me. I almost ran to the three-way mirror, turning in half-circles so I could watch the way the skirt flared out from my hips.

Greta clapped her hands together in pleasure. "I knew this dress was for you. You must keep it."

"I can't, Greta. I have nowhere to wear it." I already had a bridesmaid's dress for Jamie's wedding and since I ran around barefoot in pajamas most days it would be absolutely wasted on me.

"You will find something."

"Then let me pay you for it."

"Nonsense. We are friends, no? And you see how many dresses I have. It no longer fits me. But it fits you. You will take it."

I wanted to. Desperately. "But…"

"This will be your something blue for your own wedding. We all know you are not a woman in white."

I laughed. "Nice thought. But I am not getting married anytime soon. Like, seriously, not for a good decade."

Greta chuckled. "Ah, Maggie. You are much too serious about this relationship and wedding thing. You marry a man, it doesn't work, life is not over. You move on."

"I am not going through that more than once. Honestly, love you Jamie, happy for you, think it's great you're having this big wedding, but my ideal wedding is on the side of a frickin' mountain with the man I love and no one else around. Just us exchanging our vows. And a dress like this? Does not belong in that picture."

Greta nodded. "My third wedding was like that. We were married in an Italian vineyard, just us and the officiant. But there is no reason you cannot wear a beautiful dress for this mountainside wedding is there?"

I shook my head and went to change out of the dress even though I really didn't want to. I handed it back to her. "I appreciate the offer, Greta. It is truly a beautiful dress. But I…I just can't."

The way she pursed her lips, I knew this battle wasn't

over, but she didn't say anything else so I decided I'd call it a temporary victory and get out of there before it became a rout.

CHAPTER 19

Further wedding plans or investigation had to go on hold at that point because it was Christmas Eve and pretty much no one was available anywhere for any sort of calls or planning. (One more strike against the good ol' New Year's Eve wedding idea.)

But that was okay.

We were in a pretty good place. We had the church and pastor, we had a place for the reception, we had a caterer, we had a wedding dress, and my grandpa was doing something for the "floral" decorations. We also had enough guests to make it work and Jamie seemed on top of the cupcakes and party favors.

I did swear both Jamie and Greta to secrecy about the new reception location, though. I was just paranoid enough about the whole thing that I didn't want anyone to know we'd found somewhere until the last possible moment.

I figured I'd see if I could find some of those chartered party buses to ferry everyone from the hotel up to Greta's so that (a) no one would try driving that windy road with alcohol in their system and (b) I wouldn't have to reveal the reception location to anyone other than

Jean-Philippe, his crew, and the decorators until the actual reception.

Which reminded me I needed to sort the booze issue. That was easier at least. Since we were now using a private home for the reception I could send Matt or Jack to a liquor store with a list of what to buy.

I figured I might even send one of them down to Denver for that since there were a couple of very large liquor stores down there that would have everything we could possibly want. Tipsy's and Applewood were both good choices. Except for the local beer I wanted. That I'd get straight from the brewery.

But for the time being I had to put that all aside and prepare for the holiday.

We'd all agreed not to exchange gifts. Matt and I were too new to being a couple for me to handle the pressure of what to get him for Christmas. And Grandpa and Lesley had spent their money on their trip to Vegas. So Matt, Jack, Trish, and Sam were doing Christmas morning at the trailer so Sam could get his gifts, and then they were going to come to our house for a Christmas lunch. Jamie, Mason, Lesley, Greta, Evan, and Abe were also coming over.

Which meant I had to make sure the house was properly decorated and that there was a good spread of food for twelve people. Fortunately we'd ordered in a baked ham and were serving it cold with bread and cheese and other sandwich-like accompaniments, which meant all I had to do was prepare a veggie tray, onion dip, deviled eggs, and dessert.

Onion dip is easy enough. You just dump and stir.

But deviled eggs…

If they weren't a family tradition and didn't taste so darned good I'd probably never make them again. But there's something about that tangy yolky yumminess that goes perfectly with a good ham. So I boiled the eggs and peeled the eggs and cut the eggs and scooped the eggs and made up the stuffing and stuffed the eggs and finished it all off with a dash of paprika.

I'd made two dozen eggs' worth, which I hoped would be enough.

I like to experiment with at least one dish each holiday to keep things fresh, but deviled eggs you do not mess with. You do not put tuna in them. (Gag.) You do not put relish in them. You do not add pickles. Or lobster. Or any of the other insane, crazy things people try to put in there.

Deviled eggs are sacrosanct. You only use eggs, mustard, mayo (or Miracle Whip), and vinegar. And just enough paprika to make them look somewhat enticing. (I once used too much paprika. It was not a good thing.)

Since I couldn't experiment with the eggs, I chose to experiment with dessert instead.

And because my experiments sometimes misfire badly, I made three desserts instead of just one. All were dips of one sort or another made with variations on whipped cream, pudding, or cream cheese combined with flavors like eggnog, pumpkin, or peppermint chocolate.

I have to say…Not bad. Light and fluffy for the most part except for my failure when I tried to combine two different ways to do things and the peppermint chocolate one turned into sludge. But the eggnog one was tasty. As was the pumpkin one. Especially with ginger snaps.

They were certainly easy to make, which is always appreciated when trying to accommodate a wide range of guests for the first time ever.

🐾 🐾 🐾

I had planned on spending the end of Christmas Eve with Matt, curled up in front of a nice fire like the couple we were, but with my grandpa banished from Lesley's because of the invasion of the grandkids, that didn't happen. Instead Matt, my grandpa, and I stayed up late drinking hot cocoa with real marshmallows in it and playing Scrabble.

I was actually getting better at it. I could almost hold my own against those two. I had to be careful not to make up words, which is a bad habit of mine, or to use slang that wasn't going to be in the official Scrabble dictionary, but I'd adopted a hybrid style that combined my grandpa's love of playing multiple words at once with Matt's style of trying to play seven-letter words on triple-scores.

I still lost. But only by four points. Not bad. Not bad at all.

I have to say, it was a good night. A really good one.

And certainly better than the year before when I'd gone out for drinks to a bar with a friend of mine. There's a sad desperation to people who hang out at bars on Christmas Eve. (Not that that's wrong if you're one of those people. Heck, I was one of those people the year before, wasn't I? But that one experience did make me think that next time around I'd just stay at home alone and drink. Because being in public and drinking alone on Christmas Eve? It's just…yeah.)

Anyway. Good Christmas Eve. All prepared for Christmas Day.

CHAPTER 20

I'd like to say I slept in on Christmas Day. But who am I kidding, I had Fancy. And Fancy thought being up at the crack of dawn—or before it at that time of year—was the best possible idea in the world.

Also, it had snowed overnight. A lot. There was a solid foot of fresh powder in the backyard.

Which meant I started the day bundled up to my eyeballs shoveling Fancy a path through the backyard. I even made her two spaces where she could lie down.

And then, because she would not stop crying at me, we went for a walk. You do not understand how hard it is to walk through a foot of snow until you do so with a large black dog dragging you along at a very fast clip.

I figured that was my work out for the week.

When I returned my grandpa was seated at the kitchen table with his crossword puzzle, a steaming cup of coffee in his hand. I grabbed a Coke and joined him.

"You want me to make breakfast?" I asked.

"Maybe later. I should get out there and shovel the driveway." He quirked one eyebrow at me.

"Oh. The driveway. Right. And the sidewalk leading

up to the house that all the guests are going to need to use..." It hadn't even occurred to me to clear those. I was just thinking of Fancy when I shoveled the backyard. "I can do those after breakfast."

"Do you know how to run a snow blower?"

"No. But you could teach me. Or I can just do it by hand."

He shook his head. "I'll do it."

I would've argued further, but I knew there was no point. As old as he was and as much as I thought I was there to take care of him there were certain tasks that in his mind were "men's tasks". Mowing the lawn and shoveling the driveway were two of them.

"Okay, fine. But after breakfast."

"Deal."

I quickly shot a text to Matt asking if he thought he could make it over to clear the driveway and sidewalk before my grandpa and I were done with breakfast. He texted back that he was already on his way and almost there. I felt that weird glowy sappiness that comes with being in love. He was such a good man.

I took my time preparing fried potatoes and a breakfast frittata with goat cheese, spinach, bacon, and sun-dried tomatoes. My grandpa gave the meal a side-eye as I was putting it together because he's never been one for "fancy" ingredients like that, but I knew he'd like it. At least I wasn't trying to make hand-squeezed orange juice or something. I figured that was one part of the meal that was perfectly fine coming out of the carton, thank you very much.

Matt timed it perfectly. He finished plowing the driveway clear with his truck just as I pulled the frittata out of the oven. I went to the window and waved him inside as I set a third place at the kitchen table for him.

"Maggie," my grandpa growled as he finally looked out the window and saw what Matt had done. "I am perfectly capable of shoveling my own driveway."

I kissed him on the cheek. "I know you are, Grandpa. But Matt was already on his way over when I texted him. Let him help. Please?"

He grumbled, but when Matt came inside, he just shook his hand and thanked him. Matt gave the perfect answer. "I knew you could clear it yourself, Mr. Carver, but I wanted to try that new slow plow I got and your driveway is perfect for it. Plus, I needed to get out of that trailer. Sam has been up since five playing with some new truck Jack got him that has lots of bright lights and makes really loud noises."

"He isn't going to bring that here, is he?"

"No, sir. I will make sure of it."

"Okay then. Let's eat this thing Maggie made for us." He hesitated about sitting at the kitchen table with company, but I just ignored him and sat down. It wasn't dinner. It was breakfast.

"It's good to expand your horizons every once in a while, Grandpa," I said as I served us each up a portion of the frittata.

"So you say." He poked at the food on his plate with a frown, but he stopped grumbling after the first bite, like I knew he would.

CHAPTER 21

After breakfast I dragged out the trio of packages I'd hid in my room.

"What's that?" my grandpa barked. "We said we weren't doing presents this year."

Matt nodded his agreement.

"And we're not. These are for Fancy."

"You bought your dog three Christmas presents? When she already has more toys than can fit in her toy bin and you make her so many different types of treats it's a miracle she doesn't have to be rolled through this house?"

Even my grandpa's orneriness wasn't going to get in the way of my enjoying the holiday and spoiling my dog. "Yes. Yes, I did."

I went to the back door where I could see Fancy lying in one of her little dug out spots in the yard, enjoying the morning. "Come on, Fancy," I called.

She looked at me and then looked away. There was a squirrel in a tree. Far more interesting than me and whatever I wanted her for.

"Fancy. Treat."

That got her attention. She slowly lumbered her way to her feet and followed me inside, but not all the way to the living room. She stopped in the kitchen and stared expectantly at the spot where I stored the salmon snaps.

I knew I could either try to push and drag her unsuccessfully into the living room or I could just give in and lure her there with a handful of treats, so I grabbed a handful and held it in front of her nose and then started walking towards the living room.

She followed along after me, leaving a trail of slobber in her wake.

"Maggie…"

"I'll wipe it up. Don't worry." I threw the treats in a pile on the carpet and reached for the first bag while Fancy ate up every last crumb and then started licking around to make sure she hadn't missed anything.

"Here, Fancy. Look." I handed her the toy first. It was a hedgehog with a Santa hat that made grunting noises. I made it grunt and she lunged for it, taking it delicately between her paws and starting to gum it to death.

She's not one of those dogs that destroys her toys. No torn pieces and stuffing everywhere. She's more like a stream relentlessly wearing away at a canyon wall. You have to keep an eye on things because what looks fine one moment will suddenly turn into a giant hole along a seam somewhere the next. But that's really why she has so many toys. Because I can usually sew those little holes back up and the toy will last another year, two, or more.

My grandpa crossed his arms as he watched her. "That seems like more than enough for her. What else did you get?"

I pulled out a collar with jingle bells on it.

"Maggie May…"

"What? It'll be fun. And she only has to wear it today."

"What a colossal waste of…"

"Grandpa. It's fun."

He grumbled at me. "In my day, dogs stayed outside. They didn't have beds. They didn't have toys. They didn't go to daycare."

"And they weren't good companions, were they? But Fancy is. She's the best. And you agree, I know you do. You may pretend not to like her, but you enjoy it just as much as I do when she curls up on the couch next to you at night to watch a little TV."

"I didn't say she can't be inside. But spending your hard-earned money on…"

"On a family member. Who always appreciates what I give her." I fastened the collar around Fancy's neck, but she was still absorbed in chewing on her new toy.

That stopped as soon as I opened the last bag. One of her favorite treats which I rarely gave her anymore since I made my own treats now. The toy was immediately forgotten as her eyes fixed on my hands. She sat at attention.

I gave her a kiss on the nose. "Good girl, Fancy. Here you go." She took the treat and ran out of the room, headed for the backyard. I just smiled. I loved that dog. More than anything.

Well, Matt was running a close second. And I loved my grandpa. But Fancy still took first place. And probably always would. It's easier with dogs. No real uncertainty or challenge. They just love so it's easy to love them back.

🐾 🐾 🐾

The rest of the day went well. It was great to have so many people I knew and liked gathered together to share food and company. I know the holidays have different meanings for different people, but for me that's always what Christmas and Thanksgiving have been about: friendship, family, and good food.

We were there for hours, eating, talking, and laughing. It was wonderful. And made me so glad to be where I was with the people I loved.

But the next day it was finally time to find my culprit.

CHAPTER 22

I called Ed—Mr. Valentine's Day Breakup—first since he was local and definitely had a reason to not want to see Jamie live happily ever after.

He answered on the first ring. He sounded a bit like Eeyore on the phone, all depression and slooow talking. "Hello."

"Ed, it's Maggie Carver. How are you?" I added extra cheer to my voice to counteract his mind-numbing effect.

"Hi Maggie. I'm fine. You?"

"Good. Good. So, are you excited about Jamie's wedding? I saw you're coming."

"Jamie's wedding? Oh, yeah. When is that?"

"New Year's. You RSVP'd."

"Did I?" He thought for a long moment. A looong moment. "Are you sure? It might've been my mom. She thinks I should get out of the house more. Mooom!"

I heard his mother shout back in the background and they proceeded to have a conversation about how, yes, his mother had RSVP'd for him because there'd be a lot of pretty single girls at a wedding and maybe he could meet one and move out of her house for once and all.

As soon as he got back on the phone, I made my excuses and hung up. Glad Jamie dodged that bullet. I would've had to stop being friends with her if she'd stayed with him because three minutes in that man's company and I wanted to start pinching myself to stay awake.

But he was off the list. Can't sabotage a wedding you don't even know about.

Brad, Mr. Failed Proposal, was next. That was a fast call. He was on his honeymoon in Hawaii with some cocktail waitress he'd met in Tahoe two weeks before. At least someone had said yes to him. I congratulated him and quickly got off the phone.

I was about to make my next call when the phone rang. It was the pastor.

"Pastor Nelson. How are you? How was your holiday?"

"It was delightful, Maggie, thank you. Although, this morning was not."

I sat up straighter, knowing whatever it was I did not want to hear it. "What happened?"

"I'm not exactly sure. It seems the furnace at the church stopped working sometime yesterday, although it looks perfectly fine. But the heat was off probably all day yesterday and until I arrived today."

I bit my lip, already knowing where this was going. "Is the church okay?"

"No. A pipe burst in the basement. The one that leads to the first-floor bathrooms."

When I didn't say anything he added. "You know how cold it got last night, Maggie. None of the bathrooms have running water."

I took a deep breath. I did know how cold it had gotten. And I knew that whoever I was dealing with was the type of horrible, reprehensible person who'd damage a church to get their way.

What kind of person does that? I'm not the most religious of souls, but places of worship are supposed to be safe zones. People can be murdering one another in the streets, but never in a church. Or a mosque. Or a synagogue. Or what-have-you. You do not do that.

I glanced out my window at the sky wondering if I was going to see a bolt of lightning sometime soon. Because someone out there needed to be struck down.

"Pastor, I hate to say this, but I think you need to call Matt."

"Matt? Which Matt?"

"Matt Barnes. The police officer."

"Why?"

Bless his soul. The pastor didn't have the type of belief in other people that could see what must've happened. I had to be the one to burst that illusion. "Because I suspect that this was done by someone, it didn't just happen. Someone probably entered the church and turned off the heat after you left for the holiday."

"Why would someone do that?"

I filled him in on what had been happening with Jamie's wedding.

"But no one would do that to the church. Would they?"

"I'd like to say no, but well…Sadly I think that someone did."

There was a long moment of silence on the other end of the line.

"I'm sorry, Pastor. We'll find who did this. And Matt will punish them. I promise you."

"It's not punishment I'm after, Maggie. I believe in turning the other cheek. But I've always felt like this was a good community. It's sad to see something like this happen. I can't think of a single parishioner who would do something like this. And there wasn't anyone at Christmas Eve service that I didn't recognize."

"I don't know what to tell you, Pastor. It only takes one bad apple. And sometimes they aren't that easy to see."

He sighed. "I don't know when we'll get this fixed, Maggie. Not before the wedding day, that's for sure. I don't even know how we're going to pay for the repairs to be honest. We're not a rich church. And neither is our congregation."

I thought about Mason Maxwell and his unlimited wedding budget. And Lucas Dean and the fact that he owed me whether he thought he did or not.

"It'll be fixed in time for the wedding, Pastor, don't you worry about that. And don't worry about the cost either."

"But how?"

"A combination of someone who is in love and has a seemingly bottomless bank account and someone who owes me enough that they'll do what I tell them to."

"Maggie, please don't intimidate anyone on our behalf."

I laughed. "Don't worry, Pastor. I won't." I was going to do it on Jamie's behalf. "Stay reachable, please. I'll try to have someone there today to fix it."

"Thank you, Maggie. God bless you."

"My pleasure, Pastor."

I hung up and called Mason.

"Mason Maxwell."

"Hey, Mason. Just so you know, your wedding bill now includes some plumbing work at the church. So when Lucas Dean bills you for it, please pay."

"What happened?" he snapped.

"Burst pipe. No working bathrooms. I suspect our saboteur is behind it."

"Who is doing this?"

"You haven't thought of anyone else?"

"No. I didn't even really think Elaine was capable of it. And Jamie said the list you came up with had no one on it she'd think was capable."

"Well, Jamie's a kind person. She doesn't see the bad in people."

"True enough. But this is…Personal. Trying to ruin a wedding. And who sabotages a church?"

"Exactly. That's a new level of low that most wouldn't stoop to. Well, you think of anyone, let me know. Right now, I have to go make an unpleasant call or two. Give Jamie my love."

"Will do."

I hung up and glared at the phone. I knew I needed to call Luke. He was the best contractor in the county and the only one I'd be able to browbeat into working between Boxing Day and New Year's. But…Ugh. The man was a slug. And I'd thought that before the Katie situation.

I walked to the fridge to grab another Coke, but realized it would be my fourth of the day which was extreme, even for me.

Instead I grabbed a beer. It was only one in the afternoon, but really, did it matter?

CHAPTER 23

I'd just sat down at my command center in the dining room when my grandpa walked through. "Maggie, what are you doing?"

"What? What's wrong?"

He glanced at his watch. "It's one o'clock in the afternoon."

"I know."

"You are still in your pajamas."

"They're comfortable." (I'd changed back into them after walking Fancy. No point in wearing my sweats, which were a little snug around the waist when I could wear my PJs instead.)

"And you're drinking a beer."

"I didn't want to have another Coke."

He glared at me, hands planted on his hips. "Have you heard of water?"

I shrugged a shoulder and took a sip of my beer. "I don't drink water."

"Or orange juice?"

"That's a breakfast drink."

"Kool-Aid?"

"That's as bad as having a Coke, sugar-wise. And don't you even suggest I have a glass of milk. It was Coke or beer. I chose beer."

He stepped closer. "I will repeat that it is one in the afternoon."

"Not like I'm going to have another one. I mean, if I'd had this beer with dinner you wouldn't even mention it. But because I have my one beer of the day before five o'clock it's somehow taboo? Or wrong? That's just silly."

"What are you going to have with dinner then?"

"I don't know. Maybe I'll have…water." I knew I wouldn't. Not that I was planning on having another beer. Probably another Coke, although that was less than ideal, too.

He crossed his arms. "Fine. You can have a beer at whatever time of day you want as long as it's the only one of the day."

"Yes, sir. Thank you, Dad."

He took another step closer. My grandpa is not a man you cross.

"Sorry," I said before he could light into me about my attitude. "I'm just a little stressed is all, trying to find whoever did this to Jamie. And now someone has sabotaged the church, too."

"That's no excuse, Maggie May, for living like a slob. You can have a beer, one beer, whenever you want to. But for crying out loud, put on some real clothes. No pajamas after breakfast."

I would've traded the afternoon beer for pajamas if there'd been a choice, but there clearly wasn't.

"Why?" I asked.

"It's a mindset thing, Maggie May. You wear pajamas

all day you turn into a sloth. You just sit around and do nothing."

I gestured to the table which was full of papers. "Does this look like nothing to you? I was just about to make a very important phone call."

"Well, put on real clothes before you do. My house, my rules."

I wanted to argue, but the fact was, it was his house. So it was his rules. But I did not enjoy the fact that I suddenly felt like a twelve-year-old kid again. I stomped off to my room to change, which meant I was not in a good mood when I finally called Lucas Dean.

"Ho, ho, ho, Merry Christmas, beautiful," he said as soon as he answered. "What? No FaceTime?"

"Shut up, Luke."

"Maggie, always such a sweetheart. You should come over. Share a cup of cheer. Although I hear you're off the market these days."

"I am. Not that I was ever on the market for you, Luke. I could see through your crap from day one, thank you very much."

"Ah, Maggie. Always such a stick in the mud. It'll be interesting to see if Matt can warm you up."

I started to count to five. I needed his help and lashing out at him for being a jerk wasn't going to get me what I wanted.

Before I hit four he asked, "Why are you calling?"

"I actually have a job for you."

"It's the holiday. I'm not working until the new year."

"This is for Jamie. You owe her, Luke."

"What do I owe her for?"

"For playing her all those years. For charming her

while messing around with anyone else you could get your hands on."

He chuckled. "Jamie never seemed to mind."

"Luke. You need to do this. For Jamie."

"If Jamie wants my help, I'm happy to give it. Tell her to call me."

"Look, Luke. I do not have time for this. I am offering you paid work. And you are going to take it."

"I am, am I?" I could see his cocky smile in my mind and wanted to smack it right off his face, but instead I forced myself to take a deep breath and step back.

"This *is* for Jamie, okay? And she's not calling you because I don't want her to know about it." I briefly told him what had happened so far and about what had happened at the church. "So, see, we need you. You are the only person I know who can pull off that kind of miracle in the time we have. And, good news, Mason's paying for it. So you get a little added bonus there. A client who will pay more than full price."

He didn't answer right away.

"Luke? Tell me you'll do this. Please?"

"Alright. For Jamie. But I'm charging double time and expenses."

"Fine."

"You have any idea who's doing this?"

"No. Must be someone local, though. I just don't know who it could be. Jamie isn't one to make enemies. People like her. And Mason, I can't see him doing anything extreme enough to make an enemy that would do this. You have any ideas?"

"I assume Georgia's already on your list? Scariest woman I've ever met."

"Yeah, she's there. And my next stop. Anyone else?"

"Can't think of anyone, but if I do…I'll call."

"Alright, thanks." I gave him the pastor's number and hung up.

Only then did I cringe, realizing I'd just thanked Lucas Dean of all people. And that I'd made him part of the reason Jamie's wedding was going to be a success. Ugh.

CHAPTER 24

I called Caroline—Ms. Frenemies—next since there was a chance she was already in the area for the holiday.

"Hey Caroline," I said with my fake friendly smile on as she answered her phone. "How are you?"

"I'm so great. I just got a major promotion at work and my Italian fiancé and I ran away to the Bahamas for the holiday to celebrate. We are currently beachside sipping Mai Tais." Arrogance just dripped off of her. Made me want to gag.

My only consolation was that her fiancé was probably half-bald and significantly overweight and the promotion she'd received was not as major as she'd want me to believe.

"So you aren't going to make it to Jamie's wedding then?" I asked.

"Right. That. Isn't it going to be in like a cabin or something?"

"No. Why would you think that?"

"Well, I mean that's about all there is in the valley, isn't it? It's not like it's Aspen or Vail. When I heard she'd quit her job to move *home*, I was just appalled."

"There's actually a very nice resort here."

"That's not a resort, that's a convention center."

"It has a very nice ballroom."

"Yeah. Right. So looking forward to it." The insincerity practically oozed through the phone. "Wouldn't miss it for the world. I mean she is one of my dearest friends, after all. Sisters forever, right? Maybe I can give a toast."

"Yeah, no."

"Why not? I'm one of her bridesmaids."

I made up a lie. "They're limiting toasts to close family. So sorry."

"Oh, well, whatever. What are you doing these days, Maggie? Are you going to hook up with Jean-Philippe, again? It's like a wedding tradition for you, isn't it?"

I took a deep breath and reminded myself that I was doing this for Jamie.

"Actually, Caroline, I have a boyfriend."

"Really? Who?"

"Matt Barnes."

"Isn't he a cop now? Ew. Dating down are you?"

If that woman had been there in person in that moment she may not have survived to the wedding.

"I don't think so. He's good to me. He's funny, he's intelligent. And he's damned good-looking."

(Sorry for the cussing, but I was annoyed.)

"Yeah, but he's a cop. Isn't that, like blue collar? I mean, why'd you get a college degree for that?"

I cleared my throat to prevent myself from saying all the things I wanted to say to her uppity little…self. "I didn't go to college to get my M-R-S degree, thanks. I've got that side of things handled on my own so I can just look for a good man who'll treat me right. Which is what

Matt is. Look I gotta go. Buh-bye." I hung up.

That…. So many things I wanted to call her but I won't for politeness sake. I'm sure you can think of a few on your own.

How dare she judge Matt for, heaven forbid, choosing a career that helps people. A career that probably takes more interpersonal savvy and guts than ninety percent of people in this world even have. Not to mention the level of self-control and patience required.

What was her deal?

I was sure she hadn't sabotaged Jamie's wedding, but I decided to leave her on my list just for spite. Maybe if by the day of the wedding I hadn't yet found the culprit I could convince Jamie to let me ban her from the wedding just in case.

Or I could ask Matt to ask a friend to set a nice little speed trap for her. Or stage a quick little purse search. I'm sure they'd find something interesting enough to put her in a jail cell for the night.

(Not that he would, but I could ask. And just thinking it was possible based on his job that she'd mocked so nastily made me feel better.)

I was still wound-up when I called Bethany—Ms. Dumpster Fire—who I figured was capable of sabotaging the wedding just for kicks. But it turned out she'd taken a baseball bat to her ex-boyfriend's car and was doing a little time in jail already.

And because she'd mouthed off to the prison guards she'd lost her internet and phone privileges for a month, including the days when those emails had been sent.

That meant it was time to confront good old Georgia, Katie's mom. Not something I was looking forward to.

I'd managed to avoid her since the whole Jack Dunner affair, but seems my luck had run out. Good news: at least I was already wearing real pants, so I wouldn't have to change to go see her.

CHAPTER 25

I tracked Georgia down at the Buckin' Bronc, a dive of a restaurant/bar in Masonville that she seemed to live at. She was perched on a bar stool with some overweight, overdrunk hulk of a man at her side.

"Georgia, have a minute?" I asked, trying not to stare at how bad she looked.

She was my age, for cryin' out loud. But the years had not been kind. If I had to guess, there was probably some meth use involved given the sunken cheeks and bad teeth. What I was seeing was more damage than just booze and cigarettes could do.

She probably wasn't my culprit. The email part was too sneaky. But I had to see it through.

She sneered at me. "Why should I talk to you? You ruined my life. Ruined my baby's life. She had it good until you came along."

I thought about pointing out that when she'd had a kid at fifteen she'd kinda started down that road on her own and that Lucas Dean had started her daughter down the bad road, not me, but that just seemed mean.

(And, hey, look, if you yourself had a kid at fifteen and

your life has turned out all sunshine and roses, good for you. Congratulations. Don't read anything into what I just said, okay. I'm snarky sometimes. Especially when forced to confront a woman who could probably take me down with her pinky finger while holding a drink in her other hand.)

Rather than start a fight I knew I couldn't win, I put twenty bucks on the counter. "Because you want some easy money? And a free beer?" I gestured to the bartender.

Georgia eyed the money. I knew she wanted to refuse it and tell me she wasn't going to take money from the likes of me. But money is money and people with principles and empty bank accounts starve. So she took the twenty and shoved it in her bra.

Classy.

I hoped she'd still help, because no way was I going to get that money back, nor would I want it back.

"Where's the beer?" she asked.

The barkeep—an older man who looked like he could take anyone in the place and had the scars on his knuckles to prove it—plopped plastic cups with something resembling beer in front of us and held up two fingers. I handed him a five.

Now I knew why Georgia liked the place so much. Cheap beer.

"Cheers." I took a sip.

Good thing about cheap beer is it's just tasteless whereas cheap alcohol will burn its way right through your esophagus.

"Yeah, for you, maybe. With your family and friends to spend the holiday with. I'm all alone because…"

I cut her off. "Look. Can we get into that some other time? Right now I'm trying to figure out who's out there sabotaging Jamie's wedding. Was it you?"

She shook her head. "Don't know a thing about it."

"You knew she was getting married, though?"

She shrugged. "You hear things."

I couldn't believe that this sad, decrepit woman had once been one of Jamie's good friends. (In first grade, but still.)

"You don't blame her for Katie and all, do you?"

She inhaled snot up her nose and I tried not to flinch at the sound of it. "Nah. I blame you. You ever get married and something goes wrong there, *that* might be me. Although I'm more likely to let the air out of your tires. But Jamie and I are good. She gave Katie a chance. Tried to look out for her."

Note to self: check tires every time you get into the van because some people are horrible human beings.

"Okay. Thanks." I stood up, but then paused. "You hear anything, will you let me know? There's probably another twenty in it for you."

"Make it fifty."

I thought about bargaining her down, but I'd rather have the information than the money. "Fifty. But only if it's legit."

She grabbed my beer and downed it before I could. "Deal."

I left. One more down. But I was out of suspects and no closer to figuring out who was sabotaging the wedding. I only had four days left and I was at a dead end.

CHAPTER 26

The next morning Elaine called me and asked if I was up for taking Fancy for a walk with her and Zela. It was still colder out than I'd like but I agreed to meet her in Masonville at noon. She said the high school football field was fenced off and a great impromptu dog park when kids weren't in school.

And she was right. It was perfect. The high school is on a hill above the main road so it has this amazing view in all directions. I took a moment to just stand there and absorb the beauty of those mountains and the crisp blue sky. I don't know what it is, I'm sure some scientist could tell me, but the best blue skies always seem to be when it's a little bit too cold out. Or maybe that's just me.

Elaine and Zela joined us and the two dogs immediately hit it off, all wagging tails and excitement.

I let Fancy off leash and she went tearing through the snow. Zela chased after, making up for her lack of size with an enthusiasm that had her staying hot on Fancy's heels.

"Look at 'em go," I laughed.

"It's so good for Zela to have another dog to run around with." Elaine smiled shyly. "Thank you for meeting us."

"Of course. It's good for Fancy, too. When the barkery was open Fancy had Lulu, that's Jamie's dog, and Hans, that's Greta's dog, to play with. But since it closed a couple months ago I know she's been missing this."

I shivered and stuck my hands in my pockets. I was wearing gloves and an ear warmer, but I was still cold. "Do you know any other dog owners?" I asked.

She shrugged. "Sort of. I know people who own dogs. But not enough to get together with. It'd be weird, wouldn't it, to call someone up and ask for a doggie play date? I mean, other than you, because you offered first." She blushed so much her cheeks turned bright red.

"Yeah, I'm with you on that. I'm not very good at approaching strangers myself. That's what makes having a friend like Jamie so helpful. She'll talk to anyone and drags me right along with her."

"Margaret's kind of like that for me."

I figured anyone who insisted on having their best friend call them Margaret was maybe not so warm and fuzzy, but I let it go.

"Does she have a dog?"

"No." Elaine laughed. "She's not the dog type. I mean some people just don't have dogs, but Margaret is…She could never do the dog hair or the dirt or having to feed them regularly."

I swallowed my thoughts on that one, too. "Well, I do have a dog. And Jamie does. And once all the wedding craziness is over maybe Jamie and Lulu can join us, too, and we'll make this a regular thing. What do you think?"

Elaine bit her lip.

"What?"

"I don't…I mean, Jamie…"

"Because she's marrying Mason? Trust me, she won't find it awkward to be friends with you, Knowing Jamie she's going to make an extra effort to be your friend now that she knows you and Mason have a history."

She crossed her arms tight across her chest. "Is that what people call it these days? A history? Being engaged is having a history?"

I studied her. "Did it upset you when he broke it off?"

"It didn't surprise me. Mason's…Mason. And I'm…me."

"He saw enough in you to ask you to marry him in the first place." I had to duck out of the way as Fancy came barreling right at me, Zela hot on her heels.

"I guess." Elaine kicked at a pile of snow. "I knew I was never good enough for him. But I figured, if he wanted to marry me I'd be a fool to say no."

I grabbed her by the shoulders and looked her in the eyes. "Elaine, I don't know you well. But I've come to know Mason. And he's not a man who'd ask just any woman to marry him. He saw something in you. Something worthy."

"Margaret said he asked because he needed someone who'd keep the books and keep his grandma from pestering him. And that I was perfect for that. I could blend into the background."

"You know, I have to say this Margaret woman sounds like a real…" (I used a word I won't repeat here.)

"No. It's not like that. She's…She knows me. We've been friends since we were babies. She was just telling me the truth so I wouldn't get my expectations up and want more from Mason than I was going to get."

A little hard to argue that he'd cared more for her than he'd appeared to since he'd dumped her the minute he saw Jamie. But that didn't sound like the kind of best friend I'd want to have. There's the type of friend who tells it to you straight (which I like to think I am) and then there's someone who nastily points out every single flaw or imperfection you have to keep you down (which is what Margaret sounded like to me).

One can be useful, one needs to be removed from your life as soon as humanly possible. But when someone has spent most of their life brainwashed by that kind of Negative Nelly there's no point in coming at things head-on.

"Fair enough. If she kept you from feeling broken-hearted when things ended with Mason, then I guess it worked. But I still think it would be good to be friends with Jamie. Trust me. You'll like her. I'll introduce you to Greta, too."

"Who's Greta?"

"Oh, she was all over the papers a while back for her husband's death. Remember the body they found behind the barkery?"

"She's your friend?"

"She is. And she's a good friend to have. She stepped in when Jamie's wedding dress was ruined. She's a bit of a crazy woman, but I don't know what we would've done without her."

"What happened to Jamie's dress?"

"It was about ten sizes too big. We didn't know anyone who could fix it in time because there was all this custom beading, so Greta found her a different dress to wear."

"Oh."

"What?" I looked at her, wondering if she somehow had a line on my culprit.

"Well, um, I could've probably fixed it for her. I…" She bit her lip. "Don't tell anyone, alright?"

"Tell them what?"

"You know the custom couture hand-beaded wedding dress Margaret supposedly ordered from some Paris designer?"

"Yeah."

"I'm actually the one making it for her."

"Really?"

"Oh, yeah. No one will know the difference."

I raised an eyebrow at that.

"No, really. I…" She blushed. "I'm not good at many things, but I can sew. Really really well."

"But how is she going to use the name of some Paris designer and not get caught?"

"I based it on the woman's designs. When I'm done no one will be able to tell the difference."

"Wow. Well, congratulations on being so good at what you do that you could pull that off. But wouldn't it be better for you if everyone knew it was your work?"

She looked at the ground. "Yeah. But Margaret really wanted to be in the paper and she knew stupid Peter Nielsen wouldn't come to her wedding unless it was newsworthy."

(Peter Nielsen was the sole reporter for *The Baker Valley Gazette*, the only paper in the valley.)

"So she figured a New York chef, a six-foot tall ice sculpture, a Paris couture gown, and a pair of horses would be newsworthy enough to attract him?"

She nodded. "And she was right."

"Are the horses going to really be ponies? Is the chef really from Albuquerque?"

Elaine's eyes filled with tears. "That's not funny."

"I'm sorry, Elaine. I was just teasing. But her, not you."

"I'm getting cold, I better go. Come on, Zela." She whistled Zela to her and left without another word.

I let her go, feeling bad for upsetting her. I hadn't meant anything by it. And, really, didn't she deserve to get the credit for making such an exquisite dress instead of having her hard work passed off as that of someone famous?

CHAPTER 27

The next day Greta called me. (I'd given up on ever playing in another solitaire tournament again I was getting so many calls about the wedding, but I had just sat down to try to sneak in one little game of FreeCell when the phone rang.)

"Hey, Greta, how's it going? All the preparations for the reception coming along?"

"Yes. The food has started to arrive. You should know better Maggie than to let a French chef have an unlimited budget and creative control."

"Why? What's going on?"

"Do you think Jamie and Mason's friends are ready for frog legs and fish eggs and raw beef?"

"Ummm…Hm. Depends on if they know that's what it is. I think they'll probably try anything if it's described in French. I mean pâté certainly sounds better than liver paste, right?"

"Maggie. This is not a joke. This is Jamie's wedding."

"I understand that, Greta. But we were in a bit of a bind. And Jean-Philippe agreed to bail us out on one simple condition—that he be allowed to set the menu.

He said he was an artiste and could not be limited."

"That should not have been allowed. You must stand firm with men like that. Give me his number. I will take care of this."

"Um, Greta, we really can't afford to lose our chef three days before the wedding."

"And you will not. I will explain to this man who his audience is and that he must adjust his expectations. No raw meat. That must not happen."

"Well, I can agree with you on that one. And if you think you can bring him around without him quitting in a huff, you are more than welcome to try."

"I will not try, I will succeed."

I gave her his phone number, silently wishing I could be a fly on the wall for that conversation.

"Anything else, Greta?"

"Perhaps. There was an expensive SUV that drove up to my house this morning, but when the security guard walked towards it, the person quickly drove away. He did not get a plate. He thought they must be tourists looking at the different houses in the area. I am not so sure."

"Why?"

"You have been here. People do not come to my house that are not trying to come to my house. And there is no reason for strangers from out of town to try to come here."

"But perhaps our saboteur got wind of all of the food and party items being delivered there and was trying to check it out?"

"Perhaps."

That was a frightening possibility.

"Greta, since when do you have a security guard?"

"Since I agreed to throw this wedding. I will not let anyone ruin this for Jamie. I have told the guards to shoot anyone who steps on this property without permission."

"Shoot them? Greta, you can't shoot them." That's all we needed. For Greta's house to be off-limits because it was a crime scene. (Again.)

She sighed. "So I was informed."

"Okay. Well, keep an eye out, will you? If that expensive SUV comes back and you can get a plate I'm sure I can convince Matt to run it for me."

"I will. Now I must go."

She hung up. She might be abrupt at times, but I was pretty sure Jamie and I were going to appreciate that efficiency of hers before this was all through.

CHAPTER 28

That night I worked my fingers to the bone helping my grandpa, Lesley, and Matt put together the decorations for the church.

My grandpa had managed to get his hands on a large assortment of fresh pine boughs, poinsettias, amaryllis, and paperwhites. It gave us a lot to work with, but it was all raw materials. Which meant we had to use twine and wire to turn them into something beautiful.

(And, yes, it would've been better if we could've waited until the night before the wedding to do it all, but there was this little thing called a rehearsal dinner that we were all going to have to attend, so we had soaked everything all day to hydrate it as well as we could and sprayed it with something meant to preserve it as much as possible and were going to store the finished products in the most ideal conditions we could. You work with what you have. And thank your lucky stars that your incredibly rich friend can snap her fingers and procure the type of refrigerators you see at floral boutiques and then have them delivered right to your door and set up in your garage in less than a day.)

Thankfully Lesley was far more artistically inclined than I am, because my results would've looked like a kindergarten project not a professional wedding display without her creative guidance.

And, surprisingly, Matt was amazing at building small wreaths from the pine boughs. I didn't think he'd have it in him, but he did. My grandpa, because of all the work he did with his miniatures, I already knew would be fantastic at it.

I was the problem child. But I managed.

It was actually a really fun night. I liked seeing how my grandpa and Lesley were together even if I was still freaked out by the fact that they were married now. Such a little thing, getting married. One day that if you skipped over it on a Facebook update you'd never even know had happened. But it changed everything. It made it all permanent and important.

I shuddered. How could people believe that that was such a normal progression? Shouldn't dedicating yourself to spending that much of your life with someone be this Herculean decision that was made only in the most extreme circumstances?

And yet people made these decisions all the time. Look at Greta.

Then again, that's kind of how I think of having kids, too. I mean, unless you screw it up, that is a lifelong commitment that doesn't come with the option of divorce. And yet some crazy percentage of kids are not planned. (I just looked it up, it's close to 50%. Think about that...)

But that's why I am what I am and other people are happily married with kids. Because it turns out that sometimes you can't think about things too much or else you'll never do them. You just have to jump on in there and let the hormones set the course. That's how the frickin' species keeps going.

Still.

I think about these things. A lot.

Too much, perhaps.

Perhaps.

Anyway. Fun night. Sore fingers. Beautiful decorations as a result.

CHAPTER 29

The next morning I helped Mason transport the hand-chosen selection of rare wines he wanted to serve at the reception over to Greta's and gave him an update on where we were so far.

"How much does one of those bottles of wine back there cost?" I asked him.

"Depends on the bottle. Anywhere from a couple hundred to a couple thousand."

"Have you met Jamie's sorority sisters? I mean, sure, a few have finely-tuned palates, but the rest? You could give them Two-Buck Chuck and they'd be fine."

He chuckled. "This is my wedding, Maggie. I'm not going to hold back the good wine just because a few people won't appreciate it."

"All I'm saying is if someone walks up to one of the wine-serving stations and asks for their wine by color that you should probably have a stock of some cheaper stuff to serve them. No point in giving someone who wants the 'red' a glass of a thousand-dollar wine."

"Who knows? It might convert them to an appreciation for fine wines."

I snorted. "Not likely. You know I actually went to a wine tasting once. They had Chardonnays. The whole wine tasting, all nine glasses or whatever it was, were Chardonnays."

"And?"

"And the more expensive the glass of wine was, the more quintessentially Chardonnay with its oakiness and butteriness, the less I liked it. It turns out the French Chardonnays were a complete waste where I was concerned."

"Well, Maggie, that's good to know. But maybe not everyone is like that."

"Maybe. I'm just sayin'…Don't go throwing good wine after beer taste buds."

"I'll keep that in mind."

🐾 🐾 🐾

I made sure everything else was looking good at Greta's and that there had been no more sign of the mystery luxury SUV—who it seemed maybe was just a lost tourist—before heading home to confirm the party buses for the reception and make sure that nothing else had slipped through the cracks.

All in all, we were on track. I still didn't know who the culprit was, so I knew there was always a chance of a last-minute mess, but I was feeling good about things. Optimistic.

Of course that was before Fancy and I headed down to Denver to pick up Jean-Philippe from the airport. (He'd insisted that I had to be the one to pick him up. Said he needed the time with me if he was going to be at his best.)

When Matt heard that, he wanted to come with me, but he couldn't because he had to work so he'd have the actual night of the wedding off. I also reminded him that Jean-Philippe was no temptation to me anymore, but to make him feel better about the whole situation, I took Fancy. No way anything untoward was going to happen with Fancy in the van.

It's a long drive—a couple hours each way—but she loves drives. She puts her head right at my shoulder and watches the world go by. Or takes a good long nap.

Plus, I have the whole back of the van fixed up with a giant dog bed, non-spill water bowls, and some chew toys. (Chew toys are a must. My shredded back seatbelt is testament to what happens when a bored dog is stuck traveling too long with nothing to chew on.)

Honestly, it was like puppy nirvana back there. Passengers? What passengers? My dog was my priority.

The drive down was uneventful. It helped that it was a Thursday so there was no real ski traffic, not like on the weekends.

I managed to coordinate my timing with Jean-Philippe so that I only had to circle the airport twice before he arrived in the pick-up area.

Sure, I could've parked in the cellphone lot and waited for him to call, but I prefer that "slow-crawl, don't want to stop and get in trouble with the cops, but don't want to pass through too fast" game that all the cars play.

(Can I just say that airport pick-up and drop-off is one of the most frustratingly stupid things in the world? Do they really think that not allowing cars to stop and wait for a passenger is somehow safer? It's about as useful as telling me I can't have a half-drunk bottle of Coke and go through the security line at the airport. If I were savvy enough to have liquid explosives in a Coke bottle,

I'm pretty sure I'd also be able to get around whatever security controls they have in place. But whatever. The world is impractical and foolish sometimes. It's all about optics after all. It doesn't matter if you are safe as long as you feel safe, right? Right.)

I hopped out of the van and ran around to give Jean-Philippe a quick hug. I have to give it to the man. He was still a looker. Not tall and handsome like Matt, but dark and slender in that European way. And he was short. How had I never noticed that before? Matt was tall enough to be nicely comforting and protective when he gave me a hug, but Jean-Philippe and I were eye-to-eye, which I would've sworn up and down was not my type. But there he was and I'd fallen for it three times.

"Ah, Maggie. So good to see you." He kissed me on each cheek. "I am looking forward to this time with you. You can tell me all about this man you are bringing to the wedding and I will tell you why he is all wrong for you and you should throw him over for me."

He opened the back of the van to store away his bag. Fancy was standing there, filling the entire space. She stepped forward, eager to see who we were picking-up.

He backed up three steps, a hand over his heart like he was about to faint. "What is that beast?"

I laughed and ruffled Fancy's ears. "This is my dog, Fancy. You knew I have a dog. You've seen pictures of her."

"I did not realize she was so enormous. Why would you have a dog this big? Dogs should fit in a purse. You should carry them around with you. They should not be the size of a horse. She could eat a person."

"She's more likely to smother someone with kisses." Fancy tried to get out of the van to reach him, because she loves all men whether they love her or not, but I shoved her back inside along with his bag and slammed the door.

"Come on. Before the cops come along and tell us to get going." I opened the passenger-side door and ran around to the other side and slid in behind the wheel.

Jean-Philippe hadn't moved.

"Jean-Philippe. If you want me to drive you, you will get in this van now. If you don't, let me know and we can arrange some alternate form of transportation."

He carefully stepped closer to the van. Fancy poked her nose at him through the space between the seat and the window, and he jumped back again.

"Fancy. Back. Give the man a little breathing room." I grabbed her by the collar to keep her out of his way while I rooted around for a handful of treats and threw them in the back. Fancy immediately went after the treats, all thoughts of Jean-Philippe forgotten.

"It's safe now. Don't worry, she's not going to eat you. She probably won't even lick you. She'll just sniff at you a bit."

He got into the car, keeping a wary eye on her the whole time, but Fancy was still sniffing around for every last bit of the treats I'd thrown her. I pulled out and started the drive back home.

Once she finished with the treats, Fancy did snuffle at his hair a bit, but when it was clear he had no interest in petting her she harrumphed and laid down in the back to go to sleep.

"So…" I asked as I merged onto I-70, avoiding all the crazies who'd been caught up in the 225 exit-only lanes, "Ready to cook for a hundred and twenty-five guests?"

"Of course. I am a professional, am I not?"

"And did you and Greta talk about the menu?"

He sniffed. "Yes."

"And everything's good?"

"Yes."

"No raw meat?"

"Beef tartare is a classic. And mine has a perfect yolk on top."

"But you're not going to serve it at Jamie's wedding are you?"

He huffed. "No. I will not serve it at Jamie's wedding. Nor it seems will I serve frog legs. You women do not understand the art that is being a chef. Not being allowed to freely express yourself. But I have spoken to this Greta woman and I understand my audience would not appreciate my art. So I will adjust."

"Good." I gave him my best smile. "I'm glad you're here, Jean-Philippe. We need you."

That seemed to mollify him, which was good, for the most part, except that meant the rest of our conversation centered on Matt and whether or not he really was a good match for me. My conclusion: Yes. Jean-Philippe's: No.

Of course. I wouldn't have expected less.

CHAPTER 30

One hour after I dropped Jean-Philippe off in Bakerstown, my phone started ringing. And that one-hundred-and-twenty-five-guests number started to climb.

It seemed someone recognized Jean-Philippe. (Or perhaps, knowing Jean-Philippe, he told everyone and their mother who he was.) Whichever way it went down, as soon as word spread that *the* Jean-Philippe Gaston was catering Jamie's wedding all of the locals who'd decided not to come because they had better plans changed their minds. This was, after all, a once-in-a-lifetime opportunity for many of them.

I made a point of telling the first guests who called what I thought of people who change their mind about attending a wedding last-minute, but then one of the guests pointed out to me that Jamie had been the one to change the wedding date on everyone first. If she hadn't done that then there wouldn't have been any confusion about what day it was happening and nobody would've cancelled in the first place.

After that I shut up and told everyone they'd be more than welcome with a nice, fake smile on my face while silently worrying about just how insane the next two days were going to be.

My phone kept ringing into the night. By the time I finally went to bed at ten o'clock we were up to a hundred and seventy-five guests. And counting.

Good thing Greta's ballroom was big enough to handle that many. The question was, would the chef be willing?

🐾 🐾 🐾

The next morning I found myself very grateful that I don't speak French.

(Well, no more than to say, "Hi, I don't speak French. How much is that thing I'm pointing at?" Or, "Where is this address I'm pointing at on this piece of paper?" I find that learning at least that much of a foreign language before going to a country really helps. It's better than the standard American approach of talking really loudly and slowly in English and somehow expecting a person to magically comprehend a language they never learned.)

Because I didn't actually speak French I didn't know what my very irate French chef was saying so loudly as he paced around Greta's kitchen, banging pots and pans onto various surfaces.

But I was pretty sure all the words flowing out of his mouth were ones I'd never really want to understand. The one or two I recognized from films or books were definitely classified as profanity.

I'd waited to break the news until we were at Greta's because I was hoping the sight of the beautiful commercial kitchen associated with the ballroom would be enough to ease the pain of finding out his guest list had pretty much doubled overnight.

It hadn't helped.

Greta, of course, didn't even bat an eye at my news. She simply waved over a very competent looking young woman who'd been standing off to the side with a clipboard and issued a series of quiet, precise commands while Jean-Philippe screamed and paced and slammed things around.

Greta turned to me. "We will not do a sit down meal. We will have food stations instead. This will make it easier."

Jean-Philippe stared at her in horror and then went back to his shouting.

Greta did an admirable job of ignoring Jean-Philippe's little tantrum until he reached for a stack of fine porcelain plates in the corner, at which point she finally snapped, "Enough."

He stared at her. "You do not understand. There are now twice as many guests. How can I do this? I do not have the food. I do not have the help. I do not…"

She held up her hand and he stopped speaking immediately. That was a trick I needed to learn.

"Write down what you need. Food and people."

"We have only twenty-four hours. How can I…?"

"Write it down."

"But the food. I need…"

"Write it down. There is nowhere in this world that is not a twenty-four hour flight away, no? This is true?"

"Yes."

"Then write it down."

"But the staff…"

"Write. It. Down. Now. Before we have less than twenty-four hours and we actually have a problem." She turned away, shaking her head just enough to show her disgust. "Chefs. Take my advice, Maggie. Never marry one."

"Was one of your husbands a chef?" I asked as Jean-Philippe scribbled furiously.

"Yes. My ninth, I believe. He was Austrian. Great cook. Horrible husband." She glanced back at Jean-Philippe before turning to me. "Have you told Jamie about the increase in the number of guests?"

"No. Crap! The cupcakes."

Greta nodded.

"I can't tell her, Greta. I can't ask her to bake another hundred cupcakes on the eve of her wedding. She has the rehearsal dinner tonight."

Greta patted my arm. "Do not worry. I will see to it."

"How?"

She just smiled. "Do you doubt?"

"You? No."

"Then go. It will be fine."

"Are you sure?" I glanced towards Jean-Philippe.

Greta just stared at me.

"Okay. Jean-Philippe? Will you be okay?" I asked

He was still muttering over his list, but he nodded.

I didn't stick around to ask twice.

CHAPTER 31

On the way home I decided to swing by the church and see how Luke was doing.

I'd always loved that church. It wasn't big. But it was what I thought the quintessential church should look like. One story, white, with a peaked roof, and the mountains framing it from behind. Inside I knew there were polished wooden pews and a simple altar at the front where the pastor could deliver his sermons. There was a small reception area where people could gather before services and a couple bathrooms and the pastor's office, but that was it: a simple place to come together and pray together.

I was surprised to see Georgia lurking in the parking lot, talking to one of Luke's men.

"Georgia. What brought you to town?"

She flinched at the sound of my voice, but recovered quickly. "Sayin' hi to a friend. You got a problem with that?"

"At the church where Jamie's wedding's going to be held?"

"How'm I supposed to know that? I just needed to see Zeke for a minute."

I looked back and forth between the two of them. Something was definitely up, the question was whether they were conspiring to ruin Jamie's wedding or it was something completely unrelated like a little drug deal between friends.

"I will if something happens with this church to keep Jamie from having her wedding here tomorrow. So keep that in mind."

Georgia hunched her shoulders and turned away from me. "Told you I don't have a problem with her."

"Okay, then."

I started to walk into the church and then turned back. "Oh, and Georgia?"

"Yeah? What?"

"If I come back out to my van and have a flat tire, I'm calling the cops. Got it?"

She sneered at me, but then made a straight line for her beat-up old truck and peeled out of the parking lot. Good enough. I wasn't trying to make friends.

🐾 🐾 🐾

I found Luke in the basement, doing a final walkthrough with the pastor. Luke was good-looking in that laid-back, seedy, let's break a few laws and keep it casual sort of way. It was an interesting contrast to the portly little pastor with his balding head who had to be no more than five-two.

"We all good for tomorrow?" I asked.

Luke nodded. "Sure are, gorgeous. You here to give me a thank-you kiss?"

I ignored him. "Pastor, you agree?"

"I do." He took my hands in his. "And please, tell Mason and Jamie how grateful we are for this. Without their help…" There were tears in his eyes and it made me a little teary, too.

"I will. I'm glad they could help. And I'm sure they are, too."

I squeezed his hands one more time before stepping away. "I better go. I have to check on all the other arrangements before the rehearsal dinner tonight."

I hurried outside. Man, the things I'd do for a friend.

🐾 🐾 🐾

I checked back in with Greta. She'd already procured for Jean-Philippe an additional six prep staff, all qualified enough to meet his exacting standards, and all of the food except for the lobster tails had already arrived or was on its way.

I decided I didn't want to think too closely about what regional events might be missing staff and/or food they were expecting to use the next day.

Money, it can buy pretty much anything if you're willing to use it and know the right people.

CHAPTER 32

The rehearsal dinner was at the country club. (Fortunately *that* hadn't been cancelled.) Although it did require me to dress up, which bleh. Of course, it also required Matt dressing up and I have to say he cleaned up very nicely indeed. I had myself one very attractive boyfriend who somehow made all the mess of looking pretty feel worth it.

We were two of the first guests to arrive so we found Mason and Jamie huddled together in the entryway chuckling about something on his phone.

"What's so funny," I asked.

Jamie showed me the phone. There was a text on it that read, "Hey baby. Thank you so much for last night." And below that another one, "I'm going to miss you when you get married. Maybe we can still keep in touch after?" and then a series of emojis.

"Who texts somebody an eggplant?" I asked.

All three of them looked at me like I'd said something really stupid.

"What? What did I say?"

Matt just kissed me on the cheek. "There are so many

reasons I love you. Just when I think you are the smartest woman I know you say something like that. It's adorable."

"I don't want to be adorable. I want to understand what I'm missing."

Jamie quickly explained what the series of little images at the end of the message meant. At which point I blushed bright scarlet. "What? Are you serious?"

She nodded.

"Who…?" And then it finally dawned on me that we were looking at Mason's phone. On the eve of his wedding. "Who sent these, Mason? Who is thanking you for last night? On the eve of your wedding?"

He smiled a little smugly. "Someone who clearly didn't check to see how I spent last night before sending those messages."

Jamie grinned at me. "You want me to explain that one, too?"

"Oh shut up. I got that one, thanks. So…Some random stranger sent you text messages to make it look like you were having an affair. But you know you're not. So what good does that do them?"

Jamie handed Mason back his phone as his parents walked in the door. He walked over to greet them while Jamie answered my question. "Whoever it was called Mason's phone and asked for me, supposedly because they couldn't reach me on my phone. And while they were chatting with me about my customer satisfaction with my wedding dress," she raised an eyebrow at that one, "the text messages came in."

"Ah. I get it. So someone made sure you'd see them."

"Umhm. Seems they thought I'd believe them and call off the wedding last-minute over my cheating fiancé."

"But they messed up by mentioning last night."

Jamie laughed. "No, they messed up by thinking I would ever believe something like that of Mason. And, honestly, do you think Mason would ever get involved with a woman who uses emojis?"

I looked over at the man who stood with perfect posture in a conservatively cut expensive suit, put together from head to toe. "Good point. So that attempt failed."

"Yes it did." Jamie beamed a smile at us before walking over to kiss Mason's cheek and loop her arm through his.

Matt put an arm around my shoulders. I leaned into him. "You know what this means, don't you?"

He nodded. "Someone's still trying to ruin this wedding."

"I hope that was their last try, but I'm afraid it wasn't." I told him about seeing Georgia at the church earlier that day. "It might've just been two friends talking, but given what's been happening…"

He nodded. "I'll have Ben run by the church a couple times tonight, just in case. He's on duty and I'm sure he won't mind doing it for Jamie's sake."

"Thanks." I was ready for this wedding to be over. Not that I didn't want my friend to have her happy day, but it was stressful constantly trying to think about how else things might go wrong or scrambling to fix them last-minute.

CHAPTER 33

The morning of Jamie's wedding dawned cold and clear and beautiful. For a brief moment, I let myself believe the worst had passed and we were fine. I was even smiling as I walked Fancy down the icy streets of Creek.

But then my phone rang.

It was the pastor's wife. Telling me that he was violently ill and wouldn't be able to complete the ceremony that day.

Coincidence? I doubted it.

As soon as I dropped Fancy off at home, I drove to their house.

(I know. How rude. The man was too sick to officiate a wedding and there I was at eight in the morning on his doorstep, knocking loudly. But I hoped our little saboteur had finally slipped up.)

"Ms. Carver? What are you doing here?" The pastor's wife was a very friendly, plump, older woman who I'd never actually seen be rude or mean to anyone ever. So even though she probably wanted to tell me to go away, she didn't.

"I need to know everything the pastor ate in the last

twenty-four hours."

She lifted her chin. "I didn't tell you he was sick to his stomach. I just said he was unwell."

"But he is, right? Like food poisoning kind of sick?"

She sniffed like the very topic was offensive to her. "Yes."

"I think someone put something in his food."

"What? No. Who would do such a thing?"

"The same person who'd turn off the furnace in a church in the hopes that the pipes would burst so no one could get married there."

"Oh, this is horrible. What is the world coming to?" She waved me inside and led me to the kitchen. "Well, it can't be anything I ate or I'd be sick, too, right?"

"Right. Probably."

She glanced around with a big sigh. There were tins of food everywhere. "It had to be this time of year, didn't it?"

"Is this all from your parishioners?"

She nodded. "They know we don't like to receive money, so they try to feed us. Unfortunately, Pastor Nelson has a bit of a sweet tooth."

"Well, let me see what I can find." I started making my way through the various stacks of food everywhere. Some were still sealed, so those were easy to eliminate. There were also some that she swore he'd never eat and some that they'd both tried the day before.

That left a stack of about fifteen various plates and tins.

I looked through each one, but none of the names were familiar. Not until I reached the last one.

"Elaine Parks is a parishioner of yours?"

"Oh, yes. She's an absolute sweetheart. Such a help."

"And he ate one of these?"

"Of course. They're Jerry's favorite. He had at least three of them yesterday even though I told him they'd ruin his appetite." She blinked. "You can't possibly think Elaine…"

"She was engaged to Mason at one point, wasn't she?"

"But Elaine? No. It couldn't be. She's too nice."

I held up the plate of chocolate brownies. "She's the only one whose name I recognized…Do you have her home address?"

"I really…"

"I'll get it from Mason if I don't get it from you."

She lifted her chin. "Then do that. Because she couldn't possibly have done this."

"Fine. But I'd suggest you throw those brownies out."

"Oh, I couldn't. They're his favorite."

"Look, lady. Something here made your husband horribly sick. Honestly, you should probably throw it all out just to be safe."

She stared around the room. "But, there's so much."

"Your tummy, not mine. Will the church be ready at four?"

"I told you, Pastor Nelson can't do the service."

"But we can still use the church can't we?"

She pressed her lips together. "Who will officiate?"

"I'll figure it out. Just have the church ready, please."

"It's a house of God."

"And we'll respect that. Do you really want to reward this person for sabotaging your church and poisoning your husband?"

She thought about it for a long moment and finally shook her head. "No. You can use the church."

"Thank you."

☙ ❧ ☙

I called Matt as I walked to the car. "Hey, Maggie. What's wrong?"

"I think Elaine poisoned the pastor."

"Elaine? No."

I filled him in on what I'd found.

"I still can't believe it."

"Yeah, neither could the pastor's wife. But he's puking his guts out and had at least three of those brownies yesterday and I didn't recognize any of the other names, so…I think I better check it out."

"I'll meet you there."

"No, that's fine. She's harmless. I need you to do something else for me."

"Sure. Anything."

"Research who has to officiate a wedding in Colorado. I seem to think you can just do it yourselves, but I need that confirmed. And if that is the case then call my grandpa and ask him if he's willing to lead the ceremony."

"Couldn't Mason have one of his judge friends do it?"

"Probably. But at this point, I'm keeping everything in the family where I can control it."

"Okay. Will do. But, Maggie?"

"Yeah?"

"Please don't actually kill Elaine. I'd rather not have to date a woman who's in prison."

"Haha. Funny."

"I wasn't kidding, Maggie."

I rolled my eyes. "Fine. I won't kill her. I'll just put the fear of me in her so she doesn't do anything else to screw up this wedding."

"Maggie…"

"Look, I'm not going to do anything to get myself arrested, alright? But I am going to have a little chat with that woman about why she's doing this and tell her to knock it off. Good enough?"

"Good enough."

I hung up and called Mason. He wanted to know why I needed Elaine's address the morning of his wedding, but I told him he didn't need to know and he was smart enough not to press me on it.

CHAPTER 34

Elaine lived in a surprisingly tidy cabin just outside of Bakerstown. As I drove up I could see Zela outside barking, but no sign of Elaine. Zela was agitated and ridiculously happy to see me. She kept circling my legs as I walked from the front gate to the door, barking at me.

I stopped to try to calm her, but she just kept barking and circling. I did manage to touch her coat as she circled. She'd been outside a while. Not enough to freeze, thankfully. I remembered Elaine talking about the heated dog house she'd bought her.

Clearly something was wrong. Elaine might be the type of person to try to ruin her ex's wedding, but she didn't strike me as the type of person to harm her dog.

I knocked on the front door. No answer.

I knocked again. Still no answer.

I thought about walking around the perimeter and peeking inside, but I had a wedding to get to and a saboteur to confront, so instead I tried the doorknob. It turned. Her house was unlocked.

(Don't tell anyone, but my grandpa's house always is, too. In the mountains you don't expect trouble.)

Before I could debate how smart it was to walk into someone's house uninvited (my prior experiences doing so hadn't always gone so well), Zela pushed past me and ran inside. Her bark changed. It was the "someone get in here now there's a problem" bark.

I wanted to follow her, but I knew I probably shouldn't.

I called Matt.

"Hey, Maggie. What's up?"

"I'm at Elaine's. Something is off. Her dog was locked outside and going nuts. I tried the front door and the dog ran inside and is now sounding very alarmed. I'm going in."

"Maggie. Wait for a cop to get there."

"I can't, Matt. But you can stay on the line with me. That way if something happens, you'll know."

"At least let me call someone."

"I'm going in now. You can hang up and call someone or you can stay on the line and make sure I'm safe. Your call."

"Maggie," he growled at me, but he stayed on the line as I eased inside.

"Elaine? It's Maggie Carver. Are you here?"

The door opened onto a small kitchen that looked like it had come straight out of the sixties. There was a little metal table pressed up against one wall with a peeling laminate top and an old white and pink fridge next to it with the curved lines of that long-ago decade.

On the counter sat a container of cocoa right alongside a bottle of syrup of ipecac.

That'd do it.

"Maggie? Talk to me. Are you okay?" Matt asked.

"I'm fine. I haven't found Elaine yet. The dog's barking in the other room. But there's a bottle of ipecac in the kitchen right next to a container of cocoa."

"Really?"

"Yeah." A little too obvious, if you asked me. I stepped towards the doorway from the kitchen to the rest of the cabin. "Elaine? Are you here?"

There was a small living area divided in two. One side barely fit a recliner and a small television set atop a bookcase. The other side was dedicated to three different sewing machines as well as a workspace for prepping. A dressmaker's dummy stood in the corner, empty. A loft area above appeared to have a small bed.

But Zela was standing at another door, barking. I assumed that one had to be the bathroom. (I hoped for Elaine's sake it was. If not, that meant she had to use an outhouse and well, I wouldn't wish that on anyone, not even the person who might've tried to sabotage my best friend's wedding.)

"Matt, this doesn't look good…." I approached the door.

"What are you seeing?"

"Zela's stopped outside a door. I have to assume it's for a bathroom. If Elaine's in there, she's not responding. Do you want me to wait until a cop gets here?"

"No. Open the door. We need to know what we're dealing with."

"Okay." I turned the handle, trembling. As angry as I was with Elaine for what she'd done, I really wanted her to be okay. I'd seen enough dead bodies for a lifetime.

Zela shoved through the door as soon as she could. The barking stopped, but that was almost worse, because it was replaced with low-level whining. I couldn't move the door more than about eight inches, but it was enough to get my head in for a peek.

Elaine was on the floor, eyes closed, breaths shallow. There was a note next to her. It was printed off of a computer. It said, "I'm sorry. I had to do it."

Really?

"Maggie?" Matt interrupted my thoughts.

"Call an ambulance. Elaine's down. She's still alive, but you need to get someone here as soon as you can."

I hung up on him. I needed to think.

CHAPTER 35

While I waited for the ambulance and cops to arrive, I turned back to Elaine's living room. There was something that was bugging me about it, but I couldn't figure out what. I slowly walked around the room, looking at everything I saw, trying to figure out what was so off.

(I know. You probably think I should've shoved my way into the bathroom. Problem is, I don't know CPR. So there was nothing useful I could do except probably crack her ribs. Plus, emergency response in the valley is really fast. I figured it'd only be a minute or two before the paramedics were there and they could do a much better job of things than I could.)

Almost every surface had something homemade. There were doilies on the bookcase, mostly crocheted, a few tatted. There were cross-stitches in frames on the walls. And perhaps a water color as well. I saw a small ledger next to the recliner and flipped through the pages without really reading them. It looked like detailed handwritten lists of supplies she'd bought for various craft projects.

The bed, what I could see of it from where I stood, was neat and tidy. Me if I'd had a bed in a loft I'd never make it because the risk of hitting my head on the ceiling would outweigh my desire for tidiness.

Maybe that was it. Maybe that was what was bugging me.

Everything was put away. There wasn't mail lying around or dirty clothes thrown anywhere. Everything had its place. And was in its place.

So why would Elaine leave the ipecac syrup and cocoa on the counter? If she'd taken the brownies to the pastor, she would've cleaned up first. There weren't any dirty dishes in the sink. So why were those two ingredients out on her counter?

And would a woman who hand-crafted seemingly everything, including her own wardrobe from what I could tell, really print out a suicide note on a computer?

No.

It didn't make any sense.

Just as I reached that conclusion the paramedics came barging in and I was swept out of the way while they managed to get the bathroom door removed.

"She's alive. Barely. Let's get her out of here."

As the paramedics worked to put her on a gurney, a cop who'd arrived in the meantime asked me if I knew what she'd taken.

"No idea. I'm sorry. I don't think she took it deliberately, whatever it was."

"What do you mean?"

I walked him through the whole "this doesn't fit" theory I'd developed. He clearly wasn't buying it.

"Look. Just, humor me a bit, please. And treat this like

a potential murder instead of an obvious suicide attempt. My boyfriend, Matt Barnes, he'll vouch for me."

"Oh. You're Matt's girl, huh?"

"Maggie Carver."

He didn't look any more convinced than he had before and I wondered what exactly Matt had been saying about me at work. (Or, more likely, he was basing all his opinions of me on that slam piece Peter Nielsen wrote that cast both me and the police department in a very bad light.)

"Just…Maybe make sure no one can get to her for a few hours at least?" I asked.

"That we can do. Now come on. You can't stay here." He radioed in his status as we walked outside. "The dog hers?"

Zela had followed the paramedics to their vehicle and was barking loudly as she tried to get around them to reach Elaine.

"Yes."

"Then I'll call animal control."

"No. Don't. I'll take her."

One of my worst fears has always been something happening to me and then Fancy being left alone with no one to care for her. No way I was going to let that happen to Zela if I could help it.

"It's protocol, ma'am."

"Just let me take her, please?"

He hesitated for another minute, but finally nodded. "Fine. Take her. But if something goes wrong…"

"Understood. She'll be in the best of hands, I promise." I glanced towards the house. "But can I go back in real quick and grab her food and toys and things?"

"Yes." He didn't look happy, but as long as he let me do it I really didn't care.

I grabbed up the food and some toys and treats. I was tempted to grab the bottle of ipecac, too, but I figured it either didn't have any prints on it at all or the only prints were going to be Elaine's since it was so obviously a plant by whoever had done this.

Although I was still no closer to knowing who that was. I had five hours until the wedding ceremony was supposed to start and I was at square one.

Actually, I was at *less* than square one.

CHAPTER 36

Zela barked the whole way to my house, but she calmed down when I finally got her inside and she saw Fancy. They tore through the house and into the backyard. Ah, to be a dog whose only concerns were food, sleep, and play.

I hoped Ms. White would be okay watching three dogs instead of two (she was also watching Lulu for the night). I'm sure she would once she understood the circumstances.

My grandpa crossed his arms and glared at me. "Well? Where'd you go this morning? We have ten minutes until we're supposed to meet at the church and put up all the decorations. I told you I'd help, Maggie, I didn't say Lesley and I would do all the work."

"I know. I'm sorry. I will be there to help."

"What about the dogs? You're just going to leave a strange dog in my house?"

I rubbed the back of my neck. "I hadn't even thought of it, honestly. Maybe she can come with us."

"Maggie."

"I'm sorry, Grandpa, but things have been moving fast this morning." I explained to him everything that had happened since the pastor's wife called. "I didn't even eat breakfast. I just ran out of here to see if I could figure out who'd done this. And now I need to call them again to see if Elaine actually brought over those brownies or not. And I need to call Mason to see if she has any family that need to know she's in the hospital. And…"

"You need to eat."

"That, too."

"I'll make you a sandwich while you call the pastor and Mason."

"But the church…"

"We can be a few minutes late. It's going to be a long day and you need to eat."

I gave him a quick kiss on the cheek. "Thank you."

He just grunted, but he did go to the kitchen and start fixing me up a roast beef sandwich with Swiss cheese. He even threw in a dill pickle and a handful of chips.

I called Mason first. I hated to tell him about Elaine on the morning of his wedding, but I had to know if she had family.

She didn't. None he'd ever met. And the closest she came to friends was Margaret Kepper who not only was getting married that day, too, but had also sounded like a bit of a bully to me.

"I can run by there," Mason said.

"No. It's your wedding day. Just focus on that."

"Jamie would understand."

"Oh, I'm sure she would. But you can't tell her about this."

"Why not?"

I sighed. "Because the fact that Elaine's in the hospital and the pastor was poisoned means that whoever this is who's trying to ruin your wedding is officially dangerous. I don't want that hanging over her head today."

"Shouldn't she know? In case whoever it is comes after her?"

"Good point. Fine. I'll tell her." She was at her mom's in honor of tradition.

"Did you just say that the pastor was poisoned?"

"Yes. Syrup of ipecac. He can't do the ceremony."

"So who is going to do the ceremony then?"

I tensed. "My grandpa will."

There was a long silence on the other end of the line.

"Maggie, you do understand that my family is one of the most prominent families in the valley, don't you?"

"Yes. And?" I sat back, just waiting for it.

"So there will be judges and lawyers and doctors and other upstanding members of society there?"

"Yeees."

"And your grandpa…"

"Has a colorful history?"

"That's one way to put it."

"Mason."

"Yes, Maggie?"

"Did I make this thing happen? Even though I hate weddings and only had ten days to do it in?"

"Yes."

"And are you seriously going to tell me now that my solution to your latest issue isn't good enough for you? That my *family* isn't good enough for you?"

Another long pause.

"Well, are you? Because as much as I love Jamie and want this day to work out for her, I can wash my hands of this whole mess right now. Instead of me and my grandpa spending the next hour or more at the church decorating it for *your* wedding we can just sit at home and play Scrabble."

"You wouldn't do that to Jamie."

"No, I wouldn't. Lucky for you. Now. Do I need to tell my grandpa you don't think he's good enough to lead the ceremony?"

He sighed. "No. It's fine. As long as Jamie and I end this day a married couple and everyone comes out of it alive, I'll be happy."

"Good man. I'll see you at the church. "

I hung up.

Yes, I had badgered the groom into accepting my less-than-perfect solution to the pastor problem, but I did not care. I could rely on my grandpa. No one was going to take him out before the ceremony even if someone were inclined to try. Mason might prefer some chichi judge to preside, but I wasn't taking chances at that point.

🐾 🐾 🐾

Jamie was my next call. "Maggie! Can you believe it's the big day?"

I forced myself to sound cheerful. "No. Time flies."

"Greta just arrived with the dress and it's so exquisite. And the hair and makeup ladies are here and we're drinking champagne and…"

"Don't drink too much champagne, okay? Remember, you have to walk down an aisle with close to two hundred people watching you."

"I won't. Just a bit to take the edge off. I'm so excited!"

"And I'm excited for you."

"Then why aren't you here?"

"Because someone needs to put up all the decorations in the church and I can't just ask my grandpa and Matt to do that. It wouldn't be fair."

"But your hair and makeup."

"It'll be fine. I'll try to swing by after. Save me champagne."

"I will. You know, it could be you next…"

"No. No, no, no. We are not going there today. That topic is off-limits as of now. Look. I have to go, but I called for a reason."

She was immediately serious. "What is it?"

I filled her in on what had happened that morning. "I've got it handled, okay? My grandpa will step in to lead the ceremony and you guys can self-solemnize."

"What?"

"It sounds dirty, but it just means you sign the wedding certificate instead of the pastor. I had Matt look it up this morning and he texted me a link. You'll be fine. You're still getting married today. But I called because I need you to be careful. Don't trust anyone."

"But I thought you said Elaine was the one who gave the pastor the brownies?"

"Eh. That's what someone wanted us to think, but no. It was too easy."

"So who was it?"

"I don't know. Could be a couple people. Just be careful, and…check the tires on your car before you leave the house, okay?"

"The tires on my car?"

"Something Georgia said to me. Just channel a little bit of me today, alright? Question first, trust second."

"Okay. Fine. I will. But promise you'll try to swing by for hair and makeup?"

"I'll try."

That left one final call to the pastor's wife. She confirmed that Elaine hadn't given them the brownies directly. They'd been left at his office at the church the day before. Which led me to make one more call.

"This is Georgia. What do you want?"

"Hi, Georgia, it's Maggie."

"What do you want?"

"Any chance you were at the church yesterday to drop off some brownies?"

Silence.

"Georgia, Elaine is in the hospital. She may not make it. Now I can either call the cops and tell them you're the one responsible and you can spend New Year's Eve in jail for attempted murder…"

"What? I didn't try to kill no one. What do you take me for?"

"Those brownies? They had syrup of ipecac in them. The pastor has been sick all morning. Did you do that?"

"No."

"But you know who did."

"Not really."

I pinched the bridge of my nose. "What does that mean?"

"Some guy I didn't know came into the Buckin' Bronc and offered me twenty bucks to drop those brownies off at the church."

I quietly banged my head against the wall. "I offered you fifty for any information that might be related to whoever was sabotaging Jamie's wedding."

"I know. That's why I told him I wouldn't do it for less than a hundred."

Of course she had.

"What did this guy look like?"

"Rich."

"Height? Weight? Hair color? Age? Eye color?"

"I don't know. He drove some fancy SUV. Wore sunglasses. Wasn't really memorable otherwise."

"Okay. Fine. And, Georgia?"

"Yeah?"

"Next time someone counters my offer, give me a chance to outbid them, would ya?"

"Will do."

I hung up, wolfed down the sandwich my grandpa had made me, and was at the church only ten minutes late.

(I left Zela and Fancy at the house. They were already fast asleep in the living room by the time I went to leave and I couldn't imagine them getting into trouble in the hour we'd be gone.)

CHAPTER 37

Thirty minutes after I arrived at the church, my phone rang. It was Georgia.

"Hey Georgia, what's up?"

"That fancy man?"

"Yeah?"

"He came back. Offered me a hundred bucks to do a job for him."

"What job?"

"I don't know. I said I had to call you for a counteroffer. He ran out of here as soon as I reached for my phone."

"You get a better description of him this time around?"

"Still looked rich."

"And?"

I could almost hear her shrug through the phone. "Not young. Not old. Dark hair. A little taller than me."

"Happen to get a plate on that SUV he was driving?"

"No." The way she said it made it sound like the most absurd suggestion she'd ever heard.

"Okay, thanks."

I hung up.

"Who was that?" Matt asked.

I told him about the call. "So I guess keep an eye out for a fancy SUV. And some average-looking rich guy."

"Any idea who it could be?"

"None. I mean, Jamie's dated a few average-looking rich guys over the years, but none that would want to ruin her wedding this bad. Plus, this has to be a local, doesn't it? I mean, who else would know about Elaine and her brownies? Or be able to spread the rumor that the wedding was cancelled? Or know to track down Georgia to have her be the one to deliver the brownies?"

My grandpa joined us. "All good questions. But they won't get the rest of these garlands hung. Now get back to work."

"Yes, sir."

I didn't want to leave when we were done. It looked so nice and I was worried what might happen in the hour until the ceremony started, but I needed to get dressed and check on Fancy and Zela. Plus I had to talk my grandpa into wearing the tuxedo Greta had sent over when I called to tell her about the latest developments. We'd both agreed jeans and flannel shirts were fine for day-to-day wear but not for standing in front of the county's finest leading a wedding ceremony.

My grandpa surprised me. I thought he'd fight me on the tux, but when we got home and I pulled it out of the clothing bag his only concern was whether it would fit well enough for it to look good on him.

(It did. I'd never seen him look so dapper. And unlike some men who can only look comfortable in one type of clothes, he looked just as put together and in control in the tux as he did in his jeans and flannel shirt. Character shows through.)

I was the one who wanted to throw a fit about my outfit.

The bridesmaids' dresses Jamie had chosen were pastel pink. Floofy pastel pink. I looked like someone had stuck a big bunch of cotton candy around my thighs. For a moment there I kind of wished someone had sabotaged the bridesmaids' dresses, too. I would've been far happier in that gorgeous blue gown I'd tried on at Greta's.

But Jamie was my best friend. So if I had to spend a day looking all soft and pretty, I'd do it, with a smile.

I glanced at the clock. I had just enough time to run over to her place to get my hair and makeup done by the professionals. (One of the great parts of living in a small town. Everyone who lives in the town is only five minutes away, maybe ten at the most.)

"You okay, Grandpa?" I asked.

"I'll be fine. Where are you headed?"

"To Jamie's. She has someone there to do everyone's hair and makeup."

"Good idea." He glanced at my feet. "I assume you have different shoes to wear at the actual ceremony?"

I laughed. "Yes. No snow boots for the actual walk down the aisle. Although they are more comfortable…"

Ms. White arrived with Lulu as I was racing to my van. I gave her a quick wave and winced as I realized my grandpa was going to be stuck explaining to her the extra house guest. Hopefully she'd be okay with it. If not, the wedding might just end up with a few extra canine guests.

🐾 🐾 🐾

I don't know what instinct made me decide to go the extra block out of the way that would take me by the church on the way to Jamie's house, but I'm glad I did. Because there was a fancy SUV parked in the back corner of the parking lot. One I certainly didn't recognize.

I pulled my van up behind it and jumped out.

(Yes, I know. Stupid. The minute I saw the SUV I should've called the cops. Whoever was trying to sabotage Jamie's wedding had already proven themselves to be dangerous. The last thing I needed to be doing was try to confront them on my own. But it seems my adrenaline reaction is always fight over flight. So I charged on in.)

Good thing I did, though. I barged through the back door of the church and right into a man with two gas cans at his feet. He must've just arrived and paused to assess his surroundings.

"What are you doing?" I asked. (Throwing in a few cuss words for good measure.) "This is a church. Were you really going to burn it down?"

"Get out of my way," he growled.

"No. This is over. Who are you? Why are you trying to ruin my friend's wedding? And what is wrong with you that you'd desecrate a church? And hurt a poor innocent girl with no friends?"

"What are you talking about?"

"Elaine? You poisoned her. And the pastor. Who poisons a pastor?"

"I didn't poison a pastor."

"You didn't pay Georgia to deliver brownies to the pastor yesterday?"

He paused to think about it. "Yeah, I did that."

"Well, those brownies were poisoned. And I found the woman who supposedly made them unconscious on her bathroom floor this morning."

"That wasn't me. I just paid the lady to deliver them."

"But this is." I gestured towards the gas cans.

Reminded of the gas cans, he tried to lunge for one, but I got in the way. It cost me a hard shove into the wall, which hurt like no one's business, but at least he didn't get his hands on the gasoline.

He pushed past me and out the back door before I could stop him and maneuvered the SUV around my van by pulling onto the church lawn.

I immediately called it in to the cops. And, unlike Georgia, I had a license plate to give them. As soon as I gave them that information I also called Matt to tell him what had happened. He promised he'd call the police station and make sure every cop in the area was looking for the guy. He also told me he was dressed and ready and would head to the church so I could go meet up with Jamie.

We weren't going to take any more chances at that point.

CHAPTER 38

Jamie and the other bridesmaids were all giggles when I arrived. Clearly they had been enjoying the champagne a little more than necessary. But I told myself that was good. You should be all happy, bubbly on your wedding day.

Caroline looked me up and down. "Maggie, how is it that you can make any outfit look like trash?"

I gave her my best smile. "It's a special skill. I've been practicing it for years."

I took the glass of champagne from Jamie and downed it in one go. "Where are the hair and makeup crew that'll magically transform me into something presentable?"

"Right through here. And don't listen to Caroline, she's just jealous because you always look good even when you look bad."

I tried to parse that one and decided it wasn't worth the effort. I was pretty sure it was meant to be a compliment and that's what counted.

I sat down in the torture chair, closed my eyes, and let the ladies get to work with their hairsprays and blushes and eyeliners and hair pins.

"You're such a treat to work on," the makeup lady whispered. "You just sit there so perfectly."

"That's because I've gone to my happy place so I won't think too much about what you're doing to me. It's what I do when I go to the dentist, too."

She trilled in laughter, but I was serious. It is what I do at the dentist and when someone is intent on turning my hair into a shellacked mess that can stand up on its own.

Jamie leaned close as they were putting on the finishing touches. "Anything else happen that I should know about?"

"Nope. You just focus on the fact that you're about to marry the man of your dreams."

She beamed at me. She was so happy she was almost glowing. "I am, aren't I?"

My phone started to ring just as one of the other bridesmaids ran into the room and pulled Jamie away.

"Hey, Matt. Did you get him?"

"We did."

"And? Who is he? Why is he doing this?"

"His name is Johnny Tinson."

"Tinson? That sounds familiar." But it didn't sound like someone Jamie had dated. "Hey, wait. I know where I heard that before. There's a Bobby Tinson getting married today to Margaret Kepper. That makes total sense."

"What does?"

"He must be the groom's brother or something."

"And? Why does that make sense?"

"Because I bet she was jealous when Jamie moved the wedding. I bet it ruined all her big plans to be the center of attention. Mason's family is a big deal around these parts. People probably cancelled on her when Jamie moved the wedding. So she thought if she could ruin Jamie's wedding she'd get all the attention again. And the newspaper coverage."

"You really think someone would poison a pastor, almost kill a woman, and try to burn down a church just because they were upset that someone had stolen their limelight?"

"Yeah, from everything Elaine said, I do. Are you going to pick them up?"

"Who?"

"Margaret and Bobby."

"We have no proof they did anything wrong. And it's their wedding day."

"I don't care, Matt. You have to pick them up. If you don't they'll keep trying to ruin Jamie's wedding."

"Maybe not. Maybe it's too late at this point. Maybe they'll just focus on their own wedding."

"I doubt it."

"We have nothing to charge Johnny with, let alone Bobby or Margaret."

"Georgia saw Johnny."

"Georgia is Georgia. Not the best witness."

"I saw him, too. At the church with gas cans."

"But what did you see? A man standing in the back of a church with some gas cans near him."

"Matt, I know this is our guy."

"But there's no way to prove it."

"Matt…"

"Maggie, I serve the law. And the law protects people's rights. Innocent until proven guilty. And we have no proof here."

Jamie came back into the room. "Are you ready? It's time to get to the church."

"Yeah, I'm ready. Gotta go, Matt." I hung up on him.

I really hoped he was right and that it was all over. But I didn't believe that. I would've been much happier if he'd just agreed to arrest everyone instead of being all ethical about it.

CHAPTER 39

We were all walking out of Jamie's house, ready to pile into the limo her father had rented for the drive to and from the church and reception when my phone rang again.

This time it was Mason. I glanced at the limo and then at my phone. "You guys go ahead. I can drive the van over."

"Are you sure?" Jamie asked.

"Yeah. I better take this. And I don't want to hold you guys up. Go."

They piled into the limo, Jamie with her princess dress and the other bridesmaids in their pink cotton candy floof, giggling and talking non-stop about the reception. To be honest, I was kind of glad Mason had given me an excuse to avoid cramming myself into a small contained space with that much estrogen.

Don't get me wrong. I have a few very close female friends that I wouldn't trade away for the world. But surround me with a group of girls packed together like that, especially a giddy group of girls? I'm ready to run.

"Mason. What's up?" I asked, heading towards my van.

"We have a big problem."

I wanted to bury my face in my hands but I couldn't because of all the stupid makeup on my face. "What now?"

"Someone dumped a bunch of hay bales all over the road that leads from my house to the church. It's going to take at least an hour or two to clear them."

"They're just hay bales."

"It's a mess, Maggie. Will you tell Jamie? I'm going to be there, but it might be a while."

I shook my head. "No. Not acceptable. Be more creative."

"What?"

"You need to be more creative about solving this problem. Can you go around it?"

"Not in the limo."

"Mason…What about in a truck?"

"Too snowy."

I was starting to get annoyed. "What about on a snowmobile?"

"I…" He paused. "That might work. But then…"

"Just get around the hay bales. I'll have Matt take care of the rest."

I hung up on him. Not nice, I know, but I was running low on patience by that time and anyone who wasn't a part of the solution was a part of the problem. I called Matt and explained to him what had happened. "Can you send someone to pick up Mason and whoever else is with him? I assume it's his groomsmen. So maybe six people?"

"I'll call Jack."

"Jack? Are you sure?"

"Unless you want me to abandon the church to go get Mason. Or you want to send your grandpa off to do it."

I took a deep breath. "No. That's fine. Send Jack. Thank you."

"Are you headed this way?"

"No. I have something to take care of first."

"Maggie…"

I hung up on him, too.

CHAPTER 40

I used my phone to figure out where Margaret Kepper's father's farm was located and headed in that direction. I figured I had a few minutes to spare before the wedding started and it was time to end this thing once and for all. The article I found on the farm included a picture of Kepper. She wasn't an attractive woman, not by conventional standards. Her teeth were bizarrely prominent. But she was well-polished, so I'm sure most people saw her as respectable and likeable.

Not me. She was slime in my book and I was determined to let her have it.

Of course, if there's one lesson I keep having to learn over and over again in life, it's this one: Do not act out of anger.

My first car accident when I was sixteen-years-old, I gunned the car to clear an intersection where I was taking a left turn because I was angry at someone who'd just run what I thought was a red light for leaving me hanging out there in the intersection. Unfortunately for me and my temper and the driver of the car behind him, a second car went through the light and I smacked right into him.

I should know by now that acting out of anger is a very bad idea.

And yet…

That's exactly what I did when I drove over to the Kepper Family Farm.

Fortunately for me, there was a guard on the gate who refused to let me through. And my boyfriend knows me far too well. A police cruiser pulled up about a minute after I did. Officer Ben Clark was driving, Matt was in the passenger seat, and somebody was in the back, but I couldn't see who.

Matt got out. "Maggie…"

"I'm tired of this, Matt. It has to end. Now."

"And it will." He turned to the guard on the gate. "Are Ms. Margaret Kepper and Mr. Bobby Tinson on the ranch?"

The guard nodded.

Matt opened the back door of the SUV and pulled out the guy from the church. He perp-walked him over to the gate guard and then released him.

"Let me make this clear. I think this man here along with Margaret Kepper and Bobby Tinson have been trying to sabotage a friend of mine's wedding. That ends now. If any of those three leave these premises for the rest of the day, they will be arrested. I am leaving Officer Clark here to monitor the departure of any guests from this property with orders to arrest any of those three individuals on sight. Is that understood?"

He glared at them until both the guard and Johnny Tinson nodded.

"Good. Now enjoy your wedding, like we intend to enjoy ours."

He walked over to me. "Care to give me a ride to the church?"

"Sure."

As I walked around to the driver's side, he added, "By the way, I kind of like this whole look you have going on. Very Warrior Princess."

(I'll leave out my reaction to that little comment. Good thing Matt doesn't take me seriously. He just laughed. Well, I always did say I wanted a man who'd ignore my anger but pay attention to my tears. Somehow I tend to forget that, though, when I'm angry.)

CHAPTER 41

We were the last ones to arrive at the church. All the guests were already there and seated. I quickly switched out of my shoes and lined up with exactly two minutes to spare.

Jamie grabbed my hand. "The decorations are gorgeous. Thank you."

"Thank my grandpa. And sorry they don't match the dresses."

"That's okay. It's all okay. I get to marry the man I love today and that is all that matters." She squeezed my hands, her eyes starting to tear.

The wedding march started.

I glanced into the church. Mason and my grandpa were at the front, waiting. The pews were full of guests. It was time.

I pointed to the two flower girls and gestured them towards the aisle. They were absolutely adorable twin second cousins of Jamie's, both five years old, wearing little pink frilly dresses and with bows in their hair. They tottered down the aisle, spilling white petals left and right.

Behind them came the ring bearer, a little boy in a tuxedo whose mom had to run up and help keep him on track when he suddenly stopped midway down the aisle and looked like he was going to cry.

And then the parade of bridesmaids started.

Jamie is a great person. Love her to death. But her third cousin who she hadn't spoken to in at least six months did not need to be a bridesmaid. Nor did her best friend from high school who was married with three kids and who she hadn't spoken to since number two was born.

But that was Jamie. She had to include everyone.

So we stood there and waited while eight bridesmaids and matching groomsmen walked down the aisle. Even though I was technically the maid of honor and Matt was not the best man, I walked down the aisle with him. Because if there was any man on this planet I was going to walk down any sort of aisle with, it was him. Mason's law school buddy Mitch, who was the best man, walked with Caroline and good riddance to them both.

By the time I reached the end all I wanted was for it to be over soon because I was not used to wearing heels anymore and I certainly was not used to wearing them while standing in front of a room full of important people.

But then it was Jamie's turn.

I almost cried. She was glowing with happiness. And so beautiful in that dress that Greta had given her. And her father looked so sad and proud at the same time. It was a perfect wedding moment.

And to see how Mason watched her as she walked towards him. When I saw one single tear slide down his cheek I had to look away so I wouldn't start bawling.

No matter what I might think of him, in that moment I knew he was the right choice for her. He might be uptight, but he'd shown time and time again how much he loved her. And that look in his eyes as he took her hand from her father?

Perfection.

My grandpa smiled at both of them and then turned his attention to the crowd. "Ladies and gentlemen, we are gathered here today to witness the joining of these two bright lives together."

The rest of the speech was short and sweet, but I wasn't really listening, I was just trying to keep it together so I wouldn't turn into a horrible, crying mess.

I almost made it, too, until Mason had to say his vows. And then the way his voice wavered as he promised to love my friend forever and his hand trembled as he put the ring on her finger? And the way Jamie started to sniffle? It was just too much.

Fortunately Jamie's mom was in the front row and armed with plenty of tissues. At that point I figured I'd done my duty and sank down next to her and sobbed while a woman with the most amazing voice sang a song about forever love.

When that was done, my grandpa stepped forward once more. "We have witnessed the joining of these two wonderful people. Now let us celebrate the new Mr. and Mrs. Mason Maxwell."

We all cheered as they walked down the aisle, beaming with happiness.

It was wonderful.

Maybe it wasn't what Jamie had planned down to the littlest detail, but all the parts that mattered had happened. Given the circumstances, I considered that more than an accomplishment, I considered it a miracle.

Now all that was left was to hope that Greta and Jean-Philippe would come through on the reception.

CHAPTER 42

As I waited for everyone to exit the church, I found myself cornered by Mason's grandmother. She's ninety-five years old and *seems* incredibly frail, but that woman…

She's fierce.

"You're next." She nodded with all the certainty of a woman who's always gotten her way for close to a century.

"Next to what?"

"Get married, dear. Mason tells me you and Matthew Barnes are an item."

"We've been dating, but I seriously doubt we'll get married anytime soon." I looked around for someone to rescue me, but no one was nearby.

"How old are you?" she demanded.

"Thirty-six."

"That's not young. I married Mason's grandpa when I was seventeen. You better get married soon."

I gritted my teeth. "And why's that?"

"The clock's ticking, young lady. If you don't get married soon, you won't have kids."

I was tempted to explain to her that kids can in fact be conceived outside of wedlock and that some women actually don't want kids at all, but decided I really didn't want to give Mason's grandma a heart attack on his wedding day.

Of course, me being me, I still had to say something. I settled for, "You know, they actually say forty is the new thirty."

"Not where your ovaries are concerned, young lady. Tick-tock."

How had I ended up in this conversation? And what business was it of hers if my ovaries were shriveling up and dying as we spoke? She wasn't family. Mine or Matt's. And yet, somehow we live in this world where random people can have an opinion—and voice it—about a woman's reproductive plans.

What the…

I looked around again, desperate for someone to save me and saw Matt leaning against the wall on the other side of the church grinning at me. That little…He knew. And he was leaving me to her. Like throwing the weaker lamb to the wolves.

"Speaking of Matthew Barnes, I better go grab him before someone else does, yeah?"

"Good thinking, dear. A catch like that, you better lock him down while you have the chance."

Right. Because men are these wayward creatures that will just blow away if they aren't nailed to the floor with wedding vows and babies.

I hurried away from her as fast as I could in three-inch heels.

"Did you get the 'you're next' talk?" Matt asked me.

"Yes. Why didn't you save me?"

"Because she would've probably forced me to propose to you right here and now and I didn't want to hear you say no in front of a witness."

"With her as a witness I might've said yes. That woman is scary."

"Oh, if that's the case..." He grabbed my hand and took a step in her direction.

"Stop. That is not funny."

He tugged my hand gently, but then his phone started ringing. "I better take this."

While he answered the call I slipped out of my heels. I figured no one was watching me anymore and my tights would survive the barefoot walk to the reception area.

Lucky for me someone had come to lead Mason's grandma away but I wasn't going to chance running into her again by moving from that spot for at least another five minutes.

Matt hung up and glanced at me.

"What? Who was it?" I asked.

"Ben. He had good news. Of a sort."

"What's that?"

"Bobby and Johnny Tinson were just arrested trying to sneak away from the Kepper Ranch."

"Really? That's great news. Now we can have a reception without worrying about them doing something else stupid. Any chance they confessed?"

"Actually. Seems Bobby isn't as good as Johnny at keeping his mouth shut. He already said enough for Ben to tie them to the water damage to the church."

"What about Margaret? I know she had to be the one that hurt Elaine."

"Nope. Nothing on her. And she's still at the ranch."

"Wait…Ben was the only officer watching the ranch, right?"

"Right."

"And he just arrested Bobby and Johnny and I presume is bringing them in for holding?"

He nodded.

"So who's watching the ranch now?"

"No one."

I crossed my arms and glared at him. "Matt."

"What?"

"Who do you think is behind all this? Bobby Tinson? Do you really think he thought all of this up? No. It's Margaret Kepper. She's the only one with enough of a motive."

"Okay, so it's Margaret Kepper. I can agree with that."

"And your officer just drove off and left her alone to do whatever she's going to do."

"Where would she go? No one knows where the reception is."

"I wouldn't bet money on that. First, that SUV was seen at Greta's a few days ago. So they already suspect. And when I was at Jamie's I heard her mention it to the bridesmaids. All it takes is one and since Caroline was there I wouldn't be surprised if she picked up the phone and called Margaret Kepper herself."

"We can't arrest her if she hasn't done anything, Maggie."

I glared him down trying to perform some sort of Vulcan mind control to sway him to my side. (Fancy's the master of that. She stares me down and suddenly I'm reaching for her treat bag as if it was my idea to give her just one more.)

It wasn't working, but then his phone rang again.

"Matt Barnes."

I watched intently as he said, "She is? What did she say?" And then "Uhuh. Okay. Well, pick her up."

He hung up.

"Well?"

"Elaine woke up. She never made any brownies at all. That must've all been Margaret. It seems Margaret came by last night for a final fitting on her dress and suggested they drink some champagne to celebrate. Elaine drank a couple of glasses and then started to feel ill so ran to the bathroom where she passed out. And Margaret just left her there. Next thing Elaine knew she was in the hospital."

"Got her!"

Matt gave me a long look.

"And I'm glad to hear Elaine is okay, too," I added.

His phone rang again. This time his end of the conversation was, "She's not? Well, find her."

"What now?"

"She isn't at the ranch. You were right. The security guard said she left right after Ben took Bobby and Johnny into custody."

"Then we better get to Greta's."

He glanced at my feet. "Barefoot?"

"My boots are in the foyer. Let's go." I ran down the aisle, dug out my boots, and sat on the ground to put them on.

"I'm driving," he said, twirling his keys as he waited for me.

"No. You drive too slow."

"Not in my police vehicle, which is parked right outside."

"I thought you were off duty."

"I am, but I figured with everything that had been happening better have it handy."

I flashed him a smile. "Even better. Lights and sirens. Let's go."

CHAPTER 43

We made good time getting to Bakerstown. It was winter in Colorado and starting to get dark so we didn't make *that* good a time, but we definitely got there faster than we would've in my van. And Matt, thankfully, is actually willing to speed when he's in his cop role. (Other times he seems to think the speed limit is actually an upper limit. Crazy man.)

We were one curve in the road away from Greta's when I saw a fancy SUV pulled over to the side of the road and a small figure in a big snow coat climbing up the mountainside towards her house.

"Pull over," I shouted.

I jumped out the door before he even stopped and raced towards the figure on the hillside. I stopped at the edge of the road. "Margaret Kepper. Stop where you are. It's over."

She glanced at me just long enough for me to confirm it was her and then turned back to her uphill climb.

"Oh no you don't." I plowed into the snow—which was up to mid-calf and higher than my snow boots—and chased after her.

She tried to run away, but I wasn't having it. I dove at her, wrapping my arms around her thighs and took her down face-first into a snow bank.

It turns out I'm a fierce powderpuff player and that when we used to do midnight girls vs. guys "tackle" games I dominated. (Maybe because I was the only one actually trying to play tackle football while the other girls were coming up with clever plays like "everyone strip down to their bra so the boys are too distracted and we can score a touchdown.")

Anyway. I took her out. Sure, I could've just let Matt grab her, but she'd tried to ruin my best friend's wedding. I had feelings about that and they needed somewhere to go. Dive tackling the culprit into a snow bank seemed like a good use for them.

She tried to elbow me in the face, but I dodged it. "What is wrong with you? Seriously. Stop already."

"Jamie Green ruined my wedding. What did I ever do to her that she hates me so much?"

"Jamie doesn't hate you. I'm pretty sure she doesn't even know who you are."

That seemed to take all the wind out of her. She slumped into the ground and started to cry. "I planned my wedding a year in advance. And then she goes and changes her date last minute and everyone cancels on me so they can go to her wedding instead. Just like in high school."

"What'd she do to you in high school?"

"I was going to throw this big party at my dad's ranch and everyone was going to come and it was going to make me popular. But then Jamie suddenly hooks up with Dan and convinces him to throw a party at his ranch that same night. And no one came to my party. She ruined everything."

"I bet Elaine went to your party."

"Elaine doesn't count."

"Yeah, those friends that are always there for you no matter what, worthless aren't they? I mean who wants those when you can have the type of friends who cancel when something better comes along."

She stared at me, confused.

"Just in case you missed it, that was sarcasm. You don't deserve a friend like Elaine. And I hope she finally sees that now."

I stood up as Matt joined us. He eyed me up and down for a second. "You're going to need to change."

"Why?" I glanced down. "Oh. Right."

My tights were torn in at least three different spots and my knees were a little bloody. And somehow I'd managed to tear a huge section of the floofy little skirt on my dress so that it was less-than-decent now.

"Your hair, too."

I reached up to touch it. It was still sprayed into oblivion, but it seemed a whole section had come loose from its pins and was sticking out at an odd angle.

"Well, good thing I already know Greta has a dress that'll fit me then. And that she has about ten guest rooms. I'm sure one has a brush I can use. You mind driving me up to her place before you take this crazy woman in?"

"Oh I'm not taking her in." He pulled Margaret down the hill and locked her in the back of the vehicle. "I'll let Greta's security call someone who's actually on duty tonight." He pulled me close for a quick kiss. "This is

New Year's Eve and I'm going to spend it with the woman I love, not filling out paperwork."

"Good man. Smart man." But if he proposed to me…We were going to have words.

CHAPTER 44

Not only did Greta let me borrow the gorgeous blue dress but she also let me take a wonderfully hot shower to wash away the chill of burying myself in a snowbank while wearing a short dress. That also meant I could wash out all the hairspray and wear my hair loose and falling down my back, although I was likely to pull it into a sloppy bun before the night was out.

When I finally joined the party I found Matt and Greta waiting for me. Matt let out a low whistle. "Now that is a dress that works."

"I told her it is hers. It can be her something blue on her wedding day. Even if her wedding day is on the side of a mountain alone with the man she loves."

"Is that what you want?" he asked me.

"Can we just get through the rest of *this* wedding before we try to go there, please?"

Matt kissed my cheek. "As you wish."

"Greta, how's Jean-Philippe getting along?" I asked.

"See for yourself." She led me to the kitchen and I peeked inside.

Jean-Philippe was like I'd never seen him before. He's

usually over-the-top dramatic or almost catatonically relaxed, but in the kitchen he was a man in his element. He was cutting something up, while tasting something else, and then turning to shout in French and English and who-knew-what other languages at the others who were preparing the food under his supervision.

It was organized chaos at its finest.

Greta eyed him appreciatively.

"Remember what you told me, Greta. Never marry a chef."

"I was not thinking of marrying him." She winked at me and took another step into the kitchen. In an odd way they were a good match.

I left them to it.

As I stepped into the main room I almost bumped into my grandpa who was loitering near the door. "How's Jean-Philippe?" he asked.

"Leave him be, Grandpa. If anyone needs to defend my honor at this point in time, it's Matt, not you." I hooked my arm through his and led him towards the nearest table. It was filled with a huge assortment of delicious-looking finger foods.

I snagged myself some sort of crostini appetizer that was positively decadent. Figs and foie gras with honey drizzled on top if I had to guess.

"Thank you again for everything you did today," I told him.

"You're welcome. Jamie's like another granddaughter to me. I was happy to help."

I nodded to where Lesley was talking to someone on the other side of the room. A ring flashed as she raised her left hand.

"So I take it you're telling everyone you're married now?"

He nodded. "We're ready to start our lives together."

I grabbed another bite of food—this one some sort of butter-soaked lobster bite—and swallowed it down so fast I almost didn't taste the buttery goodness.

"Grandpa? Is Lesley going to move in with you? With…us? Or are you going to move in with her? Or…?"

"Don't worry about it, Maggie. We'll figure that out next year."

But I did. And next year was only a few hours away.

Matt grabbed my hand and bowed over it like a gentleman. "My lady. May I have the pleasure of your company?"

"Of course."

I let him lead me around the room, sampling all the delicious food and talking to the other guests. It was so different to be at a wedding as part of a couple. It was…almost fun.

We ran into Greta again on the other side of the room, daintily eating a stuffed mushroom from a table that was clearly labeled as vegan.

"So Jean-Philippe did honor the guest's wishes, did he?" I asked. "He actually came through with some healthy foods for all of Jamie's friends?"

Greta laughed. "No. The man was too upset for that. I brought in a specialist."

"Ah. Smart woman. Just don't tell anyone they aren't eating food by the famed Jean-Philippe Gaston."

She smiled. "Their loss, no?"

I let Matt pull me into a slow dance before moving on

to inspect the desserts. Jamie's cupcakes were center stage like some sort of display straight out of *Cupcake Wars*, but nearby there were also a series of small cakes that could easily serve another hundred guests as well as a large fresh fruit display and a chocolate fountain.

"Greta did well," I told Matt.

"So did you. You really pulled this together." He brushed a strand of hair behind my ear. "So, you want a wedding on the side of a mountain, do you?"

I must have looked as panicked as I felt, because he laughed and pulled me close. "Does the thought of spending forever with me really scare you that much?"

"No. It's just…It's too soon."

"Three months is too soon?"

"Yes. Definitely. It's all raging hormones at this point and no sense. I have flaws, Matt. I'm sure you do, too."

He chuckled. "So when is enough time?"

"Definitely not three months, that's for sure."

He took my chin in his hand and stared into my eyes. "But not three years either, Maggie."

"At least wait until spring, would you?"

"Done." He turned and started to walk away.

"What? No. Wait? I wasn't…"

He turned and winked at me. "Come on. Let's go congratulate the happy couple. And, I promise, no more talk of weddings for the rest of the night."

I hurried after him. "But that spring thing…I didn't really mean…"

He kissed me. "No more talk about it tonight. Let's just celebrate our friends' happiness and let tomorrow bring what it will."

🐾 🐾 🐾

The rest of that night was the best New Year's Eve I'd ever celebrated. Finally I was where I wanted to be, surrounded by friends, family, and a man I loved. Not to mention I'd been instrumental in pulling off an awesome party and getting a crazy, psycho person locked away.

Not bad. Not bad at all.

A POISONED PAST

AND PUPPERMINTS

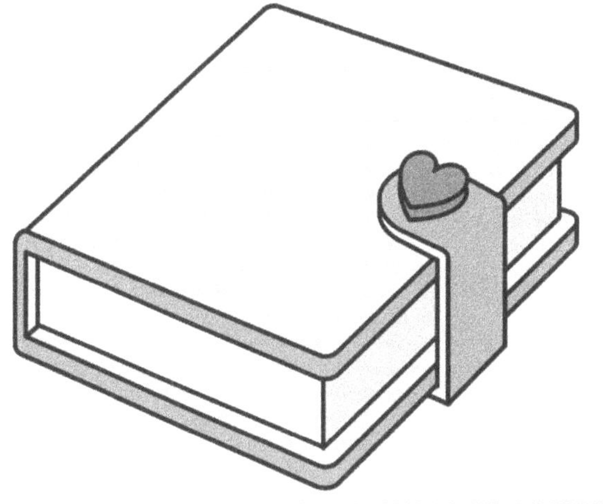

A MAGGIE MAY AND MISS FANCYPANTS MYSTERY

ALEKSA BAXTER

CHAPTER 1

As I drove along the narrow two-lane highway towards the only supermarket in the valley, I was not a happy camper. Sure, it was a gorgeous day. Winter, so not exactly warm, but the skies were a bright, clear blue and there wasn't a single cloud in the sky. I was surrounded by the beauty of the Colorado mountains, covered in evergreens and capped in snow. The barbed wire fences that kept the local cows where they belonged off the highway were ruggedly picturesque, as were the farm houses at the end of rutted dirt roads.

A heckuva lot better view than when I'd lived in DC, that's for sure. Then a trip to the grocery store had meant merging onto a four-lane road with only power lines, overpasses, and buildings visible no matter what direction I turned.

Finally, at the age of thirty-six, I, Maggie May Carver, was somewhere I actually wanted to be.

Problem was, it was the day before Valentine's Day.

Honestly, one of the worst holidays on the planet. It's supposed to be about showing your love for someone, but I have to tell you I stopped finding it an enjoyable holiday after about third grade. Prior to that it was all cutesy and fun and I gave ridiculously over-the-top little valentines to my crush—a cute little blonde boy who lived down the street and who I'd declared my boyfriend whether he wanted to be or not.

But after that it started to be about who was popular and who wasn't. And if you gave a *boy* a valentine it was far more than just some cute little card. It was a declaration of war if *that* girl in your class liked him, too. Or it suddenly meant something more than "Hey, you're cute" or "I like you because you're my friend."

And Valentine's Day as an adult? Well, let's just say that for many years I was the woman in black when I bothered to remember the holiday even existed. (Jamie, my best friend, was of course the one in bright pink. Then again, she was also the one receiving more than one bouquet of roses or sweet little notes from her various admirers each holiday.)

But what made it even worse was that now I had an actual boyfriend. Matt was wonderful. Tall, dark, handsome. A good person. (A good kisser.) And somehow bizarrely okay with being with me despite all my flaws.

Which meant I really, truly wanted to erase the holiday from the map. See, Valentine's is easy if you're a guy. You buy a dozen roses or a box of chocolates or a pair of earrings or a bracelet or something sexy and lacy, and you're done. Easy peasy.

Generic as all get out and not showing the slightest bit of thought or personalization, but a woman can't really object if you remember the day and honor it with one of the classic gifts.

Oh, stuffed animals holding hearts work, too, of course.

But for a woman. You don't really buy a guy roses. Or chocolates. Or stuffed animals. Or earrings. Or some little sexy, lacy thing.

I mean, I guess you could.

(I'm now having inappropriate thoughts about Matt and some little sexy, lacy thing that I will stop talking about because he's MINE and you don't need to be going there with me. But he'd look good in it if he'd be willing, which he probably wouldn't.)

So, anyway. It was the day before Valentine's Day. Matt and I were running away to the Creek Inn for a fancy little dinner and a nice night together the next day (which he wasn't going to let me pay for either, taking that option off the table), and I was headed to the grocery store trying to at least find a good card for him.

Which was also not going to be easy. Go with the funny option and he'd start to wonder if I cared enough. Go with the serious, "you're the love of my life" option and maybe he'd run for the door. Or, worse, he'd frickin' propose, which I was not ready for yet either.

Seriously, I think I'd have an easier life if I just never thought about anything at all. But I do.

Which is why I was in a surly mood when I finally made it to the store and located the card aisle with its helium balloons trailing curled string and bright pink and red colors everywhere.

I took my time, reading each and every card, trying to find the one that was lovey-dovey enough to let Matt know I cared, but not too much. (Advice to Hallmark— you need a better selection of cards for the ambivalent among us. And not just for Valentine's.)

I'd just found one that was going to have to be good enough when Mr. Lewis shuffled his way towards me.

He'd been a semi-regular customer at the café when it was still open, although he'd never been much of a talker. He'd come in most days for lunch, sit in the far corner, and eat a bowl of soup by himself. He didn't even bring a book or play on his phone. He just stared out the window as he slowly sipped spoonful after spoonful of soup and then left again, always with a generous tip.

He was a tall man, slender, probably mid-50s, but stooped like a much older man. I'd figured he was sick with cancer or something the way he carried himself, but I'd never asked.

In other words, every time I saw the man I just wanted to give him a hug and tell him it would get better. But instead I always gave him his space and tried to be as quiet and kind as I could. This time, though, I figured it wouldn't hurt to at least say hi.

"Mr. Lewis. I haven't seen you in a while. How are you?"

He turned to me and I could see tears in his eyes.

"Are you okay?"

He shook himself off like a dog shaking off water. "Yeah. I, um." He stared at the floor for a long moment, fists clenched, clearly trying to master his emotions.

I stepped closer. "Is there anything I can do?"

He sniffed and turned back to the display of various stuffed animals piled upon the shelf, their hands clutched around red roses or hearts with silly words on them like "Be Mine". He covered his mouth with his large hand for a moment, pulling himself back together. "Which is your favorite?" he asked.

"My favorite?"

"Of the stuffed animals. I always get her one each year, but I never really know which one she'd want. She's been gone so long."

I desperately wanted to ask who *she* was, but I suspected that if I did he might just break right there and then. And I wasn't sure he'd ever be able to put himself back together again if he did. (I've been there myself a few times.)

I reached for the shelf. "You know, I've always been partial to pandas. And this one here with the big eyes is pretty darned cute." I handed it to him.

"Good choice. Thank you."

He started to turn away.

"Mr. Lewis, can I buy you a coffee or something?"

He shook his head. "No. I'm fine. You have a nice day, Miss Carver."

He shuffled away, shoulders hunched, head down, the panda clutched in his big hand. I wanted to run after him and insist that he let me buy him a bowl of soup or something. But I knew he wouldn't appreciate the interference. And, honestly, I wasn't sure what we'd talk about. We'd never exchanged more than a dozen words at a time in all those days he was coming into the café. That was Jamie's side of things (I was responsible for the barkery), so she'd had far more interaction with him than I had.

Plus, sometimes those pleasant but shallow interactions are the ones you need most in life, you know. Those quick exchanges of a few words here or there with someone who doesn't know what's going on in your life so they can't ask about it and remind you of what's weighing you down. (Or is that just me?)

If I forced him to tell me who he'd lost—because he clearly had lost someone—then I'd become yet another person to look at him with pity. And who needs that?

So instead I grabbed a bag of salted caramel dark chocolate hearts off the shelf for Matt's "gift". I figured even if he didn't want to eat them, I would, and hey, it's the thought that counts. (I'm lucky that Matt likes a woman with a few extra curves here or there. Or that, if he doesn't, he's smart enough not to say anything about it.)

But as I walked towards the checkout, I couldn't stop thinking about poor Mr. Lewis.

CHAPTER 2

That night it was just my grandpa, Lesley, and me at dinner. They were so cute together, exchanging a quick kiss before they sat down at the table, my grandpa in his usual jeans and flannel shirt and Lesley all polished up and perfect with her snow-white hair pulled back into a classic chignon. Hard to believe that two people in their eighties could be so unabashedly in love, but they were.

I'd been all worried that when they got married they'd move in together and expect me to move out, but the reality was even stranger than that. They'd decided to keep their own houses, since both of them had lived in their homes for forty-plus years and neither one wanted to move.

But during the day my grandpa was frequently over at Lesley's or she was over at our house. They'd have most lunches and dinners together and then after dinner they'd often sit and snuggle on the couch, holding hands and talking softly until about eight o'clock when my grandpa would drive Lesley home.

(Needless to say, I'd taken to spending a lot of time alone in my room at night. It's awkward to be the third person in the room with an affectionate couple.)

I'd asked my grandpa if they ever thought they'd move in together at some point and he'd shrugged. "Maybe. If we ever get to the point where we can't easily go back and forth."

"I don't understand. Why get married if you're not going to live together? You're basically dating 1940's-style. You could've done that without the whole marriage brouhaha."

(Lesley's family had not reacted well to the news of their marriage.)

He chuckled. "We got married because we wanted to show that we're committed to one another. Also, because Lesley and I both grew up in a generation that believes that if you're going to have sex…"

I held up a hand. "Oh no. Stop the conversation right there, thank you. My grandpa and sex never need to be in the same sentence ever again. Sorry I asked. Carry on. Do your thing. Whatever works for you."

When he started to open his mouth to say something else that I knew I wasn't going to want to hear (or picture) I hurried from the room.

So there we were, almost two months later, with Lesley over for dinner as usual. She'd taken over dinner duties so dinner was fancier than something I'd normally whip up. There were steamed green beans, mashed potatoes with gravy, and a pork loin roast that smelled like heaven. All served in the dining room on my grandma's best china and with the television turned off.

(I have to say I missed the meals my grandpa and I used to eat while tucked up on the old, worn couches watching the Justice Channel, but the food was definitely an improvement.)

When Fancy—my almost four-year-old Newfound-land—laid down at my side and I put her sharing plate on the floor, Lesley glared at us, but I ignored her. That was one fight I was not going to lose in the home where I was living. Fancy got her sharing plate. Period. End of.

She was lady-like about it and it kept her from begging or barking or otherwise disturbing the meal, so too bad that Lesley thought it was barbaric to have a dog eating off of a plate next to the dinner table. She was just going to have to get used to it.

That and a few other things.

Don't get me wrong. Lesley was a wonderful woman. She was great for my grandpa. I personally liked her a lot. But she had some notions about how women should live their lives that didn't always synch with mine, which had caused a little bit of tension. But we had politely agreed to disagree.

Or, more realistically, she would subtly mention her views to me and I would subtly ignore them. Honestly, I figured if I never married Matt a big part of the reason would just be to annoy her.

(I once took this test about how susceptible you are to influence and it turns out I am so unsusceptible to influence that if you actually want to push me to do something you'd be better off pushing me to do the opposite. Turns out I become a brick wall when I realize someone is trying to manipulate me.)

So, anyway. There we were at dinner. They were being all newly in love and gooey while I brooded about the pressure of spending my first Valentine's with Matt and while Fancy drooled a small puddle onto the floor waiting for me to notice her and give her a bit of food off my plate.

To distract myself from my maudlin thoughts I said, "I ran into Mr. Lewis at the grocery store today. He was buying a stuffed animal for Valentine's for someone, but he looked like he was about to cry."

"Oh. That poor man." Lesley shook her head.

"What happened?" I asked.

She glanced at my grandpa. "How long ago was it? Ten years?"

"Maybe as many as fifteen."

"It could be fifteen by now. You're right."

They both nodded.

"What?" I asked again.

"His daughter was killed. Right after high school graduation. He'd raised that poor girl by himself. She was such a sweetheart, too. So bright and beautiful. And then, just like that, gone." Lesley sighed.

"Never did find out who did it." My grandpa squeezed her hand. "I think that's the hardest part. Not knowing who did it or why. Such a tragedy. She was his only child. He lived and breathed for that girl. He was at every single game when she played baseball for me. When she was in middle school he worked two jobs to save up so she could attend a special summer camp for gifted kids. And when she got into college, I don't think there was a man more proud than he was."

I sat back. "That poor man. I never knew."

My grandpa nodded. "He doesn't talk about it much. He doesn't talk to anyone much since it happened, really. He used to be a tractor salesman. One of the most outgoing and gregarious men you'd ever meet. Always out and about. Always had a firm handshake and a ready smile. But after Julie died, he couldn't do it anymore. He quit his job. Probably spent the first five years at home, never going anywhere except the grocery store."

"I guess that changed some over time. He used to come into the café for lunch. But he did keep to himself."

"Yeah. After those first few years I saw him around more. He'd nod hello, but it was clear he wanted to be left alone still."

"He was like that at the café, too. He'd order his soup and then just stare out the window, not trying to talk to anyone." I poked at my food, no longer hungry. "That poor man. He seemed so sad today. I wish there was something I could do for him."

My grandpa glared at me. "Don't you even think about it, Maggie May."

"Think about what?"

"Trying to solve that murder. Just because you've lucked into solving a few crimes here or there doesn't make this your business. That man has moved on with his life. Let it go."

But he hadn't moved on with his life. From what I could tell he was stuck in some gray half-life. Ten or fifteen years later and still buying your dead daughter a Valentine's present? It was touching, but it wasn't the action of a man who'd moved on with his life.

Maybe what Mr. Lewis needed was closure.

"Maggie May…"

"What? I didn't say I was going to try to solve the murder. Heck, I hadn't even thought of doing so until you mentioned it."

But now that he had…

Why not see what I could do? Not like I was doing

much with my days other than playing too much solitaire and reading too many books. (Not that you can ever actually read too many books in my opinion, but all that sitting on couches or chairs for hours and hours each day does start to affect the body. I had "reader's back" from curling up on the couch for too long too many days in a row.)

"Maggie May, don't go stirring up old hurts. Let this go."

"I heard you the first time, Grandpa." I flashed him my most brilliant smile. "What do you guys say to a game of Scrabble after dinner? You up for it?"

My grandpa narrowed his eyes at me. He knew when I was deliberately changing the subject. But he didn't push me on it. "Sure. Sounds like fun."

"Great."

The whole rest of the dinner I tried to figure out the exact right approach to use on Matt—who in addition to being my wonderful boyfriend was also a cop—to get access to the old case file. That seemed to me to be the best place to start. No use bothering Mr. Lewis about it until I was sure there was something I could do to help.

CHAPTER 3

The next night Matt and I drove through the winding canyon between my grandpa's house in Creek and the Creek Inn for our special Valentine's dinner.

Matt had dressed in a pair of nice black slacks and a white collared shirt, the top two buttons undone. He looked stunning with his dark hair and blue eyes and I gave myself a little mental pat on the back for snagging him when all the single girls in the county had wanted him. (Or at least I assumed they had. In small towns your pickings are pretty slim so a guy like Matt goes fast. Not that I'd had any attention whatsoever of falling for him, but when a man that great crosses your path, it's a little hard to ignore.)

I'd made an effort at dressing up, too. I was wearing my one remaining little black dress and had even put on makeup and done my hair, although I'd decided that due to the winter season and my aversion to heels that I could pair it with some cute furry snow boots instead of proper dressy shoes.

Matt, bless him, didn't even mention my unusual choice of footwear. He just told me I looked beautiful, gave me a kiss on the cheek, and handed me a small box of chocolate caramels.

(So many reasons I like that man…)

The Creek Inn not only had a great dive bar (where Matt and I had played pool on what I thought of as our first not-date), but it also had a gorgeous five-star restaurant attached to the hotel portion that was decorated to the hilt for the holiday with red roses and pink hearts and lots and lots of candles.

It was the only place with white linen tablecloths within a twenty-minute drive of Creek. (That's what you get when you live in a town of about a hundred people in the Colorado mountains. Lots of beauty, but not lots of dining choices.)

They had classical music playing in the background to set the mood which was decidedly cozy with about a dozen tables scattered throughout the place. We'd probably been lucky to get a reservation—although we did have an in with the owners, Evan and Abe—but then again, the price point for the dinner was probably out of reach for most of the more established couples in the area.

Abe greeted us as we walked in the door with a kiss on each cheek and led us to a snuggly little table in the back corner. "The best table for my favorite couple."

"Thank you," I told him as he held the chair for me, something I have always found incredibly awkward and honestly makes me want to avoid all fancy restaurants.

(I'm always worried I'm going to sit too soon or not soon enough and make an awkward fool of myself. That and what to do with your napkin and your fork are enough to scare me off of any sort of formal dining, but for the chance at a romantic evening with Matt I was willing to suffer through it.)

They were serving a special menu for the night that included a choice of lobster or steak for the main course (yum) and came with wine pairings, which I love. We each made our selections and then while we waited for the first course I told Matt about running into Mr. Lewis at the grocery store the day before and asked if he knew anything about the death of Julie Lewis.

(I know. You shouldn't discuss death or murder at a Valentine's Day dinner with your sweetheart, but unfortunately for Matt and our romantic evening, that dinner was the first time I'd seen him since running into Mr. Lewis, and I hadn't been able to stop thinking about the poor man since.)

Matt took a long sip of his wine instead of answering, his blue eyes narrowed.

"What?" I asked. "It was a simple question. Do you know anything about the murder of Julie Lewis?"

"Maggie May…"

"Oh, you sound like my grandpa. I'm bored, Matt. There are only so many books I can read and so many games of solitaire I can play. And Fancy's only up for a short walk every day so not like I can take up snowshoeing or something like that. And I refuse to be that person who sits on the couch all day watching TV or lives on Twitter telling everybody how offended they are by some innocuous comment. You have a job. I have…nothing."

"So you're going to dig into some old murder because you don't have any good hobbies? I'm sure Lesley could teach you how to crochet. Or you could volunteer down at the library. Or the YMCA."

"I already know how to crochet."

"You do?"

"Yes. And cross stitch. And tat. And paint ceramics. And hand-bead things. The only thing I could never get the hang of was knitting. I made the mistake of learning to crochet first and then I always wanted a hook to grab my yarn with."

He grunted. "When did you learn how to do all of that?"

"I must've been bored when I was a kid. But unless you want a cross-stitched fishing scene for your wall for Christmas next year, I'd suggest you don't encourage me to get back into handcrafts."

"So you think we'll still be together next Christmas, huh?" He flashed me a devilish grin.

"Matthew Allen Barnes. I thought we were giving all that relationship talk a little bit of time off."

"It's Valentine's Day. What better day to talk about your relationship than on Valentine's?"

I thought about it for a second. "Pretty much any other day. This day has enough pressure on it as is. No need to go adding a relationship talk on top of it."

He leaned forward. "It's just that there are some decisions I need to make soon and I'd like to know where we stand."

"Together. Isn't that enough?"

"Like the song asks, are we written in the stars or written in the sand?"

I rolled my eyes. "Don't be absurd. If I didn't want to be with you, I wouldn't be. And just because I don't want to talk about it doesn't mean I'm not serious about you. You know I'm not good at all of this relationship stuff. Now can we just talk about murder instead, please?"

"You're going to have to talk about where we're headed at some point, Maggie."

"Yeah, well, not just yet, okay? So, murder. Julie Lewis. What do you know?"

Before Matt could answer, Abe came to our table with a gorgeous shrimp cocktail for Matt and a bowl of French onion soup for me.

"Oh that looks amazing, Abe," I said. "You have outdone yourself. But you and Evan shouldn't be working on Valentine's. You should take the day to celebrate together."

He chuckled. "And miss one of the most profitable restaurant days of the year? Never. February 14th is just a day. Evan and I can celebrate when we go on our Bahamas cruise next week."

"Bahamas? Ooh. Nice."

"It will be. We always try to get away for Evan's birthday. It's the perfect cure for the late-winter blues. You two should try it. Run away for a long weekend together somewhere nice and warm."

I grimaced.

Matt smiled. "Yes, we should. You're right."

I plucked one of the extra-large shrimp off of Matt's plate, dunked it in cocktail sauce, and took a big bite to hide my consternation as Abe left to greet a couple who'd just walked in the door.

(The last guy I'd liked enough to go away with for a weekend, that weekend had ended the relationship, so I wasn't at all interested in trying that again anytime soon. Not even for Matt.)

Next I took a bite of my very gooey delicious soup (which was made perfectly with the cheese all golden brown and melted over the sides of a sturdy brown crock like it should be) before saying, "So? Julie Lewis. What do you know?"

Matt shook his head as he tore a piece of bread off the loaf in the center of the table. "Not much. I wasn't here when it happened. As far as I know they never had any real suspect. And I don't remember there being any ugly details either, so I assume she wasn't assaulted. Just one of those tragic things that happen."

"A murder. That's never been solved."

"True."

I tilted my head. "I'd figure that must be quite the black mark on your department, not solving that murder…"

"Maggie…"

"What? I'm just saying…Think what a hero you'd be if you could solve it." I took another bite of my soup trying not to make inappropriate noises at how good it tasted.

Matt leaned back in his chair and crossed his arms. "If *I* could solve it. Not you?"

"Well, I could help. But you're the cop after all." I batted my eyes at him.

"And the only one who can get you access to the old case file."

"That, too."

He shook his head and tore off more bread.

"You're going to destroy that thing, you know." I nodded at the doughy clump of bread in his hand.

"Yeah, well. Maybe this isn't my idea of a good romantic dinner conversation."

I winced. "Sorry. Change of subject. Your choice."

"Okay." He leaned closer. "Where do you want to go for a weekend getaway? You want to drive or should we fly?"

Now it was my turn to want something to tear into tiny little pieces. Unfortunately, Matt had already demolished the loaf of bread, so instead of answering I focused on taking a very deliberate bite of my soup.

"Maggie, if you don't even want to spend a couple of days with me how can we plan for a real future together?"

"Hey now. That's…not…fair. I mean, granted, we haven't had much opportunity for quality alone time between Jack living with you and me living with my grandpa, so getting away for a few days makes some sense. But traveling together is tricky. It can ruin relationships."

"So, what? We should never travel together? You know that living together is messy, too, right? Maybe we can have a relationship like your grandpa and Lesley where we never live together even after we're married. Is that what you want? Because it's not what I want."

I huffed a breath and put down my spoon. "No. That's not what I want. I just want a little bit of time to enjoy what we have before we start adding things on top of it that can break it."

He took my hand and held my gaze. "My love for you is not that fragile, Maggie. One bad weekend is not going to break it."

So he thought. But he'd never been alone with me for an entire weekend either.

I bit my lip.

"Nor is one bad Valentine's dinner where you ask me about a murder and tell me you think that going away for a weekend would be too much for us to survive."

"Well, when you put it that way…Fine. What do you think of Guatemala?"

"Guatemala? I think it's a good country for being kidnapped in." He chuckled. "How'd you come up with that one?"

"There's a very beautiful lake there. Lake Atitlan. And last time I was there it had a very beautiful resort right on the lake with a botanic gardens on the grounds. It's one of my favorite places and I've always wanted to go back."

"How long did it take to get to this resort? *After* you flew into the country?"

"Half a day maybe?"

"Not exactly a good weekend choice. Maybe we should start with something a little bit closer for our first trip as a couple. Something that doesn't require shots. Like Arizona. Florida. San Diego."

I grimaced. If I was going to leave Fancy behind for a weekend I wanted it to be worthwhile.

"Okay, so you don't like those ideas. What were you thinking?"

"Iceland? Norway? Quebec? Argentina?"

"For a weekend?"

"A long one. Leave on a Thursday, come back on a Monday."

We stared at each other for a long, long moment.

"See?" I finally said. "Not so easy is it? Maybe we should just sit on it for a while. In the meantime…"

He sighed. "Murder. Fine."

"There are so many reasons I love you." I squeezed his hand and turned my attention back to my soup before it cooled off too much to be enjoyable. Although,

with French onion soup I'm not sure that's even possible,
to be honest.

🐾🐾🐾 439 🐾🐾🐾

CHAPTER 4

Two days later Matt came over for dinner, a small file folder tucked under his arm.

"What's that?" I asked when I saw it.

"After dinner."

"Is it what I think it is?"

He shook his head and kissed me. "You are a bizarrely blood-thirsty woman, do you know that?"

I stuck my tongue out at him. "Am not. I'd be perfectly happy to never see another dead body or photo of a dead body in my life. What I am is motivated to help those who can't help themselves. And for some odd reason that seems to involve dealing with murder a lot of the time."

"So I've noticed. I'll put the folder in your bedroom."

I was tempted to follow after him to take a quick peek at what he'd brought me, but I knew he wouldn't let me. I'd always thought I wanted a man who'd stand up to me, but it was mighty annoying sometimes. Not so annoying I didn't want it, mind you. Just annoying enough to make me growly when it actually happened.

I was probably not the most polite and patient throughout dinner. My grandpa and Lesley were focused on the used book sale at the library that weekend, but all I wanted was to be done so I could go see what Matt had brought me. Knowing this, Matt chose to draw the conversation out more than normal until I finally kicked him under the table and he gave me a wink.

"Dessert?" Lesley asked when everyone had finally finished. "I made an apple pie."

"Ooh, that sounds good. But there's something I need to look at first. Matt?"

My grandpa cleared his throat as I held my hand out to Matt.

"What?" I asked.

"This is my house, young lady. I expect a certain level of decorum."

I blinked. "Decorum? Oh. You thought…?" I pointed at Matt and then back at myself. "Oh no. Not with you guys here. No. Matt brought me over the Julie Lewis murder file. I just wanted to look at it. It's in my room."

"Why don't you bring it out here? We can all look through it. Lesley and I might be able to help."

"Okay. Be right back." I ran for my bedroom, hoping that my cheeks were not as bright red as they felt.

I mean, I was almost thirty-seven-years-old. I shouldn't be embarrassed if I was in a long-term exclusive relationship and that meant *relations* with the guy in question. But I have always been one to not want to talk about that. Or acknowledge that it happens.

Not because I don't think it's fine and great and something that people should do when they want and with whomever they want to as long as all parties are legal and consenting. (And out of high school when one of those parties is Lucas Dean.) But it's just not something you discuss.

Ever.

Honestly, the way I blush around those conversations as well as anyone who decides to strip down a little too much, you'd think I was raised a couple hundred years ago. Or Amish.

I mean, my parents were hippies for crying out loud. But I somehow inherited the recessive "let's not discuss that" gene.

Anyway. Let's not discuss that.

I grabbed the murder file and returned to the dining room. "Is this all there was?" It was only about half an inch thick.

"Yep. Well, that and the physical evidence which I obviously was not going to bring here. But there's a list of what's in the box inside the folder."

I opened the file. I'd figured the first thing on the first page would be some big photograph of the body or a smiling high school photo of Julie, but maybe that only happens in TV shows. What was on top was the coroner's report. It was…sparse.

The basic gist was that she'd been struck by some hard object at least three times. The first must have been from the front, because she'd broken her forearm, probably blocking a blow, and then the other two were to the left side of the head making the assailant right-handed.

All clothes were on. No sign of sexual activity, consensual or not. And she was legally drunk, but just barely. She'd died sometime between two and six in the morning.

She'd been found around noon the next day in the woods off of a small pullout from the highway about a mile from her house by a tourist who'd stopped to take a photo of the mountains nearby and decided to let his dog out for a break. The dog had started barking uncontrollably and when the man went to investigate, he found the body.

He wasn't a suspect because he'd spent the night before in Denver at his parents' house for their wedding anniversary where a large number of guests had seen him.

Her dad hadn't yet reported her missing at the time she was found because he'd come home from a night shift at his second job at a gas station and immediately gone to bed at seven that morning. As far as he knew she'd spent the night at her best friend Barb's house. He only found out she wasn't at Barb's when the cops knocked on his door to tell him she was dead.

I shuddered, imagining what that must be like. You go home, fall asleep exhausted assuming your child is safely asleep over at a friend's house, only to be awakened by the cops banging down your door to tell you she's dead.

It reminded me how every single day is the best day in someone's life and the worst in someone else's. Every. Single. Day.

And that poor man…

My grandpa took a sip of his coffee. "He was working that second job so Julie wouldn't have to work when she went to college. Trying to build up enough extra money so she could really make the most of it. She was the first in her family to go."

"And this Barb? What do you know about her?"

My grandpa shook his head. "Never met her. She didn't play on the baseball team with Julie."

"I knew her from the library," Lesley said as she served us each a slice of apple pie and a scoop of vanilla ice cream. "She had a boyfriend she was always with. They were joined at the hip. Tim I think it was? Tall boy. Played football. And baseball. Blonde."

"Oh, Tim Holt. He played for me, too. He and Julie were good friends back then. We called them the Dynamic Duo."

My grandpa coached the co-ed kid's baseball team in town, but it was only for elementary school kids. Once middle school rolled around and the official school sports started up, there was no more need for summer baseball.

"Either one of them still around?" I asked.

Lesley shook her head. "No. Both went away for college. Some small community college. In-state, I believe. Or maybe Kansas. Never came back. I think they got married after college. I can't remember. Tim's mom was a single mom. Always kept to herself. Barb's family only lived here a couple years. They were tied in with the ski resort in Bakerstown somehow, but left after she graduated."

I glanced at the handwritten notes in the file. "Can you read this?" I asked Matt.

He took the file from me and squinted. "Yeah. It says that the night she died Julie was at the lake with Barb, Tim, and a bunch of other kids. There are about ten names here. Julie was supposed to go home with Barb, but started talking to some stranger who crashed the party—seems there were a number of people from out of town who were staying down by the lake where the party was who showed up throughout the night. Barb tried to find her and couldn't. She assumed Julie must have left with the stranger and left without her."

He scanned the rest of the notes in the file. "Cops interviewed everyone staying at the lake that they could as well as all of the kids from the party. A few kids did remember Julie talking to some guy, but no one saw them leave together, and the guy's friends all swore he was alone at the cabin when they returned around midnight. He also didn't have access to a vehicle. The friend who'd driven them all up there for the weekend had left earlier that night to return to Denver for some sort of family emergency. And…that's about it."

I grabbed the file back and glanced at the coroner's report again. "And no signs she was moved. She wasn't killed at the party or at the lake. Which is about twenty minutes from her house?"

Matt nodded.

My grandpa took the file from me and thumbed through it. He shook his head. "Not much to go on, is it?"

"Why didn't they do more?" I asked.

Matt gave Fancy a small amount of ice cream on her sharing plate, ignoring Lesley's pointed look before he answered. "How much could you do back then? The internet wasn't what it is now. No social media posts of the party. No cellphone cameras documenting every moment. No text messages. And without sexual contact, you have no DNA. All they could do was talk to people and hope someone saw something, but no one did."

"That's horrible."

"Well, that's sometimes how it works. Even now."

"But they didn't try to figure out who might've wanted her dead."

"According to the notes, no one really had a problem with her."

Fancy smacked her plate with her paw and I gave her a look. She knew better than that.

"Well, someone was obviously lying," I said as I dropped a small bite of crust on her plate.

"Probably. But who? And how much do you push on a grieving teenager when you have no real reason to push?"

I drummed my fingers on the table. "Well, they're not teenagers anymore are they? And sometimes people realize keeping a secret isn't worth it anymore." I glanced at the file and then back at Matt, biting my lip. "So…About that weekend away you wanted…"

"Let me guess, Kansas? Assuming Barb and Tim Holt live there now?"

"Well, why not? Kill two birds with one stone."

He shook his head. "Maggie May. How about you talk to a few folks around here first and then if we still need to, we'll head over there to see what they have to say?"

"Deal." I squeezed his hand. "You know you're the best, right?"

"I'd feel better about that if I didn't hear you tell Fancy the same thing at least three times a day."

I laughed. "That's different. She's the best dog in the world. You're the best boyfriend. Now, let's put this aside for the night so we can enjoy our pie and ice cream."

As I finished off my slice of pie I was already putting together my game plan. I needed to figure out where each of those kids who'd been at the party lived now and then I needed to re-interview them. *After* I spoke to Mr. Lewis.

That was going to be the hardest part of all.

CHAPTER 5

The one day each week Mr. Lewis hadn't come into the café was Tuesdays when the Baker Valley Pizza Company had their weekly lunch buffet. (Don't ask me why they only did it once a week or why they thought a Tuesday was the day to do it, but I was glad that's how it worked, because it meant I knew where to find him the next day.)

He was already seated at a table by the window, his plate filled with three small slices of pizza—one pepperoni and two meat lovers. He also had a side salad smothered in ranch dressing at his elbow and was staring out the window as if the rest of the world didn't exist.

"Mr. Lewis." I paused next to his table.

"Miss Carver. How are you?" He smiled at me and I wondered how I'd never noticed that lingering sadness in his eyes before.

"Well, I don't know. Can I join you?"

He looked like he wanted to say no, but he nodded and waved at the lacquered wooden chair across from him. I'd grabbed myself a slice of pizza before I approached so I'd look like I belonged, but I wasn't really feeling hungry and suspected I might not even get a bite in if he was unhappy with what I had to say.

He returned his attention to his meal, like I wasn't even there.

"So, um, Mr. Lewis….I, um, I told my grandpa about running into you at the grocery store the other day and he told me about what happened to your daughter."

He glared at me, clearly wanting me to leave.

"I'm sorry. I know what it's like to have people talking about you after you've lost someone. Like they can't talk to you about it to your face, but they're always right there whispering about it behind you, asking one another what's wrong with you and then salaciously sharing the news back and forth. *Oh, well didn't you know…*"

I shuddered and took a bite of my pizza just for something to do.

We ignored each other for a minute or so, and then I continued. "I, um, I lost my parents in a car accident. And then I lost my boyfriend in a skydiving accident. So I know what it's like. I mean, maybe. I know it's never exactly the same for everyone and none of the people I lost were murdered, but, well. I've been there, you know? With the people, talking."

He nodded. "I'm sorry for your loss."

"Thanks. And I'm sorry for yours."

Such generic words, but how else do you convey sympathy?

We both ate in silence for a few moments and then I finally gathered up the courage to continue. "My grandpa told me they never found who did it. Who killed your daughter."

He nodded.

"And, well, with the barkery being closed…I have some time available. I thought I'd look into it. If that's okay with you? I don't want to stir up bad memories, but if it was my daughter I'd want to know, you know?"

I scratched at my fingernail as I waited for him to respond. He didn't look at me straight away. Just stared at his plate, shoulders hunched.

"Mr. Lewis? I don't want to do this if it'll hurt you too much."

He fisted his hands on either side of the plate, still not looking at me. "I used to call them. Every month. I'd ask what leads they'd found. I'd ask when they were going to find the man who'd killed my baby girl. And they always told me the same thing. They'd done what they could. Unless someone who'd been there told them what happened, there was nothing more they could do."

He shook his head once, slowly, and his right fist banged softly on the table. "I tried talking to her friends. The ones who'd been there that night. But they had nothing to say. And when I came back again they avoided me. They wouldn't answer the door. They wouldn't answer the phone. They told me they didn't know anything. To leave them alone. To let them live their lives. The sheriff finally came by my house." He choked on a laugh. "Told me I had to stop. That I had to let it go. Move on. Get back to my life."

His hand trembled as he laid it flat on the table. "So I did. I let it all go. Except her birthday. Valentine's Day. Every year I buy her a stuffed animal. She loved stuffed animals, even at the end. Ready to go off to college and she still loved stuffed animals." He smiled softly before burying his face in his hands.

I wanted to reach out to him, but I didn't. I sat there awkwardly and waited, my fist pressed to my mouth.

He met my eyes and I knew that he could see the tears that matched his. "Do you think you can find him? Whoever did this to my daughter?"

"I don't know. But I'd like to try. Sometimes people remember things later. Or sometimes they don't tell something in the moment because it's a source of embarrassment or they're worried they'll get in trouble, but years later it doesn't seem like such a big deal. And sometimes people cover for one another in the moment and regret it later. There's no harm in trying."

I hoped.

He nodded. "Okay. What do you want to know?"

"Can you tell me about her? What was she like? My grandpa said she was a bright soul. Good at sports, headed to college. That you raised her from a baby?"

He nodded. And then for the next forty-five minutes he told me stories about his daughter. Jules, he'd called her. How it had just been the two of them after her mother passed away. And in every single word I could hear the love and pride he'd felt for his daughter. It made me miss my parents so much, to be reminded of that kind of love and support, but I just smiled and let him talk.

I didn't take notes. I didn't want him to feel like it was an interview. I just let him talk and talk and talk. And I thought about how lucky that girl had been to be so well-loved and to have such a great parent. And how I didn't care what I had to do, I was going to find the sick you-know-what who'd taken that man's daughter from him and broken his life.

Because he did not deserve that. (Not that anyone does.)

But it hit me, right there in the chest. I could give this man a measure of peace. I could help him put this in the past and begin to heal.

I could find the answer.

CHAPTER 6

That afternoon I drove over to the library in Creek to work with Lesley (who was the former librarian and also knew a lot of people) to track down all of the individuals from the party that were listed in the file.

The library was in a sleek modern brick and glass building on the outskirts of town and had two conference rooms and complementary computer stations along one wall. It was big and airy and modern and I kind of hated it. I much preferred the old library that had been crammed into two small rooms at the top of the courthouse and packed so tight with books it felt like a dangerous adventure to navigate through the stacks.

Good news was that more than half of the kids on the list were still in the area more than ten years later. (In the valley, if you don't go to college, you don't generally leave. If you do go to college, then you usually never come back except holidays.)

She helped me put together a list of current employers, current addresses, and phone numbers and also told me what she knew about each one.

After that I drove by Mr. Lewis's house. I expected it to be weighed down by grief like he was, but it wasn't. It stood tall and straight, the white fence and the blue siding bright and clean and perfect.

It puzzled me until he let me inside and I realized that all of Julie's spaces—her room and the living room and the outside—were pristine, but that all of his spaces—the kitchen and his bedroom which I glimpsed as he led me to her room—were worn and neglected.

Seeing that made my chest ache, but I hid it from him. He had enough to deal with already. He showed me her room with the trophies and ribbons and class guide to CU still sitting on the desk, the colors bright pink and white and green.

On a shelf by her desk I spied a set of four yearbooks. "Do you mind if I take these with me?"

"What good will those do you?"

"It'll let me see who her friends were. See the kind of things they said when they signed them." Maybe there'd be some mention of a secret a parent wouldn't know.

He shoved his hands into his pockets. "Fine. Go ahead."

We retreated back to the living room where the wall was dominated by framed photos of Julie's smiling face. She was everywhere. If I hadn't known what had happened, I would've looked through that house and expected her to walk through the front door any moment with a bright smile on her face, pale brown hair swinging out behind her.

"Thank you for letting me see her room," I told him. "It helps. The more I know her the more I'll be able to figure out who might have done this to her."

"You think it was someone she knew?"

"I don't know. It could be."

"Everyone loved Julie. No one she knew would hurt her."

I wondered if that was really true. Every person, no matter how good they are, no matter how nice, there's always someone who doesn't like them even if it's only because of how good they are or how nice. And Julie had been a bright star who excelled in sports and academics. She wouldn't be the first to be hated for that.

"I hope you're right, Mr. Lewis. Although that will make it harder to find the killer if it was just someone passing through." I clutched the yearbooks closer. "Well. I better get going so I can get started."

"Wait." He left the room and came back clutching a bright pink journal in his hand. "You should have this."

I held my hand out. "What is it?"

He hesitated before handing it to me. "I had to read it," he murmured. "I had to make sure there wasn't anything in there that the cops would need to see. It was better that I read it instead of them."

He glanced down at the journal, a frown on his face.

"She would've understood," I told him

"Would she?"

I carefully took it from him. "I think so. She'd want you to have done everything you could to find her killer. And she'd understand if that meant you had to read her diary."

He looked at it for another long moment. "Some of the things she said in there…I didn't know…She was so mad at me sometimes…"

I squeezed his arm. "As someone who was once a teenage girl myself, let me assure you, we all say things in our diaries that aren't what they seem. It's a safe place to vent. But from what I've seen here, I expect your daughter loved you very much."

I didn't know if it was true at the time (turns out it was), but I figured she was dead and it was what he needed to hear.

"I better go, Mr. Lewis. Thank you for this."

He nodded, but he was somewhere else, lost in his thoughts, as I let myself out the door and drove home.

🐾 🐾 🐾

I curled up in my bedroom that night as my grandpa and Lesley cuddled on the couch in the living room and read her diary.

As I read the entries, I could understand why Mr. Lewis had hesitated to hand it over. If I were him I wouldn't want to lose that connection to that person I'd known. She was so alive on the page it was hard to realize she wasn't still out there somewhere, dreaming and planning and making her way in the world.

It was page after page of teenage angst and dreams and triumphs. A crush on a boy at summer camp. A fight with her dad. Worries that no one understood her. Worries that everyone saw right to the heart of her. Fear. Excitement.

I knew her dad had probably been hurt by those passages when she was mad at him, but it was right there on every page how close they were. She'd taken him for granted as most teenagers do, but I hoped he'd also seen how much he'd been a valuable part of her life.

I made a few notes. Barb was her best friend, but there was a sort of frenemies thing going on there. Especially when Barb and Tim hooked up, because Julie and Tim had always been so close. She hadn't dwelled on it much, but it was there to see between the lines. A bit of tension between the three of them.

There were other things to note, too. Julie had been pretty squeaky clean, but she'd talked about how once graduation was over she'd have a summer of freedom, a great time between all the responsibilities and pressures of high school and all she wanted to accomplish in college. The party that night was going to be the beginning. The first time she'd ever tried alcohol.

Put it all together and she'd been a girl looking for a little adventure and taking some risks she'd never taken before with a best friend who probably wasn't going to have her back.

And the worst had happened.

I made a list, too, of all the people who'd signed her yearbook. It was a small class, but it looked like her circle of friends was even smaller than that. About five girls, four boys. Flipping through the pictures I could see that the girls were all friends and three of the boys were, too.

But the fourth boy, Dennis Clay, wasn't in any of the other pictures. No sports. No school activities. His school picture showed a boy with too much acne and ill-fitting glasses whose thin-lipped smile probably hid a pair of braces.

He'd gone to college, but he'd come back. According to Lesley, he'd done it to take care of his mom after a serious fall that she'd never recovered from. She was homebound and he worked remotely as some sort of IT consultant from the home where he'd grown up.

It was only about a mile from the Lewis residence. And in the direction where her body had been found.

He'd signed Julie's yearbook with "love", which made me wonder about his feelings for her. But he hadn't been at the party, so no one had talked to him at the time of the original investigation.

I decided I would. It was as good a place to start as any.

CHAPTER 7

I pulled up in front of the small one-story home with green wood siding at the edge of Masonville and took a deep breath. There was no reason for Dennis Clay to talk to me. Who was I really other than some bored busybody digging into events that everyone else had left behind them? But I hoped that maybe that love he'd signed in Julie's yearbook had meant there was some sort of affection for her hidden away that might make him at least moderately friendly towards me.

The place was small but tidy—what I could see of it under the snow that still lingered on the ground. And the station wagon in the driveway was old but also well-tended. So it seemed either Dennis or his mom took pride in their home. That was a good sign, I thought.

I rang the doorbell, but didn't hear anything and no one came to the door, so I opened the metal screen and knocked on the wooden door which still had a wreath up.

About a minute later the door opened to reveal a tall, good-looking man in his early thirties wearing gray sweatpants and a long-sleeved black shirt. I was taken aback for a moment. I knew some men hit their growth spurt after high school and that when the acne and glasses were replaced with clear skin and contacts they were even sometimes downright good-looking, but I wasn't prepared for that to happen right then.

"Dennis Clay?" I asked, trying to hide my stammering surprise.

"That's me." He flashed a grin with perfect white teeth. "And you are?"

"Maggie Carver. I live over in Creek. Lou Carver is my grandpa? I also ran the Baker Valley Barkery and Café until last October."

"Right. The dog bakery. Didn't work out so well?"

"Actually we closed it down because my business partner married Mason Maxwell and they're going to tear all the buildings in the area down and replace it with a fancy schmancy pet resort. So the barkery will be back, but in a bigger and better format."

"Ah. Well. Congratulations. How can I help you? We don't have a dog, I'm afraid." He smiled again. He'd definitely come up in the world since high school.

(Not that I was the least bit tempted. I had Matt. Plus Dennis was a little on the young side for me. But I was making a mental list of all the local ladies I knew who weren't too old or too settled to be interested. I suspected that if he was like other late bloomers I knew he now had all the looks, but none of the moves to put them to good use. Maybe I could introduce him to Elaine…)

"This is a little awkward. But I was hoping to talk to you about Julie Lewis."

He took a half-step back. "Julie? Why do you want to talk to me about her?"

"You signed her yearbook."

He crossed his arms. "She was a popular girl. I'm sure lots of people signed her yearbook."

"Not all that popular, actually. Please? Can I come in and explain why I want to talk to you?"

He glanced over his shoulder. "Fine. But you'll have to keep your voice down. My mother is sleeping."

"Okay. Thank you."

He stepped aside and gestured me towards a nice new leather couch. I sat on the edge of the seat, wishing he'd directed me towards the kitchen table instead—easier to make eye contact that way.

He didn't sit himself. He stood off to the side, arms crossed. "So. Explain what you want. Are you a reporter, too?"

"No." I rubbed the back of my neck. This was going to sound so ridiculous. "Her father was a customer at the barkery. I ran into him buying her a birthday gift at the store."

"Valentine's Day, right?"

I nodded. "He seemed so sad. I mentioned it to my grandpa and my grandpa told me about Julie. And…well…I have some free time and I've solved a couple of murders lately and so I decided to look into what happened to Julie and see if I can't figure out who killed her."

He grunted in surprise and sat down on the other end of the couch, burying his head in his hands. "Why me? Why are you here?"

"Because no one interviewed you back then. At least, it wasn't in the file. You're the only one who signed her yearbook who wasn't at that party that night."

"You think I did it." He leaned back with a soft laugh,

laying his arm along the edge of the couch.

"No. Did you?"

"No. But then, why talk to me? I wasn't at the party as far as you know. You don't think I did it. What can I do for you? Why come here?"

"Well I had to meet you to make that decision. I couldn't decide you weren't a murderer based on one signature in a yearbook. But now I'm pretty comfortable it wasn't you. I figure someone who killed a girl isn't going to sit back so relaxed right after I've told him why I'm here."

He shrugged. "Makes some sense."

"The, um, the other reason I wanted to talk to you was because, well…" I studied the ceiling, trying to find a polite way to phrase it and realized there probably wasn't one and that he was smart enough to know what I was getting at no matter how I sugar-coated it. "You, um, you struck me as the type of guy who was maybe on the outside looking in. And so perhaps saw a lot that others didn't and could give me an insight into Julie and her friends and who might've wanted to hurt her."

He chuckled. "So in other words, I looked like I was a loser who spent all my time pining after Julie and would know everything about her."

"Basically."

He laughed again. "Probably the most accurate description of my high school years I've ever heard. What do you want to know?"

"Who were her enemies? What kind of girl was she? Was she as good as she seemed?"

He laced his hands behind his head and stared at the wall. "She was kind to everyone, including me. I fell in love with her freshman year when some of the bigger football players stuffed me in my locker. She not only made them let me out she got right in their face and told them off until they apologized. And then she went to Tim and made him swear to look after me. Told him it wasn't right for bigger guys to pick on weaker guys. Told him that only losers would do something like that."

"And Tim looked out for you after that?"

"He did. Julie had him wrapped around her finger. Until Barb showed up sophomore year and stole his heart. Or, well, something."

"Something?"

He gave me a knowing smirk. "He was a fifteen-year-old boy. Barb was generously proportioned and generous with her attentions to Tim."

"So you don't think he really loved her? I heard they got married."

"I can't say anything about the marriage. I don't know about that. I think Tim was always in love with Julie but he couldn't say no to what Barb offered. Did lust turn to love at some point? Maybe. Especially after Julie died. I could see it happening. But before that? I think Tim just enjoyed having someone who made him the center of her world."

"And what did Julie think about it? About Tim and Barb?"

He thought for a long moment. "I don't know. I never saw her act jealous. But maybe that's because Tim didn't give her up for Barb. He still hung around Julie just as much as before, he just had Barb attached to his side while he did it. I'm not really sure Julie cared one way or the other."

"And other guys? Did she have anyone she really liked or anyone she dated seriously?"

"No. Not really. Julie was all about sports and school. Her dad sacrificed so much for her, I know she wanted to prove herself to him. She didn't even ditch school on Senior Ditch Day. She and I were the only two seniors in school that day."

"Why?"

"We were taking this elective class on Economics and the teacher told us he was going to give a quiz that day. Said that we could show up and prove how much we valued our education or we could miss class and show that we didn't. You know what the quiz asked?" He shook his head and grinned.

"What?"

"What's more important to you: hanging out with your friends or getting a good education?"

"That was the quiz?"

"Yeah. He was a bit of a, you know."

"Oh yeah. I had one of those in college. Probably one of the reasons I didn't end up a physics major."

He chuckled. "So, anyway. That was Julie. Dedicated. Not all that interested in boys as far as I saw."

"What about girls?"

He jerked in surprise. "Huh. Never thought about it before. But no. I didn't see any of that either. It was just study and sports for Julie."

"Did that shift once she got into college? Or once the end of the year rolled around?"

He drummed his fingers on his knee.

"Dennis?"

"She was a good girl. She didn't deserve what happened

to her. That's about all I can tell you."

We heard the sound of rustling from the back of the house and he abruptly stood up. "My mom's awake. I need to go check on her. It was nice to meet you." He walked to the door and held it open for me.

I scrambled to join him. "Okay. Thank you. I appreciate your help."

"Yeah."

I was barely out the door before he closed it firmly behind me.

Interesting.

I suspected there was more that he could tell me, but he obviously wasn't willing to do so and I had no reason to push. Yet.

CHAPTER 8

I dropped by the auto shop where one of the guys who'd been at the party, Hank, worked. He was that guy who was probably the lovable joker in high school. A little large, a little doughy around the edges, but always good-humored and there with a laugh.

He shuffled a bit as he joined me in the small office that smelled like motor oil, tucking a dirty red rag into the back of his overalls.

"Boss said you wanted to see me?"

"Yeah, Maggie Carver, Lou Carver's granddaughter." I held out my hand and he shook it. It was just like the rest of him, friendly and a little soft around the edges.

"Nice to meet you. So? What brings you in?"

"Well, I'm looking into the murder of Julie Lewis. You knew her, right?"

"Yeah. Grew up with her. She was good people, you know? Always willing to stand up for the underdog."

"She ever stand up for you?"

He nodded. "A few times. She also stood up to me a few times. I was one of the bigger kids in middle school. I let it get to my head a bit. Until Julie knocked some sense into me."

"That habit of hers ever create any enemies?"

"Nah. Everybody loved Julie."

"Even Tim?"

He grabbed the dirty rag back out of his pocket and started to rub at a spot on his hand.

"Something there you want to tell me?" I asked.

"Look, Tim loved Julie. Forever. More than just friends love, you know what I mean?"

I nodded.

"But Julie didn't see it. Or if she saw it she pretended she didn't. And it worked because there was no one else either. It would've broken Tim's heart if she'd gone off with someone else, but she never did."

"No sweetheart? No crush?"

"Nah. Julie was all about sports and studies. That night by the lake? The night she disappeared? That was the first night she'd ever joined us. Usually it was about a dozen of us down there, hanging out, drinking beers on the weekends. But Julie never came. She'd go to the movies with Tim and Barb or she'd have a game. But when it came time for all the rest she wanted to go home."

"So what changed?"

He shrugged. "She graduated. No more classes to worry about. No more sports to play. She had a free summer ahead of her."

"And she was going to take advantage of it?"

He chuckled. "As much as someone who doesn't know how to take advantage of it can. I swear, she had two beers that night and she was drunk. And then she started flirting with one of those older dudes who'd crashed the party and Tim lost it. He stepped in and threatened to call the cops on the guy if he didn't take off."

"How'd Julie feel about that?"

"She got angry. Stormed off. Tim went after her."

I tried not to show my excitement at that little tidbit. "You see her again after that?"

He thought about it for a long moment. "No. I saw Tim later. He and Barb were getting into it. I couldn't hear what they were saying, but it was clear she was furious with him. But that wasn't new. She was always on at him about something or other."

"I heard they got married."

He shrugged and put the red rag back in his pocket. "Sure, why not? Julie was gone and Barb was as good as anyone else Tim was going to find. At least he was her whole world."

"Do you think if Julie hadn't died Barb and Tim would have ended up together?"

He shook his head. "No. I'm pretty sure Tim was working up the courage to tell Julie how he felt. You know, one of those 'no chance like the present' situations. They weren't in school together anymore. Worst case scenario, she'd turn him down and he'd spend the summer with Barb and then go away to college. Best case scenario, he'd spend it with Julie and then, who knows?"

Out in the garage someone dropped a wrench and I flinched. "So he wasn't going to break up with Barb first?"

"Why lose the bird in the hand, right?"

"Ouch. So that guy she was talking to that Tim got upset about. What was he like? Could he have come back around later? Or could she have gone to meet up with him?"

Hank glanced towards the garage where another car had just pulled up. "Maybe. I wasn't paying too much attention to him. He was definitely older than us, but not that much older. Younger than I am now. College-age, probably. And good-looking. All the girls at the party noticed him. So he could've arranged to meet up with Julie later. Or could've gone after her wherever she disappeared to. I mean, she had to leave that party somehow. It wasn't walking distance from there to where they found her."

"You're sure of that?"

"Positive."

"Could she have hitchhiked her way home? She didn't live far off the highway."

He glanced towards the garage again, clearly eager to get back to work. "No. Julie wasn't the type to make stupid mistakes like that."

"So you think she might've gone off with a strange guy she met at a party but she wouldn't hitchhike?"

He shrugged. "Well, those are two different things, aren't they? I mean, hitchhiking, while drunk, late at night, along a highway, that's the set-up for a horror film. But meeting some guy at a party and spending time with him? That's life."

(More than one woman had found out that didn't always turn out so well either.)

It sounded like I needed to talk to that guy she'd met at the party.

I wanted to ask more questions, but I saw Hank's boss looking our way. "Okay. Thanks. Anything else you can think of? You ever see Julie and Dennis Clay together?"

"Dennis Clay and Julie? That loser?" He shook his head. "No. Julie was nice to everyone so I'm sure she said hi to him in the hallway or whatever, but I never saw them speak or anything like that. You think he did it?"

"No." Best to shut that one down right away. "He'd signed her yearbook, so I was just trying to figure out where he fit into things."

"Oh, I could see that. He had a thing for her. Most of us did, though. And she was too kind to shut him down completely." He moved towards the door. "Anything else?"

"Nope. That's it. Thank you for your time."

"My pleasure." He ambled back into the garage, taking the teasing of his fellow workers with good humor.

I watched him go wondering if that lovable teddy bear surface hid anything more sinister underneath, but I really couldn't see it.

So it looked like my choices for the moment were Tim, the potentially jealous childhood friend, and Rick, the older guy who'd dropped in on a high school party and hit on a girl he didn't know. Or, if Hank was wrong, whoever it was who'd given Julie a ride home from the party that night when she tried to hitchhike her way home.

CHAPTER 9

I managed to talk to the others who'd been listed in the report as being at the party and were still local. None of them had anything exciting to add. Most of them confirmed what Hank had told me. That Julie wasn't the party type. That she'd only had a few beers before she was pretty drunk. That she was flirting with the older guy who'd showed up at the party with a couple friends from a cabin further down the lake. That Tim hadn't taken it well. That they'd stormed off together. That no one had seen her after that, but Tim had come back and gotten into it with Barb, and they'd eventually left together.

So the big question was where Julie had gone after she and Tim fought. Which is why I asked Matt if he'd meet me at the Belgian Cafe for dinner. I would've been happy to fill in my grandpa and Lesley on the case, but wheedling a trip to Kansas out of Matt seemed like something that required one-on-one time. And since neither of us had our own place…

(Something that I had never really had a need for before when I had my own place, oh irony of ironies.)

The cafe was a medium-sized Belgian restaurant outside of Masonville that catered to the tourist crowd and generally employed fresh-faced twenty-somethings from Eastern Europe on temporary work visas, which meant the service was prompt, efficient, and not particularly chatty or interested in our business. Just what we needed.

Matt glanced around as he came to join me at a table tucked into the back corner near a roaring fire. "This was an interesting choice."

"I figured it was the closest to privacy we were likely to get."

He nodded. "Speaking of…"

"Speaking of what?"

"Privacy. You and me. Our living situation."

I'm pretty sure the sounds I made at that point in time weren't exactly coherent. "Why do we need to talk about *that*?"

"Maggie…I told you I needed to make some decisions. And I need to know if you're on board with them or not."

I tensed. "I thought you'd already decided not to re-enlist."

"I have."

"So what other choices are there?"

He laughed. "If you hadn't noticed, I'm living in a two-bedroom trailer with two other adults and a small child. It's not ideal."

"Well you can't move in with me. You saw how my grandpa was the other night when he thought we were going to run away to my room for a few minutes. And he still makes me set the table when you come over for dinner."

"As much as I like and admire your grandpa, I have no interest in living with him."

The waitress came by and I ordered a Coke without even thinking about it. (I should've probably ordered a shot of whiskey to go with that Coke the direction the conversation was going…)

"So, what then?" I asked.

He leaned forward, trapping me with those intense blue eyes of his. "I thought maybe we could look for a house together."

I'm pretty sure my eyes almost bugged out of my head. "You want to buy a property together?"

"Yes. Since you're not ready to get married…"

I laughed, almost hysterical. "Oh, see, I'd rather get married than buy a property together. A good prenup can take care of most of the issues if a marriage goes south. But *buying* a property together? Oh, no. You have to work together on making the payments and on maintenance and on deciding when and whether to sell or not…No. That's a recipe for disaster."

He sat back and glared at me. "Maggie. I can't do this. You won't marry me. You won't buy a place with me. Has it ever occurred to you that maybe I'd like more than having a few dinners a week together?"

The waitress came by with my Coke and a beer for Matt. I took a deep breath, gathering my thoughts.

Finally, I said, "I'm sorry. That was just a gut reaction. I wasn't thinking about how you'd feel about it when I said it. I told you, I'm not good at this. I'm not good at thinking about someone else's feelings or needs when I make decisions. Or say things."

I put my hands flat on the table and took a deep

breath. "So let me step back for a second and think this through."

He took a sip of his beer and stayed silent as I thought about it.

"What's your ideal solution?" I asked him.

"We get married. And buy a place together."

I worked very hard to hide how much that thought scared the living daylights out of me. "Right. Of course. But you'd be okay with us buying a place together in the meantime?"

"Yes."

I drummed my fingers on the table. "What about renting a place together?"

"I'd like to stay in Creek if possible. And there aren't any good rentals available. I checked."

He had, had he?

"Are there any places to buy?"

"A couple." He leaned forward. "But I figured if you were on board with it, that we could approach Roy Jackson's daughter and ask her if she was willing to sell. The place has been empty since her father died and as far as I can tell she's not even trying to rent it out as a holiday rental."

"Not much demand for that in Creek, is there?"

"No."

My fingers drummed faster and faster until I finally forced my hand flat on the table.

It *would* be nice to spend more time with Matt. Especially without chaperones around.

And living next to my grandpa would solve one of my concerns. One of the reasons I had moved to Creek was to take care of him. And just because I'd fallen in love and my grandpa had made it clear he didn't really need my help didn't mean I wanted to be all that far away from him, just in case.

Living next door would be almost perfect.

(Honestly, living about three houses away would be better. Give everyone a little bit of privacy. But next door meant Matt could shovel his driveway for him and he wouldn't have much room to complain since it was right there. And we could drop by to check on him or he could drop by if he wanted without much effort at all.)

I stared into the fire for a long, long moment. "It's a really good idea, Matt."

"But…" He crossed his arms and glared at me.

"What if…"

"No."

"What? I didn't even finish my sentence."

He sighed. "You were about to say something about what if we don't work out. How awkward it would be that I'm living there in a house next to you and your grandpa. And how do we manage the finances if we split. Can I afford a house without you? If I have to sell, who is there that would buy? Am I about right?"

I pressed my lips together. Yes, but now I couldn't say it.

He shook his head. "How is it that you could willingly jump out of planes for fun and quit a lucrative job to move to a small town in Colorado and start a business most people would tell you was going to fail, and yet you can't give us a chance?"

"I am giving us a chance."

He leaned forward and held my gaze with his. "Maggie. Do you really think we're not going to work out? What do you see that I don't?"

"I see myself. I'm not an easy woman to live with. Ask my grandpa. And I'm on my good behavior with him because he's my grandpa. I can be very difficult."

"So can I."

"I can be moody."

"So can I."

"I can be mean sometimes. I don't want to be mean to you."

He squeezed my hand. "Maggie, when you decide to spend your life with someone you can't expect it to always be perfect. We're going to get on each other's nerves. We're going to be mad at each other. Or at something else and take it out on each other anyway. I'll probably leave the bathroom sink full of hair after I shave sometimes. And you'll probably leave too many dishes in the sink. But that's life."

I grimaced. "It sounds very messy and complicated."

He laughed. "Because it is. But if you love someone, you deal with it."

"I do love you, you know."

"But…"

I pursed my lips. "Let's get through a weekend away together before we start putting our credit ratings at risk."

"A weekend away together? Is that why we're here? So you could convince me to take you to Kansas to talk to Tim and Barb Holt?"

I shrugged. "Pretty much. But it will be a good test of our ability to get along for an extended period of time, too. We could drive…"

He pulled out his phone. "Where do they live? Salina?"

"Umhm."

He punched in the location and then showed me the phone. "Eight hours. One way. That's a lot of driving for two interviews."

"Tim is the key to this, Matt, I know it. He can tell us what happened after Julie left that party."

He put his phone back away. "Do you think he killed her?"

"I don't know. If she'd been killed at the lake, I'd definitely suspect him. But everyone said he came back and he and Barb left together. But he will know if she went off somewhere, like with that older guy."

Matt leaned forward. "You sure we can survive sixteen hours in a car together?"

"No. But if we can't do that, we definitely shouldn't be buying a house together. So does that mean you'll go?"

He nodded. "We should make sure they'll be there before we make any big plans, though. I'll call Tim tomorrow from the police station. Make it official."

"You're the best, you know that?"

"I am. And you should snap me up while you have the chance." He winked. "Now. Tell me what you found out so far that makes you think this trip is necessary."

CHAPTER 10

I told Matt about all of my interviews, especially the fact that Dennis Clay seemed to be hiding something but I wasn't sure what. He promised to run everyone involved's criminal record the next day. Character usually shows through eventually. How often do they solve some cold case and end up tying it back to someone who went on to kill others before finally ending up in prison, right?

(By my unscientific study of real life cold case TV shows and news coverage I'd say it's about 60% of the time that the killer they finally identify is someone who ended up in prison for other murders or crimes of violence or who was at least suspected in other murders even if they'd never been charged. Then again, I'm pretty sure there are other studies out there that say that people's gut instincts about frequency of events are often highly wrong. But it seemed like a good path to go down either way.)

We did actually manage to spend most of the dinner talking about things other than murder as we split a very yummy serving of steamed mussels in a garlic white wine sauce and pommes frites. (Which for the uninitiated were basically just really tasty skinny French fries.) I loved that I could talk to Matt about pretty much anything for hours on end and never get bored or terribly annoyed.

Don't get me wrong. He's definitely his own person. We sometimes disagree, for sure. I mean, he's ex-military and small town Colorado and my mom was part of the (failed) Great Peace March. But he isn't the type of person who has to win an argument at all costs. Or who looks down on an entire class of people. He judges people by their actions, which is all I think you can really ask for.

So we had a lively discussion, but no active disagreements. And, because life is life, some of our conversation was about TV shows and the locals we knew. (Jamie and Mason were back from their month-long honeymoon in Paris, so we talked about getting together with them at some point. Maybe with Greta and Jean-Philippe—who'd ended up hitting it off a little more than I'd expected at the wedding and were now having a trans-Continental affair.)

Matt and I shared a sweet kiss outside the restaurant and then he followed me home before heading off to his own over-crowded trailer.

My grandpa was just pulling into the driveway when I arrived, so I waited for him.

"You just get back from dropping off Lesley?" I asked.

"Sure did."

We opened the front door to see Fancy curled up on the goldenrod couch. She opened one eye to look at us as we came inside and then went back to sleep. Good guard dog she was. (Although I knew if we'd been strangers walking in the door that she would've jumped off the couch and started barking. She's not an attack dog, but you don't need to be when you're a hundred and forty pounds and have a very loud bark.)

"You and Matt have a good dinner?" he asked.

I took a deep breath. "Sort of. Hey, can I ask you a question?" I'm not usually one for asking anyone else's advice, but I couldn't see my way forward with Matt. I didn't want to lose him, but things were moving so fast.

"Alright. Shoot."

"Over dessert, though." I grabbed us each a serving of carrot cake and we settled in at the kitchen table.

"Lesley is going to lecture me on having two slices of cake in a day," my grandpa said, taking a large bite.

"Just tell her I had a really big one. Or that Matt came over for dessert and had one. But, really, when she makes that good a carrot cake, what does she expect?"

I happen to be a bit of a carrot cake snob. It doesn't keep me from trying a slice every time I run across it, but I have certain standards that must be met to make a good carrot cake. Namely, it has to be moist. None of this dried out brick thing you sometimes get at the store. And not gummy. Don't ask me how to explain that better, but with some places, especially the grocery store, their carrot cakes are just downright gummy. It's like moisture gone wrong.

But the most important, make or break, factor in a good carrot cake is the frosting. It has to be a cream cheese frosting. None of this sugary stuff. It needs to be creamy and tangy and smooth and not leave a lingering sugar film on your tongue.

Weirdly enough, my MBA program served the best carrot cake ever. I would've killed for that recipe. But Lesley's carrot cake was a close second. I could've eaten it for breakfast, lunch, and dinner, it was that good.

The only thing I didn't like about carrot cake was that I really wasn't supposed to give any to Fancy because of the nutmeg.

I sent her outside with a doggie ice cream instead.

"So?" my grandpa asked, taking a sip of his coffee. "What did you want to know?"

"Well, I guess it's more that I need some advice."

He raised an eyebrow as he took another bite.

"Matt suggested we buy a house together because I won't marry him," I said as fast as I could to get the words out.

He looked at me, puzzled. "Has he asked you to marry him?"

"No. But I've made it abundantly clear that I think it's too soon."

He nodded, thinking. "And what did you tell him about buying a house together then?"

"That I'd rather marry a guy with a good prenup than buy a property with him?" I buried my face in my hands and groaned. "Ah! What am I doing, Grandpa? I love him. But…"

"You're scared."

I nodded and took another bite of cake, savoring the rich taste of the frosting that she'd layered in the middle.

He set down his fork and studied me for a moment. "What would be worse: losing Matt and always wondering what it could've been? Or marrying him and having it not work out?"

I poked at my cake, moving the plump raisins she'd included off to the side and back again. "I know I'm supposed to say that losing him would be worse." I set down my fork.

"But…"

I sighed. "But if I can't make things work with a guy as great as Matt, then I can't make things work with anyone. So in that sense marrying him and having it not work out would be the absolute worst."

My grandpa took a sip of his coffee and studied me for a long moment before setting the mug down and leaning forward. "It seems to me that if you can't even give a guy as great as Matt a chance, then there's no one you will give a chance."

I looked away. "Good point. Ugh. Why can't life be simple?" I shoved a giant bite of cake into my mouth and gazed longingly at the fridge wishing it wasn't too late to have another Coke.

(It's actually never too late to have another Coke, my real issue was that it wouldn't be a cold one because I don't keep them in the fridge in a failed effort to limit the number I consume per day and I don't like ice getting in the way of my sugar and caffeine fix.)

My grandpa finished off his cake and dropped his fork on the plate. "Life *is* simple, Maggie May. You're the one that's making it hard by digging in your heels every step of the way." He stood up and patted my shoulder. "Maybe you should stop fighting and just let life happen."

I shuddered. "Who would want to do that?"

"Most everyone." He put his plate in the sink and turned to look back at me. "I'm sure you'll make the right decision once you've had some time to think about it."

He left me sitting alone in the kitchen with my half-finished carrot cake and a drooling Fancy who'd finished off her ice cream and come back to see what she could get out of me. I knew what he thought the right decision was. And what Jamie, Greta, and probably the local mailman thought the right decision was, too.

But…Ugh.

Since I didn't want to think about it anymore, I turned my mind to the murder of Julie Lewis instead. I still needed to get ahold of that guy she'd been talking to at the party. His name and former phone number were in the file, but he'd moved on since then.

Fortunately, we live in such a creepy world that one little internet search turns up pretty much anything about anyone these days.

(I occasionally get bored and Google my old friends—or high school classmates who were never friends—to see what they're up to now. I don't find blogs or LinkedIn profiles most of the time, but I do find results that tell me approximately how much they earn per year, what their net worth is, whether they're married or not, what their home address is, and who their closest associates are. It's disturbing, quite frankly, but it is a good way to find out when that girl you really didn't like in high school gets divorced for the third time.)

I pulled out my laptop and looked him up. According to the search results from whatever random sites tell you too much about strangers, he was living in Denver about two miles from where he'd lived all those years ago. It offered to let me pay to unlock his actual phone number, too, but I didn't.

(I had this weird suspicion that the results were real

but the service itself was a scam of some sort meant to steal my money. Like those pirated book sites—which I would never use, by the way, because what kind of person steals from a creative like that when there are plenty of free books at the library. I figured half of those sites didn't really have the book but did have a lovely virus on offer that would infect your computer and steal your bank account information when you downloaded from them. If they didn't, they should.)

Luckily, I also found an employer website.

Turns out Rick was an accountant. And reasonably good-looking as the witnesses had mentioned. But he also looked a bit like a jerk. You know that spoiled kind of guy who has always had someone there to bail him out of trouble? They always seem to have this "I'm the man" vibe to them? Well, he definitely had it. I can't describe it, it's something in the tilt of the chin or the quirk of the lip.

Whatever it was, I really didn't like him as soon as I saw his photo.

I was willing to bet he'd have some postcard-perfect picture somewhere on his desk with his attractive blonde wife and two adorable children, all of them in matching clothes that involved khaki and bright pastels, seated on a perfectly green lawn.

And he'd be a golfer, too.

Only question was, was he the type to kill some teenage girl he chatted up at a party? Could be. I could see a scenario where she started something she didn't want to finish, he forced the point, and then got scared she'd tell someone about it and killed her to keep her quiet. But there hadn't been signs of that on the body.

So what would it be? He drove her home and on the way home tried something and she ran and he went after her?

No. That kind of guy was a coward at heart. If she'd run he'd've just left her and gone back to his cabin. Plus he supposedly didn't have access to a car that night.

Which meant as much as I didn't like his appearance, he probably wasn't my killer. But he still might know something useful. Matt and I could drop in on him on the way to Kansas or the way back. I wanted to see his face when I talked to him. So much of communication is about body language and not the words someone actually says.

With that cheery plan in place, I went to bed. But I didn't sleep well.

Stupid love and all its stupid complications.

CHAPTER 11

The next day I dropped by the police station to see Matt and the results of the reports he'd pulled on everyone. It was just down the street from my grandpa's house and the weather was decent enough that I chose to walk.

I tried to take a moment and breathe in the clear, crisp air and appreciate the beauty that comes with living in a small town in the Colorado mountains. Creek wasn't big—about forty homes total, half of those converted mobile homes—which meant it was nice and quiet, no ambulances or fire trucks speeding by to disturb the peace.

Some would probably find it boring, but I found it refreshingly peaceful.

The police station was a single-story brick building with just a handful of jail cells. Most people who had to be in jail there didn't stay long before they were transferred out or released. Marlene, who manned the front desk gave me a quick smile and wave as I stepped inside.

Matt was tucked away at his desk, no sign of Officer Clark who shared the desk facing his nor of the cops who used the other two desks on the opposite side of the room. I could see someone in one of the glassed-in offices behind that, but otherwise the place was quiet as a tomb.

I shuddered at the memory of the interrogation room that was down the hall past that as well as the holding cells. One night there had been enough for me for a lifetime.

Matt waved me over with a big smile. "Ben's off today, so you can use his seat."

"Are you sure he won't psychically sense that I was here and arrest me for it later?" I asked, not entirely joking. (He had it in for my family.)

Matt shook his head and held out a small stack of paper. "Here you go. Three hits. You want me to grab you a Coke?"

"Yes, please," I beamed at him as I thought once more about how he was the best boyfriend in the world.

(What? Other women like diamonds and furs, I like Coca-Cola and a man who doesn't judge my choice of footwear.)

I thumbed through the pages and frowned.

You know what they say about assuming you can judge people by appearances? Well, seems I was bad at it. Because when Matt finally pulled the criminal records for all of the individuals tied to Julie Lewis, two of the three with any sort of record were Dennis Clay and Hank.

Hank it seemed had a history of getting drunk and punching things. And people. No lovable teddy bear after all, but a belligerent angry drunk who'd been arrested on more than one occasion and had even thrown a couch off a ten-story balcony when he was in college. (Which happened to end his college football career.)

And Dennis Clay had a restraining order filed against him by a girl in his dorm freshman year of college who said he'd followed her around everywhere and made her feel uncomfortable. A girl he'd never dated, just had an infatuation with.

I figured it had to be pretty bad if she'd felt the need to file an actual restraining order with the cops for it rather than just deal with it through campus housing or by peer pressure on him to knock it off.

(Not that I think that's the ideal way to handle things. It's more that most women hesitate quite a bit to make something like that "official" so I'd expect a woman who wasn't in fear for her life would've exhausted all other options first.)

"What's wrong?" Matt asked as I stared at the reports.

"Dennis just seemed like such a nice guy when I met him. I mean, sure, I saw that socially awkward thing in his yearbook photo, but he seemed decent when I met him. I was going to try to fix him up with Elaine. And now to find out he's a creepy stalker…"

"Maybe he's learned his lesson since then. There was no allegation of physical violence, just not knowing how to walk away when someone wasn't interested."

I rolled my eyes. Leave it to a man to say that. "They granted a restraining order against him, Matt."

"Let me check something." He turned to his computer and typed away for a bit, humming to himself as he looked at this or that, moving things around with his mouse, his eyes lighting up as he hit print a few more times.

"Well? What are you finding?" I finally asked.

He handed me the printouts with a triumphant smile. "Mitigation."

"Care to explain?"

"There was a dropped assault charge filed by the woman when she was in high school. I followed that trail and found that the man who'd been charged—who was her boyfriend at the time—was later sent away for five years for beating a different girlfriend into a coma. And some other things around her family indicate that maybe she came from a pretty rough background."

"So?"

"So…maybe—don't yell at me for it—this was a woman who expected men to be dangerous. So when Dennis followed her around she didn't see it as a harmless infatuation, even though that's what it was."

I threw the pages on the table and crossed my arms. "It's still creepy to have some guy follow you around. I had some guy do that to me at a job I had in college and it made me physically ill to go into work with him."

"But did you think he was going to harm you?"

I sighed. "No. Being socially awkward and creepy is not the same as being dangerous. Although I just feel so disappointed with Dennis now to find that out about him. And I really don't like to excuse that kind of behavior even when it's not dangerous. People should know better."

"You're investigating a murder, Maggie. You have to be able to separate out awkwardly unlikeable people from dangerous people."

Rather than go on a feminist rant about how men rarely have to deal with this kind of crud (that was not the word I used in my mind), I just glared at the desk for a long moment before I spoke again. "Fine. So Hank and Dennis stay on the list as suspects because of their records. But really, we're no closer to finding our killer than when we started. Which means Denver and Salina this weekend."

Matt nodded as I read through the last record he'd found. It was for Amy Haverson, a friend of Barb and Julie's who'd been at the party. Unfortunately, there was going to be no interviewing her. She'd taken a quick and ugly turn towards hard core drugs after high school that had led to homelessness and ultimately killed her five years later.

But I did wonder why she'd taken such a downward turn. Maybe she'd witnessed the murder. Or committed it.

But how was I going to prove it?

Honestly. Coming up with new dog treats was so much easier than investigating murder. Too bad there were only so many I could come up with. Although I was almost done perfecting the recipe for my latest treat: Puppermints. Very witty, don't you think? And very minty, too.

CHAPTER 12

Matt came to my house at nine in the morning on Saturday for our drive to Kansas. We'd decided we'd drive to Salina that day, interview Tim and Barb on Sunday, drive back to Denver that night, and then interview Rick on Monday before heading home.

Three whole days together.

Lots of it in a closed, cramped space. I mean, not really that closed and cramped. It's not like we were driving a two-seater convertible or something. We were actually taking my van which was reasonably roomy.

It just *felt* like it was going to be an incredibly small space since all the expectations for our future were coming along for the ride.

(I know. I was pathetic. One of the many, many reasons I'd stayed single for as long as I had. Most men weren't worth the mental gymnastics I went through to date them.)

Fancy ran to the door when I grabbed my rolling suitcase and looked at me with her big amber eyes.

"You have to stay here, kiddo."

She stared at me like I was breaking her heart.

"It's just a few days."

She ran to where her leash was hanging and back over to me. For someone who couldn't talk she certainly knew how to communicate.

"I took you for a walk this morning. Specifically because I knew I was going to have to leave you behind. You'll be fine. Grandpa will give you lots of treats."

She continued to stare at me, all eager anticipation.

"Come here." I led the way into the kitchen and gave her a doggie ice cream. She ran outside to lay in a snowbank and eat it as I hurried back to the front door where Matt was waiting.

"Let's get out of here before I start trying to figure out how to bring her along. I've got the suitcase, you grab the two cases of Coke and the cooler."

"Two cases of Coke? For three days?"

"I drink more Coke when I'm stressed." I led the way to the van and threw my suitcase in the back. "I'll probably only need four a day, but why risk running out? Plus, you might actually want one for yourself."

Matt looked like he wanted to say more about my addiction, but he just set the cooler and two cases of Coke in the back next to my suitcase before grabbing his bag from his vehicle. "Okay, then. Let's get this party started. Who's driving?"

I blinked. "Well, it is my van…"

"True."

"But you want to drive don't you?"

He shrugged. "Whatever you want."

"Oh no. That's not going to last the whole trip. You better have some opinions, buddy, or you're not going to survive the next three days."

He raised an eyebrow at me. "Is that so?"

"It is. I'd rather you legitimately disagree with me than have no wants or needs of your own. But I'm going to drive."

He laughed. "You are, are you? I thought you wanted me to have opinions."

"I do. But I can't drive in Kansas. So I'll drive to the border and then you can take over."

As we got into the van he asked, "Why can't you drive in Kansas?"

I grimaced, remembering the last time I'd passed through and been pulled over within ten minutes of crossing the border. "They're on top of speeders like nobody's business and I don't want a ticket." (Another one.) "So since you drive slower than my grandma, you can drive in Kansas, I'll drive in Colorado."

"A strange solution, but I think it works."

Relationship test one, passed.

Before we pulled out of the driveway I hooked up my ancient iPod through the cigarette lighter. (I had an old van.) "What music do you want to listen to?"

"No talk radio?"

"No. I want to enjoy this drive not imagine creative ways to kill myself or the rest of the world." I handed him the iPod and started the van. "Figure it out. Pretty much anything on there I'm willing to listen to."

He scrolled through. "Greek music?"

"Okay, almost anything on there."

"Thai language lessons?"

"Matt…"

"You did say pretty much anything on here. And I've always wanted to learn Thai." He flashed me a wicked grin.

"Very funny. And before you go there, let's skip the French language lessons, classical music, and opera, too. They were phases I was going through, but none of them really stuck."

"Yes, ma'am. I think this playlist will work."

As the sounds of a Blood, Sweat, & Tears song started, I nodded my head. "That will definitely work. Congratulations, Matthew Allen Barnes, you have passed couple-road-tripping-together tests numbers one and two."

"And we're not even out of the driveway yet." He leaned back. "How many tests are there?"

"I don't know, but it's a lot. Hand me a Coke, please?"

Matt raised an eyebrow, but he grabbed me a Coke from the cooler and even opened it for me. "Test number three? Will you give your girlfriend a Coke without making a comment when she asks for it way too early in the morning?"

"Sure, why not, since you passed that one, too. Although barely." I took a sip of the Coke and placed it in the cup holder before backing out of the driveway.

As I turned onto the highway I silently prayed to whoever might be listening that we'd be as comfortable together when we returned as we were right then.

CHAPTER 13

We stopped for an early lunch in Arvada. There was this incredibly good little family-owned Italian place I knew right off the highway. It only had six tables in the whole place and was hidden away in a little strip mall, but they made the best calzone in the world and I wasn't about to miss the chance to have lunch there if it presented itself.

"I have to agree that was a delicious calzone," Matt said, polishing off his half of the meatball calzone we'd ordered. (The things were so big there was no point in ordering one for each of us.)

I grinned. "I think that's road tripping test number ten passed, then."

Seeing the slight tightening around his eyes, I reached across the table and squeezed his hand. "And now I stop mentioning that from here on out because it's no longer funny, is it?"

"Not particularly."

I took a sip of my soda and tried to think of a way to ease the tension. "What was your impression of Tim Holt when you talked to him?"

"Nice guy. Happy to help with anything we needed.

He's a school teacher, you know."

"Really? I didn't see that coming."

"Middle school science."

"Not exactly the type of guy you'd think could be a killer." I glanced at the menu, tempted to order dessert but then decided against it and instead waved for the check.

"Nope. Not at all."

"And Barb? They're still together?"

He nodded. "I don't know what she does. Maybe stays home with the kids. There was some tension there when he mentioned Barb. Not sure what caused it. He said he'd make sure she was there when we came by, but I had the distinct impression it would mean a fight to make it happen."

The waiter brought over the check and Matt handed over a credit card before I could even reach for my purse. He gave me a look that made it clear I wasn't going to be paying for a single meal the whole weekend.

I pursed my lips and sat back, choosing to just accept it since I secretly liked it anyway. "Interesting. Could be that Julie's death has always put strain on their relationship, so he's not looking forward to telling Barb the cops are investigating it again."

"Could be." The waiter brought back the slip and Matt signed it. He glanced at the last couple of bites left on my plate. "You ready to get back on the road?"

"I am." I regretted not finishing every single bite, but I was stuffed to the gills. That's okay, I'd forgotten that I now had a boyfriend. Matt quickly finished off the little bit I'd left and held the door for me as we made our way back out to the van.

A Poisoned Past and Puppermints

As I settled into the driver's seat, I thought about how I actually liked road trips. I liked driving down a nice flat highway with my music playing, letting my thoughts wander where they may. But it was an adjustment to have someone in the car with me. Not a bad one per se, just an adjustment.

Fortunately, like I said before, Matt and I can talk for hours and get along just fine.

"So," I said, as we pulled back onto I-70. "Tell me what foreign country you'd most like to visit and why…"

And so it went for the next six hours of driving across the very, very flat and boring plains of Colorado and Kansas.

(If you've never been there picture flat plains that stretch in all directions, cover them with snow, and have the only mountains anywhere nearby in your rearview mirror and you'll have an idea of what most of that drive was like. It was just Matt, me, and the semis all driving a little faster than we should.)

(Until we hit Kansas and Matt took over and drove at exactly one below the speed limit the rest of the way. I guess every guy has to have a flaw. Or in this case, an advantage, since we passed three cops along the way.)

I was glad the weather was good, because when the winter storms really get going they close the gates across the highway and you aren't going to get anywhere until that particular storm is past. And as much as I liked Limon, I didn't really want to get stuck there.

It was almost dark by the time we pulled into the parking lot of the La Quinta. I knew it well. I'd stayed there with Fancy on the way to Colorado. It was dog-friendly, which is always my biggest criteria when traveling with her. We'd passed through in the summer so the place had been full of travelers and their dogs and their RVs. This time around I wondered if Matt and I were the only guests in the place.

It didn't matter, though. We just needed somewhere serviceable to lay our heads for the night, which it definitely was. Although it did make me miss my girl. But one quick call to my grandpa who assured me she was fine and all was good.

CHAPTER 14

The next day we met Tim and Barb Holt at their house. There were half a dozen different kids' bicycles scattered across the lawn even though it was winter and you'd think there wouldn't be any need for bikes. But from the look of the place they could've been left there in the summer.

It was nice enough. Two stories with a combination of brick and wood paneling, painted an odd shade of yellow that was almost mustard yellow but not quite. It showed its age in the cracked driveway and faded wood around the windows, but overall it was a home I could see myself being fine with. (Except for the color.)

Tim answered the door with a toddler on his hip of indeterminate gender. The kid was cute. Lots of curly blonde hair flopping into his or her eyes and wearing a white t-shirt with a koala and red stains on it. Tim looked much like he had in high school with blonde hair and an athlete's build.

"Hey there. Sorry for the chaos. Babysitter will be here in a few." He held out a hand to shake. "Tim Holt."

"Matt Barnes."

"Maggie Carver."

We each shook his hand.

"Any relation to Lou Carver?" Tim asked as he shook my hand.

"My grandpa."

"Great man. Best times of my life were playing baseball for him. He's the reason I ultimately got a scholarship to play in college. Come in." He turned back towards the living room. "Barb's in the kitchen, feeding the rest of the kids a snack. I swear, they're like locusts. They'll eat anything and everything if given the chance."

The living room was much like the front lawn. There were plastic toys everywhere and I wondered how Tim could brave walking barefoot through that mess. Me I'd be wincing in anticipation of a Lego brick in the bottom of the foot with each step. But not only did he do it with ease, he somehow managed to do so without stepping on a single toy along the way.

(I wasn't quite so lucky. Fortunately, the hard piece of plastic I stepped on didn't break, just turned my ankle a bit.)

I glanced around. School pictures covered the walls along with one wedding photo of Tim and Barb where they looked like kids themselves.

"How many kids do you have?" I asked.

"Five. Numbers three and four were unexpected twins. And number five was simply unexpected. But we get by. And it's great to have all these little guys running around. Can't wait until they're a little older and I can teach them all how to build a model volcano."

"Tim. Get in here. I need your help," a woman's voice snapped from the other room.

Tim grimaced and moved towards the kitchen, the kid still balanced on his hip.

After he'd disappeared around the corner I glanced at Matt. "You don't want five kids do you? Or even three?"

"I don't know. It's kind of a fun idea to have your own basketball team."

"Matt…"

He tugged my ponytail. "Five? No. But at least one or two."

"You know I'm old. That might not happen."

"You're not that old. You're not even forty."

I shook my head. "Hey, just because celebrities make it happen when they're like fifty does not mean that most of us mere mortals can. I'm already in the geriatric pregnancy stage."

"Geriatric?" He laughed, but I nodded.

He looked a little more somber as he said, "All I ask is that you're willing to try. Are you willing to try?"

My gut clenched. Marriage was one thing. Kids? That was taking responsibility for the molding of another human being. For eighteen years. And then being there forever for them. I liked the idea of being really old and having a bunch of grandkids running around for the holidays. It was the in between step I wasn't particularly interested in.

(Don't get me wrong. I think kids are great. They're fascinating little bundles of contradiction and strange questions. And just adorable in general up to a certain age. But it's like puppies. They're cute to look at, but hell to raise.)

"Maggie? Are you willing to have kids?" The look he gave me was so intent I wouldn't have been surprised if he was reading my soul.

I inhaled deeply. "In for a penny, in for a pound, right? Which means that if I agree to marry you, I'll agree to have kids. We'll need something to bind us together for all those years after all."

"Our love won't be enough?"

I shrugged. "It better be if we can't have kids."

I wasn't going to explain to him how impossibly crazy I think it is to expect two people to live parallel lives for that long if they don't have kids or a business or a common purpose that keeps them somewhat on the same path. No need to put even more pressure from my craziness on what was already a fragile situation.

The doorbell rang. I'd never been more glad for an interruption in my life.

Tim came back, a different child balanced on his hip, this one in a panda t-shirt but otherwise much like the first one. "That'll be the babysitter. Hopefully. Either that or a Jehovah's Witness. And if it is a Jehovah's Witness, man are they going to be surprised when I thrust Pam into their arms."

Fortunately for the imaginary Jehovah's Witnesses— because they always seem to come in pairs, don't they?— it was the babysitter. A teenager with braces and freckles who quickly managed to lead the little troupe of kids up the stairs with promises to play at least three different games, none of which I recognized. She had Pam tucked onto her hip, the other matching toddler gripped by the hand, and a girl of about eight trailing along behind with a baby in her arms as she herded a boy of about five ahead of her.

"Wow." That's really all I had to say about that.

Matt caught my eye and grinned. "Like I said, a basketball team...Could be fun..."

🐾🐾🐾 503 🐾🐾🐾

CHAPTER 15

We settled down in the kitchen. Barb offered us both a beer even though it was only eleven in the morning. She'd clearly already had at least one herself. It was hard to tell whether it was the booze or the babies that had aged her so fast, but where Tim looked much like the kid he'd been in high school she looked like a worn-out version of someone my mother's age.

She plopped down in a chair across from us. "Tim said you're looking into Julie's murder."

"We are," I answered.

"Well, don't know what we can tell you." She took another sip of beer. "She went to that party and then disappeared and then they found her body. That's all we know."

"You were supposed to be her ride home that night, weren't you?" I asked.

"Yeah. Wasn't our fault she wasn't around when it was time to go. Probably off with that older dude she'd been flirting with." Barb slanted a glance towards Tim who'd hunched his shoulders at her bitter tone.

"I wanted to wait for her," he mumbled.

"No point when she wasn't going to have any interest in leaving. And I wasn't going to stick around while she got it on with that dude."

"Is that where she went? Are you guys sure?" I asked. Tim nodded.

"That wasn't clear in the police report."

He stood up and grabbed himself a beer from the fridge. "We told them about the guy. They talked to him, didn't they?"

"They did. But you didn't tell them you were sure that's where she'd gone. You just said they'd talked at the party."

He took a long swig of beer.

Matt leaned forward. "Can you tell us what happened that night?"

Tim stayed standing by the fridge. "Not much to tell. Julie came to the party with us. Some guys we didn't know showed up. She started talking to one of them. They left together."

"That's not what we heard. We heard *you* got in a fight with her." Matt focused on Tim with a laser-like intensity that made even me squirm.

Tim took another long swig of his beer. "So I said some things to her before she left. I didn't like the look of the guy."

"You didn't like the look of him, but you let her leave with him?" I could almost feel the intense spotlight of Matt's gaze as he focused on Tim.

"It wasn't like that. It was…" Tim sat down at the table and ran his hand through his hair.

Barb sat back, arms crossed, a sneer on her face. "Go ahead. I know how you felt about her, don't I?"

He stared at a spot in the center of the table. "Julie came to the party with us. It was the first time she'd been to a party like that. First time she'd had anything to drink. And then she's all tipsy and this guy shows up and he's all into her and she's giggling and flirting back. I told him to leave. I told him I'd call the cops because he wasn't invited and it wasn't his property. And he left."

"Alone?" Matt asked.

"Alone. And then Julie turns on me and starts screaming at me that I had no right to do that. That she could make her own decisions." He shook his head, clearly disagreeing even all those years later.

"What happened next?"

"She stormed off." He crossed his arms.

"And?"

We waited as Tim worked the metal tab loose from his beer can. "And I went after her. We…said some things."

"Oh just tell them, would you?" Barb finished her beer and crumpled it up before throwing it towards the trash can. (She missed.) "You went after her and confessed your love for her. Told her you were looking out for her because you didn't want her to get hurt. Because you loved her and always had. Because she was the only one for you."

I glanced back and forth between the two of them. Tim wasn't surprised by what she said. "Were you there, Barb? Or did he tell you about it later?" I asked.

"I was there. I followed after them. Got close enough I could hear the whole sorry mess. But here's what matters." She rested her forearms on the table and it shifted under her weight. "When Tim was done, Julie left to go after that guy. Tim and I left the party together. She was fine when we left. And we never saw her again."

"That true?" Matt asked.

Tim rubbed at the back of his neck. "Yeah. Julie left, headed in the direction of that guy's cabin, and we went home without her." He downed the last of his beer and stood to throw it and Barb's in the trash can.

"Where'd you go?" I asked.

"My house," Tim said.

"Yeah, we had to kiss and make up," Barb sneered.

I glanced at Matt, but he shrugged. "Okay then. Thank you. We appreciate the time."

We made our awkward goodbyes and got out of there as fast as we could. Nothing more we were going to get out of them and I desperately wanted to get away from that lovely example of marital bliss.

As he merged his way onto I-70, Matt finally spoke, "I don't think we'd ever be like that, Maggie, no matter how bad things got."

"No? Do you think they were like that when they first got married? You think that's what they thought their lives would become?"

"Maybe. You notice when they got married and when their first kid was born?"

"Good point."

He grabbed my hand and squeezed. "You know why I know we'd never be like that?"

"Why?"

"Because I'm not settling for you. You're exactly who I want to be with and who I love."

I squeezed back. "And you're exactly who I want to be with."

To change the subject before we got way too sappy, I said, "So. Looks like we're going to have an interesting interview with Rick tomorrow."

"That it does. He may have been the last one to see Julie alive."

CHAPTER 16

We met Rick at the accounting firm where he worked. It was located on the second floor of a three-story office building tucked into the curve off Havana Street in Aurora. The hallway carpet was a thin, faded beige and the stairs we had to take to reach the second floor were narrow and steep. But the offices themselves were nice enough.

Rick had clearly put on a few pounds and lost a few inches of hairline since his picture on the website was taken. He also seemed to have developed an inordinate fondness for hair gel. It was not a good look.

But he still had attractive green eyes and good teeth. I could see what Julie had found interesting about him all those years ago.

He led us to a conference room with four gray fabric chairs arranged around a black table. "Can I get you a coffee? Tea?"

Matt took a coffee, but I waved him away and grabbed the Coke I'd brought out of my purse. "Brought my own, thanks."

That broke some of the tension in the room. He settled

down across from us. "So? This is about that girl who got killed, huh? The one up in the mountains?"

Matt nodded. "The one you flirted with the night she died."

"Well, yeah. She was a good-looking girl, you know? She started talking to me, I started talking back. And then that friend of hers came and shoved in. Crazy guy. Threatened to call the cops just because we'd dropped in on his party. I took off. She was pretty, but not that pretty. And I had my own beer back at the cabin."

"That *crazy guy* says the girl followed you when you left the party."

Rick turned his coffee cup this way and that until it was perfectly aligned with the edge of the table, but he didn't answer.

"Did she?" Matt finally asked.

"Yeah."

"Why didn't you tell the cops?"

He grimaced. "I don't know. I didn't really want to get into it with them."

"Get into what?"

He scratched at his ear. "She followed me back to the cabin, right? My buddies had gone on to another party, so it was just us."

"Umhm. And?"

"And she was pretty." He shrugged as if what he was about to say was obvious. "So I made a few moves."

I tensed, but the coroner's report had said there was no sign of any sort of sexual contact, willing or otherwise.

"And?" Matt asked.

"And when I tried to take it past a little bit of kissing, she freaked out. Said she didn't want that. Pushed me away." He frowned like he couldn't understand why a woman might do such a thing.

"And then what happened?" Matt asked as I glared daggers at Rick and he pointedly avoided looking my direction.

"I said a few things. I don't like women who promise and don't deliver." He flicked me a glance but quickly looked away when I returned it with pure contempt. Such a class act. To know he was saying something rude, but not keep it to himself.

"And?" Matt asked again, a little more forcefully this time.

"She got all teary-eyed. Said I was mean. That she'd never promised me anything. I told her to go back to her little high school party, but she didn't want to. Said she didn't want to see that guy she'd gotten in a fight with. Asked if I could give her a ride home."

"What did you do then?" Matt asked, his voice carefully neutral, while I fumed silently.

"I said sure, why not. Figured she might warm up a bit if given the chance, you know?"

I tried very hard not to move. This was it. He was our murderer. He'd given her a ride home, she'd refused him again, and he'd killed her.

"And did you give her that ride?" Matt asked, closing the trap.

"No. Turns out Dave had left for some family emergency while I was gone. Which meant I didn't have a car to drive her home with."

I managed not to show my disappointment.

"So what happened then?"

He glanced my way. "She asked to use the phone in

the cabin. Called some guy. He came and picked her up."

"She didn't go back to the party?"

"No. Just stayed and drank my beer until the guy got there. And the guy who picked her up? That guy would never have been invited to a party in high school. Short, glasses, acne, braces. He'd hit the trifecta of loserdom."

I valiantly refrained from pointing out how he'd listed four attributes, not three.

"Do you remember what kind of car he was driving?" Matt asked, glancing my way for a brief moment.

I made an effort to calm myself back down. I don't know how it works, but when I really, really don't like someone it's like I'm drilling a hole in their skull. The whole room seems to feel it even if I don't say a word. (Comes in handy when I need customer service to notice me, but incredibly awkward the rest of the time.)

Rick glanced my way again before he answered. "A station wagon with wood paneling. I remember I made fun of it. Suggested to her that she'd be better off staying with me than getting in that piece of junk, but she ignored me. Just begged the guy to get her out of there."

"Alright. Thank you." Matt stood, so I did, too.

Rick held the door for us, but I ignored him entirely. He may not have killed Julie but he was still a creep.

Matt and I were silent until we returned to the van. "Dennis Clay," I said. "That had to be who picked her up."

"You said he was hiding something."

"I didn't think it was murder." I backed out of the parking space with a little more speed than was probably safe.

"Well, only one way to find out. I'll have Ben bring him in for a formal interview this afternoon. You can watch from observation."

A Poisoned Past and Puppermints

I wanted to just drive by his house and confront him, but Matt was right. If he really was the killer, then the cops needed any confession he gave on tape and handled properly under the law.

That didn't mean I had to like it, though.

CHAPTER 17

We went straight to the police station when we reached Creek. They already had Dennis Clay in the interrogation room when we arrived. He was angry, I could see it in the way he held the glass of water they'd given him, his knuckles white from the tension.

It was further confirmed when he snapped at Matt as soon as Matt entered the room. "When can I leave? I need to get home to my mom. And I have work to finish today."

Matt sat down across from him with a casual grace. "I'm sorry to bother you with this, Mr. Clay, but you understand that the murder of a woman is serious business even if it happened over a decade ago."

"So now the cops are investigating this, too? Not just that woman who dropped by my house uninvited? What did I say to her that you decided to haul me in here like a common criminal?"

"Nothing. Although she did think you were hiding something." Matt paused long enough to give Dennis a meaningful look. "It was the interview we conducted with Rick Patterson today that led to you being brought in for questioning."

"Who is Rick Patterson?"

"Who do you think he is? Think back to the events surrounding Julie's death and tell me who might've pointed us in your direction."

Dennis's upper lip twitched as he glared at the corner of the room.

"Look, Mr. Clay, you can come straight with me about what you know about the death of Julie Lewis or I'll build my case without you. But your silence won't save you."

He stared at Matt, looking genuinely shocked. "Save me? I didn't hurt her."

"Then tell me what you know about the events surrounding her murder. And why you didn't come forward at the time."

He pushed away from the table and rubbed his hands on his jeans. "I didn't hurt her."

Matt spread his hands wide. "Okay. I'll believe you. For now. Are you willing to give a DNA sample?"

Dennis shifted in his seat. "I thought she wasn't…hurt…that way."

"She wasn't. But there have been incredible advances in DNA testing since she was murdered. We can tell if someone touched her. It's called touch DNA. Did you touch her, Dennis?"

"Not like that." He pressed his lips together and stared into the corner. "It wasn't like that."

"What was it like, Dennis? Tell me."

He fidgeted some more before finally answering. "She called me. It was late. She was clearly drunk. She was crying. She said she was down by the lake and needed a ride home. She asked me to come pick her up."

"Why you?"

"Because I lived nearby? Because she knew I'd be home? Because she knew I'd do anything for her? I don't know."

"So you picked her up."

"Of course I did. Julie Lewis called *me* to help her. What was I going to do? Say no?"

"Did she tell you why she needed the ride?"

He shook his head. "Not really. She…She didn't want to talk. I tried, but she just huddled against the door and cried the whole way home. I asked her if that guy had done something to her and she shook her head, but that was all I could get out of her."

"You didn't like that, did you?" Matt snapped as he leaned forward. "You did something about it. Here you were, being the nice guy, picking her up from that stupid party, and she wouldn't even talk to you."

"What? No. It wasn't like that." He crossed his arms and hunched downward in his seat. "She was so sad. I didn't know what to say to her. I didn't know what to do. So I just drove her home."

"Is that all you did? You didn't pull over on the side of the road and try to get a little payment for the favor you were doing her?"

"No! Not at all. I'd never do that to Julie."

Matt leaned in even more. "Then why didn't you tell anyone about it when she was found dead the next morning? Didn't you want to help the police find her killer?"

He rubbed at his face. "I didn't think it mattered. She wasn't killed at home, right? And I knew if I told people that they'd react like you are. They'd accuse me of doing something to her. But I didn't do anything. I just picked her up and gave her a ride home. That's all."

"Can anyone confirm your story?"

He shook his head. "No. Her dad wasn't home when I dropped her off. My mom would've been able to tell you I got a call and was back by midnight, but she's in and out these days. I doubt she could remember one specific day like that. Not all these years later."

Matt stayed silent, watching Dennis until the tension in the air became almost unbearable.

Dennis shook his head. "I didn't kill her, I swear. I'll take a lie detector if you want."

"What about that DNA?"

"She was in my car. I squeezed her shoulder when she was crying. She may have my DNA on her. But not because I did anything to her."

Matt glanced towards where I stood watching the interview. "Anything else you can remember about that night?"

He shook his head. "She told me thank you when I dropped her off. Told me I was a true friend, someone she could always count on. She didn't say it, but there was an implication that someone else wasn't a true friend. And, no, I don't know who it would be."

"Did you see anyone else at the party?"

"I didn't see a party. I picked her up at some cabin. It was just her and some older guy. I don't even know where the party was supposed to be compared to that cabin, but it definitely wasn't anywhere within sight."

Matt nodded. "Okay. Stay in town. We may need to talk to you again."

I waited long enough for him to walk Dennis out the

front door and then joined him at his desk. "So now what?"

"I don't know. We have a better timeline than the original investigators had. We know Julie made it home safe, assuming Dennis is telling the truth, and I think he is. But phone records don't show any calls to or from her house that night. So someone had to go to her house and pick her up. Or she had to leave to meet them. But who? And why?"

"That's the million-dollar question, isn't it? Who would come to Julie Lewis's house in the middle of the night instead of calling her? And who would she go off with at that time of night?"

"Exactly. Well, I better write up the interviews we did for the file. And then, dinner? Say six?"

I nodded. "I'm sure Lesley will have whipped up something interesting."

He caught my hand. "I prefer your cooking to hers, you know."

I laughed. "That's because you've never lived with me. Just know that sometimes I think that onion dip, chips, and a hunk of cheese is a perfectly acceptable dinner."

He grinned. "Sounds good to me. As long as you're occasionally okay with a can of tuna fish and some Doritos."

I gave him a kiss on the cheek and headed home, still trying to figure out what had drawn Julie Lewis away from her house in the middle of the night. (Assuming Dennis was telling the truth, of course.)

CHAPTER 18

Fancy practically bowled me over as soon as I opened the front door. I sat down so she could crawl all over me and lick my face until she finally calmed down. "It was only two nights, you goof," I told her.

But in dog-world I'm pretty sure any absence over an hour is a lifetime. She trailed after me as I put my bag away and stashed the leftover Coke in the kitchen pantry. (I still had six cans left, which considering that I'd put six in the cooler and started with two cases, was pretty good really.)

I checked the stove top which had a big batch of split pea soup cooking, and took a deep deep breath of the yummy smells coming from the bread maker. No signs of my grandpa or Lesley, so I figured they'd run somewhere real quick until dinner was ready. Never the best idea to leave food cooking on the stove without supervision, but they probably hadn't gone far or for long.

When I settled on the couch, Fancy jumped up next to me and stared at me, not lying down like she normally would. "I'm right here. I'm not going anywhere again anytime soon, okay?"

I couldn't imagine leaving Fancy for a month like Jamie and Mason had with Lulu when they went to Paris. I mean, Paris. But, Fancy. She hadn't asked me to take responsibility for her, I'd made that decision on my own. And since I had, I tried to do the best I could by her even if that meant no really good, lengthy vacations for a decade.

At loose ends and determined not to spend the time until dinner playing solitaire, I called Jamie.

"Maggie. How'd it go?"

"Well, we had some interesting interviews. I mean Barb Holt is…"

"I don't care about that. You're the only person I know who would combine interviewing people about a murder with your first getaway with your boyfriend. I'm sure that kept things interesting, but I want to know how your first weekend away with Matt went. Are you still together?"

"Yes, we're still together. Although he asked if I want kids." I shuddered.

"And what did you tell him?"

"That if I agreed to marry him I'd agree to try for kids, too."

"If? Maggie. Come on now. Who are you going to find that's more perfect for you than Matt?"

I pinched the bridge of my nose. "I don't know. Probably no one. But marriage is a big deal."

"Not really."

"How can you say that?"

"Look, Mason and I were great together before we got married and are even more great together now. Marriage didn't change anything."

"It's permanent and binding, Jamie. You have to like go to court if it doesn't work out."

She laughed. "Maggie, you are so crazy. Do you want to lose him?"

"No."

"Then marry him."

"He hasn't even asked." Fancy gave me a glare before jumping off the couch and going outside. She's not a fan of loud voices.

"And if he did, what would you say? Because you know darned well that if you give him the slightest indication that you're interested he'll ask."

I made some sort of noise that probably sounded like I was dying. "I don't know."

"He survived a weekend with you. In a van. For hours on end. Do you like him less now? Or more?"

"Probably more."

"Then marry him."

"He hasn't asked."

"He will. Soon. And when he does, you better say yes."

I rolled my eyes. "Just because you're happily married doesn't mean I will be."

"Maggie, you're never going to be perfectly happy. But you'll be much happier with Matt in your life than without him. I know you. Trust me. So say yes when he asks."

I narrowed my eyes, suddenly suspicious. "He hasn't talked to you about this, has he?"

"I am your best friend."

"What did you tell him, Jamie?" I snapped.

"I told him you were very skilled at avoiding discussions you didn't want to have. And that if he waited for you to give him the green light to ask he'd never get it. But that if he pushed the point and just went ahead and asked you that you'd almost certainly say yes."

"Jamie!"

"It's true."

I slumped down. "Doesn't mean you should've told him."

"Don't worry. You have until spring."

"Spring?"

"Better go. Mason just got home." She hung up.

When was spring? Months away, right? Like May?

I frantically searched for the first day of spring on my phone. Turns out it was in the middle of March. I had less than three weeks.

Matt was probably going to ask me to marry him in less than three weeks. No wonder he'd been talking about buying a place. And kids. For him this was right around the corner.

For a second, I forgot how to breathe. I wasn't ready for this. I needed…years. Decades, even. Centuries, really, but unfortunately the human life span didn't allow for that one.

I glanced at Fancy who had come back inside and gone to sleep at my feet, snuffling quietly to herself. I'd always wanted a dog, but had never found the time for one. And then Fancy came along. She had nowhere else to go—nowhere good at least—so I'd taken her on.

It had changed my life entirely. Probably for the good.

No. Definitely for the good.

I hated big commitments. They never made sense to me. They were so lasting and final. I'd taken Fancy on and for me that was a commitment to ten years of living my life differently, putting the needs of another living creature above my own. But it worked out okay, because she really couldn't tell me when I messed up and was easygoing enough to just roll with it.

But a human being would have opinions. And marriage was a commitment for the rest of my life not just ten years.

Jamie was right, though. If Matt asked I wouldn't be able to tell him no.

Fancy moved in her sleep and her paw stretched out to rest against my leg. I looked down at her for a long moment and sighed. As much as I didn't like to make them, big commitments were usually worth it.

CHAPTER 19

The next day I asked Mr. Lewis if he'd join me for lunch. We went to a BBQ joint in Masonville and I told him everything we'd found out about the night Julie died and then I apologized to him for not finding the killer.

"Don't be sorry. You found out more than the cops did back then. You really think Dennis Clay was telling the truth?"

I nodded. "I knew he was hiding something when I talked to him that first time. And after we talked to Rick Patterson, I thought maybe he was hiding the fact that he'd done something to Julie. But I just don't see it. Matt really grilled him and he held up."

I took a bite of my BBQ pork sandwich and managed to suppress my groan of pleasure. I don't eat BBQ often because even I know that too much fat is probably bad for your heart, but, man, that stuff is good. Especially the bits with the crispy fat…Mmmm.

"Had Julie ever snuck out of the house before that night that you knew of?" I asked.

"No."

"And why did she leave? Why not just let whoever it

was into the house? She had to know you weren't going to be home for hours." I dipped my fries in the tangy barbecue sauce, relishing that mix of tartness and salt and starch. It was hard to focus on the conversation when the food was so good.

"That's easy enough to answer. My neighbor at the time, Ms. Franks, had horrible insomnia. She was up most of every night. And she took it upon herself to keep an eye on Julie. Every time Julie was up past midnight Ms. Franks would let me know. Not only that, she'd tell me which lights in the house were on and if there was a car in the driveway, what kind of car it was."

"Did that happen often?"

He shook his head. "Only a couple of times."

I forced myself to ignore my food for a few moments. This felt important. "And when there was someone over, who was it? Before that night, I mean."

"Tim. Always Tim."

"Not Barb and Tim?"

"No, just Tim. When Barb and Tim went anywhere together they always drove her SUV, because it was new and fancy. But Tim had access to an old pickup truck that had been his grandpa's. It wasn't really safe for the road, but he only lived a couple of miles away so it was safe enough to drive to our house and back."

"Did Ms. Franks see anything on the night Julie died?"

"I never asked her. I always assumed Julie didn't make it home."

"And she didn't tell you? She sounds like the type that would've immediately given you full details when she heard about Julie."

I snuck another fry dunked in barbecue sauce while he rubbed at the back of his neck, thinking. "She had a stroke right around then. Might've been the same day they found Julie. I can't remember, I was so numb, so lost. They moved her into a home. She passed away a few months later."

I stored that fact away for later, but I had a more promising lead to explore first. "What about Amy Haverson? How close was Julie with her? There were some photos in the yearbook and one or two mentions in her diary, but that's about it."

He shook his head. "They were never really close. I mean, same age, grow up in the same small town, you don't tend to have a lot of choices about your friends. But Amy was always a little on the wild side. She was always testing to see where the lines were. Led her to make some bad choices. Julie stayed away from that."

"That fits with what I know of her. Amy overdosed five years ago."

"I know. Her dad and I were friends. She was headed that way from a very young age."

"I was kind of hoping she'd had some involvement in Julie's murder and spiraled from there." I took another bite of my sandwich. It wasn't as good when it wasn't hot.

He shook his head. "I don't think so. But her dad still has all of her things. You want me to give him a call? Maybe she had a diary like Julie did."

"It's worth a shot."

Believe it or not, we spent the rest of the meal talking about the television show *Chopped.* It turns out we were both fans and they'd just had a barbecue special episode we'd both watched. Discussing that episode led to a long discussion about other episodes we'd watched. My personal favorite was the April Fool's episode with the caramel-covered onion. I'd liked all the misdirects with foods that weren't what they seemed. His favorites were the teen competitions because it reminded him of what amazing potential kids have.

It was a nice meal overall. And good to see him share a meal rather than eat alone and stare out the window at nothing for once. I promised myself I'd try to make a habit of it after the investigation was over. It was good for both of us, really.

🐾 🐾 🐾

Turns out Amy did have a diary. Or a journal of sorts. Actually three of them. They were more pictures than words. Lots of dark, angry, black drawings of tortured faces and dripping blood. It was hard to reconcile those images with the relatively clean-cut yearbook photos I'd seen.

I asked her dad about it. He was a short man whose large belly pushed against the seams of the white shirt he'd tucked into a pair of old jeans.

"She wanted to dye her hair black junior year of high school. I told her if she did I'd send her off to live with her aunt who was a former Marine. Same with when she tried to wear ripped jeans and black t-shirts with violent images on them. The threat worked until she turned eighteen that June."

"Did she stay around here after that?" I glanced around the small, cramped living room. There wasn't a single sign in that room that he'd ever had a daughter.

"Nope. She blew out the birthday candles on her cake, walked out the front door, and hitched the first ride she could find." He glanced out the window to where we could see the interstate running by half a block away.

"How'd she react to Julie's death?"

He shrugged. "I think she wished it was her. She had this idea that she was destined to die young. Said she couldn't believe goody-goody Julie had beat her to it. But other than that, it was like it didn't happen."

"Did she hang around with anyone that summer?"

"Not really. Not that I saw. No one came by. I know she went out to the lake to party like the other kids, but other than that she wasn't close to anyone." He scratched at his belly. "I tried to talk to her. I did. I worried so much about her, but…" He shrugged. "I wasn't very good at it. I got impatient. And angry. And then she'd leave. And that was that."

"Have you read these?" I put my hand on the journals he'd dug out of the closet.

"From time to time. She used to leave them lying around the house. But I didn't like what I saw, so I stopped."

I wondered if that had been her way of trying to communicate with her father. Not every kid can talk to their parents, after all. "Well, thank you for letting me borrow them. I really appreciate it."

"Keep 'em. Not doing me any good anymore."

"Oh, no, I wouldn't want to do that. You never know when you might change your mind."

He nodded, but it was clear he wanted them gone for good. I quickly made my excuses and got out of there.

CHAPTER 20

Exploring those journals was fascinating and disturbing at the same time. When I'd read Julie's diary it had felt familiar. We'd grown up in different places and under different circumstances, but we were a lot alike. High achievers comfortable in our own skin and our belief that life was going to work out.

But Amy's journals were an insight into a type of worldview I'd never experienced and honestly struggled to understand. Not a worldview in the sense of what she thought of other people or her religious or social beliefs, but in terms of how she approached the world and what happened in it.

It was mostly drawings, but those drawings combined with the few words she used were all about the darkness in life, about failure and loss and inevitable decay. About not feeling comfortable with who she was and who the world wanted her to be.

A part of me wanted to believe that she was the killer, because then there'd be some logic or explanation for what I saw on those pages. Some inner corruption that was reflected outwardly in what she did. But after reading all three journals I knew she wasn't the killer.

She was just a sad, lonely girl struggling with depression and with a parent who didn't understand the bleakness that filled her soul, and so couldn't give her the help that might have saved her from the path she'd gone down.

I set the journals aside and went to find Fancy to snuggle with for a few minutes. Of course, Fancy isn't a snuggler so as soon as I sat close enough to her that she thought I was going to actually intrude on her space she got up and moved to the other side of the room with a look like, "What is wrong with you person? Boundaries, please."

"Everything alright?" my grandpa asked, coming into the room.

"No." I told him about the journals and about how sad it made me to think how many people walk through the world with that kind of inner darkness eating away at them. I finished with, "From what I could tell, she had a decent enough life, Grandpa. But she was so…angry and sad and confused."

"You can never know what someone else is carrying around inside. And you can never understand how much that life that seemed good to you wasn't for her. I can't tell you how many times I've seen it with the kids I've coached over the years. For the ones who fit into the lines that their parents draw for them, life is easy. It's charmed. But every few years I get a kid through who seems like they should have it all worked out and they're drowning. Because who they are inside doesn't match what the world they live in wants them to be." He nodded towards the door. "Jack, Matt's brother, was one of those. He had the looks and the brains and the charm to be anything he wanted to be. But he messed up all the time, because his dad wanted him to be something he couldn't be."

(Jack was quite the gentleman criminal before he finally decided to turn it around.)

"Matt turned out fine, though," I said.

"Yes and no. Matt struggled, too. Don't think he didn't. But he found a way out—the military. If he hadn't found that path, I don't know where he would've ended up."

It's hard to realize that someone you love could actually have turned out completely different given just a few different choices along the way. But it's true. Our choices drive us down certain paths but then those paths turn right back around and shape us into the people we become. Which is why the paths we choose are so important.

Like marriage. Twining your life so closely with anyone else is bound to change everything from that moment forward.

"Grandpa."

"Yeah?"

"Do you think I should marry Matt?"

He shook his head. "That's your choice to make. But please make it soon before you drive all of us crazy. As they say, it's time to put up or shut up."

Fancy rolled onto her side with a loud grunt as if agreeing with him.

I glanced at those journals again. Who did I want to be? The person who saw darkness and despair down every possible path? Or the one (like Jamie) who saw it all as one great, wonderful adventure that was bound to work out one way or the other?

I'd always had faith in my ability to accomplish things. Jump out of a plane and land in one piece, no problem. Quit my job, move halfway across the country, and open a business not many people would find interesting, done. Get an MBA, sure. Get a promotion, absolutely.

But people always stymied me. They were these fathomless black holes that I could throw my love or interest or attention at, but what happened after that was a great, vast mystery I didn't really understand or trust.

I trusted Matt, though. To my core. Which meant, it seemed, that I was going to have to get married.

Damn it. (Sorry for the language, but, really, a moment like that called for it.)

CHAPTER 21

I wanted to solve Julie's murder first, though. Which meant actually figuring out who had lured Julie away from her house that night.

I sat down with a piece of paper and started writing down names.

Hank. A violent drunk. Definitely capable of hurting her. But I couldn't see Julie leaving her house with him. They weren't especially close. Plus, he'd probably just passed out at the party. He'd be a suspect if she'd died there and not near her house, but she hadn't. So he was out.

Amy. A sad, depressed teenager with dark thoughts. It wasn't outside the realm of possibility that she'd want to hurt someone else, but there'd been an entry in her journal from the night of the party, and I didn't see her writing that entry and then leaving her house to go kill Julie.

Dennis Clay. Another probably sad and depressed teenager. He did have that restraining order from college, but he hadn't tried to hurt that girl in college, he'd just been uncomfortably attentive. And I couldn't see him hurting Julie. Pining after her? Sure. Making her uncomfortable with his awkward attempts to get to know her? Absolutely. (Been on the receiving end of that once or twice, myself.) But I believed him when he said he'd driven her home that night and then left.

Rick (the you-know-what). Hadn't had access to a car. And if he'd been going to do something I'm pretty sure it would've been before driving her home, not after. He didn't even know where she lived either, come to think of it.

Tim and Barb. I didn't know. Maybe. But why was I thinking of them as a unit? Because Lesley said they were always joined at the hip? Or because they were still together?

I realized I shouldn't be thinking of them that way. I should be thinking of them as two very different people with very different needs.

Tim. Had told Julie he loved her and she'd walked away. I could see him going to her house that night and trying to make it right. Trying to get back that friendship they'd shared all those years. Or to make his case again.

But would he then kill her? For what? For rejecting him? That's definitely the danger point in most abusive relationships, the point where the woman tries to leave. But they'd just been friends. Would he really kill her like that? And there were no signs he was an abuser either.

He was strong enough to do it, though. And he was certainly one of the people Julie would probably leave her house for.

Which meant he had to stay on the list. He was my strongest possibility so far.

Barb. She'd heard Tim confess his love to Julie. She knew she was his second choice. And that he was willing to give her up for Julie if Julie said yes. Had she lured

Julie out of her house so she could take care of her competition for good?

But would Julie leave her house in the middle of the night for Barb? They were friends, but were they that close?

(Me, I'd only leave the house if someone was in a dire emergency that required immediate action. Otherwise I'd be like, "Why are you at my door? Do you not understand that it's the middle of the frickin' night? Go away and come back at a decent hour." But I'm also anti-social and rude.)

I tried to put myself in Julie's shoes. She'd gone to her first party. She was drunk for the first time. She'd flirted with some guy who turned out to be a jerk. Her best friend of forever had confessed he was in love with her. She'd had to call the guy she probably knew was in love with her but that she wasn't interested in for a ride home. And now she was home, all alone.

That summer was supposed to be this great, wonderful adventure where she got to let loose a little after so much drive and passion, but the first night had been an absolute disaster. Who could she talk to about that? Not her dad. He was at work. So a friend? But which one?

Barb?

I could see her agreeing to go off somewhere with Barb to talk it through except for the Tim situation. That was awkward. But if she confessed to Barb that she didn't want Tim, would that make it doable?

Maybe.

We knew Barb and Tim had left the party and gone back to Tim's house together. But what if they didn't stay together? Then it could've been either one of them.

Or what if they had? What if Barb had turned on Tim that night and they'd had a huge fight and she'd said that if he really loved her he needed to take care of Julie. That she was coming between them. That if he really cared about her, he'd help her do something about it for once and for all. Would he do that for Barb?

Did they have that dynamic?

I wasn't so sure.

Then again, they were clearly miserable in their lives, but still together. *Something* was holding them there. But what? Mutual guilt over the murder of Julie?

Of course, people stay in awful relationships for any number of reasons, and 99.99% of the time it's not because they killed someone together.

For Barb it could be thinking she'd won the prize and now being stuck with Tim even though it turned out all he could offer her was an average life in a small town.

For Tim it could be about duty. Or religious belief. (I hadn't seen signs of religious belief in their house, though.) Or it could be figuring there was nothing better out there or staying for the kids.

(The worst reason to stay in a relationship ever from my observations.)

So maybe their misery had nothing to do with Julie's murder.

I didn't know. And I didn't know how to find out.

What I did know is that I needed some fresh air.

I grabbed Fancy's leash. In less than two seconds she went from a snoring, slobbering mess to wide awake and on her feet, staring at the door. (Must be some doggie survival trick, because I certainly can't pull that off.)

"I take it you're up for a walk then?" I asked as she

came over to let me leash her up.

As we stepped outside, I cursed under my breath. How had I forgotten that it was winter in the mountains of Colorado, which meant it was *cold*? (I try not to go for walks when I can literally see my breath.) Ah well. Too late to go back once a hundred and forty pounds of eager dog started pulling me down the street.

CHAPTER 22

That night Matt came over for dinner and I talked through my suspect list with him and my grandpa. Lesley was at her youngest grandkid's school pageant and my grandpa had managed to excuse himself. I didn't blame him. There's a point where kids move from adorably incompetent to just horrendous sounding and little Bobby was at that age. The only people who were going to enjoy that particular performance were besotted parents or grandparents.

Since Lesley wasn't there I'd made dinner. Spaghetti casserole. There's just something about massive amounts of Velveeta melted over noodles, spaghetti sauce, and spicy sausage that really works well together. Pair it with some nice crunchy French bread and real butter and it's a winning combination.

(Then again, any meal that involves cheese is already halfway to delicious in my book with the exception of gorgonzola which I swear is a sign that evil lurks in the corners of the world. I will never forgive those gorgonzola mashed potatoes that absolutely ruined a nice, juicy steak for me back when I was basically living on room service meals.)

As I judiciously fed Fancy small bites of cheese and noodles—I didn't think she needed spicy sausage—I asked Matt if he could maybe call Tim and ask him if he and Barb had spent that entire night together. "At least then we'd know whether to look at them as a couple or on their own."

"I'd rather not if we can avoid it."

I must've frowned at him, because he chuckled a bit and added, "If I'm going to go back to them for another interview I want more information and I want them in an interview room."

"You can't possibly think of bringing them here with five kids in tow."

"I will if I think they're murderers." He stabbed a piece of sausage with his fork. "But we need a lot more to go on before we make that decision. There was nothing in Amy's journals?"

"No. She wasn't much for words. And it's hard to know which of the drawings were real events and which were fantasies. There were some pretty disturbing drawings in there. Lots of Barb and Julie and a few others. For example…"

I ran over and grabbed the most recent journal and flipped through to show them one of the sketches. "See, here's Barb and her face is all twisted up in a snarl. And here's Julie with her head down reading a book. And then here's Amy on her knees, crying. But they're all separate images. See that? They're on the same page, but there's no way to know if they were drawn at the same time or if they're supposed to be connected."

My grandpa flipped through the sketches, raising his

eyebrows at what he saw. "Is there any pattern?"

"Maybe. Barb is usually looking mean when she's drawn. Julie is usually daydreaming or disconnected from what's happening. A few of the other girls look mean sometimes, too. And Amy generally looks angry or hurt. Which pretty much confirms what I already knew about Barb, which is that she's a, you know. And that Julie was off studying and playing sports most of the time."

My grandpa showed me a drawing. "Tim?"

"Yeah, probably."

Matt took the journal from my grandpa and showed the page to both of us. "Look at who he's watching."

I nodded. "Julie. But then that also confirms what we already knew. One big ol' love triangle that Julie was oblivious to. Do you kill over that? If you're Barb? Or if you're Tim and the girl you love rejects you?"

My grandpa took the list of suspects and glanced at it. "You left off one possibility."

"What's that?"

"A stranger."

"But she was half a mile from her house. Do you really think she walked half a mile in the middle of the night by herself and then just happened to stumble upon someone who decided to kill her but not do anything else?"

He shrugged and handed it back. "It's still a possibility."

I tossed the journal and list aside in disgust. "I wish that busybody, Ms. Franks, was still alive. Mr. Lewis said she knew which cars came by, license plate and all. Someone like that, she probably kept a written record of it. But Mr. Lewis said she had a stroke right after Julie died."

"Hm." My grandpa reached for his non-existent cigarettes and then frowned when he remembered he no longer smoked. "It's a long shot, but her son is a bit of a hoarder. It's possible he actually kept his mother's things."

"It's been over ten years."

"What would that matter to a hoarder? Of course, if it turns out he did keep a notebook of hers that says who came by that night, that will make him even worse than he is now."

I shuddered, thinking about the few episodes of that show on hoarders that I'd watched. Give me an episode of *Intervention* any day, but *Hoarders*? Ugh. No. I draw my line at…ugh. I won't even say it. Just, no.

"Maybe we don't have to tell him if we find something," I said.

"Good luck with that."

I glanced at Matt. "Are you up for it? Swinging by his place tomorrow to see what he kept?"

He nodded. "Sure. I'd like to see this solved as much as you would at this point. Even if it means wading through piles of old newspapers."

"And worse. Don't forget the worse." I shuddered.

CHAPTER 23

The next day we drove out to Beau Franks's house. It was a one-story house on the edge of town. It looked weary but not neglected. The paint was fresh enough, the window screens were well-repaired. But there was a sag to the house that made me feel like it might collapse in a puff of dust any day.

Matt banged on the door. He was in his uniform. (Which looked mighty nice on him, I might add.) This was a quasi-official visit. His boss had kind of sort of signed off on my participation in the police investigation. (Mostly because he knew not signing off wouldn't change my involvement and at least this way he looked like he was in control of the situation.)

Beau, when he finally opened the door, was much like his house. His clothes were clean enough. He didn't smell or anything like that. But he looked worn and on the point of collapse. A cat wove its way between his legs before shooting outside after prey only it could see. The odor wafting through the door was decidedly musky, but not rotten like I'd feared it would be.

"Beau Franks?" Matt asked.

"That's me."

"Officer Barnes. And this is Maggie Carver. We'd like to ask you a few questions if you don't mind."

Beau angled his hip against the doorframe, clearly blocking us from coming into the house. It was not a warm enough day to be having any sort of lengthy conversation on the front step, so I added, "We can do it in the police SUV if you'd rather we didn't come inside."

He glanced towards the SUV. "That thing have prisoner locks?"

Matt answered. "It does."

I added, "But I can sit in the back if you'd like. You can sit up front with Matt."

He raised his eyebrows in surprise. "Understand that I'd like to invite you in, that's how my mama raised me. But it's not fit for company in here. I haven't cleaned up in a while."

"Understood," Matt said, with a casual smile.

Beau glanced at the SUV one more time. "What's this about?"

"The murder of Julie Lewis. She was a neighbor of your mother's. We think your mother may have kept a record of who she saw at her neighbors' houses and that this could help us figure out who killed Julie."

He nodded. "No need to go to your SUV for that. She did keep records. Come on." He slipped on a pair of snow boots that were sitting by the door and led us towards a large shed perched near the side of the house. We had to truck through about six inches of snow to get to it. Clearly it wasn't a place he went to often.

He pulled a string of keys out of his pocket and unlocked the small padlock on the door. The hinges creaked as he pulled the right-hand door open, pushing snow out of the way a few inches at a time until there was room to see inside.

It smelled…stale. No mildew or rot or decay, just…stale. Like the air hadn't moved in a century or two.

"This is all my mama's stuff. I never had the chance to go through it, but didn't want to get rid of it neither."

"Any idea where the record we're looking for might be?" I asked looking at the boxes piled all the way to the ceiling, at least two deep along the walls.

"Nope. But the boxes are labeled. See? *Kitchen. Bedroom.*"

Matt nodded to him. "Do you mind if we take some of these boxes with us to look through?"

"You'll bring them back when you're finished?"

"Yes, we will. Any particular room you think is most likely?"

He thought about it for a minute, his face completely blank. "Kitchen or Bedroom, probably. Could also be the Living Room."

Well, that narrowed it down, didn't it? At least we could skip the bathroom boxes.

Beau rubbed at his arms. "Well, I'll leave you to it. Lock up when you leave if you don't mind."

He trudged back to the house. Matt took a gingerly step into the shed.

"Are you sure you want to do that?" I asked.

"Seems sturdy enough."

"I'll take your word for it." I stayed outside, shivering.

"It's also warmer in here."

"I'll still take your word for it."

He laughed. "So. Where do you think we can set up these boxes?"

"I would say my grandpa's house, but not knowing what might be lurking inside those boxes, there's no way I'm bringing them anywhere near where I have to sleep. So maybe…the community center in Creek?"

The community center was a large single-room brick building that was always too cold, but did have a nice assortment of long folding tables and uncomfortable chairs to go along with them. It didn't get much use in the winter months since the furnace that was supposed to heat it was usually on the fritz.

"Good idea. Let me make some calls."

CHAPTER 24

Matt made his calls while we warmed ourselves up in the SUV. It only took about ten minutes for him to confirm that no one was using the community center, to arrange to use it for the next week, and to get permission from his boss for the whole operation. We had to wait another ten minutes for someone to run us over the official crime scene camera so we could document the location of the boxes before we moved them.

As we sat in the SUV with the heaters blowing at full blast making my skin so warm it almost gave me shivers, I said, "You know. I think at this point this is definitely a police operation, which means you really don't want some untrained person like me handling those boxes."

Matt leveled a gaze my way. "You're not getting out of this that easy, Maggie May."

"Who said I was trying to get out of this? I'm just worried about the integrity of the investigation. This is physical evidence we're talking about."

"And I'd maybe believe you if you hadn't already handled both Julie and Amy's diaries. But since you did, I suspect this has far more to do with spiders than evidential procedure."

"Not just spiders. I'm also not too thrilled about running across any of those squirmy little bugs with too many legs and pincher mouths. And mice. And mice droppings. And who knows what else. Have you ever watched that hoarder show? Ew."

"Don't you want to catch a murderer?"

"Absolutely. And I have no doubt that you and whoever helps you will find the record you need to do so. Don't *you* want to catch the murderer?"

"I do. Which is why I will be sitting in that freezing-cold community center, wearing plastic gloves that make my palms itch, sorting through the effects of a woman who has been dead over a decade. But I'm not doing it alone. You got me into this, you're staying in it."

I shook my head. "See, this is the kind of crap you get yourself into when you decide for better or for worse. Moldy boxes in freezing concrete buildings."

"When you decide for better or for worse?" Matt grinned at me.

I held up a finger. "After we find the killer. And not until spring. But, yeah. If you ask, I'll say yes. I would've just set the whole thing up and sprung it on you, but I know you're the traditional type so you'll want to ask and make it all official. Let me just tell you now, I don't pretty cry, so prepare yourself."

He leaned back against the door, a big grin on his face. "Alright. I will. And what did you mean set the whole thing up and spring it on you?"

"Something like this is best handled like a Band-Aid. Just get it over with. You ask, I say yes, we do it, done. The less delay and anticipation, the better. You know I actually had a friend who was engaged for two and a half years? Her engagement lasted longer than the marriage. Crazy. Seriously, I do not need one special day of my life taking up that much mental space."

"So just get it over with, huh?"

"Yes."

"As soon as possible?"

"Yes."

I didn't think it was possible, but he grinned even more than he had been before. "Alrighty, then. But it's not getting you out of helping me with these boxes. I love you, but I don't love you that much."

"Haha. Funny." I glanced in the rearview. "Maybe we can get Officer Clark to do all the work."

"Not likely. Come on. Let's lock and load."

CHAPTER 25

Officer Clark did help us load the boxes into the back of Matt's SUV and his own. The whole time I kept waiting for a spider to crawl on my hand or for the bottom of a box to be suspiciously damp. But maybe because everything had been stored in a shed that was often below freezing for over a decade, we didn't run into a single bug or mouse. It was amazing. It gave me hope that the task wouldn't be all that horrible.

But once we unloaded the boxes at the community center that was the end of Officer Clark's involvement. He said he had to go man a speed trap outside of Bakerstown. I suspected he was making it up, but Matt wasn't going to stop him when that was where he was headed.

Which left Matt and me standing in the middle of the community center surrounded by ninety-two boxes of old lady belongings.

(My apologies if you're an old lady yourself, it's not meant to be an insult. It's just that older people acquire some strange belongings, especially those who lived through the Great Depression. There was half a box of neatly-folded wrapping paper that had clearly been saved from prior packages for reuse. I could appreciate the desire not to waste something like that while at the same time really wishing she'd been much younger and much less interested in holding onto anything that wasn't absolutely necessary.)

There was also an entire container of pens that were almost all dried out. (In a perverse moment of boredom, I uncapped a number of them and tried them on a notepad that only had three sheets left. I didn't think Beau would miss it.

"Maggie…" Matt said, from across the room where he was sorting through a box that seemed to be mostly plastic coat hangers. "These are still her belongings."

"Do you honestly think her son, after more than ten years, is going to miss a notepad from the Quality Inn that has three pages left on it?"

"No. But it's the principle of the thing. Plus, the sooner we find where she recorded the activities of her neighbors, the sooner we can be done with this. And get on to better things." He grinned at me again and I knew he was thinking about our wedding.

Why had I told him about that? What was I thinking? Now I couldn't back out.

I returned to my set of boxes with a renewed effort, more to channel my nervous energy than because I wanted to speed things along faster than they were already going.

As much as we tried to hurry, it still took a lot of time. Matt insisted that we photograph the exterior and interior of every box we opened, assign each one a number, and then create an inventory list of what was in the box. I saw the point in doing so, but it was still tedious.

On my tenth box I finally found one of Ms. Franks's day planners. It was one of those big ones that have two pages devoted to each and every day. The ones she preferred didn't have the times listed already, they just had the day of the month and a bunch of skinny lines. She wrote in the time of day herself and then a bunch of illegible scrawls next to that.

"Matt."

"What?"

"Is this shorthand?" I still hadn't bothered to learn it myself, but I remembered very well that he knew how to use it. I hate being at a disadvantage like that.

He took the day planner from my hand. "It is."

"What does it say?"

"7:15 JL left house. Wearing blue coat. 7:20 Bus picked up JL. 8:25 CL left house. Black shirt, no coat." He flipped through the pages, scanning each one quickly. "And that's pretty much what it says for each and every day. Different coats or different times, but it looks like she noted down when the five or six people who lived within view of her house arrived or left, every, single day."

"That's it?"

"Oh, there are also notes about the mailman in here. And it seems one of her neighbors had a new couch delivered at one point. There are also some notes about the weather, but only on days when it rained or snowed from what I can see."

"Any opinions? Thoughts? Feelings?"

He shook his head. "Nope. Just facts. She would've made a good investigator, actually." He glanced at the cover. "Too bad this is the wrong year."

I pointed to the box I'd pulled the planner from. "Not the only one, I'm afraid. I'll double-check, but I suspect that since this box came from the bedroom that these are the ones she'd already filled in. But this is what we're looking for. At least we now know they exist."

Matt went back to his boxes, whistling happily to himself. I mentally grumbled as I quickly scanned the rest of the day planners in the box. A decade of monitoring every little detail of her neighbors' lives, but not the one day I needed.

Figured.

CHAPTER 26

It took another hour and an encounter with one very ugly spider for me to finally find the day planner I needed. It was buried at the bottom of a box that included a set of twelve paper-towel-wrapped glasses, a roll of duct tape, two pairs of scissors, three baggies worth of rubber bands, a spool of twine, two screwdrivers, and a hammer.

(Someone really hadn't put much thought into their packing. The fact that those glasses survived that hammer was amazing. They almost didn't survive my excited squee and reach when I saw the corner of the day planner at the very bottom of the box and started to pull it out without removing everything else first.)

Matt was at my side almost instantly, helping me to carefully remove all twelve glasses before I pulled the day planner free. I immediately handed it to him.

"So?" I asked, practically dancing in place as he flipped through the pages.

"Give me a minute to get to the right page."

I peered over the edge of the day planner as he continued to flip through. I knew I shouldn't have given it to him until I found the page we needed. Never give a slow driver something that you need done in a hurry.

"Maggie."

"I want to see."

"Found it." He turned so we could both see the relevant pages.

We scanned the entries. There was Julie leaving for the party. There was Julie coming home from the party. Both included the make and model of the vehicle and the license plate.

But that was the last entry. Dennis Clay bringing Julie home.

I cussed. "I thought we had it." I leaned against the table just long enough to realize that was a very bad idea.

"Maybe…" Matt turned the page and I jumped back up. "Ha! Look."

He pointed at an entry right at the top of the page. 3:20 in the morning. Make, model, and license plate for the vehicle that picked her up.

"That's it. We have them." I made Matt flip back a page. "So it was Barb. Or Barb and Tim. Right?"

"Looks like it. Definitely the same vehicle and they did admit to picking her up and taking her to the party."

"We got 'em!" I did a little hip shake dance around the room, singing the words a few more times. "We got 'em, we got 'em."

"Maggie. Not so fast."

"What do you mean?"

"This is still just circumstantial evidence. A woman who is dead and can't testify about what she saw wrote something in a day planner over a decade ago. I doubt they'll even be able to use this if it comes to a trial."

"But they did it."

"Just because one of them—and we don't even know for sure which one or even if it was Barb or Tim—killed her, we don't know which one. We don't know how, we don't know why. It's not going to be enough to bring a case against them. If we don't get a confession, we won't be able to close this case."

I cussed. "They killed a young girl who had her whole life before her. They deserve to pay, Matt."

"But which one? Maybe it was an accident."

"An accident? She was struck three times. That's not an accident."

"Some people lose it in the moment. They don't even know what they're doing."

I crossed my arms and glared at him. "Murder is murder."

He set the day planner on the table. "If only it were that simple."

"But it is. One or both of them picked up Julie Lewis at three in the morning, drove her to that pullout off the highway, and attacked her. People don't go around carrying large dangerous objects in their hands. Whoever did this had to deliberately grab whatever they used when they talked to Julie."

"I don't disagree with you, Maggie. I'm just saying that we won't really know what happened until whoever did this tells us. Until then it's just a guess. And a guess isn't going to get us a conviction."

I thought about it. Darn it, he was right. "So we need to bring them in for questioning."

"They live in Kansas. And have five children. We can't bring them in that easy. We need more."

I paced the room, thinking. "Barb's family moved away, right?"

He nodded.

"But Tim's mom is still around. We could try her."

"Maybe."

"And the vehicle. They don't still own it, I don't think. Maybe they sold it to someone around here."

"Julie wasn't killed in the vehicle. She was killed on the side of the road."

"But whatever was used to hit her, wasn't left there. It was in the vehicle. After. And…Well."

He nodded. "And there could be DNA."

"Maybe. Long shot. Especially if it's been used by someone all these years."

"It's still worth a try. Let me see what I can find out tomorrow at work. And then we'll put together a game plan. But, Maggie?" He took hold of my shoulders and held my gaze.

"Yes?"

"You can't tell anyone what we found. Not yet. Especially not Mr. Lewis."

"He deserves to know, Matt."

"And he will. When we have something concrete to tell him."

I pulled away and paced the room again. "What if we never do? What if this is as close as we get to finding the killer?"

"Then we tell him we tried and we couldn't find the killer. We do not tell him about the entry in this day planner or the vehicle it identified."

"Why?"

"Because what do you think he'd do?"

I stopped and crossed my arms, pouting. "Confront them."

"Exactly. Imagine that. Poor Mr. Lewis driving to Kansas, banging down their door, accusing them of killing his daughter, and likely getting arrested for it. That man does not deserve jail time after everything else he's been through."

I pressed my lips together and glared. "Then we damn well better find the killer. Or else I'll be the one driving to Kansas to confront those two."

Matt kissed my forehead. "We'll do what we can. And if that includes my taking your car keys away until you calm down, I'll do that, too. Can't have my future wife going to jail now can I?"

I shuddered at that word—wife. Ugh. The things we do for love…

CHAPTER 27

Matt did some digging around the next day. It turned out that Barb's parents had given her a brand-new car for her birthday that fall and she'd given the SUV to Tim's mom who hadn't had a reliable vehicle up until that point. His mom was still driving it. Which meant that if we inspected the vehicle, we'd be giving away a key piece of information to our suspects.

(Look at me, saying "we" as if I was any part of that conversation whatsoever. Matt was still keeping me in the loop, but things had developed to the point where it was his job to bring everything home and I was just a cheerleader on the sidelines.)

It took about a week, but they finally arranged for Matt to re-interview both Barb and Tim at the police station in Salina. No way they were going to get permission to bring them back to Creek, not without a confession.

Since I had absolutely nothing going on in my life, I went with him. Our *second* long car trip together. This one with a small little snowstorm that left somewhere between an inch and three inches of snow on the road. I, ironically, seem to do better in severe weather driving than in good weather because I know I have to maintain focus. (Most of my early car accidents involved some form of "ooh, isn't that interesting" distractions while someone ahead of me stopped unexpectedly.)

Matt, on the other hand, kinda crumbled when it snowed. He was already a slow driver, but Matt and snow? A turtle could've driven faster. So after about ten miles of that, I made him switch with me even though we were in Kansas and it meant I might get a ticket. I figured better a speeding ticket than strangling my boyfriend to death for driving so slow he might as well be in reverse.

We made it. (Eventually.)

Matt decided to interview Tim first, figuring that he hadn't been involved that night and would quickly turn on Barb. Or, on the off chance he had been involved, that he was the most likely to feel incredibly guilty and break.

The station didn't have a separate room to stand in and observe like we had in Creek. But there was a recording room where the action played out live on a computer monitor. The officer who was assisting Matt didn't really want to let me watch, but Matt took him aside and convinced him to do it anyway.

Tim didn't look nervous at all. At least no more than the average person would when brought into a police station for questioning. As he waited for Matt he played some game on his phone that involved swiping things around.

But when Matt stormed into the room, Tim immediately dropped the phone in his lap and sat up straight.

Matt threw his folder down. "Were you there?"

"Where?" Tim shook his head, clearly bewildered.

"There when she was killed?"

(We'd had the officer advise Tim of his rights before Matt entered the room so that Matt could be a little bit of a drama queen right off the bat.)

"Who? Julie? No. I told you I don't know who killed her! Don't you think I'd tell you guys if I did? I loved Julie. She was my everything." Tim looked genuinely surprised by the accusation.

"So what does that make Barb?" Matt asked.

Tim let out a deep sigh and slumped in his seat. "My wife."

"Aren't you supposed to marry the woman who's your everything?" Matt said it with just enough of a sneer that even I felt offended by his tone.

Tim put his phone on the table like a man going to his execution. "I would've. I loved Julie."

Matt crossed his arms and glared down at Tim. "Did you? Seems you were quick enough to pick up with Barb when she came around."

"It was...I didn't realize...I mean I'd always loved Julie since we were little. But I didn't realize it was that kind of love until...it was too late." He spun his phone in little circles on the table, not looking at Matt.

"Too late? You told her you loved her that night."

"And it all went wrong. She didn't want me."

"Do you blame her? She'd spent the last year or more watching some other girl hang off your arm every minute of every day and then you suddenly tell her you love her? What did you expect her to do?"

Tim buried his face in his hands. "I know. I screwed up. I never thought it was a possibility, you know?" He threw himself back in his chair. "I thought she was gonna go away to college and meet some guy who had everything. But then at that party she started talking to that jerk loser and I realized *I* was better than *that*. That if she'd go for him, she'd certainly go for me."

"So you tried."

"Yeah."

Matt slammed the table. "And she turned you down. Told you she didn't want you."

Tim rubbed his hands through his hair. "It wasn't like that. She was drunk and she was mad at me for chasing that guy off. For always being around but never being the guy who wanted to be with her. And when I told her I did want to be with her, then she just got even more mad because I'd waited so long to tell her and what were we supposed to do now. Barb was her friend."

He slumped even further in his chair.

Matt waited him out.

"And then she left. I think…" Tim pressed his lips together. "I think looking back at it now, that we could've worked it out when she sobered up. She'd think about it and we'd talk about it and we could be together. I actually woke up the next morning hoping that's what would happen."

"But that's not what you thought in the moment, was it? Not as she was walking away from you to go after that jerk loser, as you put it."

He buried his face in his hands. "No. I thought it was over. I thought I'd lost my best friend in the world." I could barely hear him he was so quiet.

Matt leaned in. "Tell me what happened after you left the party with Barb."

Tim glanced at Matt and then turned his body away towards the corner, his shoulders hunched.

"Tim. I need to know. Were you with Barb when she killed Julie?"

He whirled back around. "Barb didn't kill Julie. She was with me the whole night."

"Then how was her car spotted in front of Julie's house at 3:20 that morning?"

"What are you talking about?" He seemed genuinely surprised.

Matt showed him a picture of the day planner and then the photocopied image of the relevant page. "Ms. Franks, who lived across from Julie, noted down everything about her neighbors. What they wore, when they left the house, when they returned. And who parked in front of their house. She had a stroke the day Julie was found. But she'd recorded this entry before she did. See this?"

Tim stared at the page.

"That indicates that Barb's car was parked in front of Julie's house at 3:20 the morning she was killed. So I'll ask again, were you there when Barb killed Julie?"

He sagged forward like every bone in his body had just dissolved.

"Tim. Tell me what happened. Tell me which of you killed her. We do have enough to arrest you with this. Do you really want your children to go into foster care if they don't have to? You need to stop protecting her."

He shook his head slowly back and forth. "I never knew. But...All these years. No wonder..."

"No wonder what?"

"It makes so much sense now."

"So it *was* Barb?"

He shook his head again, still lost in his own world. "No. Not Barb."

Matt finally sat down. "Then who was it?"

Tim sort of laughed, but it was a wounded sound. "I think it was my mother."

CHAPTER 28

I definitely hadn't seen that coming.

But as soon as he told Matt he thought it was his mother, Tim let everything out. Through sobs he explained that he and Barb had gone back to his house that night, but they hadn't tried to make up. It turns out that Tim had a bit of a routine when he was angry and upset. He'd pop a whole bunch of pills and talk about wanting to die until Barb convinced him to throw them back up. There were no medical records of it, because she always managed to convince him in time.

That night it had taken a little longer than normal and enough of the meds must've gotten into his system to make him especially woozy. He didn't quite pass out, but he was out enough to not really be aware of what was going on around him.

He said he had vague memories of his mother coming home that night, drunk. He'd thought at the time that she was mad at Barb and screaming and shouting about how Barb had ruined his life. But looking back on it now, he realized that his mother must've been talking about Julie.

His mother didn't have a working car. She bummed rides to and from work with co-workers or neighbors. And to and from the bar with "friends". So she must've taken Barb's SUV that night and gone over to confront Julie. Because he did clearly remember Barb being there with him the whole night.

After he finished, he bent over clutching his stomach. "I can't believe…All these years. They both knew and…"

Matt patted him on the shoulder and left him alone in the interview room to come find me.

"What do you think?" I asked as we both stood there in that cramped, too hot space and watched Tim rock back and forth on the computer monitor, sobbing.

"It rings true to me."

"Me, too."

"But now I have to convince Barb to tell us what happened that night. Because it's still just conjecture and guesswork at this point. We still don't have a case."

I nodded. We didn't have one yet, but we would. I knew Matt would get the story out of her.

🐾 🐾 🐾

Unfortunately, we had to wait a few hours to actually interrogate Barb because she was clearly drunk when the cops brought her in. (Tim had come alone and we'd let him because of the kids. But seeing the state she was in, I sure hoped that babysitter had been around, too.)

By the time she finally blew a number below the legal limit I was on Coke number five for the day and ready to be done already.

Matt sat down across from her. "Do you know why we're here, Barb?"

She sneered at him. "Julie Lewis. I told you we left that party and that was the last I ever saw her."

"But you know who killed her."

She shook her head. "No I don't. Tim and I went to his mom's and that's where we stayed the whole night."

"That's not how Tim tells it."

She laughed, once. "And what does he say? Because as I recall that night he was mostly passed out, wasn't he?"

Matt leaned forward. "He wasn't so passed out that he missed you and his mom having a fight."

"So we yelled at each other. That wasn't anything new. She thought he could do better than me. She didn't want her baby boy tied down at such a young age. She thought he could go pro if only he wasn't distracted by me."

"But that's not what you were fighting about that night, is it?"

Barb crossed her arms and rolled her eyes. "It's been years. I can't remember the conversation."

Matt pulled out his photocopy of the journal entry from Ms. Franks. "Do you know what this is?"

"No."

"It turns out Julie's elderly neighbor had insomnia. And she liked to write down every single visitor that came to Julie's house."

"So?"

"So this record says that it was your vehicle that was at Julie's house that night."

"Well, duh. We picked her up for the party."

"At three in the morning?"

Barb leaned forward and looked at the license plate number that was clearly visible on the page.

She shrugged one shoulder. "It wasn't me."

"Who was it? Who did you give your vehicle to?"

She shook her head, but refused to answer.

Matt leaned forward and fixed her with a glare. "I have to admit Barb, you don't strike me as the best mom in the world. But I'd hate to see those kids of yours lose their mom for a crime she didn't commit."

"Exactly. I didn't do anything."

"You had material information relevant to a police investigation and you failed to disclose that information. You can go to jail for that. Unless you help me now. Tell me what you know. Who killed Julie Lewis?"

"If I tell you, do you promise to leave me out of it?"

"You'll have to testify. But I think we can probably leave it at that."

"Fine."

Barb crossed her arms, closed her eyes, leaned her head back, and told Matt everything she knew about that night.

According to her, Tim's mom had come home from the bar, seen him barely conscious, and started screaming at Barb about how she was ruining his life and was no good for him. Barb screamed right back and told her it was Julie's fault not hers that he'd taken the pills. And then she told her what had happened that night.

Tim's mom was furious. More furious than it warranted, in Barb's opinion. She demanded Barb's keys so she could go over there and tell that girl to stay away from her boy for once and for all.

Amused by the idea Barb had happily handed over the keys and went to curl up with Tim who was passed out in bed. She was asleep by the time Tim's mom returned.

The next morning Barb found Tim's mom sitting in the kitchen, red-eyed like she'd never gone to bed.

She asked his mom what had happened the night before. According to Barb, his mom refused to tell her but did suggest that Barb clean up her vehicle before someone came by. When she went out to her SUV there was a bunch of mud on the wheels, so Barb started to hose it down. Tim's mom came out a minute or two later and took something wrapped in a rag out of the backseat. Barb didn't get a clear view of what it was, but she suspected it might be a tire iron.

She said she'd thought about driving by Julie's house or calling to see if she was okay, but she hadn't. Instead she'd stayed with Tim pretending everything was fine until Mr. Lewis called and told them that Julie had been killed. When the call came in and Tim started screaming, his mother had walked out of the house and hadn't come back until the next day.

Barb never spoke to Tim's mom about what happened that night. Never asked her why she'd done it. And never told anyone, not even Tim, what had happened. But as soon as she could, she got rid of the SUV. She gave it to Tim's mom out of spite. And to protect herself, just in case anyone ever came looking.

"Do you feel sorry for what happened to Julie?" Matt asked.

Barb shrugged and looked away. "She was my friend. But she was also going to take everything I'd ever wanted away from me."

He left her there, staring into the corner of the room, her face completely blank.

CHAPTER 29

We drove back from Salina in silence for the first couple of hours. I hadn't even remembered to start up my iPod, so it was literally silent except for the slush of the snow against my van's tires and the occasional thwack of the wiper blades.

Matt held my hand as I drove. And I held his. We needed that connection. That tie to something good. Something pure.

Because the death of Julie Lewis was just one big tragedy that could've been avoided in so many ways. That poor girl, everything had gone wrong for her that night. She'd never had that chance to grow up, to make mistakes and find love. To travel and explore and grow and see life in all its many aspects.

And worst of all, we still didn't really know why.

🐾 🐾 🐾

The next day Matt arrested Tim's mom. I sat in the viewing room as he led her into interrogation. She was a tiny woman, probably not even five-two, but she had a wiry strength to her. This was a woman who'd been knocked down by life and come back up swinging. Her voice when she finally spoke was the gravelly voice of a lifetime smoker.

"Do you know why you're here?" Matt asked as he settled into the seat across from her.

"Tim called last night. Told me you'd talked."

"So you want to tell me what happened?"

She met Matt's gaze, but didn't answer.

If she didn't confess, I wasn't sure we'd have a case. I mean maybe we could prove it. Use Barb's testimony, but a drunk bitter woman didn't strike me as the best witness in the world. And we wouldn't be able to use the entry from Ms. Parks.

When it became clear she wasn't going to speak, Matt leaned forward. "You know the part I don't get? Why? I mean, what had Julie Lewis ever done to you? Or to Tim? Every single person we talked to said they were close friends. That they were good for each other. So why kill her?"

"Do you have kids?" she asked.

"No."

"Then you wouldn't understand."

"Explain it to me. Please."

He held her gaze until she finally looked away. "Did you know, I had Tim when I was seventeen?"

Matt nodded and waited for her to continue.

"My parents kicked me out when they found out I was pregnant. I went to the father, but he wanted nothing to do with it. I had plans, you know. I was going to move to LA, become an actress. But I didn't, did I? I stayed in this worthless place, gave up all my dreams. All for him. For my boy."

I studied her in confusion, still not understanding

why she'd done what she had. Matt, being the good cop he was, didn't say anything.

Finally, she continued. "I didn't like Barb much. I worried he'd get her pregnant and that would be that, but I figured he'd outgrow her after high school. Sure, they were going to go to the same college, because she was that kind of girl, but I figured he'd get there and he'd see all the other girls on campus and he and Barb would be over by Christmas. In time for him to really start focusing on baseball and make something of himself. He had potential, you know? Lots of potential."

Matt nodded, but still didn't speak.

"But Julie. When Barb told me what had happened that night. That he'd confessed his love to her and she'd rejected him and he'd tried to kill himself. I knew he'd never outgrow that. He'd always pine for Julie. Always want her. And she'd ruin his life. So I went over there to tell her to stay away from him."

"Why'd you leave her house?"

"I didn't know where her dad was. I wanted to have a one-on-one conversation without him around. He was always the type to step in and defend people like that," she said. "So I told her Tim was really sick and upset and needed to see her. I begged her to come with me."

"And she went?"

She nodded.

"Did you mean to kill her?"

She met his eyes for a long moment and then looked away.

"Ms. Holt? Did you mean to kill her?"

She shrugged her shoulders.

"Why the turnout?"

"It was close, it was private. I figured I could say what needed saying without anyone to interrupt."

"And then you went back home."

She nodded. "And then I went back home."

He leaned forward. "What did you do with the tire iron?"

"Trash."

"Are you sorry for what you did?" he asked.

She laughed softly. "You know, I was trying to look after my boy. Keep him from making the same mistake I did. But Julie's death drove him right to Barb. No way he was going to give her up after all they'd been through together. He never even played one season of baseball in college because of her."

"I met their kids. They're cute. And he's got a good job. He's a teacher."

She looked at Matt, her eyes dead. "Yeah, but he could've gone pro."

I turned away. I'd seen enough. It was time to tell Mr. Lewis who'd killed his daughter. And why.

CHAPTER 30

I met Mr. Lewis at his house. He invited me in and we sat in that living room of his with all the pictures on the wall of Julie.

"Did you find the killer?" he asked me, lacing the fingers of his large hands together as he sat on the edge of the couch, every line of his body taut with tension.

"We did."

His knuckles went white as he clutched his hands tighter together. "Who was it? Who killed my little girl?"

"Melody Holt. Tim's mom."

He stared at me. "Why? Did she say?"

"She said it was because she thought Julie was going to ruin his life. That he wouldn't pursue baseball if he fell in love with Julie. Honestly, it didn't make a lot of sense to me."

"That's because you never saw Melody and John."

"John?"

"Tim's father." He shook his head. "Melody was an amazing actress. When she talked about moving to LA everyone agreed that they'd see her on the big screen someday. But then she fell for John. He was horrible to her. He knew she loved him, but he was always hanging around other girls or saying horrible things about Melody to his friends. Didn't keep him from sleeping with her, of course. When she ended up pregnant, John cut off all ties. Said the baby wasn't his. Left for college and never looked back."

"But why kill a girl over that?"

"Melody had big dreams. Dreams that John took away from her. Dreams she placed on her son. And Julie…I can see how she'd remind Melody of John." He grimaced. "I loved my girl, but sometimes she treated Tim the way John treated Melody. Just took for granted that he was there for her and always would be. Didn't give back to him what he gave to her."

"I'm so sorry, Mr. Lewis."

He reached over and squeezed my hand. "Don't be. You found my daughter's killer. Something I never thought would happen. Thank you."

"You're welcome." I gave him back Julie's diary. "I think you should read this again. I know you probably saw all the times she was angry with you the first time you read it. But I hope if you read it again that you also see what I saw, which is how close you were and how much she loved you and knew what a great father you were."

I gave him a quick hug and left before I started crying. It was hard to be reminded of what it was like to have a parent that loved you that much. I had Matt now and my grandpa and the friends I'd found along the way, but nothing in life could ever compare to having parents who truly cared for you. I'd lost my parents when I was too young, but I would always have their love with me.

A Poisoned Past and Puppermints

It was the most precious gift they'd ever given me and something no one could take away.

CHAPTER 31

Spring in the Colorado mountains. I'd like to say that the birds were singing and the flowers were blooming and that it was a balmy sixty-degrees Fahrenheit, but this was Colorado in the mountains in the middle of March. Which meant that the first day of spring was forty degrees with a few inches of snow on the ground.

I was bumbling around the kitchen, dreading Fancy's daily walk when my grandpa strolled through, nuked himself up the leftover coffee from the day before, and poured it into a travel mug.

"Where are you headed this early?" I asked.

"Out."

I frowned at him. "Out? Out to where? It's six-thirty in the morning."

"I know."

"I thought we were having breakfast this morning. You told me to wait for you."

He winked at me and glanced out the window. "My mistake. Guess you'll have to have breakfast with Matt instead."

I'd known it was the day Matt was going to propose,

but I'd thought he'd do it that night not before the sun was even up. I expected to freeze in panic, but I didn't. I was actually kind of sort of looking forward to it. The investigation of Julie Lewis's death had changed me. In a good way.

I followed my grandpa to the door and waited for Matt to walk up the front walk.

"Happy first day of spring," he said, looking slightly nervous. "I brought you this."

It was a bright yellow tulip in a small green pot.

"I know you don't like flowers because they just die, but I figured this one would be okay because it's potted."

"It's beautiful, thank you," I said, feeling teary for some inexplicable reason.

I glanced down the street and saw Lucas Dean coming out of his house. He was not going to be a part of my special moment, no siree.

I stepped inside, pushing Fancy out of the way, as I walked towards the kitchen. "Come on, come inside before you freeze. I was just about to cook breakfast. My grandpa asked me to wait for him last night, but I guess it was just one big bait and switch, huh? You guys had this whole thing planned out in advance? Well, I hope you like bacon and eggs, because that's what's on the menu."

I would've kept blubbering on, but I turned back at the kitchen doorway to see Matt kneeling on one knee. He would be a traditionalist, wouldn't he?

My throat went dry. I desperately wished I had a Coke in my hand. Or even water. Or maybe vodka. Lots and lots of vodka.

He held his hand out towards me and I stepped towards him, but Fancy beat me to the punch. You don't kneel down on the level of a dog that big without her thinking it's about her. She started licking his face like crazy and wagging her tail and jumping around.

I burst out laughing. "Fancy. Stop it. Go on. Get away. Shoo." I shoved her towards the kitchen. "Go outside."

She ducked me and went back towards Matt. He stood up, laughing, too. "Well, I expect if you're not into all the other trappings you won't mind if I do this while standing?"

"Not at all" I said, softly, afraid I was going to burst into tears at any moment.

He pulled a small red ring box out of his jeans pocket. His hand was trembling. I wanted more than anything to reach out and cover it with mine, but I didn't. I pressed my fist to my lips and waited.

He met my eyes. "Maggie May Carver, will you marry me?"

He opened the box.

The ring inside was perfect. (For me.) It had a band each of white gold and rose gold entwined together and engraved with roses. No big stone to get caught in my hair for the rest of my life. No gaudy amount of diamonds to make me wonder if he'd blown all his money. Just a simple symbol of our love.

"It's beautiful." I smiled at him, tears in the corner of my eyes. "You remembered."

"I did. So? What's your answer?"

I laughed. "Oh, right. Of course. I have to actually answer."

He nodded and looked at me, waiting.

"Yes. Yes, I'll marry you. Of course I will."

He pulled me into a big hug and spun me around in a circle, which caused Fancy to go absolutely crazy and start barking at us very loudly.

"Shush, Fancy," I said when he finally set me down. But then he kissed me and I pretty much forgot the entire world for a moment. How was I lucky enough to have found such an amazing man?

"You want to try it on?" he asked when he was done taking my breath away.

"Try on what?"

"The ring."

"Oh, right. Yeah. Sorry. I'm just a little flustered, that's all. No food, no Coke, and a wedding proposal. I'm not quite in my right mind."

"Well, let's take care of that, shall we? One Coke coming up and then I am going to make you the best cream cheese stuffed waffles you've ever had."

"I thought you couldn't cook?" I said, following him into the kitchen where he pulled an almost perfectly frozen Coke out of the freezer. (He and my grandpa had definitely been conspiring on this one.)

He winked. "I've been practicing. Jamie's been giving me lessons. She said you really like a man who can cook."

"That is definitely true. Although I was willing to overlook it for you."

"No need." He kissed me on the cheek and pushed me towards the kitchen table while he whipped up the most delicious looking breakfast I'd ever had.

I took a sip of my Coke and slid the ring on my finger. It fit perfectly. As I admired it, I said, "I'm going to have to call Jamie. She probably already knew you were going to propose, but I should tell her I said yes. Oh, and my grandpa, too."

Matt gave me an odd look. "Actually…Speaking of that…"

"What?"

"Well, you did say you wanted things to happen fast, right? You didn't want to spend a lot of time and energy on preparing for a wedding."

I nodded, suddenly nervous.

"Well, if you really meant it, I thought we could get married today."

It's a good thing I hadn't just taken a sip of my Coke or I would've spit it out. "Today?" I squeaked.

He tensed and nodded. "Yeah. What do you think?"

I blinked as I tried to get my brain back into working order. "Um."

I glanced out the window. "Where were you thinking we'd have it? Because my personal preference for getting married at the top of the canyon probably isn't going to work so well today what with all the snow."

"I know. And…" He winced. "Don't be mad at me, please…"

"About what?"

"I know your ideal wedding is just the two of us on the side of a mountain."

I nodded. "In theory."

"But your grandpa said there was no way his granddaughter was getting married in the town he lives in without him there."

"Okay, that's fine. I would kind of like to have him there."

He stepped closer, still looking like he expected me to

lose it at any moment. "And of course that means Lesley."

I was starting to see where this was going. "Right…"

"And Jack said he better be invited, too. I mean, he is my brother."

"Which means Trish and Sam."

He nodded.

"And I expect Jamie and Mason want to be there, too?"

He nodded again. "And Greta. And Jean-Philippe. And Evan and Abe. And if we're going that far…"

I sighed. "You have friends and co-workers who'll want to be there, too."

He nodded.

I sat back, my visions of a quiet intimate promise between just me and Matt suddenly blown to bits. Then again, there wasn't a single person he'd listed that I wasn't willing to have there.

He sat down across from me and took my hand. "We can still have the wedding you want, just the two of us. All I care about is getting married to you. Today or when the snow actually thaws or whenever. And wherever. What matters is us, Maggie."

I sighed. "Well, now that you mentioned everyone, it does seem only fair to include them." I took a long sip of Coke. "It's just that I don't want to plan it. They're such a hassle and such an expense." I glanced at the living room. "Maybe we could just ask everyone to drop by this weekend and you know, say our vows or whatever."

"We could." He grinned at me. "Or, better yet, we could get married today at four o'clock and you could let those friends of yours, who love you very much, put the wedding plans they've been making into effect."

I raised my eyebrows. "Wedding plans they've been making?"

"They have it all. The flowers, the venue, the guests, the dresses, the food. All I have to do is make one phone call and it happens." He held up his phone. "So? What do you say? Are we going to do this thing or not?"

I bit my lip, feeling one last shiver of fear. This was it. This was the make or break moment. "Go ahead. Let's do this. On one condition."

"What's that?"

"We invite Mr. Lewis, too."

Matt nodded. "Already done."

EPILOGUE

At four o'clock on the first day of spring in the small Colorado mountain town of Creek I found myself standing in front of a red wooden door wearing a beautiful sapphire blue dress with a fitted bodice and long skirt that flared from my hips but wasn't poofy. (The one I'd tried on and borrowed at Greta's for Jamie's wedding if you remember.)

Because it was cold out, I also had a (fake) white fur wrap around my shoulders and matching blue snow boots on my feet. (It was nice to know my friends knew me well enough to know I'd refuse to wear skinny little heels.)

That red door belonged to the house next door to my grandpa's, the one Matt and I were going to move into that day, immediately after the ceremony.

Matt hadn't bought the house, thankfully—marriage and joint property ownership on the same day would've been just a little too much for me—but he had arranged to rent it for three months with an option to buy if we liked it.

My friends had transformed the place into a magical (and warm) winter wonderland with a gigantic tent in the backyard and thousands of little white lights strung everywhere.

I hadn't had to do a thing but show up. Matt and I ran to the courthouse first thing to get our marriage license and then Jamie and Greta whisked me away for a day of prepping and pampering which involved lots of yummy finger foods (courtesy of Jean-Philippe) and probably a few too many Bellinis.

It made for a nice relaxing day even if I had been forced to sit through hair and make-up. The make-up took an inordinately long time because the woman kept stepping back from doing my eyes and saying, "Oh, look at that, how gorgeous," every few minutes. Honestly, it looked good when it was done, but not one hour of my life good. But, hey, I was being accommodating so I just let it happen.

Thankfully the woman who did my hair kept the hairspray within manageable limits. She took small sections from the front on each side and braided them back and then let the rest of my hair fall loose and curled down my back. (It was long at that point, too. I hadn't realized I'd grown it out as much as I had.) She then tucked in matching blue, lavender, and white baby roses through the braided sections, gave it a small bit of spray, and that was it. Not too bad. Something I could live with.

Jamie and Greta were my bridesmaids. They had long lavender dresses that complemented my dress perfectly. And matching lavender boots, which made me laugh. (Something I desperately needed as the moment of reckoning drew closer.)

When it was finally time, we hopped into a limo and drove over to the house.

It had been transformed. No longer was it a small ranch-style house in need of a good paint job. Now it was covered in little white lights that gave it a charming fairy-tale sort of feel.

I stopped in front of the door, scared to go inside. This was it. This was the end. Or the beginning. Or just one more day along the continuum. A day that could be just like any other except for how scared I felt.

I didn't want to get this wrong. Not the wedding. If I got the wedding wrong we'd just have something to laugh at for the next fifty years. No, it was life with Matt I didn't want to get wrong. I swore to myself in that moment I would try the best I could to make him happy.

Before my thoughts could spiral towards how hard that was going to be, Jamie pinched me. "Enough. Go inside. We're freezing out here."

"But…"

"Maggie, if I have to grab you by the ear, drag you inside, and force you to say these vows, I will. Don't doubt it." Since Jamie is normally the most laid back of people her vehemence surprised me, but it had its intended effect. I opened the door and stepped inside.

It smelled delicious. I'd expected French cuisine because of Jean-Philippe, but that's not what I smelled. "Is that…?"

"Yep." Jamie squeezed my hand. "Your grandpa made some of your dad's green chili, your grandma's pinto beans, and your mom's homemade tortillas."

I instantly wanted to cry. Happy-sad tears, knowing they couldn't be there to see me get married but would be there in spirit through their signature dishes.

"You can't tell me that right before the wedding," I

wailed. "I'm going to cry all my makeup off." I stared at the ceiling and blinked rapidly for ten seconds to keep the tears from falling.

"Sorry. I forget because you're not usually one to cry."

"Yeah, well, when the tears come, they really come, so let's try to get through the ceremony before that happens, shall we?"

My grandpa stepped into the living room just then. He was wearing a black tuxedo with a lavender cummerbund and looked downright dapper.

"Grandpa." I gave him a quick hug. "Thank you. Jamie told me about the green chili, pinto beans, and tortillas."

He gave me an extra squeeze. "You're welcome. I figured that was the best way to have them be part of the day with us." His voice was rough as he said it.

"Don't you start crying or I'm never going to be able to hold it together," I told him.

He wiped a tear from his eye. "Okay. No more tears. This is a happy day. For both of us."

I probably would've just broken down into tears at that point, but fortunately Jack, Trish, and Sam arrived.

"Maggie, Maggie, Maggie," Sam cried running over to me with a big grin on his freckled face. He was in a little tuxedo himself, the lavender of his bow tie a perfect complement for his red hair. "Guess what?"

"What?" I asked, smiling at his enthusiasm.

"I'm your ring bearer. And I get to ride Lady down the aisle."

That definitely cleared up any lingering desire to cry. I turned to Jack who gave me a wicked grin. (He was as tall, dark, and handsome as Matt but I'd always had the feeling that kissing him would be like taking one gigantic step down the path to ruin.)

I stalked over to him. "Lady? Is this the Lady I think it is?"

"If you mean the incredibly well-behaved and docile miniature horse, Lady, then yes."

I crossed my arms. "You're telling me that there's going to be a miniature horse at my wedding."

He winked. "That's what you get for not wanting to plan your own wedding."

I glanced over at Jamie who shrugged back at me. "It seemed like a fun idea at the time."

I closed my eyes and took a deep breath, reminding myself that if it went wrong it was a funny story to tell. The only thing we had to get right was Matt and I exchanging our vows. That was it. That was all that had to happen. Matt and I promising to be together forever.

I frowned. "What about Fancy? If Lady is going to be in the wedding, then Fancy should be, too."

Jack grinned at Jamie. "Told you."

"So you did." Jamie nodded. "Fancy will be in the wedding if you want her to be. Matt found her a matching leash and collar. And, um…"

"What? What now?"

"Jack found a groomer who temporarily dyed the tops of her ears blue."

Yep, definitely no lingering desire to cry at that point. "You dyed my dog's ears blue? Let me see her," I snapped.

Jack left and came back with Fancy on a sapphire blue leash that matched my dress and with the hair on the tops of each ear dyed blue. I had to admit, the ears actually looked pretty cute. And Fancy certainly didn't seem to notice the difference. Plus she wouldn't be able to shake it off like she would've if they'd tried to put bows on her.

She was also wearing her Go-Pro camera harness. "Didn't I mention?" Jack asked. "She's the official wedding videographer, too."

Before I could lose it, Jamie gently touched my arm and pointed to where an actual videographer was walking around capturing footage of the event. "But not the only one," she said.

I nodded and took a deep breath. Okay. It was unorthodox, but no denying it was also just the right type of wedding for me. (And Matt. Couldn't forget Matt.)

"What do you think, Fancy? You ready to do this thing?" I asked her.

She looked around the room at everyone and then yawned and laid down. Leave it to a dog to put things in perspective. It was just another day. A lot more going on, but just another day.

So I told myself until they opened the back door and I caught a glimpse of Matt standing at the front of the crowd in a tuxedo with a bright blue cummerbund that matched my dress and his eyes, a flower-covered arch festooned with white lights and blue, purple, and white roses behind him.

He was gorgeous.

And scared.

And then he saw me. And he smiled, a smile so bright it hurt. And those frickin' tears came back and threatened to overwhelm me.

"Let's get this over with," I said.

Not that I meant it in *that* way, but we only had so long before I was going to completely lose it and as I'd already told Matt, I do not pretty cry.

As Trish helped Sam onto Lady—whose bridle matched my dress and who had flowers woven into the little braids in her mane—Jack came over to me. "He's the best guy you could ever hope to marry. You know that, right?"

I nodded. "I wouldn't be marrying him otherwise."

"If you ever break his heart, I'll steal your dog."

I laughed and glanced down at Fancy. "My dog? What kind of threat is that?"

He shrugged. "I figured I'm good at stealing things. And aside from Matt, Fancy and your grandpa are the two things you love most in this world. I'm pretty sure if I tried to steal your grandpa, he'd shoot me. So Fancy it is."

I laughed again, my tears once more banished for the moment. "How about this. I won't break his heart, you don't need to steal anything, and we all have our happily ever after. Deal?"

"Deal."

Greta came over. I knew she'd wanted me to marry someone rich and old for my first husband and save Matt for a later marriage, but she squeezed my hand and said in her German accent, "He will make a good husband for you, Maggie, I know it."

"So do I. Thank you."

Jack held his arm out to her and they walked out the doorway as the sound of some sort of beautiful music played in the background. Mason and Jamie followed right behind.

And then it was my turn.

My grandpa handed me a bouquet of lavender, blue, and white roses and held his arm out for me. "You're making the right choice, Maggie."

"I know." And I did. Matt was exactly the right man for me. I didn't expect it to be perfect—life never is—but if there was anyone I wanted to tie my life to and let change me in ways I couldn't even foresee, it was Matt.

As I stopped in the doorway I saw Abe and Evan, their skin nicely tanned from their vacation. Mr. Lewis, his eyes already full of tears. Elaine, sitting quietly by herself in the back. Lesley, as polished as ever in a darker purple dress that complemented the colors of the wedding. Jean-Philippe who gave me an entirely inappropriate up and down appraisal and then winked at me. Matt, waiting nervously. Jack, standing at his side with a roguish grin. Mason, all serious and sober next to him. And Greta and Jamie beaming smiles at me.

These were my friends.

My family.

I'd always thought that I wouldn't want to go through my wedding day because it would be too painful without my parents there. But looking around at all those faces I realized that even though some of the people I'd loved most in this world couldn't be there that day that I still had plenty of love in my life.

I hadn't come to Creek looking for this, but I was glad I'd found it. And I'd be forever grateful for the twisted, crazy path that had brought me here.

I took a deep breath and stepped forward, a smile on my face, my grandpa and Fancy by my side, to start my next big adventure.

🐾 🐾 🐾

Maggie May and Matt finally got their happily ever after, but the murder and mystery doesn't stop here.

If you want to see how Maggie and the crew handle the events of Spring 2020 then check out **A Housebound Holiday.** *Otherwise, the next mystery can be found in* **A Fouled-Up Fourth** *where Lucas Dean finally gets his due. Both are also included in the final Maggie May and Miss Fancypants collection.*

ABOUT THE AUTHOR

When Aleksa Baxter decided to write what she loves it was a no-brainer to write a cozy mystery set in the mountains of Colorado where she grew up and starring a Newfie, Miss Fancypants, that is very much like her own Newfie, in both the good ways and the bad.

🐾 🐾 🐾

You can reach her at aleksabaxterwriter@gmail.com or on her website aleksabaxter.com.